REIGN OF CINDERS AND GLASS

FATED FAIRYTALES BOOK 1: ELLA AND THE DARK PRINCE

LINSEY HALL

VERONICA DOUGLAS

Magic Side Press

ABANDONED CHURCH
SIGGY'S HOUSE
SILVERTHORN
UPPER TOWN
LOWER TOWN
ELIA'S MANOR
THE BLOODVALE
N

1

———————

Ella

The rising moon peeked over the dense crown of oaks as the sun sank lower toward the horizon, making the shadows of the trees stretch toward me like long, dark fingers. An icy shiver tickled my spine. The safety of our manor house was miles behind me now, with only the cursed forest ahead. I'd have to turn around soon.

"Damn you, Belle," I muttered as I followed the path deeper into the woods.

It had been five days since I'd seen her last. My sister was often gone for a day or two, either guiding the immortals from the castle on their hunts or gathering wild herbs for the royal larder, but she'd never been gone this long. Not five days.

Our stepmother hadn't shown the slightest concern. "She'll turn up when it suits her," she'd said. "She always does."

But I couldn't shake the unease that had rooted in my gut. Something was wrong, and if my stepmother wasn't going to do something about it, I would, even if that meant searching every corner of the ancient forest.

I pulled the hood of my coat over my braided silver hair and patted the little rat who nuzzled my neck. "Don't worry, Pip. I won't get us lost."

He gave a soft squeak of encouragement.

Although the forest had always been a place where my sister and I could escape our troubles, a part of me hated the cursed woods, not because they were rumored to be haunted, but because they were a prison for every human in the valley—an impenetrable barrier that prevented anyone from venturing too far beyond the grasp of our masters, the Lords of the Bloodvale. The immortals.

Bloodsuckers.

Yet as cruel as our masters were, whatever lived in the heart of the forest was worse—or so the rumors said. Hunters and trappers disappeared in the deep woods all the time. Sometimes, their mangled bodies were found, but more often, they simply vanished. The villagers spoke of ghosts and monsters and magic. Although I didn't necessarily believe all of the rumors, I was experienced enough to know something was lurking out there beyond the reach of civilization, and that I shouldn't be caught out past sundown.

Hopefully, Belle hadn't ventured too far.

I touched my father's hunting knife to make sure it was there, then hitched up my skirt and trudged uphill toward the ancient oaken sentinels that marked the edge of the *true* wilderness, the part of the forest where few mortals ventured. My pulse quickened at the sudden shift in the air—thick and damp and riddled with the earthy scent of decay. An unnerving silence fell over the woods, prickling my skin. It was like the silence of anticipation, as if the creatures and trees were waiting for me to do something.

The hush came every time, and I'd never understood why. When I'd tried to explain the sensation to Belle, she'd told me, "Maybe it's just the way the woods welcome you."

Tonight, it felt more akin to a warning.

I quickly found the silver bark pine that marked the head of the path Belle had forged during years of daily forays into the woods. Blackberry tendrils had already encroached on the trodden dirt trail in her absence, their thorns snagging on my dress and pricking my legs.

Over the next hour, I checked all our childhood haunts—the wading pool with the smooth skipping stones, the ancient hollowed-out oak where Belle would pick wildflowers each spring, and the secret glade—but I found no indication that my sister had passed by.

As the sun sank behind the canopy, the shadows deepened, transforming familiar trees and stones into ominous forms. I glanced up at the sky. Twilight was fading quickly, which meant I had about twenty minutes before darkness enveloped the woods.

Pip scampered along my shoulder and tugged on a loose thread on my coat. I smiled down at the little brown and white rat. He twitched his tiny pink nose and looked up at me with wide eyes that seemed to say, *It's getting late.*

I scratched him between the ears. "We'll go home soon, I promise."

I had one last place to look before heading back to the manor, so I fetched a shelled walnut from my pocket as an apology. Pip plucked the nut from my fingers and began nibbling at it contentedly as I headed up the path.

Most of the villagers thought it was peculiar the way I talked to animals, and a few had spread ugly rumors. I didn't care. Belle and Tarran, the farm boy up the road, were the only ones who didn't give me a hard time about it—one of several reasons why they were the only close friends I had.

And now Belle was gone. It was like half my soul had been cut away.

It didn't take long to reach the hideout that we used to escape to when our stepmother was being particularly cruel. The dense trees opened onto a low, grassy outcrop overlooking the Bloodvale. It had been years since we'd been here last, but the fallen trunks we'd used as a fort remained.

I set Pip down to nibble on the vegetation while I searched the clearing for any indication that Belle had visited the outcrop recently, but the blades of grass were fresh and untrampled.

"Where are you?" I sighed as I gazed out across the glittering lights, relishing the cool evening breeze against my heated skin. A winding river split the valley in half, fed by the mountains in the north. It cut through the town, dividing rich and poor, with Castle Silverthorn perched on a high cliff above. The fortress with its towering spires was both breathtaking and horrible, a symbol of the power the immortals held over us all, rich and poor alike.

Was Belle somewhere in there?

Although she frequently visited the kitchen, she'd always warned me to stay as far away from the castle as I could. "Never visit Silverthorn, Ella. The immortals are ruthless, and they take what they want."

Perhaps she'd stopped there to sell her latest harvest and had drawn the eye of a lord. Would he have forced her to pay the blood tithe? Would he have kept her there against her will?

I shivered, and my stomach twisted at the thought of Belle offering her blood to one of those vile creatures.

I let my gaze drift to the long carriage road winding through the farms toward the far end of the Bloodvale. "One day, we'll get out of this valley and forge our own path."

A branch cracked behind me, and I froze.

Was something out there?

Goosebumps rippled along my arms, and my heartbeat accelerated. I scanned the shadowed tree line, but the thick vegetation obstructed my view. The woods were silent, nothing unusual. Still, I couldn't shake the unnerving sensation that I was being watched.

I scooped Pip out of the grass and quickly began making my way back along the path.

My fingers brushed the hunting knife at my side. *Calm down, Ella. The bloodsuckers feed in town and in the castle, not in the forest.*

But if it wasn't a bloodsucker, then what was it?

I took off in the direction of home, moving as quickly as I could. The rustling of leaves and snapping of branches sounded behind, and I stole a quick glance back.

A dark shape flashed through the trees at the crest of the hill. My stomach curdled with dread. Humans didn't run with such speed.

Immortal.

Pip scampered into the crook of my neck, his poor little heart fluttering against my skin. "Hang on tightly, Pip," I muttered, then hitched up my dress and began to run, my breath coming faster and faster. The sounds from the trees followed, quickly closing in. The path split before me, the left fork heading toward the manor and the other veering deeper into the woods. There was no way I could outrun an immortal, so I went right, barreling toward the hollowed-out oak Belle and I once used as a fort. It'd be a tight fit, but if I could squeeze inside, I'd be safer than out in the open.

A man's laughter echoed through the trees behind me, nearly drowned out by the sound of my thundering heart. I crashed through ferns and thimbleberries, cursing the silence of the woods as I tore through the underbrush. Gods, if I were lucky, the bloodsucker would mistake me for a wild boar.

A rock slipped beneath my foot, and I crashed down, skinning my forearms. With no time to think of the pain, I shoved myself to my feet and kept running. *Fates help us now.* The woods awoke in an explosive fury of noise—melodic cries of warblers and thrushes joined the symphony of chaotic cawing and hooting, while chittering and clicking rose from the underbrush, as if the entire forest were calling out in warning.

I'd never heard them so agitated. What was going on?

I leapt over a fallen trunk and burst into the clearing with the weathered oak. Nestled in its lightning-scarred bark was a gap large enough for a small person to fit through. A cloud of crows descended from the sky and fluttered into the branches overhead, their piercing shrieks no doubt drawing the attention of every creature in the forest.

"Shh!" I scolded. "You're drawing attention to me! Get out of here!"

I froze as the birds above all went silent.

"What's a pretty little human like you doing so far out in the forest after dusk?" a smooth voice asked from behind me.

My breath stilled, and I turned slowly.

A male stood in the dim light at the edge of the clearing. He was tall and gracile, his light brown hair tied back in a low ponytail. He was beautiful and severe and ageless.

An immortal.

I palmed the hunting knife tucked into my waistband. The male's amber eyes tracked the movement, and the corners of his thin lips quirked. "A playful one, aren't you?"

Even though we both knew the blade was next to useless, it gave me courage. I forced out an even tone. "I'm meeting my father. He's a skilled hunter, so I suggest you be on your way."

A slow grin cut his marble cheeks, and he took a step toward me. "Then we'd better be quick. I wouldn't want to keep Daddy waiting."

2

Thirty minutes earlier, sundown.

Cassius, Prince of the Bloodvale

I ducked beneath the crooked branches of the oaks and spurred my stallion up the forested slope. Foam dripped from the corners of his mouth, and his midnight flanks glistened with sweat, but I pushed him harder.

A fallen immortal was stalking my woods, and I would hunt him down.

The bastard had already massacred two families living at the edge of the valley. He'd torn another man limb from limb in front of his wife, then nearly drained her dry. Undoubtedly, more corpses would come to light in the coming days.

The brutality of the murders went beyond the blood tithe humans paid us for protection and the right to live on our lands. This was the work of a wild creature, an immortal who'd forsaken civilization and given into their thirst, going mad with a lust for blood.

While we called ourselves immortals, some still whispered the ancient word for what we were: *vampires.*

I prayed to the Fates that the rogue was my brother Valen,

returned home at last. It had been fifty years since I'd seen him. Fifty years since the madness had taken hold and he'd abandoned the throne, leaving the kingdom to me.

I'd forgive the bastard a hundred murders if he'd just return and take his rightful place. Fates knew I'd never wanted it.

I spurred Tenebris faster, my fangs bared in anticipation, yet I didn't let hope take control or cloud my mind. I'd left the chains of emotion behind long ago. My brother was the only one I'd ever cared for, and he was gone.

Hoofbeat by hoofbeat, we ascended the ridge, not stopping until the trees thinned and the valley stretched out before me. Shadows had consumed the forested vale, but the edges of the clouds still shone like they were on fire. I saw no beauty in it, only relief. The blinding light of day would no longer burn my eyes and hinder my search.

I reined in Tenebris, and we stopped in a clearing on the ridgeline, the best vantage point in the Bloodvale. My castle rose from a cliff above the river on the eastern side of the valley, its spires streaked by the last rays of the setting sun.

I scowled out of habit. The place was a prison filled with vipers—the simpering courtiers plotting and scheming behind my back, and the meddling high council, trying to control my every move.

Valen had been born into that world, not I. As a second son, I'd spent my youth defending our borders and was far more at home among the gnarled trees of the cursed woods, despite the monsters that lurked in its shadows.

Hoofbeats thudded on the hillside behind me, and moments later, Aamon, the Master of the Hunt, pulled his winded steed alongside mine. "You're a madman, Cassius. Searching in the daylight and charging through the woods like that. How do you expect to find the bastard?"

Ignoring my advisor's protests, I pointed across the valley.

"The first attack was there, near the village, two days ago. The second was there by the river last night. And a hunter spotted him further upslope early this morning. He's moving this way, but only in the dark."

Aamon grunted and gave a faint nod. "You mean to cut him off."

"I mean to keep looking through the dawn if that's what it takes." I inhaled deeply but caught no scent of my brother or any other of our kind. We were predators, and although our eyesight was keen in the dark, scent was by far our most powerful sense.

"He's not upwind," I said. "We should keep looking."

I lifted the reins, but Aamon placed a hand on my shoulder. "I know who you're looking for, Cassius. It's not him."

I turned to face my old friend. "What do you mean?"

Aamon's blond hair hung about his face, dislodged by the hard riding, but his glacial eyes betrayed no sign of exhaustion or doubt. "It's not your brother. No matter what form his madness took, Valen wouldn't do this. It has to be an outsider driven insane by the mists, or perhaps one of our nobles giving in to his demons at last."

"We can't be sure."

Aamon shook his head as he repositioned his brace of flintlock pistols. "You must stop this. I'll help you hunt down the savage, but you must accept that your brother is not coming back. It's been half a century. You must do your duty. You must forget him and wed. You *must* take the throne."

And as soon as I did, my brother would become an enemy of the kingdom.

My lip curled as a low growl tore from my throat. "If there is any chance, I will keep searching. *That* is what I must do."

"Your friend is right, Cassius," a craggy voice said behind me.

I spun Tenebris around and dropped my hand to the hilt of

my sword. I had the speed and strength to tear someone apart with my hands, but a blade was far cleaner.

An old woman sat cross-legged on one of the protruding boulders. Her right hand clasped a long walking stick, while the left held an open flask of strong whiskey, its scent wafting on the breeze.

My hand relaxed and left my blade. It was the Fates-damned seer.

She'd lived in these woods as long as our family had ruled and had been old when I was young, centuries ago. Whatever she was, and whatever powers she possessed, the spell that repressed magic in the Bloodvale didn't suppress her foresight.

The Triad—our kingdom's high council—didn't like her, but our father had always cautioned us to keep our distance and do her no harm. *Who knows what evil tampering with the Fates-touched witch could bring down on our family?*

I eased Tenebris forward. "What are you doing out here, old woman? You're a long way from your cottage, and the forest isn't safe for travel."

Despite my keen hearing, I hadn't heard her approach or caught her scent. Had she been here all along, lurking in the shadows, or had she just appeared out of thin air?

"Old woman?" The seer chuckled, giving me a foxlike grin. "You're not so young yourself, Prince Cassius—though I'll admit you wear the centuries better." She winked with one eye, the other covered by a patch. "And as far as your *thoughtful* warning, I've nothing to fear from your kind."

I narrowed my eyes. Did she already know about the fallen immortal stalking the woods? "Then what do you want?"

"Only the honor of serving the Lord of the Bloodvale." She gave a mocking half-bow from her seat. "I offer counsel, should you desire it."

A muscle in my jaw tensed at her tone. "Then say your piece and be done with it."

The seer took a swig of whiskey and tucked the flask beneath her cloak. "I know you miss your brother, my lord, but you need to accept that you're not the one destined to find him."

Her words crashed over me like meltwater from the high mountains, chilling my skin. How much did she know?

I buried my surprise and steeled my expression. "We shall see."

The old woman shook her head. "I don't doubt your determination, but Valen isn't the one you should be looking for."

I straightened in the saddle as a shadow crossed my face. "Then you think I should be looking for a bride, like all the other fools in this realm? A queen to seal my throne?"

Her good eye laughed with mischief, and she swept her hand out in a flourish. "I simply wished to remind you that the choice of a queen should not be made lightly, Your Highness."

The council would have me pick a bride during a grand masquerade ball. It was a tradition dating back to long before our family had taken the throne, but the ridiculousness of it galled me. If I were forced to marry, I would pick a bride who would leave me to my own affairs. A woman was the last thing I needed or desired in my life, even less than the crown.

"Trust me, there is no lightness in it for me." I tugged on Tenebris's reins, beginning to back the ebony brute away. "Have you any wisdom, or are you here simply to mock my affairs?"

"Wisdom?" she said. "No one has wisdom, but I will give you a warning from the Fates."

Her good eye flared with an unearthly light, and Tenebris backed away as the shadows of the night stretched and flowed around the old crone. The air thrummed and turned cold.

She raised her hand and pointed to me. "Heed me, Prince Cassius. If you fall in love, the woman you choose will destroy everything your father built. And if she ever takes the throne, she will make your people pay the price of their thirst. Choose a bride *wisely*."

The wind stirred the branches overhead, and then, just as quickly, it died. The shadows dropped away from her, and the energy prickling the air subsided, but her words made a chill race over my skin, and I couldn't shake the feeling of power in the place.

Fucking hell. I didn't need the old witch messing with my mind.

My mouth turned down. "If *do not fall in love* is your warning, then don't worry yourself, Grandmother. I have no love left in me."

"I can see that, my prince." She chuckled as she rose and shook her head. "I wish you the best of luck with the ball and a long and happy marriage." With that, the seer turned and began hobbling stiffly down the ridge and into the woods below.

I opened my mouth to call out after her, but a flock of crows burst into the air above the dense trees in the valley, filling the forest with haunting cries. They screeched and dove down the slope, attacking something I couldn't see.

I sat up and pulled Tenebris's reins, preparing to ride.

The old woman glanced at the birds and then back at me, and her lips twisted in a self-satisfied smile. "Oh, my. Seems like there's a bit of trouble ahead. Imagine that."

3
____

The immortal circled me, his eyes blazing with blood lust. I thrust my hunting knife in front of me, trying to stop my arm from shaking.

How did you kill a bloodsucker? The legends said either a knife to the heart or by cutting their head from their spine—both unlikely options, considering the size of my blade and my ineptitude at fighting.

But that didn't mean I couldn't make him hurt.

The immortal's eyes gleamed with amusement, settling on my skinned forearms. "What do you think you'll do with that little thing? Poke me in the heart? Skewer my eye out?"

I tightened my grip on the blade. "I was thinking more along the lines of slicing your balls off."

He gave a sick, condescending chuckle and stepped forward. "I think not. But it does give me some wonderful ideas about what to do to you."

He leapt.

But instead of him taking me to the ground, the air between

us exploded into a whirlwind of screeching black wings as the murder of crows fell upon him from above. He bellowed and clawed at the air as they viciously pecked at his face and eyes.

I bolted toward the hollowed oak, the only refuge in sight. The immortal would never fit through the opening, unless of course he managed to pry apart the trunk, which wasn't out of the realm of possibility. I dropped onto my bruised knees at the base of the scorched tree. Pip leapt off my shoulder and scurried into the safety of the brush as I angled my body to fit through the narrow gap.

Before I was halfway inside, strong hands gripped my ankles and wrenched me out of the tree. Icy fear streaked through me as I clawed at the dirt and leaves. The immortal flipped me over and clamped his hand around my throat, cutting off my breath. His mouth tightened, and deep red scratches marked his cheeks and neck.

"Now you've made me angry." Ice crystalized his tone as he yanked me up and held me dangling in front of him.

Dizziness crept into the corners of my vision as my lungs screamed for air, but I still had my knife. I rammed it into his chest again and again, as fast and as hard as I could, until it lodged deep between his ribs. It was a far cry from his balls, but it would still hurt like hell.

He released his grip and stumbled back, my knife protruding from his chest.

"You foolish cunt." He pulled the knife out, then flung it into the dirt, well out of my reach. "I was going to let you live, but now I think I'll drink you dry. I'll make you beg me for death before I'm done."

Although my throat ached and stars clouded my vision, I grabbed a broken branch from the ground and held it out like a spear. "I'm afraid I'm not the begging type."

I knew that I had no chance of ramming it through his chest

like a stake, but something about the way it felt in my hands gave me a sense of power—the feeling that somehow, I was connected to the forest. That the woods would give me strength.

The bloodsucker bared his fangs.

Then the ground beneath me shook with the sound of crashing branches and thundering hooves. I spun as a cloaked rider on a midnight stallion erupted into the clearing and charged straight for me.

I dove for the ground, the force of the impact whooshing what little air I had from my lungs. The stallion vaulted over me and landed squarely in front of the bloodsucker. The rider pulled back on the reins, and the stallion's front legs pawed the air before it came to a stop. He turned the horse and guided it in circles around the immortal, its hooves stomping the dirt in warning.

Who was he?

The male wore a crisp black uniform and silver-trimmed cape. The only people in the Bloodvale who could afford such fine clothes or a warhorse like that were the lords who lived in the castle.

That meant I had two bloodsuckers to evade, one of them a high lord.

Wonderful.

"What are you doing in these woods?" The rider's deep voice was laced with violence, his attention focused entirely on my attacker.

Had he even seen me?

I began slowly creeping backward toward the trees.

"I was taking the blood tithe, as is my right, Your Hi—"

"You have no rights," the lord growled. "Not anymore. I've seen your work. This was no tithe. You've lost control. You've become a butcher. An animal."

The bloodsucker backed up a step and glanced at me, his

face contorted in rage. "What does it matter if I have a little fun with my food? We're the predators, and they're the prey. It's my right, by nature."

"You're mistaken," the dark rider said as he loomed over my assailant. "I'm the predator, and *you're* the prey. It's time you learned what fear really is." He pulled on the reins, and his stallion reared. "*Now run.*"

For a second, my assailant hesitated, and then, in a blur of movement, the immortal vanished into the trees as the horse's hooves crashed back down onto the ground.

The rider watched him go, but instead of pursuing, he turned his steel gaze on me. An icy shiver snaked down my spine, and my heart sputtered. Beneath the hood of his dark cloak, raven-black hair framed a hard, chiseled face. It was his brooding eyes, however, that stole my breath and sent panic fluttering in my chest. I found myself paralyzed, unable to rise or even move my legs. Was this how the lords hunted? Incapacitating their prey with terror?

I dropped to my hands and knees and bowed my head, partly out of respect and partly just to break away from those eyes. "Thank you for saving me from that bloodsu—" My throat clenched as I realized what I was saying. "From that immortal, my lord."

He was going to peel the skin from my bones.

The lord scoffed with contempt and pulled off his hood. "Get up."

I scrambled to my feet and adjusted the cowl of my coat.

The moonlight kissed his flawless skin, accentuating his sharp jaw and full lips. His ebony shirt and trousers clung to a powerful physique that could only have been honed through battle. His gaze felt as if he were unraveling me, layer by layer. "Who are you?"

Fear surged through me. I didn't want to give him my real name, but he'd probably sense if I were lying. "Ella DuPonte," I answered, substituting my stepmother's maiden name instead of my own—Marquette.

"Ella." My name fell from his lips like a sin, and for some unfathomable reason, his deep voice stirred something equally dangerous low in my belly. I'd never heard my name spoken in such a sinister and seductive timbre.

The rhythmic plod of hooves echoed behind us, and a second rider broke into the clearing, stealing my attention from the predator in front of me. He was an immortal as well, with strong shoulders and blond hair. "Have you gone mad?" the other rider shouted, and then his eyes fell to me. "Oh."

The raven-haired lord angled his head and cast a withering expression at the rider before turning back to me. "What are you doing in the woods at night? Alone?"

His tone was cold with an undercurrent of anger, and I felt his judging eyes skate down my body before landing on a loosened strand of my silver hair.

I quickly tucked it behind my ear, a storm of conflicting emotions raging inside—fear, hatred, intrigue. I loathed that he made me feel anything at all.

"I was looking for my missing sister."

"If she's as foolish as you are, then she's already dead."

His words sliced through me, and my throat tightened—both out of fear that it was true, but also with deep resentment. The immortals were callous, soulless monsters who thought of us as no more than property, only good for bedding and feeding.

I met his stony expression with one equally as hard. "Why are two lords wasting their time with a foolish human like me?"

"Why indeed?" the blond rider asked curiously, scrutinizing me with something between amusement and boredom on his sharp aristocratic features. He also wore a midnight cloak, but his boots and clothes were not as finely tailored as those of the lord before me.

The muscles around the dark rider's eyes tightened, and the corners of his lips curled in a feral snarl, revealing the tips of two ivory fangs. He guided his steed closer to where I stood and circled me slowly.

The fire inside my chest quickly transformed to fear, but I held my ground and glared up at him.

"These woods are not a pleasure garden," he said disdainfully. "They're not safe, nor are the creatures that dwell in them. So, if I were you, little mouse, I'd run."

The lord shifted his weight, and with a subtle tug on the reins, the black stallion turned and launched itself into the trees in the direction that my assailant had fled. His cloak billowed out behind him, and in the light of the rising moon, I could make out the royal insignia concealed on the underside of the thick fabric.

Was he part of the royal family or just one of their bannermen?

The second rider gave me a final smirk, then followed after the high lord, leaving me alone in the deeply silent woods.

Pip climbed up the back of my leg and onto my shoulder, and I let out a long sigh of relief. He was okay.

That made one of us.

I glanced down at my hands, which were stained black with blood in the faint light. I had attacked one of the immortals.

The shock of it made my hands tremble. Justified or not, harming an immortal was an *executable* offence. Would they find the knife wounds I'd given the bastard and come for me? They knew my first name and had seen my silver hair. No one else in the village had hair like it. The high lord might hang me from the battlements for all to see, an example to our kind: never touch an immortal.

A shudder shook me, and I glanced up at the moon shining brightly against the sky. For a moment, I'd thought the rider was my savior.

I'd never been so wrong.

4
____

I fled the woods as quickly as my feet would carry me and didn't stop running until I reached the farm road that led to our manor.

I had no doubt the high lord would catch the bloodsucker who'd attacked me—which gave me a cold sense of relief—but I wanted to put as much distance between the immortals and myself as possible. The last thing I needed was for the lord to take an interest in me. With any luck, he'd ignore the knife wounds in my assailant's chest. Hell, maybe he'd butcher the creature and not even notice what I'd done.

I tried to steady my breath. They'd been hunting *him*, not me. I didn't matter. I'd be okay, and so would Belle.

By the time I reached the manor, I almost believed it.

The two-story stone house wasn't enormous, but it was home and always filled my heart with joy. Rosebushes lined the sides, their blossoms the palest pink. They bloomed almost all year round, except in the coldest months. I assumed it was something in the soil because we didn't need to do anything special to care for them.

Despite the relief of home, my troubles tonight were far from over. A light flickered in the sitting room windows. It offered no comfort or warmth. Belle wasn't there—it was my stepmother, Lucille, waiting like a wolf.

I slipped through the gate and hurried through the back door into the dark kitchen. I quickly latched the door behind me and pressed my back against it, my chest still heaving from the run, my mouth dry. Tarran had told me that the immortals couldn't cross a threshold uninvited. It had to be true, right?

Probably not.

"Ella." My stepmother's icy voice cut through my thoughts— a stone-hard summons. I'd stayed out far too long, and there would be a price to pay.

"Coming!" I quickly cleaned the blood from my hands and arms, then scooped Pip off my shoulder and placed him on the old wooden counter. "Stay here. I'll be back," I whispered under my breath.

"I'd better not have to call you again," my stepmother said, this time with an edge of iron.

"I'll be right there!" Hanging my coat, I smoothed my hair and dress and headed into the warm light of the sitting room.

My stepmother sat straight-backed at my father's oaken desk, her hands folded in her lap. She was an austere woman wearing a dark, high-necked dress; two ever-present silver bracelets were her only adornment. "Where were you?" Her eyes flashed as she rose, scooping up the papers that littered the desk. "You're a sweaty mess. You weren't with that farm boy up the road, were you? Gods help me, I will teach you a thing or two if you were."

I shook my head. "I was out looking for Belle, and I lost track of time."

"And your senses. Your sister's problems are her own damn fault. She'll show up when she's good and ready, and I'll whip her hide for it. Trust me, you don't want to be there beside her."

I'd be beside her, whatever came.

"How can you be so callous?" I asked, my voice low but quaking with anger. "Aren't you worried at all?"

My stepmother shoved the papers into her lockbox, turned the key, and slipped it back into its hidey-hole in the floor. "Of course I'm worried. But I have people out looking for her—people who know what they're doing. I do not need you lost as well."

My chest tightened. She had people looking? Why hadn't she told me or included me? I knew my sister's patterns better than anyone. It was like there was always a wall between us, like my stepmother lived a secret life that she wanted me to have no part of.

She replaced the wooden slat over the hidey-hole and dragged the rug back over it, then glanced at the old clock on the mantle. "Searching for Belle is no excuse for returning so late. Do you have any idea how long I've been waiting for dinner?"

"I ran into an immortal in the woods."

The words slipped off my tongue like it was the simplest thing in the world, like it was just gossip or something that had happened to someone else.

My stepmother froze, and her lips tightened into a taut line. "Don't you dare lie to me, not about that."

"I'm not. It was near where Belle gathers herbs. There were three of them—two lords and a fugitive."

Her face paled. She crossed the room in two steps and grasped my jaw, turning my head left, then right, to examine my neck. "Did they bite you?"

Fear thrummed beneath the anger in her voice.

"No."

She released me forcefully and then inspected my arm, pulling up my sleeves. "You reckless girl, do you have any idea what kind of mess you could have gotten yourself into?"

Of course I did. We all lived beneath the specter of the bloodsuckers.

I pulled out of her grasp. "I'm fine. I got away."

"It's a miracle you're not worse off. I hope they scared the foolish straight out of you, because the Fates know I haven't been able to. You should never have been in those woods to begin with."

Belle and I went out there nearly every week to pick berries for her breakfast or herbs and mushrooms for her tea. "I go out to gather with Belle all the time. You've never stopped us before."

"Yes. And now we're looking for her."

The words punched me in the gut. My neck heated, and I turned to leave before I said something I'd regret, but she caught my hand. "Promise me you won't go searching in those woods again."

I let out a deep sigh, doing my best to smother my frustration. Wherever Belle had gone, it wasn't there.

"I won't," I promised.

Some of the tension left my stepmother's body, and she slumped back down on her chair. "Why the Fates thought it fit to burden me with two willful girls and no husband, I'll never know."

"Neither will I," I muttered.

As if she were the only one who'd lost my father.

She looked up. "What was that?"

"I'll go prepare dinner."

Her lips pulled back. "Dinner for one. Maybe a growling belly will help this lesson sink in."

"Of course," I said, and headed to the kitchen, just glad to be free of her. Pip was sitting where I left him, teeth bared at the door like a savage little thing. I scooped him up and put him on my shoulder. "You mustn't let her see you. She'd snap your neck."

He chittered angrily as I began to prepare a rushed meal.

"She's just worried for Belle and me. I can't hold that against her," I explained. "Her anger gets the best of her."

A proper stew or hot meal would've taken hours, so I laid out a board with soft cheese, cured meats, and the rest of the morning's baking. Then I tossed together a quick salad with garden greens, the last of Belle's mushrooms, and onions from the cellar, and dressed it with my homemade vinaigrette. Even though I hadn't made a portion for myself, I licked a bit of dressing from my finger, savoring the sweet and tangy taste of defiance.

I brought the meal and a flagon of farm ale to the table where my stepmother waited. Hopefully, she'd indulge in the beer and be asleep by the time my work was done.

"You'll do your sister's chores tonight as well as your own," she said as she picked up her fork and prodded at the cold fare.

Of course I would. Who else was there to do them?

"And polish Clorinda's and Thisbe's saddles. I may go riding tomorrow, and I don't want to give people the wrong impression about us."

My stepmother was capable of that all on her own. She was a bitter woman, but I knew she'd had a good heart once. Before Father had died, she'd often been kind, even nurturing at times. I clung to those memories when she was at her worst.

I refused to forget that part of her, even if she had.

Dismissed, I rushed back to the kitchen and cleaned the mess. I gave Pip a hunk of cheese, then leaned back against the counter and took a deep draught of the ale. It was cold from the cellar, and the bubbles soothed my parched throat. Perhaps it violated the spirit of her command, but not the letter. Of course, that wouldn't stop her from tanning my hide if she caught me with ale on my breath, but I had no intention of spending another minute in the house. I had hours of chores ahead of me.

I closed my eyes and exhaled, trying to savor the moment of rest—but instead of finding a place of calm, my thoughts filled with *him*. The dark rider. A vision of terror. Impossibly cold and beautiful, mounted on his stallion. I could still feel his eyes boring into me. My chest tightened, and my pulse raced. There was fear in me, but also something else. A flutter in my stomach.

Just nerves.

I grabbed a lantern and lit it, suddenly extremely thankful for the hours of work lying ahead of me. I knew I wouldn't sleep unless I was dead exhausted. Pip gave an annoyed squeak and grasped for another crumb of cheese as I snatched him up and headed out into the farmyard.

I herded the chickens back to the coop in a din of outraged clucking, then counted them quickly. I found the last renegade hiding behind a dilapidated haybale and escorted her back to the others, then sealed them in. "It's dangerous to be out after dark, you silly thing," I said as much to myself as to her.

I fed the milk goats, who were all too happy to ignore their dinner and nuzzle my hands, here and there trying to sneak a bite from the sleeves of my dress. I'd learned that nothing was so delicious as the forbidden taste of fabric.

Pip hid behind my neck as I poured a little milk for the cats who prowled the farmyard. They purred as they rubbed around my ankles, and I scratched one on the rump, but Pip gave my ear a savage nip. "Fine, I'll stop," I told him. "No cavorting with the enemy."

My feet were aching by the time I finished the chores and cleaned up the kitchen, but I still had to deal with my stepmother's prized mares, Clorinda and Thisbe.

The horses nickered and stamped the floor as I entered the barn.

"I'm sorry I'm late."

Thisbe bit at me.

I unlocked the special cabinet where I kept the oats and some apples. They fought each other over the bucket of oats and then nearly took my fingers off going for the fruit. I filled their trough, then set about brushing them. Clorinda's haunches tensed, and I scooted back, narrowly avoiding a kick. While Thisbe was aggressive, Clorinda was the treacherous one.

I could talk the temper out of a goose, but those two had never warmed up to me, despite every attempt to win their favor. They were the only ones on the farm who didn't do a lick of work—aside from my stepmother, who treated them like they were little goddesses.

After I cleaned the stalls, I threw myself into vigorously polishing the saddles. Needless punishment or not, I took pride in my work, and I was going to make them gleam.

"Ella?" a male voice whispered.

I jumped back, knocking over the lantern and looking wildly about for a pitchfork or a stake. I seized the bucket of oats and held it in front of me like an incredibly stupid shield.

The man slipped into the barn. "Ella, it's me!"

Not a man. An idiot farm boy.

My cheeks heated. I dropped the bucket and scrambled to right the lantern before it set the place on fire. When I stood, I threw a handful of dirt at him for good measure. "Tarran, you son of an ass, what the hell were you thinking, sneaking up on a girl like that at night?"

"I'm sorry, El," Tarran said, with a broad grin splitting his lips. He shoved his hands in his pockets. "I saw the light. You're not usually so jumpy."

He'd known me since we were young. Unlike most boys, he'd

never made me feel like an outcast because of my lavender eyes or silver hair—but he could be a pain in the ass sometimes.

Still, it was almost impossible for me to stay angry at him.

I sank down on a haybale. "I was almost bitten by a bloodsucker tonight, and you nearly gave me a heart attack sneaking up on me."

The smile drained from his lips, and his broad shoulders knotted with tension. "Are you serious? Are you okay?"

I was suddenly reminded how much he'd filled out in the last few years. Although we'd been friends since childhood, thinking of him as a boy was unfair. He had strong arms and a square jaw and would be rather handsome if you cleaned the dirt off—though of course, he was nothing like the dark rider. *That* was a different kind of man. Statuesque and perilous. Gorgeous and forbidden.

I self-consciously dusted my dress clean. "It's nothing I can't shake off."

Tarran stalked over, his posture vibrating with protectiveness and concern. "You weren't bitten, were you?"

Suddenly, we were very, very close together. His eyes locked on mine, and there seemed to be unspoken words hanging on his lips.

It was too close, too much, after all that had happened. I slipped away, needing a little room to breathe. "No. I wasn't bitten. I swear I'm okay."

"Good. I was just worried."

Tarran was always worried and always looking out for me. His attentions were kind, even flattering, but sometimes it felt like he didn't see the strength I had—that I *had* to have.

I returned to polishing the saddle. "What are you doing here, anyway? It's late, and if my stepmother caught me speaking to you—"

He glanced at the door as if he wanted to make sure she

wasn't lurking, then crossed his arms and leaned against a post. "I know, but I need your help."

Of course he did. There was always another shoe waiting to drop.

My stomach squirmed with hunger, and I became keenly aware of how absolutely exhausted I was. But this was Tarran.

I closed my eyes and braced against the saddle. "Okay. What do you need?"

"It's Hen. My brother must have left the gate open, and she got out again. You're the only one she listens to."

Hen, his prize sow. It was the stupidest name for a pig I'd ever heard.

I rubbed the bridge of my nose. "You have to learn how to catch that pig yourself. Where are your brothers?"

"Drunk. They'll only make things worse or make a game of it and frighten her out of her mind. Please, Ella, I know it's late, but I couldn't live with myself if anything happened to her," he whispered. "She's special."

My shoulders cried in protest, but I took a deep breath and nodded. "Why not? The day can't get any shorter."

"Thank you!" He almost hugged me, but he probably remembered we weren't kids anymore because he stepped back. "I'll owe you a huge favor."

I'd add it to the list—though I'd lost count of the tally years ago.

I dimmed the lantern, and we headed outside and started down the starlit road.

"It'll be quick," he assured me. "She listens to you. And just think, you can tell me all about the bloodsuckers while we walk. I've never been close to one. What were they like?"

Terrible. Violent. Cold.

And utterly enthralling.

My gaze drifted from the dark mountains that ringed the valley to the towering spires of the castle perched at its tip. "I think some conversations are best left for the day. Come on, let's go."

5

Ella

By the time we caught the bloody-minded sow, it was nearly midnight. Tarran insisted on walking me back to the manor, although we both knew that there was nothing either of us could do if one of the bloodsuckers came for us.

I was glad for the escort all the same.

Tarran knew me well enough not to press me about what had happened, and I was grateful. I was still processing the assault. I could almost feel the bastard's hands clawing at my ankles and neck and hear his half-crazed voice echoing in the back of my mind. People whispered that sometimes the immortals went mad with bloodlust and lost control of their thirst. Was that what had happened to him?

I shuddered. They were monsters. Maybe they were all like that.

Yet I couldn't imagine the dark rider ever giving in to anything close to the madness that had seemed to possess the bloodsucker—not like that. He had a will of iron. Every motion he'd made was precise and practiced. In a way, his cold perfection terrified me more than the brutality of my assailant had. What cruelty would a man with that kind of control be capable of?

I thanked the Fates that I was free of them all.

Tarran lingered once we reached the gate. I bid him goodnight, but he gently caught my hand as I turned to leave. "Are you sure you're going to be okay, El?"

I raised my eyebrows playfully. "And what if I'm not? What would you even do? What can any of us do?"

We were just livestock to them.

He tightened his fingers around mine. "I could sleep in the hayloft. That way, I'd be near if you needed me."

The way his gaze swept over me told me that protecting me wasn't the first thing on his mind. He was strong and handsome, and I couldn't deny he was attractive—but I wasn't the only girl he looked at in that way.

I pulled away with a shake of my head. "My stepmother would have you whipped in the town square if she had any inkling that you'd lingered here all night. You'd better get going in case she peeks out the window."

Tarran gave me a rueful grin. "Well, I guess you know where to find me, should you need me." With that, he turned and headed down the road.

My smile faded as I started toward the door. Every bone in my body ached, and all I wanted was my own soft bed. That would be heaven.

I pulled the handle of the back door, and it clunked dully. *Locked.*

What little spirit I had left drained from my soul, and I placed my forehead against the unyielding door. "You've got to be kidding me."

Perhaps all the talk of bloodsuckers had spooked my stepmother—or perhaps she'd noticed I was late and was intent on teaching me another lesson. Either way, I'd be getting an earful in the morning when she realized I wasn't in my bed.

I closed my eyes. The woman was doing her best to raise us strong, but damn, sometimes she could be a piece of work.

The front door and first floor windows were also locked, and trying to climb to the second floor seemed like a great way to break an ankle or bust my pumpkin open.

Pip squeaked from where he was hidden beneath my hair, and I gave him a little scratch. "Looks like we're camping in the hayloft. At least we won't have to listen to her snoring from down the hall."

He nuzzled against my fingers and chittered in support.

My stepmother's mares snorted as I trudged into the barn and climbed the ladder into the hayloft. *Serves you right*, they seemed to say.

I sighed as I flopped my aching bones down on a pile of golden hay. It prickled my skin and poked through my clothes, but the hayloft was warm, dark, and reasonably soft. Seeing as I'd nearly been murdered a few hours back, I was pretty damn content.

I rolled over to look at Pip in the dim light. "This isn't too bad, is it, little buddy?"

He nestled down beside me, making soft little grunts and squeaks as he vigorously dug about in the hay to form a sleeping nest.

I closed my eyes and collapsed in the embrace of a deep sleep, and with it, dark dreams.

I was alone in the woods. Everywhere I looked, the shadows seemed to bend and move. And then *he* was there, fangs glinting in the moonlight. Not the bloodsucker who'd chased me, but the dark rider with his raven hair and stormy eyes.

I ran as fast as I could, with him on my heels. It seemed like the forest had come alive and was trying to stop him, but he wouldn't be deterred. The stable appeared before me. I fumbled with the latch, but he was on me in an instant, pinning me against the wooden wall. His body pressed against mine, rigid with corded muscles and as immobile as iron. I pushed back, but it was like we were moving in waves, like I wasn't struggling at all, but rather melting into him, our bodies entwining and becoming one. His hands drifted down my sides, and I felt his lips brush along my neck. *Ella.*

I gasped as I sat up, my heart pounding and skin slick with sweat.

A razor of sunlight streamed through the wooden slats, and I raised my hand to shield my eyes. Dust motes danced in the still air, and mercifully, I was alone.

"No way." Pip was nowhere to be found as I scrambled up and hurried down the ladder. "I'm not having *those* kinds of dreams, not about *them.*"

Bloodsuckers.

But it hadn't really been about them, but *him.*

The barnyard was awake, though it wasn't as late as I'd feared—just after dawn. The windows were open, which meant my stepmother had risen early. I tried the back door of the house, and it swung wide.

My skin iced the moment I stepped inside. My stepmother was waiting, still as a statue in the corner of the kitchen. I swallowed, and she stepped close, plucking a strand of hay from my dress. "Where were you?" she asked, her voice as cold and sharp as a knife, and dripping with just as much threat.

"You locked me out. I had to sleep in the hayloft."

"You were out late gallivanting with that farm boy, weren't you? I swear, if you let him touch you or take you down in the hay—"

"Fates, nothing happened between us!" I said as I pushed around her. "I had to catch his damn pig, then I came home and slept *alone*. You know when I'm lying. I'm not."

She studied my face, and at last, a fraction of the tension slipped from her shoulders. "You girls are going to be the death of me."

"We're the only reason this place is still running and that there's food on the table," I said sharply, my patience thinning.

Her lips tensed. "Which is why we should have sold it an age ago—"

"No." I said forcefully. "This is our home."

She hadn't wanted to keep it after Father disappeared, but Belle and I had fought for every inch. The manor had been his pride and joy, and it was all we had left of him.

Her brow furrowed, and lines pulled down the corners of her mouth. She was about to say something when a knock sounded at the door.

Who could it be this early?

My stepmother shooed me out the back. "I have business to attend to today, and so do you. Finish the chores and wait outside until my visitors are gone. Then you and I are going to have a reckoning to make sure yesterday never happens again."

The chickens were already protesting their confinement, so I quickly splashed a little water from the well on my face and headed around the corner of the house.

My path brought me near the sitting room window, and my stepmother's hushed voice stopped me cold in my tracks. "Have you found her?"

My heart skipped a beat, and I ducked down beneath the

window with my thoughts racing. If the visitors had come with news about Belle, then why had my stepmother sent me away? Was she afraid something bad had happened?

"The latest word is that she's been confined to the castle, but we don't know why," a man said in a hushed tone. I thought it was the village butcher speaking, but I wasn't certain.

"Could she have been caught?"

"We don't know," a woman said—the village seamstress. She was almost as hard as my stepmother and equally feared among the town's girls. "Without Belle, we don't have anyone running information in and out. We were lucky to learn this much."

My mind reeled. Belle had been running information in and out of the castle? But why? I knew she visited to sell her herbs and sometimes to guide the lords, but she'd never told me anything about the place other than to stay far away.

I leaned against the wall as my stomach tumbled. She and my stepmother had been keeping secrets.

"This is why we need more people," my stepmother said.

"More people, more chances of someone getting caught," the butcher muttered. "Those bloodsuckers know ways to make people speak, and if Belle—"

"She'd never betray the resistance," my stepmother snapped.

Everything I thought I knew about my stepmother and my sister came crashing down in a thousand glistening shards, like the world was made of glass and had been hit by a sledgehammer.

The resistance?

It was little more than a rumor, a hushed murmur in the tavern, whispers exchanged in the back alleys of town.

According to the histories, our people had revolted against the immortals three centuries ago, led by a coven of powerful mages. Yet despite their magic, the Uprising had failed. The bloodsuckers crushed the human army, executed the mages, and purged all magic from the land. They'd ruled the Bloodvale ever since, and no one had dared challenge them.

Except, perhaps, the resistance.

When we were girls, Belle and I had imagined that Father had been part of it and that he'd disappeared on a secret mission. We'd dreamed up heroic stories and adventures that he'd undertaken to fight the immortals—stories that made not knowing the truth a little less painful. Something to give us hope in this forsaken place.

But suddenly, the resistance wasn't a child's tale anymore. It was real, and my stepmother and sister were a part of it. They were living a life I'd only dreamed of in secret.

Had my father been a part of it, too?

"What are our options?" my stepmother asked, yanking me out of my astonishment.

"With the ball coming up, the castle is hiring a handful of new live-in servants," the seamstress said, her voice pinched. "That's why we came so quickly. This is our chance to get someone else inside."

"We already have someone inside," my stepmother said. "We need someone who can come and go."

"This is the best shot," the butcher countered. "We'll have to risk using ravens to communicate. The royal masquerade is almost here."

"Then who do we send? It will be *extremely* dangerous, and I'm not sure there's anyone I trust—"

The words slipped off me like rain. I wasn't even listening anymore. I was running to the back door and up the steps. I didn't care about danger or secrets or immortals. All I cared about was finding Belle.

I burst into the sitting room, breathing hard. "Send me."

The two visitors bolted upright, and the blood drained from

my stepmother's face. Her lips curled back. "What are you doing here, treacherous girl?"

She tried to drive me back into the kitchen, but I slipped around her like she was a charging sow and took up a position in the far corner. "I heard everything. I want in. I want to find my sister."

6

____

Ella

"How *dare you* eavesdrop on us!" my stepmother said as she crossed the room. "You have no idea what you're talking about."

I knew in that instant I had no chance of winning her over— not alone. I turned to the butcher and seamstress. "My sister matters more to me than anything in the world. I'll do whatever you need if it helps get her out. I'll infiltrate the castle, serve the bloodsuckers, smuggle information. You name it."

My stepmother moved between us, her anger collapsing into mortification. "I'm so sorry. I assure you, this will never happen again. Ella will never repeat a word of what she heard."

The butcher chuckled. "She has her father's spirit, that's for sure."

My father? Had the whole family been in on the secret? I fought down the bitter taste of the truth and straightened my shoulders. He could be my in.

"I *am* my father's daughter, and I want to be a part of this. I hate the immortals. You know I'd never betray you—not with my family's life on the line."

The seamstress crossed her arms, fixing me with an iron

stare. "This is about more than learning what has happened to your sister, or even getting her out. It's dangerous work."

"If Belle can do it, so can I."

"You're not your sister," my stepmother hissed bitterly, leaning over her desk. "You don't even know what you'll be asked to do."

"Does it matter? I can sew and bake and scrub and tend animals. Whatever those bloodsuckers need, I'll do it."

"And what if they want a piece of you?" she asked. "What if they want you to pay their blood tithe?"

Although my stomach churned at the thought, I straightened my back. "If it means getting my sister back, what does it matter?"

The ferocity in my stepmother's expression slipped into a deep sadness, and she looked away. "I've already lost Belle to the castle. I will not lose you, too."

My heart twisted. She'd never talked like we were worth anything at all to her, and yet it almost seemed as if she cared.

The butcher fixed me with a grim look. "You'd be in a precarious position—a servant with no protection. If they caught you spying, girl, do you have any idea what they'd do to you?"

I gave a bitter laugh. "One of them nearly killed me yesterday. As long as they rule, we're all in a precarious position."

The seamstress straightened as if someone had just prodded her with a stick. "You were attacked by an immortal?"

I took a deep breath, willing away the memory of the dark rider. "In the forest. I stabbed him before he could bite me. When a pair of lords showed up, I ran."

Silence cloaked the room as all three of them stared at me, mouths agape.

"You didn't tell me you *stabbed* one of them," my stepmother breathed.

The blood drained from the butcher's face. "To harm one of the immortals is a death sentence. The lord could've beheaded you then and there and been within his rights."

I shrugged. "He didn't. I doubt he even realized what I'd done. He was hunting the bloodsucker himself and barely noticed me. We're little more than dung to them."

"Stabbed one of the immortals..." My stepmother slowly shook her head as she sank onto her desk chair.

The butcher glanced over at the seamstress with eyebrows raised. "She can obviously handle herself, and Belle would trust her. Maybe it's not the worst idea."

The older woman nodded. "She already knows what we do. We wouldn't have to let anyone else into the circle."

My stepmother pressed her palms into the dark wood. "I can't believe you two are considering this! She's the spitting image of her mother with that silver hair. She'll stand out even more than Belle. She'll draw *attention*."

My father had always said how much I'd resembled my mother. When he'd said it, it had filled me with sunlight, but coming from my stepmother, it had always been a condemnation. As if it were something to be ashamed of.

I pulled my hair back self-consciously. "Then I'll wrap my hair. I'll dye it. I'll be quiet as a mouse and keep my head down. I won't speak to anyone. I'll work hard, and no one will notice me. You know I work hard."

"What about the manor?" my stepmother protested as the argument slipped away from her. "What about the animals? Without you here—"

"Tarran can do it. He owes me for catching his pig a dozen times over, and his father can spare him. I can pay him, too—I've put a little money away."

The seamstress snorted. "Well, you can't question her enthusiasm."

"What do you say, Lucille?" the butcher asked. "She's your ward. It's your decision."

My stepmother looked from one to the other, then to me with a mournful expression. When she spoke, her tone was hushed. "Neither Belle nor I wanted this life for you."

Maybe all they saw was danger, but they had hope. Working for the resistance was a chance to stand up to the bloodsuckers and make my life mean something. To find my sister.

"I don't care," I said. "It's the life I want. Give me this chance to *matter*."

She studied me for a long while, then closed her eyes. "Fine." When she opened them, all emotion had drained from her face. "You need to understand that we will not coddle you. You will become an asset in a greater struggle, a soldier expected to put her life on the line to protect our secrets."

"I understand."

She unlocked a drawer, pulled out an old, tattered prayer book and a long, slender knife, and laid them on the desk. "Then you will swear an oath of secrecy and obedience to our order, or this goes no further."

I stared at the book. It was matted with dark brown patches. Dried blood.

I shuddered.

"Cut your palm and place it on the book." Perhaps noticing my hesitation, she said, "We've all sworn the same oath."

I picked up the blade and drew a thin line across my skin, then pressed my hand down on the ornate circle etched into the leather cover.

My stepmother locked my gaze with ice-cold eyes. "You must swear to never betray the name of anyone who is part of our circle or to ask the identity of other members. Everyone in this room is your superior, and you must swear to obey orders and never take things into your own hands."

"I swear."

Her expression hardened. "All our lives depend on your silence and *obedience*, do you understand?"

"I do."

She placed her cold fingers on top of mine. "Then swear it on your sister's name."

"I will, by my love for Belle." I would do anything they asked if it led to getting my sister back.

"Then may the Fates bind you by your oath," she said, her voice like iron. I could almost have sworn something tingled across my skin, but a moment later, it was gone.

The others bowed their heads in acknowledgement, and I swallowed.

The butcher's solemn expression slipped away as a broad grin split his lips. "It's been a long time since we could brag that someone in the resistance had actually attacked one of the bloodsuckers."

"And there are reasons we don't," the seamstress said.

He shrugged. "Either way, I'm glad to have her with us."

My stepmother cleared away the book and blade. "There's no guarantee Ella will be hired. The immortals may take one look at her and her hair and send her home. You two should find another applicant. With a second, there's a better chance one will get a job."

The seamstress nodded. "I'll see who I can find."

My stepmother took me by the arm. "Now, if you'll excuse us for a moment, I need to speak with our new recruit."

She escorted me out of the room, and as soon as the kitchen door closed behind us, she spun me around. "I should whip you for that stunt, you insolent girl."

Her temper couldn't smother the glow within me. "Thank you for letting me go," I said, and gave her a hug.

She froze, holding me for a second, then stepped back, her

expression almost tortured. "If you don't want me to sell this place in your absence, you'd better go hire that farm boy to take care of it. It's not my burden any longer, and the application is tonight." I turned to go, but her hand tightened on my arm. "You'll speak of this to no one, and certainly not to that boy. Belle's life depends on it."

"I'll keep my promise."

As soon as she released me, I darted down the back steps and hurried along the road, finally running toward *something* for the first time in my life.

7

Ella

Tarran agreed to tend to the animals after only a little begging, but it took some strong negotiation to convince his father, and I had to promise him a little extra as a fee. I wouldn't be able to afford it long on my meager savings, but I'd heard that the castle staff were well paid. It was the only reason anyone wanted to work there, after all.

I showed him the ropes, and after an hour, he wiped his brow. "You've been doing all this yourself with your sister gone?" Sweat glistened on his biceps and made his shirt cling to his chest.

I shrugged, pulling my gaze away. "I'm used to the work. Belle's often gone."

He shook his head. "Well, I'll give it my best, though I can't say I liked the way your stepmother's horses looked at me."

"At least she doesn't expect you to do the cooking."

"Gods, no—not if she expects to live."

I laughed and self-consciously brushed a strand of my hair from my face. "Thanks for looking after the manor. It means a lot to me."

"I know."

Of course he did. We'd known each other since my father was still alive, and he'd heard me talk about how much I treasured it dozens of times. My heart ached just thinking of losing it.

"Are you okay?" he asked as his fingers lightly brushed my arm.

My cheeks heated. "I should go. I have a lot to do to get ready before I apply."

I turned to leave, but he pulled me back. "Are you sure about this? Those bastards are ruthless, and they take what they want. I can't stand the thought of one of them laying their hands on you—not again."

"I'll be fine, Tarran. Plenty of people work there."

His eyes flashed with anger. "And plenty must pay the tithe, whether they like it or not, while others don't return. I don't want you to be one of them."

"I won't." I stepped back at the protectiveness in his voice, suddenly frustrated for reasons I couldn't quite explain.

His shoulders slumped. "I'm sorry, El—I didn't mean to frighten you. I just don't understand why you're applying for work at that place when you've got more than enough waiting for you here. The castle is perilous." He glanced toward the manor, and his voice lowered. "Is it to get away from her? Has it gotten that bad?"

Tarran knew so much about my life. *Too much.* It was one reason it would never work between us. I wasn't certain he'd ever stop seeing me as the little girl struggling beneath her stepmother's thumb and start seeing the woman I was capable of being *despite* her.

I shook my head. "No, it's not Lucille."

He read my expression like a book. "It's Belle, then, isn't it?"

I'd promised my stepmother not to speak of it, but my silence betrayed me.

"Shit," he said, and ran his fingers through his dusty brown hair. "Well, then I know there'll be no talking you out of it, but please, El—be careful. If any of those bastards tries to…if they —" His voice cut off, and he grabbed me by both shoulders. "Just run for it, okay? Come back here and find me. We'll get out of here."

I gave him a sad smile. "Where is there to go?"

Nowhere. There was no escape from the Bloodvale. Nothing but an impenetrable forest filled with mists and monsters, and he knew it. Talk of running was just bravado.

His jaw hardened. "Just promise me you'll be careful."

"I will." I slipped from his grasp and gave him a kiss on the cheek, then stepped away. "But I really have to go."

The heat of his gaze followed me up the steps to the kitchen.

As I lingered at the window and watched him head back up the dusty road, the reality of what I'd signed up for began to sink in. I'd fled home along the same path the night before, terrified out of my mind and never wanting to see a bloodsucker again. Now I was planning to march straight into their lair.

I glanced up at the castle's spires, which rose above the valley like white fangs. Would the dark rider be there? The shape of him filled my mind—impossibly cold and beautiful, mounted on that nightmare beast. My hands turned to ice, and a shiver of anticipation slid down my spine. Of course he'd be there. While some lords lived on estates, a man like him belonged in the castle.

When I went back inside, the butcher and seamstress were gone, and my stepmother was sitting at her desk as she had been the day before. This time, she didn't bother to hide her papers away. Her eyes flicked up at me. "Is everything arranged?"

I nodded.

She pulled the thin silver bracelets off her wrists and handed them to me. "You'll need to wear these."

I turned them over between my fingers, inspecting the gorgeous things. They were hammered silver with facets that glinted this way and that in the light. She'd worn them for as long as I could remember.

She'd never given me anything so fine—or much of anything at all.

"They're beautiful."

"They're a tool, not a gift. I expect them back, and if you lose them, Fates help you, girl." She headed toward the door. "I'll show you how they work."

My neck heated as I followed her out of the kitchen and into the yard. She craned her head around as we walked, as if looking for something, then glanced at me. "Don't be daft. Put them on."

I slipped one around each wrist.

"There he is." My stepmother pointed to a black bird on the roof. "Our messengers are never far. Knock the bracelets together with your wrists a few times, and he'll come down to you."

She demonstrated with her bare wrists, and I imitated, clinking the bracelets against each other in what I hoped was an inviting jingle.

The bird cocked his head but didn't ruffle a feather.

I tried again, this time a little louder and longer, yet he simply gave me a suspicious side eye.

"They're slow to trust. Let me show you," my stepmother said as she reached for the bracelets.

I evaded her grasp. There were few animals I couldn't win over. I held out my hand and jingled the bracelet on my wrist as I walked forward. "Come on down, little friend. I'm not going to hurt you. I just want to talk."

There was a flurry of black feathers as he leapt off the roof and alighted on my arm, digging in rather sharply with his pointy little claws. He pecked at the bracelet. I stroked the tuft of feathers on the top of his head, and he squatted down, beak open. "You're such a beautiful birdy."

He was not. The old crow looked like he'd seen a few too many windstorms and lived off whiskey. But birds were vain creatures, and it was best not to insult them. It was the same for cats.

When I looked up, my stepmother's jaw was halfway open. "What?" I asked as I continued to groom the bird.

"They're not usually so—" She shook her head. "It doesn't matter. Watch the castle for him and his fellow ravens. If you clink the bracelets together, they'll come to you."

I opened my mouth to point out that he was in no way a raven, but then I bit my tongue. Now was not the time for an ornithology lesson. "Got it."

"Check for a message tied to their leg, and for Fates' sake, don't let anyone see you take it off or even call them, or the game will be up."

"Can I write back?"

"Only if you're desperate. If you can find some way to come home and deliver the message yourself, that would be far safer. That's what Belle would do."

It felt like a cloud had passed over the sun. It still shook me that she'd secretly been a part of all this. And now she was a prisoner or hurt or forced to be one of the immortals' thralls.

The mangey bird pecked my wrist, so I started stroking his head again. "Don't worry," I told him, glancing down. "We're going to get Belle back."

My stepmother shook her head. "Your job is not to get Belle back. Your job is to pass information and do as you're told. I won't have you taking things into your own hands and putting her or me or anyone else in danger, are we clear?"

I nodded.

Crystal. I was a soldier in the resistance now. I'd obey every command to the letter—as long as it led to getting my sister back.

"Then you'd better wash up and do something about that awful hair of yours. Application day is tonight, and you look like you've been sleeping in the barnyard."

Of course I did. She'd locked me out, after all.

Despite the anger prickling up my back, I kept my face a mask. "I will."

She turned to go, but then she stopped and looked back. "I expect the best from you, Ella, but by the Fates, if things go badly in the castle, you'd better remember that you're the one who chose this path, not me."

8

Ella

Once the last of the manor chores were sorted, I rushed to bathe and throw myself together. Belle's absence stung as I dressed. For those few times a year when we visited the fair or festivals, she'd always helped with my makeup and hair. She would've known how to make me look pleasing to the eye but not draw too much attention. As it was, I'd have to make do on my own. Fates knew my stepmother wouldn't help.

With dusk drawing near, I put on the finishing touches and followed the old wagon road into town with Pip riding on my shoulder for confidence. He might gain me a few odd stares from the villagers, but I was used to it. Each stride I took toward the castle brought me one step closer to peril, and one step closer to Belle.

Our path took me through the outskirts of Lower Town with its humble and run-down houses. Many of the castle staff came from here, where there weren't enough jobs to go around. I followed the old stone bridge across the river to Upper Town. The difference was night and day. The nicely cobbled streets were flanked by pristine townhouses, flowered squares, and bustling markets. Pip sat up and chittered longingly as we passed a delicatessen with enormous wheels of cheese in the window.

"Sorry, buddy. Not today."

The stone and plaster homes grew larger and more resplendent as I drew nearer to the castle, and I quickly realized how small and insignificant our little manor was—barely a manor at all.

I'd only been on this side of the river a handful of times before and felt entirely out of place. The gentlemen of the town wore conservative suits, while the ladies dressed in flowing modern styles tailored to follow their curves with scandalous precision.

My dress felt dull and plain and more common than it ever had. *Good*, I told myself. The last thing I wanted to do was stand out or draw attention, especially after last night. The immortals needed to see me as competent and reliable, but also forgettable.

I touched the light blue silk scarf I'd wrapped around my head to conceal my silver hair, making sure it was still in place. I hated the idea of having to hide a part of me away, but it was always the first thing people saw—that and my lavender eyes, which I could do nothing about.

I muttered a little prayer beneath my breath, begging the Fates that the dark rider wouldn't be there. He'd recognize me on the spot, and I didn't need any trouble.

I headed up the wide, winding carriageway that led up the hill to the castle gates, my gaze fixed on the white towers and crenelated walls looming above the rooftops. Castle Silverthorn had always seemed enormous from far away, but now it was oppressive. I shuddered. The people in Upper Town must have felt like the immortals were always watching.

As I rounded the corner of the last switchback, I stopped short in surprise. A line of at least a hundred milling people wrapped around the base of the castle, leading up to the gate. I'd never seen so many people anywhere except at the fair.

Were they all here to apply? Of course they were—times had been hard lately, with poor weather for the crops influencing the lives of those less fortunate.

My chances of getting hired were slimming by the second.

It doesn't matter, I said to myself. *They'll hire you because you'll work harder than any of them. You just have to find a way to show it.*

The castle was far more intimidating up close. The walls had been constructed of carefully hewn and fitted limestone blocks that probably weighed ten times as much as I did. A half dozen spires pierced the ruddy sky. Who inhabited the rooms behind the glittering balconies?

I plucked Pip off my shoulder and slipped him into my shoulder bag. "You might want to keep a low profile for a moment. I'm not sure they have any openings for rats."

I fell in at the back of the line and glanced up at the sun. It was low, minutes away from setting, and I cursed myself for not getting there sooner. Other applicants were still arriving, so at least I wasn't going to completely bring up the rear. I leaned against the stones and eavesdropped on the conversations of a cluster of three girls next to me. Some spoke eagerly of work in the castle, others of gossip from the town.

A blonde with an expensive dress and Upper Town accent leaned in close to her friends. "I've heard they're going to demand a blood tithe from each successful applicant this year."

My blood went cold. Could it be true? Would I be forced to pay it if I worked there?

The blood tithe was an ancient tradition. The immortals protected our village and lands, and in return, they could drink from any human they wished, whenever they wished. The only rules were that they were not allowed to drink one of us to death, and we couldn't be made to pay the tithe twice in a week.

It was little protection or comfort. Some of the girls from town had said that the immortals would drink from you until you went weak in the knees.

I dug my fingers into my palm. If paying the tithe was what it took to get Belle back, I'd pay it a hundred times over. She was all that mattered.

"I heard it's not so bad," another girl said, brushing ringlets of auburn hair from her shoulders. "Enjoyable, even."

I raised my brows skeptically. The way I saw it, chickens didn't like to get eaten, so there was no way getting bitten by one of those monsters was going to be anything but pain.

"So, you'd let them feed on you if they demanded it, then?" the blonde asked.

"Probably." The girl with auburn hair glanced at a trio of bloodsuckers exiting the main gate on horseback. "I mean, if it was one of those lords, could you blame me?"

I followed her gaze, and to my relief, the dark rider wasn't among them. Was one of them the blond-haired man from the night before? They didn't even spare us a glance...but then they wouldn't. They were handsome, ageless, and poised, and infinitely above our station.

Yet none of the three came even close to the flawless beauty of the dark rider. I could almost feel those pale eyes burning through me again, and shivers prickled my skin. What would it be like to pay the tithe to him?

Cruel, cold pain.

He was a predator. A heartless, frigid statue. Not a man. Not a creature capable of giving pleasure.

Yet my dream had been so, so different...

"What are you gawking at, peasant?" the blonde snorted. "You think one of those lords would even look at you?"

I started, jolted from my thoughts, and glanced back at her.

Her lips curled in a disdainful smirk. "What are you even

doing here? I don't think there are any open positions for pig farmers in the castle."

Her friends laughed, and my neck heated. Their condescending expressions were all too familiar.

I raised my chin. "I'm from a manor."

"How quaint," the girl with auburn hair said, then turned to her friend. "She's from the country. I doubt she's ever *seen* one of the lords before, let alone running water."

"You'd better hope you don't get a job," the blonde said, not taking her eyes off me. "You wouldn't last a week."

I opened my mouth to retort, but someone touched my arm and pulled me away. "Don't mind those three. They're just bitter because they keep getting rejected every year." I looked over in surprise, and a brunette about my age smiled back at me. "Why don't you join us?" She nodded toward a broad-shouldered man just a little further back in line.

As I let her lead me away, the blonde called after, "They're going to eat you both alive!"

"Is this your first time to the castle?" the brunette asked.

I forced a sheepish grin. "Is it that obvious?"

"Just a bit. The big eyes gave it away, not to mention that far-off look, like you might be imagining what it would be like to have one of those lords for yourself." She winked as we fell in line beside her male friend.

Heat rushed over my face. "It's not that. I just don't have much experience with immortals, let alone the castle or court. Have you ever been inside?"

"Once, when I applied last year. I was rejected, obviously—but if at first you don't succeed, sign up to be humiliated a second time. Or a third, like those Upper Town girls."

I looked over my shoulder. "I'm used to their type, but thanks for stepping in."

"Of course." She gestured to herself, then to the man beside her. "I'm Cara, and this is Teagan."

The man tipped his head forward. "This is my first time applying, so you're not the only one." He had strong features, curly black hair, and looked like he could lift a wine barrel over his head.

"I'm Ella," I said. "And I'm relieved I'm not the only one who has no idea what I'm in for. Do you both live here in town?"

"Lower Town," Cara said with a little pride—like being from Upper Town was something to be ashamed of, even though they were the ones with all the money. She gave Teagan a coy look. "I've known this ox since we were kids. He's the best blacksmith around."

Despite the teasing, there was admiration in her tone.

Teagan's cheeks reddened. "I'm ordinary. Cara, on the other hand, is the most promising dressmaker's apprentice in town. There'll be many disappointed ladies from Upper Town when she gets selected today."

She rolled her eyes. "I wish. If the mistress had more clients, I wouldn't be in this line. But I can't lie—I do like the idea of better pay. Or any pay, really."

"*Hazard* pay," Teagan said. "There's a reason they have new openings every year."

Cara shrugged. "It's worth the risk. I need the money for my family, and with the ball coming up in a few weeks, this might be my best shot. They'll need someone who can work on dresses and do last-minute alterations." Cara turned to me. "What's your skill?"

"My skill?" I faltered, looking around. Many of the applicants held evidence of their work. Cara had a green silk dress folded in her arms, while others had baskets of baked goods, clothing, and a wide variety of items that they'd probably made to show off their skills. It began to sink in how immensely inadequate I was, and a knot of worry twisted in my stomach. I had no expertise at anything and was woefully unprepared for the application. If I'd had more time, maybe I could have come up with something, but as it was, it had been a scramble to even get to the castle on time.

I licked my parched lips. "I'm not sure, really. I've taken care of my father's manor since he...left when I was a girl. I take care of the livestock, tend the horses, clean the house, mend the clothes, cook, and bake and even brew beer. It's a little of every-thing, so I guess my skill is...multitasking?"

Instead of giving me a pitying look, as I'd expected, Cara's face brightened. "I'm jealous. I just sew and mend dresses all day. I could never run a manor or manage all those things. I'm sure they'll be able to use you."

I wasn't so sure.

"I didn't realize how many people were going to apply," I said as we neared the main gate. "Or how stiff the competition would be."

I should have realized, though, given the poverty of Lower Town.

Cara squeezed my shoulder comfortingly. "Don't worry. There's no knowing who they'll select. I'm sure with your experi-ence, you've got a fair shot."

More like a long shot. And if I failed, I'd prove my stepmoth-er's doubts right, and there'd be no one to help Belle.

I took a deep, determined breath and set my intentions. *They will hire me. They'll see my value.*

The line began moving more quickly as it disappeared through the gateway. A pair of sentries flanked the entrance, their halberds raised, while others roughly shoved the appli-cants into a single-file line as they passed through.

I clutched my shoulder bag close to me and followed the

stream of apprehensive applicants beneath the entrance, praying that no one would want to inspect its contents.

A bloodsucker with a dark uniform tallied us as we stepped into the noisy courtyard, regarding us with a mixture of suspicion and disdain. He sneered at me and licked his bottom lip.

Hurrying my pace, I adjusted the scarf I'd wrapped over my hair. This was definitely not the day to draw that kind of attention.

More than a hundred people filled the vast courtyard. Soldiers with bayonetted muskets patrolled the perimeter. Did they expect a riot?

Outside of the castle guard, it was illegal for humans to own firearms—not that they would be effective against the immortals, who reportedly could heal from nearly any kind of wound. The ban was just another symbol of who was in control here.

Dozens of courtiers had gathered on an open gallery above to watch the spectacle like a row of colorful statues.

"I've never seen so many lords and ladies before," Cara whispered nervously. "It must be because of the upcoming ball."

My stomach swam in a wave of nausea. "Does it remind you of something?"

"A theater show?" she mused.

"I was thinking a meat market."

Shock tightened Cara's soft features, while Teagan cleared his throat and stepped closer. "What a strange analogy, Ella. Perhaps you might keep those to yourself, as I'm sure you're aware of how *keen of hearing* our masters are."

I blinked at him twice, then my chest constricted.

Of course. The immortals were supposed to have razor-sharp senses. A whisper was probably like shouting.

Teagan and Cara lived in Lower Town and brushed shoulders with the bloodsuckers from time to time, so they'd probably learned at an early age that survival meant keeping a low profile and blending into the background.

And keeping your stupid mouth shut.

I kept my eyes fixed on the ground as we shuffled into the courtyard, praying none of the courtiers had heard—at least not those making the decisions.

Cara touched my arm and whispered, "Look at the wall."

I followed her gaze, and my blood turned to ice.

The battered corpse of a male dangled from the castle wall. A wooden spike with a rope had been rammed through his chest and out the other side, like a toggle popped through a buttonhole. His hands were missing, and his body looked like it had been mauled by a wild animal.

A knot blossomed in my throat. It was my attacker from last night.

"Do you think he was a thief?" Cara asked, her voice vibrating with suppressed horror.

"He was an immortal."

She glanced at me in surprise. "Are you certain?"

Although he was bloody and tattered, I'd never forget the face of my attacker. His head drooped down, his expression frozen in horror, his eyes wide and lifeless.

Teagan nodded. "That explains why they didn't hang him on the outer walls. I doubt they'd want to advertise they can be killed to the general public."

"But why would they do that to one of their own kind?" she asked.

Teagan leaned in, pitching his voice even lower. "There've been rumors. A half dozen people have gone missing in the last week. One of the other apprentices told me that a farmer out west even had his limbs torn off, but that could be a wild rumor. Still, something has been happening, and it's been hushed by the royals. Perhaps it was this fellow."

And I'd been alone with him in the woods last night, one moment away from being ripped apart.

My corset suddenly felt like it was crushing my ribs.

Cara watched me with concern. "Are you okay?"

"I'm fine. It's just—I've never seen anything like that," I said, keeping my voice low to hide my rising panic.

"There's no way a man did that to him," Teagan said. "It had to be something from the woods. A monster."

My heart felt like it was going to break through my chest. Had I met that monster? Had he ridden a black stallion and looked through me with those relentlessly cruel eyes?

Did that monster know my name?

I shuddered. The fact that I was still alive was proof that the Fates were looking out for me—or at least they *had* been last night.

Today was an entirely different matter.

9

———————

Ella

I tore my eyes from the dangling corpse as applicants shoved past me. The sun had set, and there was a lot of confusion in the dim courtyard, but the crowd was beginning to organize into five groups.

Cara took my hand and pulled me along. "They interview us by occupation. The first line is for the armorers and blacksmiths. Next are the groundskeepers and animal handlers, followed by the entertainers, artists, healers, and the like, then the kitchen staff, and finally the household staff, which includes tailors, laundresses, maids, and servants. You'll probably want to join the last line with me."

"Hope to see you both on the inside," Teagan said. His eyes lingered on Cara for a moment, and then he slipped through the crowd toward the first line, where the armorers and blacksmiths were queued.

"Good luck!" Cara said, then guided me through the crowd toward the last line. It was by far the longest, and we were nearly the last to find spots as a handful of remaining applicants filtered into the courtyard and organized themselves.

A hushed silence fell as a woman strode out of a broad, arched entrance and onto the gallery. My eyes widened. Her clothes were more vibrant than the sun itself, and her chestnut hair was mounded in elaborate curls. Stacks of jeweled bangles wrapped around her arms, and her shoes were as red and glistening as fresh blood. I didn't know whether to be amazed or horrified. I'd never imagined clothes like that in my wildest dreams.

I wasn't the only one. A low muttering went through the crowd.

She seemed to bask in the glow of adoration, and then, with an elaborate flourish, she silenced us all by holding up a single finger. It suddenly felt like we were hanging on threads, and she was the puppeteer.

A gust of wind swirled through the courtyard, and dozens of torches along the walls burst alight, their flames licking high up the stones before settling into a steady flicker.

There were gasps of awe and surprise, and a murmur of astonishment spread.

"How did she do that?" I asked, my eyes still wide with wonder. The torches were mounted onto the outside of the stone wall, so no one could have lit them from inside the castle.

"Magic," Cara replied as I fought the urge to walk up to the closest torch and inspect it.

Magic? The only magic I knew of was the simple tricks performed by gleemen at the local fair and the dark sorcery that the town's relentlessly tiresome priests warned us about. Magic was only ever the work of demons, they claimed.

I could almost believe it. The immortals were as close to demons as a creature could get.

Silence fell again as the high lady lowered her hand and spoke. "Welcome to Castle Silverthorn," she said in a high, resonating voice that made my ears hurt. "I anticipate your stay shall be brief, as we are looking for servants fit for a king, not lazy peasants and fools looking for an easy wage."

Easy wage? I almost laughed. Everyone knew how hard it was to work in the castle. If we weren't desperate, we wouldn't be here.

She strode to the side and turned to face us again. "Let me set the rules. You will each be judged by the royal chamberlain herself. If the skills you possess are deemed worthy and fit for the castle's needs, you will be given a token—though I'm certain most of you will be found *gravely* wanting."

There were more murmurs, but she silenced them by raising a bronze coin high and letting her withering gaze drift over the crowd. "If you do not receive a royal token, you shall leave the castle grounds *immediately*. If you question the chamberlain's judgement or try to steal a token from another, you will meet a swift and bloody death." She smiled, displaying her fangs in delight. "Or a slow one, if you are particularly irksome."

My palms grew clammy.

No questions. No negotiation. Just one shot. I either passed or I didn't.

A second woman appeared on the gallery. Her blonde hair was swept back in a neat bun, and she wore an elegant gray gown with a gold watch piece hanging from a chain attached to the belt around her waist. While there was something similar about their faces, the first was like a sadistic minstrel, while this woman wielded an air of authority like a shield.

"Turn and face forward so that the chamberlain may inspect you," the brightly dressed woman said. "When she passes, you will tell her what special skill you have that makes you qualified to work in the castle. If you have no skills, please leave now and save us the trouble of evicting you."

Doubt gnawed at me.

Dealing with my stepmother was a skill few had mastered, but I doubted that would count for much here. Or alternatively, maybe it made me uniquely qualified to navigate the court. I could imagine these women would make equally cruel mistresses.

The image of Belle locked away in some lord's suite, forced to pay the blood tithe or worse, made my palms sweat.

I wouldn't fail her. I couldn't.

The chamberlain began with the first line, walking slowly past each applicant as they rambled off their skills. She interrupted most after they'd spoken only a few words, her voice sharp and cruel, like a knife pulled across a whetstone. She berated some and simply waved others off dismissively.

She handed a token to a middle-aged man who excelled at restoring antique metalware but sharply rebuked a goldsmith who specialized in filigree jewelry. Several applicants broke down in tears, but most hurried away and out through the castle gates.

The girl with auburn hair protested as she was passed over. The chamberlain spun and backhanded her across the face with inhuman force, sending the girl sprawling onto the cobblestones. Two guards stepped forward, spears lowered. "Get out," the chamberlain said to her, then turned to face the rest of us. "This is your only warning."

My stomach knotted as the auburn-haired girl rose and hobbled away, her face bruised and bloody.

The chamberlain moved on to the next line, having only selected a handful of individuals—and Teagan wasn't among them.

I wasn't sure why he was seeking a job, but like Cara, I assumed everyone here was desperate enough to risk working beneath the heels of the bloodsuckers.

I resisted the urge to reach into my handbag and give my small stowaway a scratch to soothe my nerves. Pip was close, and that was what mattered.

By the time the chamberlain reached our line, only nine applicants had been selected out of the hundreds she'd passed by.

My throat felt dry as the gray specter of a woman paused in front of Cara, scowling. "Your skill?"

Cara curtsied and said, "I make dresses for all occasions, my lady, but I specialize in gowns."

I watched the chamberlain out of the corner of my eye as she scrutinized Cara from head to toe. "Did you make your dress?"

"Yes, my lady." She held out the one she'd brought, letting it fall open in a flutter of green. "And I finished this one yesterday."

"I see." The bloodsucker regarded it for a long moment with apathy, and my stomach knotted for my new friend. The chamberlain turned to continue on, then paused and disdainfully dropped a bronze token in Cara's palm, as if she were being forced to give pennies to a beggar.

Cara's face beamed, regardless of her treatment.

My heart swelled with relief, then descended back into dread as the chamberlain stepped in front of me. I didn't have anything like Cara's brilliant green dress to display.

My gaze darted to the chamberlain's dress, searching for the pockets or pouch where she stored the tokens, then finding nothing, I met her withering gaze. Despite her callous demeanor, she was exceptionally pretty with her full lips and high cheekbones. She was like a belladonna—beautiful but poisonous.

She narrowed her hazel eyes suspiciously as she inspected me. "Is there something wrong with your head, girl?"

I blinked in surprise. "Excuse me?"

"Why is your head covered in that filthy rag?"

Rag? It had been my mother's satin scarf, and it was far from a rag. It was one of the most beautiful things I owned.

I reached up to touch it. "I—"

With a whiplike motion, she yanked it off my head and let it drop into the mud.

Shock paralyzed me, and disapproving whispers rose on the light wind. The girl at the end of our line gasped and took a few steps back. "*Witch*."

I closed my eyes briefly as I tamped down my frustration. This was why I avoided coming into the village. My silver hair was unusual, and people didn't like unusual, even though they lived alongside immortal blood-drinking monsters.

The irony of it left a bitter taste in my mouth.

Cara gave the girl the evil eye, but I just straightened my spine, despite the sting of their judgement. Let them all look.

The chamberlain's lips twitched, but her gaze didn't lift or indicate revulsion. "And do you have a skill, girl?"

I raised my chin, summoning all the confidence I could muster. "I run my family's manor. I'm a fast learner, and I'll work harder than anyone else. I can cook, clean, and tend to the stables."

She eyed me for a moment longer, then moved to the girl who'd called me a witch. My heart strained against my chest. I couldn't fail.

The auburn-haired girl's bloody face burning in my mind, I shoved down my fear and stepped out of line. I'd taken beatings before. I could do it again if it meant finding my sister. "Please," I begged, "I'll excel at any task you assign. Just give me a chance."

"You're not chosen," the chamberlain snapped. "The last girl who questioned me walked out. I assure you, you won't be so lucky—but go ahead and linger. I'm sure we'd all like a little entertainment after such a dull day."

The clicking of hooves rose in the courtyard, tearing her

attention away, and perhaps sparing me a savage beating. The three lords I'd seen earlier rode in and dismounted, passing their horses to a stable hand.

The chamberlain moved to the next applicant, having already forgotten about me.

Despair lodged in my chest.

"Go home, Ella," Cara pleaded quietly, taking my hand and giving it a squeeze. "It's not worth your life. You can try again next time, like I did."

There wouldn't be a next time. Belle needed me now, but what else could I do? If the chamberlain and her guards left me maimed, I'd be of no use to her or the resistance.

Numb, I retrieved my muddy scarf and stepped out of line. It felt like I was stepping off the top of a cliff and falling to the ground below. I headed for the gate in a daze, passing in front of the three lords. Two were eyeing the fresh recruits with interest, but the third was watching me with relentless attention.

It was the blond rider from the forest last night. A flicker of recognition flashed through his eyes.

Oh, hell.

Did he know what I'd done?

The butcher's words played on a loop in my mind: *To harm one of the immortals is a death sentence.*

Suddenly, finding a job was the least of my worries. Adrenaline pumping, I hurried toward the gate with his gaze burning the skin from my neck. I kept my eyes trained on the ground. *All I have to do is get out of here with my head still attached to my neck.*

I was almost through when the ground shook and another rider thundered through the gate in front of me. I leapt back as the monstrous stallion's hooves skidded across the smooth paving stones, and its front legs lifted into the air just in front of me as it came to an uneasy stop.

Fear froze me as the creature's hooves crashed back down.

On its back sat the dark rider, with his raven hair and steely eyes.

He pulled his horse around and glared down at me with a mix of anger and disdain. "Do you have a death wish, foolish woman?"

And then his face hardened with the certainty of recognition. *Shit.*

Clutching my scarf, I slipped around the horse and hurried toward the exit.

In a flash, he dismounted from the stallion and cut off my escape. "You."

The torchlight accentuated the angles of his face, and his eyes...Fates. They were the hue of stormy skies and just as violent. I opened my mouth, but no words came out.

"What are you doing here?" he asked.

"Applying to serve, my lord," I said, fumbling out a low curtsy at last. It was more than I'd done in the woods.

His imperious gaze burned through me, unraveling me layer by layer. "Were you hired?"

I swallowed. "No."

He stalked slowly around me like a circling wolf searching for the right moment to strike. At last, he seemed to reach some kind of decision. "Perhaps that's for the best."

The lord turned his back and walked away, leaving me as empty as the hollowed-out old oak.

Then the emptiness was replaced by rage. My opportunity had fallen from my lap, and I stood there, struck dumb like a cow-eyed farm girl.

I looked around the courtyard desperately, searching for anything I could do. The court and applicants were all watching the high lord, melting away from him as he strode toward the back of the castle.

I'd already been forgotten. Invisible, as I had always been.

Yet one pair of eyes remained fixed on me. The high lord's black stallion had paused to look back, defying his handlers with a jerk of its lead. There was something unnatural about his attention, as if he were judging me, just like all the others had.

For a second, I felt a deep, inexplicable connection with the beast. A silent understanding.

Then, with a sudden burst of fury, the black warhorse reared on his hind legs and gave an ear-splitting whinny, yanking his handler clean off his feet. He slammed his hooves down with a snort, and then, tearing free, bolted across the courtyard.

Courtiers and applicants dove away, knocking each other down as he charged through the group. The blond-haired lord lunged forward, grasping for his reins, but that only further agitated the stallion. His hooves clattered against the cobblestones as he circled the courtyard and galloped for the gate, with only me standing between him and freedom. His handlers charged, but he spun and kicked his legs out, driving them back. He looked like he was ready to vault over me to get to freedom.

The world fell away, and instinct kicked in. My sole concern became the stallion.

"Easy, handsome," I said as I stepped forward slowly with my arm raised, as I would when calming my stepmother's mares. The stallion neighed and slowed, and his ears pricked forward.

Had I been the one who'd spooked him? Why had he looked at me like that?

As the others warily hung back, I closed the distance, heart drumming. One kick could break my leg or cave in my chest. "That's a good boy. I'm not going to harm you. Nobody's going to harm you."

He watched me with ferocious eyes, and then, seemingly satisfied that I wasn't a threat, he exhaled loudly and lowered his head and walked forward. I placed my hand on his neck and stroked him firmly. A low gasp rose from the crowd, but I paid it little heed, my attention focused solely on the horse. His coat was hot and damp with sweat, and he smelled like the woods. He looked back at me and sniffed my arm.

I smiled at the magnificent creature. "I'm Ella. It's nice to meet you."

The stallion gave a soft, almost self-satisfied snort.

The silence of the courtyard was suddenly deafening. I felt them all watching me.

I felt the dark rider watching me.

The stallion had to be worth more than our entire manor. A dozen manors. And it was being handled by a peasant girl. Touching it was probably another executable offense, like me taking the queen mother's crown and plopping it on my head.

Return the horse. Avoid eye contact with the angry bloodsucker. Leave with your life.

I gently led the stallion back toward the groomsman he'd knocked down, keeping my eyes low. The man's face was pale, and he said nothing as he took the reins.

With the beast out of the way, the chamberlain strode forward, her face livid and taut with disgust. "How dare you the touch the—"

The dark rider threw up his hand to silence her and approached like a wave of midnight crashing down on me.

My throat tightened, and I took a step back. Gods, he was tall. And broad.

Tension zinged the air between us, and I met his scalding gaze. His dark hair was tousled from his ride, and the five-o'clock shadow on his jaw made my stomach flip for reasons I didn't understand.

He tilted his head. "How did you calm Tenebris like that?"

I dug my nails into my palms, trying to strangle my nerves. "I—I've a knack for animals."

"That's a warhorse, not a peasant's mare or beast of burden," he said in a low voice rumbling with threat. "Yet you know some trick his handlers do not?"

My heart felt like it was going to break free of my chest. This could be my chance or a trap. "I don't know," I said. "But if he does this often, you might give him some oats mixed with a few drops of chamomile at night."

There was a low murmur.

"*I*," he said with an incredulous growl, "might?"

"The stablemaster, I mean, my lord." I dipped low, suddenly remembering my station. Even though I hadn't fully tightened my corset, I struggled to breathe as I faced him. "I beg your forgiveness, I'd just very much like to leave in one piece."

"You will stay," he said roughly, studying my hair.

I didn't even know how to respond. All I'd wanted was a chance to work in the castle, but that now meant being trapped here with *him*. With all of them.

I looked around at the courtiers. They were staring at me, and none of their expressions were kind or welcoming. Some stared with disgust, others anger, and some with an almost hungry interest.

They were all predators, and I'd just been placed on the menu.

A muscle in the lord's jaw twitched as he gave me one final displeased look, and then he turned and walked back toward the grand stairway. "Find her a suitable position, Lorayna."

Fury flickered across the chamberlain's face, but she bowed her head. "Yes, Your Royal Highness."

The blood drained from my head, and dizziness tunneled my vision.

Your Royal Highness?

The night air pressed in on me, suffocating and thick, as he disappeared. It all made sense now—the way they danced around him, cowering and deferring.

The dark rider was Prince Cassius, the Fates-damned Lord of the Bloodvale...and I'd just told him to feed his horse oats like he was a stableboy. I was certain he'd slaughtered people for less, yet miraculously, he'd let me live.

10

Cassius

I left the commotion of the courtyard behind and strode through the entrance into the great hall, my thoughts clouded and furious.

What the fuck was the silver-haired woman doing here?

First, she'd been in the woods last night with the blood-thirsty bastard I'd gutted, and now here she was in my castle. It was too calculated to be mere coincidence. But what was her game? Was she an informant sent by one of the great houses? Or was it possible she was here of her own volition, perhaps drawn by our encounter the night before?

Whatever she was, it was trouble, and I didn't need the distraction. Not now.

"That one caught your eye, didn't she?" Aamon prodded.

I lifted an eyebrow at my counsel. "Who?"

"The girl with the silver hair?" He chuckled. "The one from the woods last night? Everyone saw the way you looked at her."

I grunted as I strode through the great hall, my lip curling at the exhaustive array of fine tableware that had been spread across the long tables to be polished. "I thought she might be a threat. I was wrong. She's nothing."

It was a lie. She was something, but I didn't know what, and I was determined to find out.

Aamon made an incredulous sound, and it took an enormous effort not to stab him. "I've seen how you deal with threats, Cassius. It's not like that."

"She has a way with horses," I said dismissively. "There will be plenty here soon with the ball approaching."

I'd never seen anyone, let alone a *mortal*, have that effect on Tenebris. And what in the hells had spooked him in the first place?

Suspicion and a myriad of dark thoughts muddled my mind, and in the center of them was her. *Ella.*

Aamon drew close. "I think you fancy a taste."

A twinge of desire rose like a long-forgotten temptress. It had been decades since I'd felt anything but apathy, let alone lust for a female. *And her scent.* The mere memory of it made my fangs ache. I shook my head. "Trust me. I have no interest in the little mouse."

He shrugged, stepping away. "Then I assume you won't mind if I take her for myself. She's quite a unique specimen, and I suspect she ta—"

I spun on my friend, gripped his throat, and pushed him into the nearest wall. Wood cracked, and a portrait of my father buckled. "Keep your hands off her if you want to keep your head."

Aamon raised his hands in surrender as a teasing grin spread across his face. "Just thought I should get some clarification. No need to get violent, Your Royal Highness. Clearly, you have no interest in her whatsoever, and of course, neither do I."

I released the cheeky bastard and exited the great hall.

Aamon cleared his throat and hurried on behind. "However, on the off chance you are feeling possessive of that one, you might wish to mark her as your own sooner rather than later. I saw the way the others were watching her, and I'm certain I'm not the only immortal who'd fancy a bite. The court loves novelty, and that hair of hers is rather breathtaking."

A vicious rumble rose in my throat. "I have no interest in claiming her. I just don't want you or anyone else to, either."

I couldn't care less about their kind, but she'd already been attacked once. I would not have it happen again. Not, at least, within the walls of my castle. It would be an afront to my rule.

That was all.

"You should have the girl work for Lorayna," Aamon suggested. "She and her sister are viciously possessive of their servants and run them to the bone. They prefer to feed from tall and brooding males anyway, so you can be sure the girl will keep her chastity intact while here in the castle." He glanced over with a wry smile. "Considering what you did to the last man who touched her, we don't need a pile of bodies turning up before the ball."

I clenched my jaw. She meant nothing to me. There was no reason for me to be protective or possessive, yet there was something about her that made me murderous.

I gave Aamon a curt nod. "Fine. I'll speak to Lorayna. After what the girl did with Tenebris, I assumed she'd be assigned to the stables, but this is a better plan."

If the girl worked in the stables, she'd be on display for every immortal in the castle.

Although I'd intended my words to signal a dismissal, Aamon pursued me like a relentless and irritating shadow.

I sighed. "Is there something else, *Lord Aamon*?"

"We need to talk about the ball, seeing as it's only three weeks away. Have you decided on the wine you want served?"

Apparently, Bianca, the Mistress of Ceremonies, had managed to turn him into her attack dog.

"Does it matter?" Avoiding the courtiers, I skirted the inner courtyard and headed up the stairs to my private wing.

"To me, of course not, but the Mistress of Ceremonies keeps asking me, and it's annoying as fuck. I'm your counsel, not a party planner."

"Better you than me." The sconces lit as I stepped into the study, hoping the solitude would ease the tightness in my chest, but somehow, it felt more suffocating. "Have her choose whatever wine she sees fit."

I dropped into one of the chairs below the stained glass window, exhausted by even contemplating the politics of the court.

Aamon strolled over to one of the floor-to-ceiling bookshelves that lined the room and pulled out a book. "I've never seen anyone throw a party with less enthusiasm for it."

My fingers thrummed the arms of the chair as I gazed absently at the empty one beside me. My brother's chair—the king's seat. Unlike the one on which I sat, the king's seat had a high back and was decorated with ornate upholstery and detailed carvings of roses and thorns, the emblem of my family's bloodline—a bloodline my brother was supposed to ensure.

"This ball wasn't meant for me." The vitriol in my voice came naturally.

Aamon stopped paging through his book and looked over at me with a raised brow. "Are we circling back to this again?"

The arms of the chair cracked beneath my grasp. "The moment I take the throne, I condemn my brother to a life of exile. You know that."

Aamon snapped the book shut. "Valen made that choice when he abdicated. He knew it meant he could never return."

Anger thrummed in my friend's voice. I knew he hated Valen

for the position he'd put me in, but I couldn't summon an ounce of anger. I would run, too, if it wouldn't leave the kingdom in tatters.

I forced my fingers to release the splintered wood. "I would have welcomed Valen home with open arms. He could have come back."

Aamon shook his head. "No, Cassius, he couldn't. The Triad would never permit it. The die has been cast, and if he's out there and still sane, he knows it."

As much as it stung, I knew he was right. The mantle of rule had fallen to me, and I couldn't give it up.

"You need to leave him behind and move forward, or the other houses will take your hesitation as a sign of weakness," Aamon said.

I released an ironic laugh. "And choosing a bride at a silly ball is a sign of strength? It's a ridiculous tradition."

"The council doesn't expect you to choose her then—just to announce your decision after the last dance. That's why you need to do the work *now*."

It felt like the walls of the study were closing in. My lips curled. "You know the ladies of this court. It's an impossible task. They're all conniving, power-hungry, and treacherous. Which I would respect, if I weren't liable to wind up staked through the heart in my wedding bed."

Aamon returned the book and leaned against the shelf. "Then we look beyond the immediate court. We scour every one of the great houses."

"The ball is in three weeks. How am I supposed to find a woman who will be a capable queen, someone I could trust and bear an heir with, but can feel no affection for?"

"No affection?" My friend laughed. "Is this about what that old woman said to you? You can't seriously believe any of that."

The seer's words echoed in the back of my mind. *If you fall in love, the woman you choose will destroy everything your father built. And if she ever takes the throne, she will make your people pay the price of their thirst.*

I cracked my knuckles. "The old woman is touched by the Fates. I do not take her advice lightly—nor should you."

"Touched by the Fates?" Aamon scoffed. "She's a *drunk*. She's touched by whiskey, not prophecy. You know as well as I do that there's no magic beyond these walls."

"There are plenty of things out there we don't understand. Things not affected by the curse over the wood."

The creatures that dwelt deep in the forest, for instance.

Aamon shrugged. "Maybe. Or she could be trying to mess with your head."

I rubbed my temples. "Everything about this situation messes with my head."

11

As soon as the prince disappeared, the courtyard burst into a flurry of commotion. Soldiers slammed the gates shut, the groomsmen shuttled away the horses, and the chamberlain began barking orders to the new hires.

My legs nearly buckled, but Cara hurried forward and looped her arm around mine to steady me. "Fates, Ella, that was incredible. Did you see the way the prince looked at you? You've certainly caught his eye."

The prince.

The plan had been to be inconspicuous. To not draw attention. Instead, I'd drawn the eye of the most powerful immortal in the Bloodvale. One who might know that I'd attacked one of his kind.

"I think I might have just dug my own grave," I said darkly.

Cara squeezed my arm. "But you're not buried yet. And just think, we've got jobs in the castle!"

I took in the imposing structure that would be our new home. Stone buildings encompassed the courtyard on three sides, creating a U-shape around us. A staircase led up to an ornate entry at the northern end of the courtyard, while a pair of towering four-story residential wings flanked both sides.

But as massive as the buildings were, they were dwarfed by a single tower rising above all the others.

I had no doubt about who lived there. I shivered, and tearing my eyes away, I turned slowly to take in the rest of the space. There were barracks, stables, and a beautiful rose garden. My heart longed to explore it, but I was certain it wasn't for common servants like us. We were little more than animals in the eyes of the immortals.

It didn't matter.

As intimidating as the castle was, a job meant that I was one step closer to finding my sister. It meant that I'd be able to spy for the resistance and maybe even help bring an end to the immortals' cruel reign. It was probably impossible, perhaps even a dream that would end with me dangling from a rope, but it was hope—and that was rare enough in the Bloodvale.

The elation of being hired didn't last long, and my smile faded as I met Cara's eyes. "I'm sorry Teagan wasn't hired."

Her face fell. "Yeah. It's going to be a long year without him."

"Year?"

"I've heard they don't let the first-years leave—not without permission. But maybe I'll find a way to sneak out." She squeezed my arm more tightly. "At least you're here with me. That will make it easier."

I opened my mouth to respond but froze. The chamberlain stood high on the steps, glaring straight at me with a murderous expression.

The ramifications of what I'd done hit me like a brick, and my stomach dropped. The woman in charge of the castle's staff had rejected me, yet I'd found a way to go over her head *in front of the entire court*. They'd threatened to kill anyone who talked back, so what would she do to me for publicly embarrassing her?

I'd just made a very dangerous enemy, and if I were going to survive the day, I'd better smooth things over.

She started stalking down the stairs toward me, so I slipped out of Cara's arm. "Get going. I'm in trouble, and I don't want to take you down with me."

Before Cara could protest, I hurried over to my new employer and curtsied as low as I could. "I'm grateful for a second chance, Chamberlain."

"You impertinent wretch." The imperious woman dug her fingers into my arm and pulled me brusquely aside, her expression ice. "You will address me as 'Lady Lorayna' or simply 'your ladyship.'"

"I'm sorry, your ladyship."

"That was quite the performance you put on back there, but you don't fool me." Her lips twitched with displeasure. "While the prince may have taken pity on you, I will not. You'll work twice as hard as the other servants, and if you cross me, you'll find out just how cruel this place can be."

The corpse hanging from the wall left no doubt. I'd grown up hearing rumors about servants who'd been crippled or left traumatized from their work, but most seemed able to endure the bloodsuckers and earned a good wage for their labors.

I'd be one of those. I was a survivor.

I nodded. "I understand. I'll work harder than anyone here, your ladyship."

Narrowing her eyes at me like I was a silly child, she said, "It's a wonder what His Royal Highness saw in an ugly creature such as yourself, but what the prince desires, he gets." She held up a bronze token. "This is your pass into the castle. Always keep it on you, and don't lose it, because you won't get a replacement or a second chance to work here." She tossed the token like she would have flicked a coin into a wishing well.

I lurched forward and caught it before it bounced off the stone step. The metal was warm to the touch, and a small rune had been etched into the surface of one side—a series of concentric circles. I didn't recognize the symbol, but something about it felt familiar.

"You're to join the household staff." Her voice was as sharp as glass. "If I hear of you causing any other kind of disturbance, there will be hell to pay. Now get out of my sight."

She was a miserable woman, but I just had to put up with her for as long as it took to find Belle. Hopefully, I'd be buried in the kitchens or with the cleaning staff, as far from her as I could get.

"Thank you, your ladyship." I hurried off in the direction that Cara and the others had gone. They were already filing into the castle through a side door rather than the main entrance. I found a bit of string in my satchel and threaded it through a small hole in the token, then hung it around my neck like a pendant and tucked it into my bodice. I drew in a bracing breath, then climbed the stairs toward the servants' entrance.

As soon as I crossed the threshold, the air snapped, and I gasped as a thousand pins pricked my skin, like I'd just stepped into a hot bath after swimming in the cold creek. The token warmed against my chest, and I stopped in my tracks. *What the hell?*

"Is there a problem?" Lorayna glowered at me from the stairs.

"No, your ladyship, I just felt something..."

She pinched the bridge of her nose as if I'd just caused her an enormous inconvenience. "The gods are certainly testing me with you."

Funny. I felt the same.

Shaking her head, she turned and headed into the entrance hall, her heels clicking on the pale marble floor.

I hurried over to where Cara and the other new hires were listening to a butler dryly explain etiquette and what was expected of us.

Cara silently mouthed, *Are you okay?*

I nodded, then covertly checked on Pip. The butler was explaining that since we were lowborn humans and repugnant to the lords, we were forbidden to use the same doors as immortals or to be in the great hall, dining spaces, or public chambers unless we had express duties there. If we were caught out of position, we would be fined and potentially fired.

Some of the other new hires were attentive, but most were looking around nervously, their expressions drawn and faces pale. Each of us had been desperate for a job, but now reality had sunk in. We were in the lions' den, surrounded by immortals with no checks on their power and the right to feed on us whenever they wanted.

A pair of courtiers glanced our way as they swept through the entrance hall. Their gazes were intent. Hungry.

I swallowed and pressed myself back against the wall as I tried to get a sense of my surroundings. Black silk tapestries hung from the walls of the entrance, the midnight cloth embroidered with twisting silver vines and crimson roses. My gaze crept upward. The ceiling was impossibly high, and I suddenly felt very, very small.

"For your first year here, you are expected to be on call at all times," the butler continued. "You may collect your most necessary personal effects from home this evening, but otherwise, you are not allowed to leave the castle grounds without the express permission of your supervisor."

Cara's mouth tightened, and my spirits sank. If I were going to get any information to my stepmother, I would have to use her mangy old crow.

The butler turned and led us through a long feasting hall. The space buzzed with activity as servants moved around the long tables, polishing silverware and ornate vases, and folding brightly embroidered fabrics. The piney fragrance of wood polish brought me back to the manor. I used that same oil to clean the furniture, only this place was the glaring opposite of home.

Lorayna stalked through the room like a wolf, berating and cursing the servants at their work, but the sound of gurgling water drew my attention to a large fountain at the head of the chamber. It was carved in the form of a dense rose thicket—the royal emblem—with streams of water pouring from the blossoms and rushing down into a dark pit.

I stopped in my tracks as we passed by and stared. There was nothing holding the fountain up. It was floating over the pit, all on its own.

Impossible. I moved toward it, my curiosity burning.

"What are you doing?" the butler snapped, jolting me back to reality.

"How is the fountain...doing *that*?"

The butler snorted. "Well, it certainly isn't physics. Where were you raised? A barnyard?"

"A *manor house*."

"Well, this is no manor house. Now, get in line. You're not here to sightsee."

My thoughts spun as I rejoined the group. It had to be magic, but a part of me felt silly even considering the thought. Magic existed in fairytales and in the myths our grandparents told us as children when we sat around the fire, but what if there was a thread of truth in them?

What if magic hadn't been fully extinguished in the Uprising? What if the immortals had kept it all for themselves? I'd seen the Mistress of Ceremonies light the courtyard torches with a wave of her hand.

The butler ushered us down the hall and through another small door, and my jaw dropped as I emerged in an enormous ballroom. The excessive wealth and opulence on display screamed undeserved privilege and power. Glorious tapestries hung from the balconies that overlooked the polished marble dance floor, and the raised stage for the orchestra was ringed with ornate gilded railings. Enormous crystal chandeliers cast a warm glow over the vast space—only they weren't suspended from the ceiling by chains, but rather floated freely in midair.

Just like the fountain.

It was madness.

"This is the grand ballroom," the butler continued. "Many of you will be working here to make sure it is perfect for the Prince's Ball."

I barely heard his words as I craned my neck back. A vibrant mural spanned the high ceiling, and as my vision sharpened, heat spread through my veins, and my pulse quickened. Naked humans and immortals graced the ceiling in all manners of embrace. It was lewd and erotic and enthralling. Rather than recoiling in terror as the immortals fed from their blood, the humans were enthralled, lost to their carnal desires.

My gaze gravitated to a strong male with dark hair at the center of the ceiling. He held a woman who leaned back in what I could only imagine was ecstasy, her right breast exposed, two crimson marks on her lower neck. Red tinged the male's fangs, and his stormy eyes seemed to follow me as I wheeled around.

I swallowed hard. There was only one immortal who had eyes like that...

"Watch where you're careening," a man snapped.

Jumping, I cleared my throat and rubbed my aching neck. "Excuse me."

He carried an armful of the new blue linens Lorayna had requested, and a coy grin tugged on his lips as his eyes darted to the ceiling. "It's fine, just don't get any ideas. Things can go from good to bad very quickly."

Did he think I was fantasizing about the bloody orgy?

My cheeks burned as he walked away.

I hurried to catch up with the group, shivering as I imagined the raven-haired immortal's gaze following me. *Keep your eyes on the ground, Ella.*

Columns flanked the sides of the long ballroom, enclosing two dimly lit galleries. Their back walls were painted like the forest, while the murals above them depicted idyllic scenes of life in the countryside. My gaze followed the elaborate composition toward the far end of the ballroom, where two curving staircases framed a royal dais. The imagery became more and more disturbing, and by the time it reached the dais, it depicted abject carnage. Blood. Bodies. Destruction.

A cold chill snaked over me. It was a depiction of the Uprising and the wholesale slaughter of my people.

"A bit dark for an entertaining hall," Cara whispered, her voice pinched.

Dark didn't cut it. It was sickening. Perverse.

The painted scenes of the woods along the flanking corridors suddenly felt just as stifling as the real ones that surrounded this valley and kept us trapped.

"I bet the royals keep it to remind us of what happens when we step out of line," she continued quietly.

The prince and his murderous bloodline deserved to be staked and burned for the atrocities they'd committed against humans over the centuries. I wished I could do something, *anything*, to put an end to it all—their reign and the horrors we continued to endure.

My fists clenched, and I bitterly glanced back at the orgies on the other end of the ceiling. "So, if this is the Uprising, what are those supposed to symbolize? I don't remember any orgies in the history books."

"You must've been looking in the wrong books," a deep voice said from above.

The prince's blond henchman stood on the balcony, an expression of amusement—and something darker—on his face. "Think of the murals as incentivization."

Refusing to be intimidated, I narrowed my eyes up at him. "Incentivization for *what*, exactly?"

As if the bastard was shocked that I could speak, his eyes rounded for a split second. "To be a good little girl, of course."

Anger burned under my skin. I hadn't been a girl for quite some time.

He gestured to the bloody images of slaughter at the back of the hall. "*That* is what will happen if you're naughty." Then, keeping his cold eyes on me, he inclined his head slightly toward the painting of the orgy. "And that is what could happen if you behave."

"I prefer my men to have heartbeats, so I'll pass."

A slow grin curled his lips, showing the tips of his fangs, and though he was gorgeous by human standards, all I felt was violence toward him.

"And who are these men?" he asked. "Because the color on your cheeks suggests your virtue is still intact."

My neck heated. "My virtue is none of your business." I turned to Cara. "Let's go."

"Watch yourself, Ella DuPonte," the lord said, his voice suddenly tinged with threat.

I froze. He remembered my name from last night.

"DuPonte." He accentuated my stepmother's maiden name. "It's curious, because I couldn't find your name in last year's land taxes. Or the year before, or in any of the last few decades."

Dread coiled around my chest. Why the hell were they looking into me? Because I'd stabbed an immortal? It had to be. And worse, the name I'd given them could lead back to my stepmother, even though she didn't use it anymore.

Trying to keep my voice and heartbeat steady, I glanced over my shoulder and shrugged. "Maybe you're looking in the wrong record books."

"I doubt that very much." He gloated. "We like to keep a close tally of the cattle."

My fists tightened, but Cara took my arm and pulled me back toward the group of newly hired house staff.

I squeezed my eyes shut for a moment, cursing my luck. If I was going to be any value to the resistance, I needed to be inconspicuous. But so far, I'd drawn the attention of the prince and his blond lapdog, not to mention the ire of the chamberlain and the butler.

Hell, I'd pulled the stunt with the stallion in front of the entire court. I drew in a steadying breath. Maybe it would be okay. No spy would be so foolish as to make a grand entrance like I had, so perhaps they wouldn't suspect me.

Or perhaps they'll never stop watching.

12

———————

Ella

We'd just caught up with the others when footsteps clattered on the floor behind me.

I turned, and pain exploded across my cheek as Lorayna backhanded me. I staggered under the force of the blow, which was more powerful than any my stepmother had ever given me —probably stronger than the town blacksmith could deliver himself.

"You silver-haired harlot," the chamberlain hissed, her voice low and full of venom.

The butler's face went white, and the rest of the staff backed away.

"Get on with you lot!" Lorayna snapped.

Cara lingered as the others hurried away, but I shook my head, and she reluctantly followed.

I pressed my hand to my throbbing cheek, my vision dancing. Still too shocked to feel anything but surprise, I curtsied. "I don't know what I did wrong, your ladyship, but I apologize."

She gave me a withering scowl. "Apparently, it wasn't enough for the prince to hire you. Now he's assigned you to work for me."

The blood rushed from my face.

No. Not her. Anyone but her.

She shook her head. "Only the Fates know why he did this to me. An undeserved punishment? A cruel joke?"

My mind raced. My time in the castle was on the precipice of disaster. The bloodsucker would do everything in her power to make my life miserable unless I could start working my way into her good graces. My life probably depended on it, along with any chance of finding Belle.

Thankfully, I had a decade of experience placating a harsh woman. I kept my gaze lowered dutifully. "I'm honored to work for you, Lady Lorayna. The prince must have seen how busy you were with your duties in the castle. Clearly, a lady of your standing deserves additional help."

Her stance softened—almost imperceptibly, but it was there.

"Perhaps he's finally recognizing my value, but don't get any ideas about your station. You're not replacing my handmaids. You'll do any task they or I assign. You'll work yourself to the bone to atone for the spectacle you've made of my authority today."

"Yes, your ladyship."

"Then follow me. I don't have time to waste."

Lorayna marched me to her quarters in a tower at the end of the western wing, and my breath stilled when I stepped inside. I knew that the immortals in the castle lived lavishly, but her chambers were beyond anything I'd imagined.

Her sitting room had a towering ceiling like a church with huge stained glass windows, gray stone walls, and silver decoration that gave the space a cold, wintry feel. Just a fraction of the wealth on display could let Lower Town feast like kings for a year.

My gaze landed on a life-sized marble statue that depicted a kneeling man worshiping a goddess who'd clearly been modeled on Lorayna. Both were stark naked, and I quickly turned away. I'd seen village boys swimming naked in the river before, but the statue left nothing to the imagination, and his adoration of her had left him as excited as a stallion.

"You'll begin work immediately," Lorayna said without sparing me a glance. "There's a pile of laundry in my suite that needs washing. Use hot water on everything but my dresses, obviously, which should be washed in cool rose water. And so help the gods, if you forget any of these orders, I will lash you until your back is bare."

Got it. Don't shrink the bloodsucker's clothes.

She crossed her arms. "After you've finished the laundry, mop the floors, and it's been ages since the windows have been scrubbed. I expect to see rays of sunshine coming through when you're finished."

Right, because immortals *loved* to bask in the sun.

It was a lot of work if she expected it done in a day. Worry crept over my shoulders. "Anything else I should know?"

She pursed her lips, then snapped her thumb and third finger. "Yes. I need you to unclog my bathtub. My sister used it yesterday, and her wretched hair gets everywhere."

Was she kidding? "I understand."

She made a disdainful sound, then glided over to the entrance. She paused with her hand on the door, looking back at me with a ruthlessly cold expression. "If I find one thing missing, or anything out of place, I will hunt down every member of your family and spike their heads in front of the castle —*understood*?"

The blood rushed from my face. "I would never think of taking anything from you, my lady."

Her lip pulled up. "Of course you wouldn't."

With that, she pulled the door shut, and I let out a deep breath. *Stay positive. Focus on why you're here.*

I might be working for a madwoman, but I was safely in the castle and one step closer to finding Belle. And since Lorayna was the prince's chamberlain, perhaps there was some piece of information here that the resistance could use.

"What do you say we have a look around?" I said to Pip as I set my handbag down and opened the top.

The little rat climbed out and sat up, clearly as awed as I was.

"Watch for cats," I cautioned.

He gave me a look that seemed to say, *I don't think I'm the one who's first in line to get bitten around here*, then darted under a settee to explore its potential for crumbs.

I wandered into Lorayna's bedroom and ran my fingers over the silky sheets and heavy comforter. I'd never imagined anything could be so soft. She'd strewn dirty clothes over the floor, so I gathered them and put them in a hamper to wash later. Crafted from the smoothest cottons, silks, and linen, each piece was like a work of art. I couldn't believe she'd just left them lying about like a filthy stoat.

Her bathroom was larger than our dining room, with a huge claw-foot tub and a spout emerging from the wall above it, along with a couple of knobs. Curious, I turned one. Water came gushing out of the pipe, and I stared, slack-jawed, as it began to steam after just a few moments.

She had *hot* running water.

There was no doubt about it now. The castle *was* magical— and even with the floating fountain and chandeliers, this was the most miraculous thing I'd seen so far. What would it be like to live in a place where you could take a warm bath without having to boil the water first?

I quickly shut it off in case the magic ran out.

The tub drained slowly because of the clog, so I splashed a little water on my face. My skin heated with its glorious warmth. If we'd had a bath like this in our manor, I would have fought Belle every day to use it first.

Magical castle or not, I had work to do. I unplugged the tub, then hunted down the laundry room and washed Lorayna's clothes. After hanging them out to dry during the coming day, I set to work scrubbing the grime off the floors and walls of Lorayna's bathroom. My eyes grew bleary, and my arms throbbed, but eventually, I reached a place of calm in the hypnotic work.

The castle might have been filled with monsters and psychopaths and magic, but hard work was something that I understood. It was familiar and safe, unlike everything else around me.

And I had Pip. I'd worried about bringing him, but it filled my heart with joy to see him scampering about and exploring her rooms.

After countless hours, a bell pealed in the courtyard outside, shattering my sense of peace. I looked up. Dawn. Had I really been working that long? When would I be allowed to stop. Never? Maybe they'd just work me until I dropped dead.

Bloodsuckers.

I got my answer forty minutes later when the door opened. Pip skittered up my sleeve and tucked himself behind my hair as Lorayna entered the room with another girl at her side.

"What are you still doing in my chambers at this time of night?" she hissed. "You're my servant, not my handmaid."

I rose quickly and curtsied. "I'm sorry, my lady. I didn't realize I was dismissed."

She rested her hands on her hips, glaring at me. "Didn't you hear the bells? They mean *get out of my space*. I need my beauty sleep without little rodents like you scurrying about and making noise." With that, she turned and stormed into her bedroom, muttering, "The girl's either half deaf or half dumb."

Her handmaid ushered me out and gave me directions to the women's residence. "The first set of bells mean dinner, which you probably missed. They'll ring curfew shortly, and it's best not to be caught out, so I'd run if I were you."

I hurried through the winding corridors, finally finding the women's residence as the last of the other servants were scuttling in.

A broad woman with gray hair and a worn ledger scowled at me as I entered. "Who are you? There are no visitors allowed in here."

"Ella," I said, and pulled my token from my bodice, showing it to her. "I work for Lady Lorayna and just started today."

She ran her finger down her list, checked off a name, and then looked back up with a frown. "Why aren't you wearing your uniform?"

I glanced down at my mother's dress. It had started the day clean and pressed but was now damp, stained, and halfway to ruin. My stomach knotted. "I was assigned work before the orientation was over, so I missed a lot of things. I don't even know where anything is in this maze."

The gray-haired woman shook her head in annoyance and went to a cupboard on the wall, muttering, "What a couple of buzzards they are, letting you destroy your best clothes." She pulled down several garments, then handed me the stack. "I'm Headmistress Alana, and I run the girls' residence, so you'll report to me at the end of each day. You're required to wear these uniforms in the castle at all times."

"Thank you, Headmistress," I said, flipping through the pile of clothes. A pair of aprons, three simple gray work dresses, a nightgown, and mercifully, a few undergarments.

She produced an old, sketched map of the castle, pointing out the places I would need to go to do my work. In addition to the central wing that held the feasting hall and ballroom, there were two primary residential wings, each augmented by imposing towers for the most powerful members of the court. The western wing, which overlooked the river and rose garden, was reserved for the high lords who lived within the castle grounds, such as Lorayna, her sister Bianca, and the blond rider who'd accosted us in the great hall. In addition to the servants' quarters, the east wing held guest rooms for visitors, as well as the small chambers belonging to courtesans and the castle's blood retainers—the poor souls whose only job was to let the immortals feed from them.

The prince and a handful of other royals lived in the soaring north tower. They had their own staff. "The royal tower is off-limits to our like," Alana emphasized.

She led me to the door on the right, which opened into a chamber with a dozen or so bunk beds. "I've assigned you the top bunk, five down, above loud Annie." She frowned. "I'm sorry about that, but all the other spots were taken earlier by the other new hires."

"I'm just glad to have a place to sleep."

After freshening up in the girls' washroom, I sneaked into my bunk. Loud Annie was already asleep and breathing hard. I quietly slipped Pip out of my bag and placed him on my pillow, then climbed beneath the thin, scratchy sheet. Pip curled up against my neck, a warm comfort in the unfamiliar place.

The shades were drawn, but the rising sunlight still filtered into the room. Because our lords were nocturnal and shunned the light, the household staff worked nights and slept in the day. Dawn would become my dusk, and dusk would become my dawn.

I stared at the ceiling, still unable to believe it. The bloodsuckers had taken my world and turned it on its head.

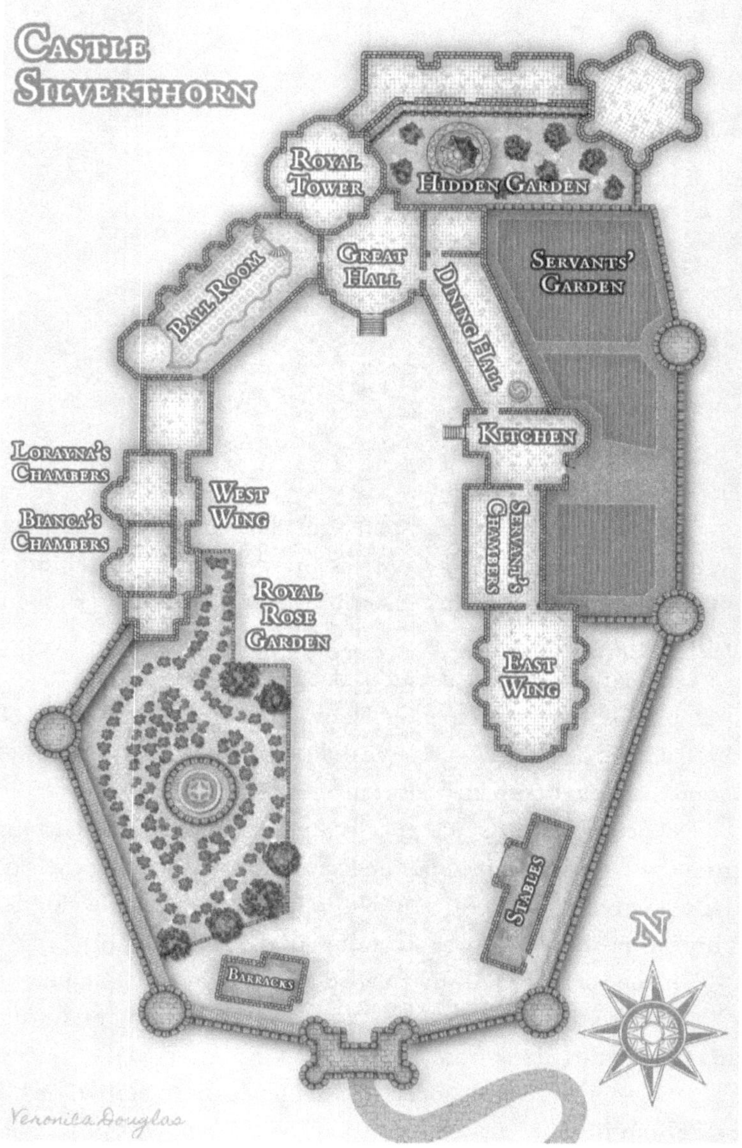

CASTLE SILVERTHORN
ROYAL TOWER
HIDDEN GARDEN
BALL ROOM
GREAT HALL
SERVANTS' GARDEN
DINING HALL
LORAYNA'S CHAMBERS
BIANCA'S CHAMBERS
WEST WING
KITCHEN
SERVANT'S CHAMBERS
ROYAL ROSE GARDEN
EAST WING
STABLES
BARRACKS
N
Veronica Douglas

13

—————

Ella

The clanging of the first bell wrenched me awake the next evening. My back ached from the hard mattress and lumpy pillow, and my eyes burned like they'd been vigorously rubbed with sandpaper.

Loud Annie had exceeded expectations, producing a gasping, pig-like snore that practically had concussive force. I thanked the Fates that Lorayna had worked me to the bone, otherwise I might not have slept a wink.

I wiped my bleary eyes and sat up, pulling back the curtain from the windows above me. The sun had gone, leaving the sky the dying red of dusk, broken by patches of dark purple clouds. This was my life now. I was a creature of the night.

The bed shook as Annie crawled out and glared up at me.

"What's your problem?" I asked, none too keen on enduring any kind of dirty look from her.

"You snore," she snapped. "You better learn to stop it, or I'll make your life a living hell."

My jaw went slack in surprise as Annie turned and sauntered toward the washroom, muttering under her breath.

I hadn't eaten since the day before, and my stomach was growling. After putting on my new uniform, I found Cara, and we headed downstairs to the servants' mess together. It was a large, low-ceilinged room with long tables, like in a tavern. I mounded my plate with a couple of warm biscuits and eggs as my stomach groaned with hunger. It took every ounce of willpower I had not to start eating before we reached the table.

The food was bland, but I savored every crumbly bite. It was the first meal I hadn't cooked since Belle had disappeared, and that alone made it absolutely glorious.

Cara launched into an excited account of her time on the household staff, making preparations for the ball. "It's going to be so amazing, Ella. A masquerade like no one has ever seen. The decorations are gorgeous—so much silver and gold. Fates, I hope we get to see it happen."

Loud Annie scoffed at the far end of the table. "They aren't going to let the likes of you in there. The waitstaff, for certain, but not seamstresses and scullery maids."

Cara stiffened. "Maybe I'll peek."

The other girl rolled her eyes. "Maybe they'll catch you and cut your head off for the entertainment of their guests. I bet they'd drink out of the stump like a fountain."

We stared at her, aghast.

"Just remember your place," Annie said with a full mouth. She finished the last bite of her biscuit and rose. "There are a lot of girls who've worked far longer and harder than you two have. You're fresh meat. You deserve nothing."

She scooped up her plates and walked away, shattering any remaining illusion I still had about what life in the castle was going to be like.

It'll be worth it if I can find Belle.

"What the hell was that about?" I asked.

Cara shrugged. "I think this place is going to take some getting used to."

A short girl with blonde hair leaned in. "Don't mind Annie. She works in the kitchens with me, and we never get to see anything but the insides of pots and dirty dishes. What you're doing sounds amazing."

"Once we finish the decorations, we're going to start adding the finishing touches to some of the ladies' gowns," Cara said. "That's what I'm really excited to see."

The squat girl snorted. "Why do you care about dresses? I want to see the males in their tight suits. Can you imagine what the prince will be wearing? He's already so handsome, my eyes almost break every time I look at him."

The thought of the prince chilled my blood. He was beautiful, but how could anyone fawn over him? He was a cold, callous statue. A heartless immortal.

And yet, he'd made my heart beat faster when he was close.

I shoved him from my thoughts and turned to the girl. "You work in the kitchens? Have you ever seen a girl with eyes like mine? Belle—she would have brought the cooks herbs and game for the lords' table."

Her face brightened. "Oh, yes! I knew there was something familiar about you!"

"Have you seen her recently?"

"No, but I'd ask the head cook, Sylvester. He deals with all the kitchen deliveries."

Before I could ask anything more, Lorayna's handmaid pulled me away. She looked to be about twenty-five and had a tight black braid and pinched features. "Her ladyship was ranting nonstop about you while I was getting her ready for bed yesterday. You'd better get to work early if you want to avoid a whipping."

The biscuit in my mouth turned to ash. I quickly bid farewell to my new friends, then followed Lorayna's handmaid, Katherine, into the halls.

"Are they all like this?" I asked. "The lords, I mean."

"Most aren't quite as bad. There's a special circle in hell reserved for Lorayna and her sister, Bianca, who is even worse, if you can imagine." A bitter smile crossed Katherine's lips. "The best thing to do is avoid the both of them like the plague."

Since I'd missed the orientation, Katherine showed me the servants' passages. They were cramped, narrow, and dimly lit. Every so often, the passage widened into a larger chamber, or we came across a door leading into a room or hallway. Most were unmarked, but Katherine pointed out the important ones as we went. I'd thought the main part of the castle was complicated, but the servants' passages were a labyrinth.

We flattened ourselves against the wall so a lady with stacks of linen could pass. "All this so the immortals can pretend we don't exist?" I muttered.

"That's part of it," Katherine answered as we continued. "On the other hand, the passages make it possible to do our job without getting constantly waylaid by immortals wanting us to do something else. Think of these tunnels as your own personal refuge from the sisters." She glanced back with a grin. "It also keeps you off the menu. You never know who's looking for a snack around here."

A chill snaked down my spine. "I have no intention of letting anyone drink from me."

"You're so certain about that? I heard you already caught the prince's eye. I wouldn't say no to that if he were interested."

The blood rushed from my face. Had everybody heard?

"He's a heartless monster. The only reason he noticed me was my hair and his horse. I'm hoping to stay as far away from him as I can."

"Hmm," she said, pausing to consider me with a long look. "I suppose the question is whether the prince will stay away from you."

14

Over the next few days, Katherine and I tended to Lorayna's every whim. We cleaned the castle guestrooms, as well as those of the courtesans and blood retainers who didn't have full-time staff of their own. The needs of the court ran me ragged from dusk till dawn, with barely time for a snack, but at least I had Cara. After work, we'd sit together, exhausted but excited to gossip about all we'd seen and heard in the castle.

Each evening, before the other girls rose for breakfast, I'd sneak out into the kitchen's large vegetable garden. After I was certain no one was watching, I'd clink my stepmother's bracelets together and try to summon her crow. Plenty of the black birds congregated on the walls of the castle above the garden, but none of them ever approached.

I finally was rewarded on my third day in the castle, when the scruffy old bird dropped down beside me. I fed him some crumbs of bread from my apron pocket, and then, making sure no one was looking, I gently picked him up. There was a tiny message tied to his leg. I plucked it off, then released him back into the air. "Don't get caught!"

He cawed loudly as he fluttered away. *I was going to tell you the same thing.*

I stared at him, stunned. Had I just heard him in my mind? I shook my head to clear the silly thought. Of course not. I was just doing the same thing I did with Pip: imagining things.

Not that it wasn't good advice. *Don't get caught.*

I retreated into the deepening shadows of the wall, then carefully unrolled the note. Although it was hard to see, I recognized my stepmother's handwriting. *Urgent. Find a broken gargoyle head in the rose garden. Key underneath. Tie to raven.*

I checked the darkening sky. While I'd had little interaction with the gardeners to that point, I'd briefly met the head gardener, Matthew, a sinewy, sun-weathered man who'd warned the new hires to keep our sticky fingers off of his beloved roses. But Matthew and his team worked on the day shift, and the night shift was still eating its breakfast. If I skipped the meal, I might be able to scout out the garden without anyone around.

I tore up the note and put it in the pocket of my apron, then headed back inside with my thoughts dancing. What was the key for? And who had put it there?

Also, I was somewhat bothered by the instruction *tie to raven.* The crow was definitely not going to like that.

By the time I reached the royal rose garden, the sun had set, leaving it draped in shadow. The flowers were brilliant blooms in the starlight, patches of white and deep red against the shadows and leaves. Technically, it was off-limits to staff other than the royal gardeners, but as far as I knew, the immortals seldom went there, and it was still very early in the evening. I glanced up at the brightly lit windows of the western wing, where Lorayna and many of the other nobles lived. I doubted anyone looking out would notice me.

It took twenty minutes of sneaking around, but I found the broken gargoyle head. It was weathered to the point that I almost passed it by, thinking it just an oddly shaped rock. Checking that no one was watching, I knelt and turned it over. My heart skipped a beat. A small silver key glinted beneath. I snatched it and stood, then let out a restrained breath before quickly walking toward the exit with the key clenched in my fist.

Who'd left it there?

Apparently, I wasn't the only one working for the resistance in the castle. Did I pass them in the halls? Could it be Katherine? Or Annie? No. Not her. I refused to let her be part of my fantasy.

"Do you like my garden?" a deep voice called from behind me.

I froze, my stomach tumbling. I knew that voice, so deep and silky. Pip did, too, and he leapt off my shoulder and disappeared into the depths of the garden.

Footsteps approached, crunching on the gravel walkway.

My palms went damp, and the key started burning a hole in my hand. With my heart hammering in my chest, I slowly turned. Head down, I dipped low and knelt on the ground. "Your Royal Highness. I didn't mean to disturb you."

I kept my eyes locked on the ground as a pair of polished black boots appeared.

"I didn't realize you had joined the garden staff," the prince said. "Are you as good with roses as you are with horses?"

I could barely think. Had he seen me drop down by the gargoyle's head? If he noticed my clenched fist, if he found the key, I'd be hung from the wall alongside the bastard who'd tried to kill me.

I pressed my hand to my chest. "No, Your Royal Highness. I'm not part of the garden staff."

He circled around me like a stalking wolf. "Then what are you doing in my garden? It is forbidden to mortals."

As soon as he was at my back, I slid my hand down my side

as casually as I could, slipping it and the key into my apron pocket. "I didn't know. I promise I'll never come here again."

He hesitated. Had he sensed my motion?

"How do you find employment in my castle?"

I moistened my parched lips. "I'm grateful to have been chosen, Your Highness."

"And your mistress, Lady Lorayna. How do you find her?"

She's an impossible tyrant who loves to watch mortal women cower before her. "I seek to please my mistress through my work."

"I see." The circling black boots paused in front of me. "Rise."

I stood, but I still didn't dare lift my eyes. Immortals could hear your pulse, it was said, and mine was pounding like a hailstorm. He probably relished it. He was probably enjoying watching me sweat as much as Lorayna liked to watch me humiliate myself.

They were all monsters.

"You haven't answered my original question," the prince said. "Do you like my garden?"

"Yes. It reminds me of the rose bushes at our manor house." I looked up, my eyes pleading. "I was homesick and wanted to see them. I didn't mean to trespass."

The prince wore a crisp black uniform with two blades at his side. He was breathtakingly perfect and severe, like a statue. His gaze was so intense, it felt like it was turning me to stone.

Did he ever smile? What would make a man like that smile?

Probably the throbbing vein on a young woman's neck.

I quickly looked away, focusing on the field of roses. "They're beautiful. I've never seen their match."

"Nor have I," he said softly. Something about the tone in his voice made the hair on my neck rise and my stomach flutter.

He reached down and snapped off a white blossom, then held it out to me. "The rose is the symbol of my house."

I stared at the brilliant bloom, and my mind went blank. The prince of the Bloodvale was offering me a flower. It probably violated decorum a dozen different ways, but I knew I couldn't refuse. I hesitantly reached up and took the stem. The prince didn't let it go, but instead met my eyes. "Roses remind me that beautiful things can be dangerous."

My breath stilled. His eyes were dangerous. Blue and gray, like clouds passing through the night sky.

He relinquished his hold on the flower and stepped back. "You'd better run, little mouse. You'll be late for your duties, and you wouldn't wish to leave your mistress disappointed."

Relief washed over me. I was going to live. I dipped low. "Thank you, Your Highness."

With the rose in one hand and the skirt of my dress in the other, I turned and ran back to the western wing as fast as I could.

15

———————

Ella

I rushed inside, slamming the servants' door behind me. Terror and euphoria churned through me. I'd stolen a key right from under the prince's nose, and I'd lived.

The key I could easily hide on my person, but the rose...what was I supposed to do with it? If I took it back to the women's residence it would only raise questions, but I couldn't throw it away. It was too beautiful, too perfect.

I twisted it in my fingers, discovering a twinge of emotion I couldn't quite explain. A fluttering in my chest.

Brushing it aside, I scurried downstairs and tucked the rose away in an old storage closet that only Katherine and I used. Then with my stomach growling from my missed breakfast, I hitched up my skirt and ran upstairs to Lorayna's chambers. Katherine raised her brows at me when I hurried in late, but mercifully didn't ask questions.

"You're lucky her ladyship already left," she whispered.

"I know."

She left me to continue my duties from the day before, and I relished the quiet to think on all that had happened.

I was halfway through washing the windows when the door to the chambers burst open.

I looked up from my work as a lady with chestnut hair swept into the room like she owned the place—except it wasn't Lorayna. It was the woman who'd announced the rules for the selection on application day. Flaunting a yellow dress as vivid as gorse in full bloom and pointed shoes the color of blood, she was both beautiful and jarring. She snapped her paper fan shut and pointed it at me. "You, there. Come with me. There's work to do."

I looked down at my rag and bucket of water, then back up at her. "Who are you?"

Her expression knotted with fury. "Are you an idiot? I'm the *Mistress of Ceremonies*. Now, come along!"

My mind raced. I didn't dare defy a powerful noble— certainly not one with magic—but I didn't dare leave and anger my vengeful employer.

I dipped in a curtsy. "I'm sorry, mistress, but I have more than I can manage today. Perhaps I could assist you tomorrow?"

She backhanded me with her fan, and I staggered, hand to my face. *What the hell was with these women?*

The woman tapped the fan against her palm threateningly. "You will refer to me as 'her ladyship' or 'Lady Bianca.' A mistress is a *whore*, like you."

So, this was Bianca. Clearly, she was as insane as her sister.

"Yes, your ladyship," I said guardedly.

She looked around at my work, scowling. "I don't know what my sister might want with a wretched little thing like you, but she always keeps the best for herself—which is why you will be working for me as well."

My mind spun. Was I going to be a toy torn apart in a siblings' tug of war? Could Bianca even pull rank like this and take me from her sister's service? There had to be a way to diffuse her interest.

I dipped low again. "I'm sorry, your ladyship, but I'm not worthy of your attention. I was assigned to Lady Lorayna's service against her wishes."

Bianca scoffed. "The chamberlain hires and fires the castle staff. Who would *assign you* to her service?"

Ah, hell.

Bianca seized my hair, her expression taut with furious curiosity. "Tell me now."

Pain lanced through my scalp, and I grabbed at her hands, but her grip was iron. Although she was lithe, and I'd spent my life working on a farm, she was at least five times as strong as I, and ten times as fast. There was no fighting her—not if I wanted to live.

"Tell me!" she ordered.

"The prince!" I squeaked as she jerked my hair again.

She shrieked with rage and shoved me backward, then began stalking the room. "How dare he favor her above *me*! I'm the *Mistress of Ceremonies*! I'm the one running his damned ball. I deserve more help than my wench of a sister." Bianca brushed the hair from her face with a practiced flourish. "Which is why you're coming with me. The prince probably just made a mistake. Whatever tasks you've been assigned by my sister, you will do them for me."

Half dazed, I followed her out the door and just down the hall. Apparently, they were neighbors.

Bianca's chambers were just as large and opulent as her sister's, but unlike Lorayna's pretentious and stately style, Bianca's rooms looked like they'd been decorated by a mad art collector—which probably wasn't far from the truth. Everything was a clash of gold and silver and a riot of colors.

"Isn't it beautiful?" she said, twirling in a circle, before flopping down on a vivid lime green and gold chaise longue that clashed enough with her gown to make a honeybee blind.

"It's breathtaking," I said, which was the truth, but not in the way she was thinking.

"Of course it is," Bianca snapped, then dramatically sighed. "Once the prince marries me, I'll redecorate the entire castle."

Fates have mercy.

She propped her hands on her hips as if she were rather proud of herself. "I want this place immaculate. The prince is fastidiously tidy, and I want to ensure there is nothing to put him off, should he visit my chambers. I need to give him every reason to choose me over all the harlots who will be vying for his hand—or Fates forbid it, my sister."

My eyebrows rose. Both her and her sister were vying for the prince's hand? It wasn't unexpected with all the chatter over the ball, but their rivalry might be something my stepmother could use.

I dipped low and kept my eyes down to hide my reaction. "Of course, your ladyship."

Bianca kept me as busy as her sister had, gleefully dragging me away from my duties and leaving me to bear Lorayna's wrath. My life became a tug of war and left me running from one side of the castle to the other, doing whatever Lorayna and her crazy sister wanted, *whenever* they wanted, at the drop of a hat.

I thought that maybe Lorayna would put a stop to it, but I soon realized it was a game to them—a competition to see who could make me fall first.

I promised myself that I wouldn't give them a sliver of satisfaction.

Unfortunately, the tug of war left me precious little time to investigate the castle or look for Belle. It was a full two days before I even had the chance to retrieve the key from its hiding place. Miraculously, the rose the prince had given me hadn't yet wilted. I briefly traced my fingers over the soft, white petals, feeling a tug of something I couldn't identify.

It's nothing. He's a monster. Put him out of your mind.

Clearing my thoughts, I scratched out a quick report to my stepmother on an old scrap of paper, then slipped into the castle gardens as dusk fell. The old crow dropped down as soon as he saw me, and I didn't even have to click the silver bracelets together to summon him.

"Thanks for meeting me," I whispered, and scratched the bird's head. Checking that no one was watching, I tied the key securely to his outstretched leg. "Sorry about this, but it's my stepmother's orders."

He squawked in protest at his new cumbersome accoutrement, so I gave him some crumbs from a dinner roll I'd brought as a reward. Once he'd eaten his fill, he took to the skies, and my spirit lifted for the first time in days. Despite the beatings and exhaustion and relentless work, I was making a difference. I'd dug up a little information and a mysterious key for the resistance.

But the feeling was fleeting, and my heart sank a little as he disappeared over the battlements. Despite all my work, I still hadn't found any sign of Belle.

An hour later, I was on my way to Lorayna's with a fresh set of towels when a flash of garish color swept into the hall. *Bianca— the monster of Castle Silverthorn.*

She paused as soon as her gaze landed on me. "Just the person I was looking for."

I immediately averted my eyes and turned toward the

nearest servants' passage as if I hadn't noticed her, but I wasn't fast enough.

"I see you there, girl!" she shouted from down the hall. "Don't you try to skulk away from me, you indolent thing!"

I stopped in my tracks and closed my eyes as she approached, begging the Fates for patience and perhaps a little relief. Pip, who had been riding on my shoulder beneath my hair, huddled against my neck, quaking.

"Trying to hide from an honest day's work, I presume?" she asked, ignoring the obvious implications of the massive bundle of sheets and towels in my arms.

"No, my lady."

She fanned herself, though the night air in the hall was cool. "The prince is going out riding alone tonight, and I mean to accompany him. Run to the stables and have one of the groomsmen saddle my horse immediately."

"Yes, my lady, I'll just put these—"

She shoved the laundry from my arms, scattering it across the floor.

When I dropped down on my hands and knees to pick it up, she put her foot on my fingers, and I yelped.

"I said *immediately*. You'll just use them as an excuse to lie about, and I'll miss my ride with the prince."

"I can't leave these in the middle of the hall. Lady Lorayna will—" My protest cut off as Bianca shifted her weight, sending a burst of pain racing up my arm.

"What my sister might do doesn't matter. I'll do far worse *right now* if you talk back anymore. Understand? You're to leave the mess you've made and go *immediately*."

She ground her foot into my fingers, and I gritted my teeth. "I understand."

The pressure released, and I scooted back, rubbing my fingers. Remarkably, they didn't seem broken.

"That's better," Bianca said as I stood. She reached into the little purse dangling at her side and pulled out a thorn. "Once the horse is saddled and the groomsman isn't looking, I want you to drive this into my horse's hind foot."

I stared down at the thorn, flabbergasted. "Why on earth—"

She grasped my jaw and tilted my face to look me in the eyes. "Your job is to do as I say and to not ask questions."

Fury boiled inside of me, but I forced myself to calmly take the thorn. I clenched it in my fist behind my back—just in case I accidentally rammed it into her eye.

"Good," she muttered, then began to preen her hair. "When my horse goes lame, the prince will have no option but to let me ride with him on the way back. We'll be pressed together in the saddle with his arm around me. It will be wonderfully romantic. He won't be able to help but notice me moving against him."

The expression on my face must have betrayed the horrid carnival of thoughts racing through my mind. Her eyes flashed with fury. "Clearly, you don't understand the first thing about romance, you stupid girl."

Clearly not, if it involved maiming animals.

Bianca bared her fangs and hissed, "*Hurry!*"

I hitched up my skirt and fled down the hall toward the courtyard. I would pay for the mess of towels later, but I knew that if I lingered any longer, Bianca wouldn't hesitate to take a bite out of me. Literally.

I ducked into the servants' passages and spiraled down the narrow stairs, then slipped through the kitchens as quickly as I could and out into the night air.

The stables, a long two-story barn made of wood and stone, were on the far side of the courtyard. The structure was dimly lit, and I slowed in awe as I entered. They dwarfed my father's barn by two dozen stalls. Constructed with heavy timbers and tight stonework, it was a step above our manor house, let alone most of the homes in the town.

A dog barked, and several of the horses stirred in agitation.

The source of the noise was a little cattle dog. It was sitting next to a large, curled-up hound who barely bothered to open his eyes.

"Hush, now!" I scolded the noisy thing.

It gave a soft whine, then promptly laid down with its head on its paws.

"What's all this?" an old, bowlegged man said as he hobbled out of a back room. He looked around blearily as if I'd just interrupted his evening nap, and his expression soured when he spotted me. "Hey, now, this place is off-limits to house staff. I won't have you hiding here to shirk work or have a roll in the hay."

I curtsied. "I was sent by Lady Bianca. She needs her horse saddled. She wants to go out riding with the prince."

The old man shook his head. "The prince is riding alone tonight. Her ladyship can break her neck riding another time."

"Please," I said as I stepped over the drowsing hound and approached. "Bianca will snap *my* neck if her horse isn't ready by the time she arrives."

He waved his hand at me dismissively. "I don't want to get in trouble any more than you do, and I'm afraid I value my own skin more than your neck. Scamper on back to your mistress. I'm sure her bark is worse than her bite."

It was not. Bianca would ruin me if she didn't get her way. My heart began to beat a little faster, and I pulled my fingers through my hair. "Did the prince directly order you not to saddle anyone else's animals?"

A moment of guilt flickered across his face. "Not exactly, but I've been the night master of the stables for thirty years, and I know when he needs to go alone. I already let the groomsmen go for the night."

I glanced around the deserted stables, absorbing the conspicuous absence of other people for the first time. Of course, tending to the horses would take a large staff. The prince's enormous destrier was already saddled and waiting, which meant I didn't have much time. I bit my lip and met the stablemaster's eyes. "The prince's horse looks thirsty. Take it out to water it and warm it up before the ride, and I'll saddle Bianca's horse while you're gone. Just point out the animal and its kit, and you can deny any knowledge of it. Someone sneaked in to do it."

He shoved his hands in his pockets and eyed me warily. "A right fool, aren't you? The prince will have your hide if he doesn't take mine."

"I'll risk it. I don't know what he'll do, but I know Bianca will send me home or drink me dry if I don't do what she says, and I can't afford to lose this job. My sister's life depends on it."

It was only a little stretch.

His expression wavered for a second, and he glanced at a horse at the end of the far line. "Do you even know what you're doing? If her saddle slips, you'll be hanged for sure. Hell, I might join you swinging."

My heart leapt. "I've saddled my stepmother's horses hundreds of times, and I'm good with animals."

The old stablemaster looked me up and down slowly, as if seeing me for the first time. "Aye, you're that one. I saw that stunt you pulled with Tenebris. If you can soothe him, you could probably saddle a bear."

I took that as a *yes*.

I gave the old man a quick hug. "Thank you."

His face reddened, and he looked down. "Well, if you end up hanging, it ain't my fault, but I'll help you as much as I can.

Name's Albert, by the way." He pointed out the mare's tack and gave me her name—Gwendolyn—then hurried toward Tenebris, clearly eager to be away if the prince appeared. "No matter what they do to you, I wasn't here when you arrived, and I don't know a thing about this. Got it? I have a family to look after myself."

I swallowed. "Got it."

"Good luck, lass," he said, shaking his head.

16

———————

Ella

As soon as he walked the prince's giant horse out into the courtyard, I grabbed Bianca's saddle and hurried into Gwendolyn's stall. Pip jumped off my shoulder and found a spot to watch. The horse tossed her mane and stamped her feet, clearly agitated. I set the saddle on the rail and brushed my hand along her neck. "I know it's late, but you're going out riding, Gwen. And I know you might not like her, but will you please help me out?"

She snorted and nudged my arm as if to say, *At least I get to leave.*

"Thank you." I situated the saddle and began securing the straps. She shimmied and huffed to let me know how she liked it fitted. Once I was certain the saddle was properly secured, I pulled the large thorn from the pocket of my apron and showed it to the mare. "Your rider wanted me to put this in your foot to make you lame."

Gwen's eyes widened, and she backed up until she bumped the end of the stall.

I tucked the thorn back in my pocket. "I would never do that to any animal—even one I didn't like—but especially not to a sweet creature like you."

The horse tossed her head. *I should hope not.*

"It leaves me in a bit of a predicament, though. Bianca will be furious."

She pulled her lips back, showing her teeth.

I stroked her neck with an affectionate smile. "No, don't nip her, or we'll both be in trouble. But perhaps you could pretend to go lame partway through the ride? She wants an excuse to have to ride with the prince."

The mare snorted. *So, she wants to take me out riding but doesn't want to ride me?*

I shrugged and grinned back at her. "Pretty stupid plan, huh?"

She stamped her hind foot and snorted again. *I'll be glad to be rid of her.*

"I bet you will," I laughed, then shook my head. I'd always talked to animals, but I'd had to guess what they would've said back. It was a little imagination and a little wistful thinking. But with the chestnut mare, it was almost like I could hear her talking in the back of my mind.

Like she was *actually* talking to me.

I arched my eyebrows as I checked the straps one last time. "Are you sure that saddle fits okay?"

Her head bobbed. *Perfect—I can actually breathe. The stablemaster always tightens it up like he thinks I'm a hundred pounds lighter than I am.* She looked me straight in the eyes, with just a hint of accusation. *We can't all be dainty little things, can we?*

"Holy Fates," I said as I stumbled back in surprise, my heart suddenly beating against my chest. Either I'd lost my wits or the horse *was* speaking to me in my head. Was that part of the castle's magic?

The horse sniffed the air. *She's here.*

I looked over my shoulder just as Bianca swept into the stables. She was dressed in a scandalously tight riding outfit that hugged every curve of her body. My jaw dropped. I'd never seen a woman dressed like that before. I wondered if her pants would rip when she mounted up. Perhaps that was part of her plan, as well.

"What are you gawking at, girl?" she snapped as she approached. "Where's the stablemaster? Is my horse ready?"

"He took the prince's horse out already," I said as I walked Gwendolyn out.

She glared at me. "If you've made me late, I'll make you bleed."

I decided not to point out that I'd been waiting for her. "Let me help you up, my lady."

She mounted Gwen, and I led them out of the stable.

The stablemaster looked up with an expression of trepidation, but it was the prince who caught my eye. He sat on Tenebris, the hard lines of his face drawn into an icy expression. "What is the meaning of this? I'm riding out alone."

I shivered as the frosty accusation skated over my skin, but Bianca simply fanned her fingers against her chest and put on a look of surprise that wouldn't have fooled a six-year-old. "Oh, I had *no idea* you were going out riding, Your Highness. With all the commotion of the castle, I needed a breath of fresh air and a bit of quiet."

"As did I," he gritted. His hard gaze found me, and something wicked flashed in his eyes. A blaze of heat raced across my skin, and I looked away. It did nothing to distill the tension that tightened the air between us.

No—I had to be imagining that. More likely, he was planning ways to punish me for this.

"How wonderful!" Bianca cooed as she spurred Gwen over.

"We can ride together and discuss the ball. I know you wouldn't be so rude as to make me ride alone."

Her voice dripped with honey and feigned naïveté. I couldn't believe the prince would be fooled—and by the expression on his face, he wasn't. "I'm going hunting."

"That's wonderful, Your Highness. I should adore seeing you in action. I love killing things myself. I'd do it more often if it were legal."

The prince's mouth opened, then shut as hoofbeats sounded from the castle gates. I followed his gaze as a female rider appeared, and my stomach tumbled.

Lorayna raised her hand as she spurred her horse into the courtyard, making directly for the prince. "Your Highness, what a surprise! I was just out for a little ride but turned back because —" Her voice cut off as her sister rode over. "Bianca? What are you doing here?"

"I was going out for a ride with His Royal Highness. It seems you've already gone. Too bad. Your horse must be tired."

The lines of Lorayna's face stretched as her skin blanched with white-hot fury. "He's not tired in the least. I was just preparing to head out, but when I heard the prince was riding, I thought I'd wait to join him. We have important things to discuss. Alone."

I stood there, gaping at their audacity. Had the sisters come up with the same plan to corner the prince?

Bianca brought her horse alongside her sister and turned her nose up. "Well, perhaps you can join him another time."

Her movements left me standing in the open. My muscles screamed for me to run and hide, but instinctually, I knew that if I moved an inch, I'd draw attention to myself. For now, I was just another servant. Invisible. A plaything beneath noticing.

Except I thought I felt the prince's gaze on me, warming my skin. Surely not.

I looked up, surprised to see him watching me instead of the sisters. I'd have given my best boots to read what was in his eyes, but of course I couldn't. His gaze didn't move from me, and I looked away first, seeking the sisters.

Lorayna's lips curled in disgust. "All the groomsmen were just leaving for the night when I was preparing to ride out. I hope you weren't so desperate that you had to saddle your own animal. I doubt you have the skill, and I wouldn't want you to break your neck, *dear* sister."

I was certain that if the prince hadn't been there, Lorayna might have tried to snap her sister's spine on the spot.

"I will leave you ladies to sort out your differences," the prince said, his voice thrumming with disdain. Without so much as a nod to either of them, he gave me one last heated look, then spurred his horse and galloped through the gate.

"You've ruined everything!" Lorayna hissed at her sister, then pinned the stablemaster with an accusatory look that nearly curdled my blood.

The truth clicked into place. Lorayna had been the one to send the groomsmen away, not the prince. It was her wrath that the stablemaster had risked by helping me, not the royal's. The old man bowed his head as his knees began to shake. "I'm sorry, my lady. I had no idea Lady Bianca was going out riding, or I would have saddled her horse for her. But alas, I was here with the prince."

Bianca tossed her hair and glanced back at me. "Don't worry, sister, your new maid saddled the beast for me. The feral little thing seems to know a thing or two about horses."

My stomach dropped as Lorayna turned a murderous glare on me. Whatever hope I'd had of escaping this debacle disappeared like smoke in the breeze.

"The stables are part of the household, and that girl is *my* servant. You presume too much upon your position," Lorayna said, ice-cold.

Bianca snorted. "I think the word you are looking for is *initiative*. Good evening, dear sister." With that, Bianca dug her heels into Gwen's side and raced after the prince.

Before I could escape, Lorayna jerked the reins of her gelding and rode over. "So, you think you can be one of the groomsmen, then, you treacherous little wench?"

Yup. I was going to die.

Rather than cower like the stablemaster, I raised my chin. "Lady Bianca pulled me from my duties and made me saddle her horse, as the stablemaster and groomsmen were not around. I only helped her out of respect for you, my lady. She *is* your sister."

Whatever happened, I wasn't going to take the kindly old man down with me.

Lorayna's deathly expression didn't waver. "Well, if you think you're a groomsman, then we'll see if you have what it takes to handle the rest of their chores. I want the entire stables mucked out and refreshed before I return from my ride—by yourself."

"The entire thing?" I blurted as I looked back at the massive building.

The sting of her riding crop lashed my shoulder. "Of course, the entire thing. Have it finished, or I'll flog you skinless in front of the staff." She turned to the stablemaster. "As for you, I want you out of my sight. You'll work the next month with no pay for this lapse, and if I hear you've helped her in any way, I'll drain you myself."

"Thank you, my lady." He bowed. "I'll leave now."

Lorayna spun her gelding around, and bending low, spurred it into motion and galloped after the prince and her sister.

The stablemaster shook his head. "I warned you no good would come of it."

"I'm sorry for getting you into this mess. You can have my pay. It may not be as much as yours, but it'll be something."

"It's not me you should be worrying about. Lorayna has given you an impossible task, and she knows it."

My heart sank as I stared at the open gates of the castle and the dark night beyond. "What am I going to do?"

"You could run, but she'd probably hunt you down and make an example out of you." He scratched his chin. "I suspect it's better to do what you can and take the beating. The sisters might be devil spawn, but I doubt the prince would let it get too far. He has a sense of justice, even if he's one of them. A good trait in a king, I suppose."

Oh, so he'd just let them *beat me a little* for obeying their orders.

"Any king that would employ those two to run his house is a monster," I muttered.

The old man shook his head. "You'll get yourself killed for talking treason like that."

"It's the truth."

He glanced over his shoulder as the castle guards closed the main gate, then lowered his voice. "There are two sides to every story. Those vipers are the daughters of a powerful duke. The old king appointed them to ease tensions between the families, so Prince Cassius can't sack them without reigniting a blood feud—although I'm certain he's considered risking it. The fact that neither of them has been staked in the hallways is a miracle, or at least a testament to their canniness." He clapped me on the shoulder. "Too bad they didn't make you a groomswoman from the start—you did a right fine job with that saddle. I hope you're just as good at cleaning." His expression wavered, and the jovial wrinkles of his face fell. "I *am* sorry about all this, lass. I'd help, but..."

I nodded. "I understand. You'd better go."

"Right. Well, good luck." He looked around sheepishly, then headed to the front gate, leaving me on my own with an impossible task as the only thing keeping the whip from my back.

17

———

Ella

My shoulders drooped, and I headed back into the stable, shutting the central door behind me. A dozen stalls stretched out in either direction. There was no way I was going to be able to muck the entire place out before they got back—not on my own, not even in a day.

But I was going to have to try.

"At twenty minutes a stall, I might be able to do it in eight hours," I muttered as I located a wheelbarrow, pitchfork, and shovel stashed in the back. "So, if I get it down to fifteen, maybe I can do it in six?"

Would they be gone that long? Probably not. I guessed that dawn was only four or five hours away. I was going to have to work harder than I'd ever worked before, and I was going to need a miracle.

I started with Gwen's stall first, pulling out all the old bedding and shoveling up the manure. Pip helped—or tried to, at least. With his tiny body, it was more moral support than anything.

The work stank, and I was sweaty and itchy almost immediately. After I dumped the wheelbarrow of waste in the dung heap out back, I hustled in and laid a new layer of hay as bedding—extra thick because she deserved it.

My chest was heaving once I finished, but I knew I couldn't rest. I had to work faster. As I didn't want to mess up Gwen's stall, I rotated the horses into the space left by Lorayna's gelding. Once each was out, I set to work, furiously cleaning, tossing old hay like a windstorm.

As I was digging out the fifth one, a wave of dizziness hit me, and I dropped to my hands and knees in the muck. My back and shoulders ached, and my head spun. I was too tired to care that I'd fallen in the manure. I just leaned against the sides of the stall and let my head thump against the wood. "I'm never going to make it."

The bloodsuckers couldn't be gone more than another couple of hours—less if the sisters irritated the prince as much as I thought they would.

The lazy old hound dog sauntered in and sat down beside me, nudging me gently with his nose.

"What am I going to do, ol' boy?" I asked.

He cocked his head to the side and raised his limp ears with a soft bark. *Help?*

"I wish. But I'm on my own with this one, and I don't think paws are going to do the trick." The laughter in my voice faded. "I think I'm royally screwed."

He threw his head back and released a mournful howl.

I shook my head. "My thoughts exactly."

A moment later, a string of ear-splitting yips burst from further down the stable.

Help! Help! Help! Help!

When the little dog didn't stop, I groaned and shoved myself off the ground. "What are you going on about?" I asked as I emerged. "Settle down!"

He was facing the central double door of the stable and barking at the top of his lungs. He didn't stop or even look at me. *Help! Help!*

Was someone out there?

I wiped off my hands and grabbed the pitchfork, then headed toward the door. The little ruffian didn't stop barking. I lifted the latch, and then I toed the door open, pitchfork held at the ready. "Who's there?"

Darkness exploded around me, and I tumbled back onto my butt, surrounded by a cloud of feathers and the piercing cries of crows. I rolled out of the way as hundreds of birds streamed in over my head.

The stable was in chaos—birds of all kinds everywhere, the dogs barking, and the horses turning about in their stalls. I crouched there like a deer in the stalker's sights, no idea what to do.

The insane little dog raced down the corridor between the stalls and circled the empty wheelbarrow once, barking all the while. In a wave of darkness, the crows followed and then began diving in and out of the stalls. They wheeled around, dodging each other and dropping hay into the wheelbarrow.

My jaw went slack. They were cleaning the stalls for me.

The stunned silence of my thoughts drowned out the noise in the room. I was in a magical castle, and it was full of magical animals. It was like I was caught up in a fairytale. If bloodsuckers could be real, and floating lights could be real, why couldn't this be real as well?

I glanced back at the open door to see if anyone else was watching the spectacle or had been drawn by the noise. The sky outside had shifted from deep black to the slightest hint of blue.

It was late, and I was running out of time.

I sprang to my feet and locked the door, then threw myself into the chaos. The horses were going crazy, spinning in their stalls and desperately trying to get away from the divebombing birds.

"Not while the horses are in there!" I shouted above the din, and the cyclone of crows lifted off and shifted their efforts to an empty stall.

I shook my head, still barely believing. *They'd listened to me.*

I opened the gate to one of the occupied stalls and motioned to the slightly spooked horse inside. "Come on, let's get you out so we can clean."

The mare turned her back and began kicking the soiled bedding into a pile, and I watched in disbelief as she trotted out and down the corridor into the last stall I'd cleaned.

"Okay, then, we've got a system now." I grabbed the brimming wheelbarrow and disposed of it on the slop pile out back. The birds followed me out, whisking away the dirty hay, so I left the door open. With their help, I could clean a dozen times as quickly and better, and soon, we had a rhythm going. Once I'd finished cleaning a stall, the crows and sparrows quickly began filling the empty stalls with fresh bedding.

Every minute counted, so I didn't dare stop working myself —that was an ungrateful way to lead, anyway. After an hour, the maelstrom of activity began to subside.

I returned the empty wheelbarrow to its spot and stretched my aching back and trembling arms. Then I looked around. The stables were probably cleaner than they'd been in a century, better than I could have ever done on my own.

It was a Fates-damned miracle.

Despite the pain coursing through me, my heart was bursting with joy and pride. There was magic all around me, and I'd found a way to be a part of it. I knew it wasn't me—it was the castle that was enchanted. But still, for a moment, I could imagine I was like one of the witches of old, talking with animals and banishing my troubles with the wave of a hand.

Granted, mucking the stables hadn't been a simple wave of the hand. It had been backbreaking, and every joint in my body felt it. My damp hair clung to the sides of my face, while my clothes stuck to my sweaty skin. I was covered with strands of hay and dust and—well, frankly—horseshit.

But I'd done it. *We'd* done it—and that was all the magic I could have ever asked for.

I grabbed a big sack of oats from the back and dragged it into the center of the aisle. "Settle down, everybody!" I said as I threw my hands in the air.

The birds squawked and cawed about me, but slowly, they came to rest, filling the rafters and rails of the stalls. Finally, the stable was quiet except for the low din of the sparrows fighting for position. Hundreds of eyes were trained on me, and my heart was full to bursting, both with gratitude and a thrill for the magic of the place.

"I don't know how much you can understand, but thank you, from the bottom of my heart. You saved my skin today, maybe even my life," I said, lowering my arms. "I'm not sure how to show my gratitude, but I hope you like oats."

I opened the sack and tipped it over, spilling its contents across the floor. The crows and sparrows descended so quickly, I had to dive out of the way to avoid becoming a pincushion. The offering began rapidly disappearing, so I poured another out a little way down, and then treated the horses to hefty portions as well.

Halfway through, the hound barked and came running from the far end. *Bloodsuckers and horses.*

"Everybody out!" I shouted to the birds, and they rose into the air, then poured through the back door into the early dawn sky, leaving me in an almost unearthly silence.

18

———————

Ella

I stole to the front door and cracked it so I could peek out, tensing as soon as I caught sight of the riders.

Gwendoyln was hobbling along, favoring her foot, just as I'd asked. But Bianca was not cuddled up against the prince.

My heart picked up.

He rode alone, a dark figure against the twilight of the early dawn sky. No matter how many times I told myself he was a monster, he was breathtaking to behold.

Her ladyship, on the other hand, was covered in mud and riding hunched behind her sister on the rump of her gray gelding. Both the gelding and Lorayna looked deeply displeased, but Bianca was beyond livid, with curled lips and fangs bared.

I had to stop myself from laughing. So much for a one-horse fantasy.

Her gaze swept over the stable, finding me, and my stomach dropped. She'd probably been brooding for hours, and now her wrath had a target. Me.

Never let them see you standing around.

"Get out of here, Pip," I whispered, and my little friend raced away.

I tried to slip back into the stable undetected, but before I could vanish, Bianca dropped off the back of the gelding and hurled herself across the courtyard at unimaginable speed, her form becoming a blur in the predawn light. My head jolted back as she seized my hair, sending a burst of pain down my neck. I twisted and turned, but to no avail. Bianca might have been built like a dancer, but holy Fates, she was as strong as a blacksmith.

"You ruined my ride, you idiot!" she screamed as she forced me to face her. "You gave me a lame horse, and one that bucks as well!"

"I gave you the horse you asked for," I gritted through my teeth.

She released my hair, and I stumbled back—then pain exploded through my cheek as her slap drove me to the ground.

"I will bleed you dry and mount your head on a spike!"

"Stop!" The prince's command slammed into me like a hammer against an anvil, and both of us froze where we were, paralyzed by the power of his voice. He hadn't shouted, hadn't even raised it above a whisper, and yet, it was deafening. Absolute authority and control in a single word.

Lord Aamon came hurrying down the steps of the castle, his hand resting on the hilt of his sword. "What the hell is going on?"

"Look what this serving wench did to me!" Bianca snarled as she displayed her mud-caked clothes. Her left cheek was scratched and bruised, and the entire left side of her body was coated in filth. Gwen had apparently chosen the rockiest, muddiest part of the woods to buck her off.

"Bianca lost control of her animal," the prince said to Aamon, then turned to her with disdain. "If you cannot handle a horse, how can I expect you to handle the ball? Should I find someone more capable?"

Lorayna's expression had gone from annoyance to boredom to unabashed delight. The bitter woman was practically glowing. Bianca, on the other hand, was as white as a sheet, and her teeth were clenched tightly.

And who was going to bear the brunt of her wrath? Not the prince or her sister. *Me.*

Bianca pointed. "She did this on purpose to sabotage me—to kill me for working her too hard! She probably put a thorn in the damned horse's hoof to make it lame."

Gwendoyln casually picked up her lame hoof, showing it to the world, then walked past me and into her empty stall, her limp miraculously cured.

"A horse knows when it has a bad rider." Aamon laughed as a broad smile lit his face. "She didn't want you riding her any more than I would."

Bianca's expression turned to ice. "Then she should be fed to the dogs."

I scrambled to my feet. "No!"

The wicked woman spun on me, fangs bared and hand raised.

Then *he* was there between us, looming over her. While Bianca was fast, the prince moved so quickly, it was like he'd been there all along, and I just hadn't seen him. She stumbled back, cowering before him. "You will never touch that horse or this girl again," he said. "If anything happens to either one, I will hold you responsible."

Her expression twisted in frustration. "They're both just dumb animals, barely any use for breeding, let alone food. Why on earth would you stand for them?"

"I am the custodian of this place and all who dwell within it, dumb animal and high countess alike. You will not question me, and you will not abuse my property."

His property?

I was nobody's property.

Whatever gratitude had been building up within me came crashing down in disgust. He wasn't standing up for me; he was protecting an investment, a thing whose life he held in his hands.

Bianca snarled, then stalked away.

Lorayna's grin vanished the moment the prince turned on her. "The same goes for you. This girl and my horses are off-limits. If anything happens to either of them, I will hold you both to account, so don't get any ideas of sabotaging your sister."

My stomach knotted as the truth of it sank in. Lorayna probably would have butchered Gwen and me just to get Bianca in trouble, and the prince knew it. I had to find Belle and get the hell away from him and the sisters as soon as I could.

Lorayna brushed something off the sleeve of her riding coat. "I wouldn't contemplate doing such a thing, Your Highness. I'm not as crass or desperate as my sister, but I will make sure no harm comes to any of your mares."

My neck heated. *Mares.*

Lorayna dismounted, and then, leaving the horse standing there unattended in the middle of the courtyard, she strode away, head held high.

I was going to pay for this twice over. Whatever those sisters decided to do to me might not leave a welt, but it would hurt where it counted.

"Where's the stablemaster?" The prince's rich voice rolled over my skin like honey.

I didn't dare meet those stormy eyes. "Lorayna sent him away, along with the groomsmen."

The prince peered inside the stables. "Then who cleaned

this place? It wasn't like this before." He stepped in and slowly looked around, then turned back to me with an unreadable expression that sent strange prickles along my skin.

My breath quickened, and I swallowed. "I did. While you were out riding."

For a moment, his reaction was utterly unreadable—but then the corner of his lips turned up as his gaze roamed over me. "Looks like it."

My breath halted for a second, and the deep heat of shame flooded my skin. I was sweaty, dusty, disheveled, and covered with mud, manure, and hay. Immortals had a sense of smell and visual acuity that was five times as strong as a human's. The dim light would disguise nothing, and my odor would tell all.

I wanted to die. I wanted to melt into the floor. I wished Bianca had maimed me so that I'd have been sent to the infirmary and out of his sight.

Hell, I might as well own it.

I straightened my back and met his gaze like a woman who didn't give a damn what a prince thought. "It's dirty work, Your Highness. I've been doing the like all my life."

Something flashed in those impossibly haunting eyes— something between surprise and curiosity—and he cleared his throat. "Seeing as the stablemaster and his staff are gone, will you put Tenebris away for me?"

His tone was gentler, kinder now. It was unnerving from an immortal. I didn't trust it for a second.

"Of course, Your Highness," I said, relieved to get away from him. I turned my back and patted Tenebris's neck. "I hope you had a good ride. Let's get you tidied up."

I loosened the straps of his saddle slightly, then offered him water and a handful of oats. As soon as he was done drinking, I led him into his freshly bedded stall. I quickly cleaned off the saddle as I would for my stepmother, then removed it and the rest of his tack, setting them aside. Seeing as he was the prince's horse and a proud fellow, I spent extra time wiping him down and checking him over before I brushed him to a glossy sheen.

I'd thought the prince would leave me to my business, but instead, the heat of his gaze followed every movement I made— burning through me like it could peel away the dirt and the grime and even my skin to reveal what was underneath.

"Is there something else, Your Highness?" I asked when I could bear it no longer.

A fleeting look showed him leaning against a post, silhouetted against the doorway. "It took months before old Albert could handle Tenebris like that, and most others who've tried got their knees broken."

I shrugged, trying to brush off the compliment. "I guess I have a way with animals."

He shoved off the post and drew closer. "And very peculiar techniques. I've never seen anyone bed a horse stall like that. It's almost like a bird's nest. Do they prefer it that way?"

I looked down in shock. I hadn't noticed it in the rush, but the birds had mounded the bedding into a shallow bowl of interwoven hay.

Oh, Fates.

My gut told me it would be very bad if anyone found out what the birds had done. Perhaps servants weren't meant to interact with the magic of the place. Perhaps they'd hang me as a witch.

I licked my parched lips. "It's an old family trick. I don't do it often—just for special occasions."

Special occasions? Fates, I was babbling like a fool.

The prince's scent—a warm and intoxicating blend of leather and vetiver—drifted over me, addling my thoughts as he asked, "Was your father a horse trainer?"

"No," I said, not daring to add anymore.

Why was the prince lingering and asking questions? He was the prince. He shouldn't care where I was from or what I was doing. I should be *invisible*.

"He wasn't a DuPonte, either. You lied about that." His voice dropped the temperature of the room.

I froze. This was the last thing I needed—the prince taking a suspicious interest. "I was terrified and didn't know you. Of course I lied."

He lifted his eyebrow. "To your prince?"

"What does it matter?" I said, masking my terror with courage. "I'm nothing more than property to you. My name doesn't change that."

Something simmered in his eyes, something I couldn't detect. "You're feral, but you're no animal. I can see that much."

Feral.

I liked that. Feral meant tough. Scrappy. A survivor.

I'd need that spirit to make it another week in this place.

I went back to brushing his horse. "I'll take that as a compliment."

"It wasn't meant as one." He stepped closer, his proximity heating my skin and stealing the breath from my lungs. "You stand out. Every time we've met, you've been up to your ears in danger with one of my kind. Just minutes ago, I had to stop you from striking a high lady. You're trouble."

He'd sensed my intent back there. Had he seen my hands tighten?

"I know you stabbed that immortal in the woods," he continued, his voice deep and threatening. "That's an executable offence."

My heart seized. Executable offence or not, I had no regrets about stabbing that bastard, and I'd do it again if I had to. I wanted to tell him that, but I saw the danger in him. Tightly coiled. Controlled. Pulsing just below the surface like a viper ready to strike.

So instead, I gave a half curtsy and said, "Thank you for not murdering me, Your Highness."

There was no way I could hide my hatred, and I was certain that was an executable offense as well. Treason, like the old stablemaster had said.

There was a long silence, and then the prince's boots scuffed as he turned and walked toward the door. Before I could release my breath, he paused and turned back. "I still want to know your real name." His voice was smooth as honey, but there was no doubt, it wasn't a request, but an order.

"Marquette," I whispered, my palms suddenly damp. "Ella Marquette."

It might put my family in more danger, but he would have found out sooner or later. There was only one person in town with silver hair and lavender eyes. For all I knew, he already knew, and was simply forcing me to admit it.

"Marquette," he repeated softly, sending shivers down my back. There was a way he rolled the word in his mouth as if he were studying it or tasting fine wine.

A slight smile tugged at the corners of his lips, as faint as the crescent moon. "Given your prodigious talents with the animals, *Miss Marquette,* I'm reassigning you to the stables, four hours every day. I want you to tend to Tenebris and my other mounts."

I raised my brows in surprise, then dipped low. "Of course, Your Highness."

My mind was racing with possibilities. A new position meant new opportunities to spy.

His smile faded as his expression hardened. "Lorayna will not be pleased, but I will make sure she understands that this is my will. Still, I would watch your back. She is a wicked woman."

With that he left, leaving my stomach churning with worry.

19

Cassius

I stalked through the castle, unable to shake the girl from my head. *Ella Marquette.*

Nothing about her was as it seemed. She acted like a simple serving girl, wide-eyed and new to castle life—but just as the dust and grime of the stables couldn't hide her beauty, Ella couldn't hide that she was something more.

What other serving girl would have stood up to Bianca for the sake of a lame mare? What other peasant, out wandering the woods, would have been bold enough to stab an immortal five times?

There was no denying she was far braver than one of her kind should be. The way she'd bewitched Tenebris unnerved me the most. The beast had a heart as black as mine, and he'd maimed more than a handful of stableboys in his time. Yet the moment she approached him, he became as docile as a palfrey.

Who in all the hells was Ella Marquette?

I vowed to dig into her family history, but as soon as I returned to my study, I found the room was already occupied.

Aamon was lounging in a chair beside my desk, while

Cassandra, the commander of my army, stood against the wall. With deep red hair that matched the crimson of her lips, she wore the simple tight black uniform of my officers, with three silver roses to show her rank.

"What's the meaning of this? An ambush?" I asked, in no mood to dicker with them this early in the night. It had better not be more problems on the western border.

Aamon pushed an envelope across the table. "The Triad sent me with a note."

I cursed and picked it up, then broke the seal and flipped the heavy paper open, revealing a short note: *We want to know your choice. Soon.*

I tossed it in the fire. The Triad—the high council that served as a check to my power and constant thorn in my side—delighted in meddling in affairs that were none of their business.

"They'll know my choice at the end of the ball, like everyone else," I grumbled.

Aamon's eyes darted to the burning message. "I have explicit instructions to light a fire under your feet."

"And you're going to follow them?" I asked incredulously. The man hated the Triad almost as much as I did.

He glanced at Cassandra. "We both think you need to get ahead of this. You don't want them forcing a woman on you. Besides, your enemies are growing active in the court, and the ball is the time to reforge alliances."

I crossed to the window and stared out at the night sky. I felt like a caged animal, and the glass was my only escape. I hated the politics of the castle.

"Lord Perrault has been busy," Cassandra said. "He's threatening families who could make you a better marriage alliance. He wants to ensure that you marry one of his daughters."

My stomach twisted in disgust. Lorayna or Bianca? "He can't be serious. Everyone knows how I feel about them."

"I'm certain he knows and doesn't care. He means to force you into an alliance."

I gritted my teeth against the thought. "There are some depths to which even I wouldn't sink to protect this kingdom. That's one of them."

If those two were my only option, I'd flee just as my brother had, kingdom and crown be damned.

Aamon leaned back, his eyes bright with laughter. "Can you imagine what kind of queen Bianca would make? Fates. She'd likely have the rest of the court put to the stake in her first week of rule and burn the castle down in the second."

That probably wasn't too far from the truth. Unfortunately, the problem went deeper than my dislike for the vicious sisters and their tantrums. Lord Perrault was cruel and a constant torment to the humans on his lands. Their lives meant little to me, but I was the Lord of the Bloodvale. It was my duty to protect them.

I shook my head. "Even with Lorayna, I couldn't risk giving their family any more power than they already have. They'd turn the Bloodvale into a living nightmare. Their family practically caused the Uprising in the first place, and now we're all paying the price, human and immortal alike."

"All right," Aamon said, rapping his knuckles on the table. "Then we've eliminated two of the dozens of eligible women in this kingdom. Immense progress. Let's keep going."

"It can't be a woman from any of the great houses. I don't want to upend the balance and start another house war."

Cassandra nodded. "Okay, then you should prioritize minor houses and outsiders, then—perhaps a foreigner, an unknown, who could bring with her new economic ties and hopefully less baggage."

Aamon nodded. "She has a good point. I like the idea of an outsider."

"They wouldn't understand the Bloodvale and its people or its history." I sighed. I wasn't sure why that was important to me, but it was. I glanced at Aamon, then looked back out the window. "It would have been easier if you'd a sister instead of brothers. Then I wouldn't have to worry about the damn politics of the thing."

"If I had a sister, I wouldn't let you anywhere near her. I'd want her to marry someone who was capable of love and affection, or at least someone who could let their guard down from time to time."

My shoulders tensed, but he wasn't wrong. I was loyal, but I hadn't been given a heart for love. I'd never had it in me. It made the seer's prophecy easier to bear, at least.

Aamon sighed and pulled a sheet of paper from the writing desk. "I assume that if I presented you with a list of all the eligible women in the kingdom, you'd find a reason to scratch off each of their names."

I ground my teeth. "Probably."

He dipped a quill in the ink and looked up at me expectantly. "Then we're going to make a list of all the impossible traits you want and see who matches the *most*."

I scowled. "Someone who is above all loyal and can be trusted."

"There goes most of the court," Cassandra muttered.

She was loyal and would have made a good choice. Although I relied on her, I felt nothing for her. Unfortunately, her family had little to offer, and unlike many of our kind, she had already taken her permanent mate.

"I want someone capable, intelligent, and independent—I don't want her to rely on me," I said.

"All important qualities in a queen," she said, as Aamon scribbled.

But it wasn't enough. A queen had to be more than cunning and capable. She had to be a servant of the land. I looked out across the courtyard, into the darkness beyond the walls. The lights from the village below melted into a flickering mass, and if I were capable of feeling anything, it might have been pity.

"The next queen must understand the royal history and the importance of keeping the peace between immortals and humans."

Like Perrault, too many in the court saw them as livestock. They didn't see their capacity or the threat they posed. My line had nearly toppled once, and although few considered it likely, it could happen again. An immortal might be able to fight ten men at once, but they couldn't fight a hundred. And there were thousands of them for every one of us.

"Student of history, with radical ideas about the value of human life," Aamon said as he wrote. "I'll check to see if there are any eligible librarians."

I glared at him. "Are you here to help or to mock me?"

He looked to Cassandra with an expression of feigned hurt. "Can't I do both?"

"Not if you want to see me wed," I snapped.

He sighed and leaned back. "What about as a *woman*? What are your tastes? You will be seeing *quite* a lot of each other."

That was another problem. I'd have to produce an heir. "I won't lie with her beyond what is necessary to perform our duty. She must know that before we marry."

Aamon squeezed his eyes shut and rubbed them with a free hand. "I'm sure that will go over well—'How do you feel about a life of chastity, your ladyship?'"

My lips curled in disdain. "She can fuck and feed from

whomever she likes, but my duties will end at continuing my bloodline. I will not risk being seduced into love or desire."

Not that I was capable of love. I was a selfish bastard who valued solitude, freedom, and most of all, my independence—all things that the crown had taken from me.

Aamon shook his head. "The drunk woman's prophecy can't have shaken you this badly, can it?"

The seer's warning made no sense to me, but something about it refused to slip from my thoughts. I felt the foreboding in it, and the power. Magic was supposed to be repressed beyond our wall, but she had it.

"I do not take it lightly."

Aamon began ticking off his list with his quill. "Loyal. Capable. Intelligent. Won't upset the balance of power among the houses. Knows our history. Values human life. And of course, completely unlovable." He looked over at Cassandra, then back at me. "You realize that you've just given us an impossible list of requirements, don't you?"

I crossed my arms. "Are you saying that you are not up to the job?"

"Of course not." Aamon folded the paper and shoved it in his pocket. "I just have to look for your opposite. Someone likeable, funny, easy to work with, and who utterly detests you—though where I'll find her, only the Fates know."

20

Ella

To hell with the prince.

Cara teased me mercilessly when I told her about speaking to him alone in the stables. "You've definitely caught his eye, El. Next thing you know, he'll be bringing you flowers."

I reddened at the thought of the bloom I'd hidden away in the storage closet. I stole looks at it occasionally. It meant nothing. I was nothing. His interest would fade like its petals.

"If the prince really wanted to do me a favor, he should've taken me off Lorayna's service completely. I would have gladly tended to the pigs or latrines as well as the horses."

"I don't doubt it!" Cara laughed.

Instead, I had the worst of both worlds—two jobs and a livid mistress.

When Katherine and I reported to work the next evening, Lorayna descended on me like a whirlwind and gave me a roasting that nearly set my dress on fire.

I braced myself and took the abuse, imagining myself bending like reeds along the riverbank. If I could endure my stepmother, I'd find a way to swallow my pride and endure the bloodsucker's sister for Belle's sake, if not my own. Lorayna could scream and yell all she wanted—it was just words and hatred, and I was stronger than both.

"How dare you put my bitch of a sister ahead of me!" she hissed as she dug her nails into my arm.

Okay, so maybe it wasn't just words. But hopefully, it wouldn't get any worse.

"Do you have any idea how foolish you made me look? Like I couldn't control my own staff—and in front of the *prince*."

I lowered my eyes. "I'm sorry for any trouble I caused, Your Ladyship, but it was your sister who looked the fool, not you. The prince seemed impressed with your poise, given the difficult circumstances."

Her fire faded slightly, and she let go. "Maybe so. But it's cost me four hours of your workday. Your insolence has robbed me of what is rightfully *mine*."

"I'll use my time there to make sure your horse is treated as well as the prince's and that your tack glistens."

"Don't think I'll expect any less work out of you here. I showed you mercy because you were new, but I expect you to do a full twelve hours of work in eight."

Of course she did. I curtsied.

With that, Lorayna left, slamming the door behind her. I released a deep breath. How was I going to find time to search for Belle when I had so much extra work to do?

"Are you okay?" Katherine asked, her face pale. "I've never seen her get that angry and not give out a beating."

My heart was still hammering, and I clasped my hands to keep my arms from shaking. "I'm fine." I forced a cheerful smile. "Let's get to work."

I was furious to the point of exploding, but there was nothing like sweat and toil to take the anger out of you.

Katherine shook her head as she fetched some rags. "Fates,

Ella. You're more resilient than I am. I thought her skull was going to burst when you didn't break down sobbing. It's what she expects."

I grabbed the cleaning supplies from where they'd been stashed and shrugged. "She may have to reset her expectations with me."

Lorayna made good on her promise to push me to my limits, assigning me two more tasks before I finished the last. My time in her service became a blur as I raced from one wing of the castle to the next, each chore chosen to make me as miserable as possible.

Albert the stablemaster took pity on me at least. He shook his head in wonder as I polished Tenebris's saddle later that night. "I don't know how you got these stables clean all by yourself, and I'm not going to ask—but I'll make you a deal. I know the sisters are running you ragged, so if you tend to their horses and the prince's, the rest of the time here is yours. Take a nap in the hayloft if you don't let the other stableboys see, and I won't say a thing."

Relief washed over me. If I had a little spare time between breakfast and curfew, I might finally be able to use it to look for Belle and explore the castle. I smiled back at him. "Thank you."

He nodded. "Just make sure the prince's horse is ready for riding first thing each evening. He goes riding almost every other day."

"Why so often?"

Albert shrugged. "Hunting he says—though he never brings anything back."

I raised my brows. "So, he's a bad shot?"

The old man laughed. "Not likely. He comes back covered in blood often enough. Maybe he hunts for blood—they say he never drinks from the vein—or maybe he's just at it for the sport and leaves the carcasses for the wolves. I don't know. Aamon is the only one who ever goes with him."

My fists tightened. Hunting I could accept, but killing for sport? It was cruel and needlessly wasteful. But then again, what else were the immortals but cruel, wasteful predators who loved to prey on lesser beings? Why would the prince be any different?

Except I suspected that he was.

Despite the extra work, my new position turned out to be a godsend. In addition to the break in my schedule, as a member of grounds staff, I had permission to freely move around the courtyard and outbuildings, as well as other places that had previously been off-limits. No one stopped me and asked me where I was going since everybody knew I was working two jobs and would likely be whipped if I delayed.

By reassigning me, the prince had put me in the perfect position to search for Belle.

I spent the next two shifts at the stables getting ahead of my chores, but on the third night, I took Albert up on his offer of a little time off and headed straight to the kitchens.

As I pushed through the large wooden door that led to the castle kitchen, a wave of heat assaulted me, along with the ear-piercing noise of clanging pots and cooks shouting orders. Dozens of staff flitted about the enormous room, carrying bowls of chopped vegetables and meats, trays of fresh herbs, and pots of soup.

"Who are you?" a towering man demanded, his moustache quivering. He wore a tall hat and apron, and had a large wooden spoon gripped in his fist.

"I'm Lady Lorayna's servant. I'm looking for the head of the kitchen. Sylvester?" I hoped I'd remembered the correct name.

"He's inventorying the pantries in the back." He nodded curtly, then turned to a giant pot bubbling over a fire.

I carefully picked a path through the organized commotion of the kitchen, dodging a scullery maid and nearly getting a bowl of chutney dumped down my front.

My nose wrinkled at the scent of tarragon, and I deftly avoided a table where one of the cooks was mincing dried bunches of the herb. After harvesting it as a child and breaking out in a terrible rash, I'd recognize the elongated olive green leaves anywhere. Unfortunately, it was my stepmother's favorite herb, and she still made me cook with it. I had to be very careful to keep my hands from blistering.

I received more than a few terse looks as I passed the various cooking stations and prep areas. A dozen storage rooms lined the far end of the kitchen, and a formidable figure, who I presumed was the man I was looking for, filled the doorframe of one. "Sylvester?" I asked.

"That's my name," the bear of a man said as he turned toward me, holding a pen and weathered notebook. His stocky build and calculating eyes were daunting, but I straightened my back. "What can I do for you, missy?" He paused and frowned. "You don't work down here, do you? Otherwise, I'd recognize you."

"No, I'm Ella. I work for Lorayna, but I'm looking for my sister, Belle. She sometimes visited here. Do you know of her?"

"Belle," he drawled, rubbing two fingers through his scruffy beard.

"She has lavender eyes like mine and used to deliver herbs and game from the forest."

His expression brightened. "The eyes! Of course, I should have recognized you instantly. Belle's a good lass. Terrible thing about her leg. I haven't seen her since she broke it."

"A broken leg?" Fear sank its talons into my chest.

"Don't you worry about her. She's in the infirmary, convalescing."

"The infirmary? *Here*?"

"Nowhere better. I heard she was out leading some lords and ladies on a royal hunt in the woods when she took a bad tumble down a ravine and snapped her leg. Lucky she was on official business, otherwise she might have died out there." He looked around cautiously, then leaned forward. "Supposedly, one of the lords offered her his blood to help speed the healing process, but she refused. Foolish, if you ask me. I'd have done it in a pinch, even if it did put me in a thrall."

I frowned. I'd heard rumors like it before: if an immortal offered you their blood, it would heal you, but you would also fall under their spell, like drinking it gave them some kind of control over your mind.

No wonder Belle had refused it.

"Could you tell me where the infirmary is? I need to visit her and make sure she's okay."

He tutted with disapproval. "Afraid that's not possible in your state, missy. They only accept the broken or infirm up there."

"No visitors?"

Sylvester shrugged. "The prince hired a fancy physician. She's absolutely mad, if you ask me. The infirmary staff have started insisting that everything needs to be boiled. They constantly scrub the place with vinegar and have a policy of absolutely no visitors. The physician says we have to be worried about letting in things we can't even see. They're a real odd bunch up there."

Things we couldn't see? Like ghosts?

I furrowed my brow. "Surely the kitchen delivers food to the patients. Perhaps I could make a bargain and take the duties of one of the staff who makes those deliveries. I promise I won't stir up any trouble. I'll be in and out."

He chuckled but shook his head. "I admire your devotion, but that won't be possible. The immortals don't take kindly to changes in staffing without prior consent. If they don't know you, they won't let you in. Just bide your time. Your sister will be better in a month or so."

I couldn't wait a month. I didn't want to wait an hour, especially with the knowledge that Belle was inside the castle and injured. I'd just have to find another ticket into the infirmary. I was certain I could inspire Bianca to whip me until I couldn't walk, but there had to be a way in that didn't leave me crippled or battered.

"Thank you for the information, Sylvester. I truly appreciate it."

I started to go, passing a table where a dozen warm bread loaves were cooling. The scent of warm wheat and tarragon wafted over me, and an idea popped into my head. I turned back to the baker and smiled brightly. "Say, would it be okay if I took one of these loaves? I missed breakfast."

He sighed audibly. "Fine. Hold on a second."

He turned to fetch a sheet of parchment paper, and I made my move. I palmed a handful of the dried tarragon and carefully slipped it in the sack before he could see.

He wrapped a loaf in the paper and handed it to me with a curt nod. "This is against the rules, so if anyone asks, it's for your mistress. I don't want handmaids down here begging for crumbs like a gaggle of hungry crows."

"My lips are sealed."

The tips of my fingers were already itchy from the tarragon by the time I left the kitchen, but my spirits were soaring. Belle was in the castle, and now I had a surefire means to get to her.

21

I'd never imagined the day would come when I would purposefully poison myself, but here I was, sitting alone in the servants' dining hall with a pile of dried tarragon leaves, the fresh bread, and some cheese I'd found leftover from breakfast.

The plan was risky, and there were a lot of things that might go wrong. Firstly, while I was moderately allergic to fresh tarragon, I didn't know how I'd react to the dried variety, which presumably had less oils and was thus less potent. Secondly, I had no idea how long it would take to react after ingested.

"You're going to owe me big-time for this, Belle," I muttered, crushing the brittle leaves into fine pieces and pressing them into a hunk of cheese. It smelled divine, and my stomach grumbled.

I ripped a piece from the bread loaf, combined it with the cheese and tarragon, then took a bite, savoring the flavor. Poison or not, the dried tarragon gave the cheese a mildly sweet anise flavor that was incredible.

Why did I have to be allergic to something so delicious?

A small, clawed paw tugged on my clothes, and I glanced down. Pip was peering up at me with plaintive, limpid eyes.

"Don't worry, I didn't forget about you."

Ignoring the horrified looks from the staff who were eating at adjacent tables, I moved to a secluded corner and fed him some chunks of the cheese.

I feel like a king, Pip said.

I stopped chewing and stared at him. "You can talk. Like all the others."

He wiggled his whiskers at me. *Of course.*

I blinked. His voice was the same as I'd always imagined it. "Have you always been able to talk? What about the other animals outside the castle?"

Pip greedily yanked another bit of cheese from my fingers. *We all talk. People just aren't very good at listening—not like you.*

I sat back as my thoughts raced. What was happening? Was it me or was it the castle? Was the castle doing something *to* me?

I was tempted to ask the others if the animals talked to them, but my reputation was already questionable. I didn't want word getting out and the rest of the staff deciding that I was indeed a lunatic.

Anyway, I had more pressing problems.

I felt my throat. It was slightly itchy, and my head felt stuffy, but it wasn't too bad. Had I gotten over my allergy?

Before I could decide what to do, Katherine interrupted my thoughts. "Ella! There you are. I've been looking all over."

Pip scrambled into my pocket to hide as I stood. "What's going on?"

"Bianca is in one of her moods, and she's nearly torn the suite apart." Katherine looked at me apologetically. "And she's shouting for you."

As we rushed back to the west wing, Katherine gave me a quizzical look. "Are you all right?"

"Fine. Why?"

"It's just that your face is really flushed."

The door to Bianca's suite was wide open, and several servants slowly backed out of her room. It was like a windstorm had ripped through the place. The tapestries had either been torn from the walls or ripped to shreds, while the furnishings had been toppled over.

"You!" Her shrill voice cut through the space like an arrow. "This is all *your* fault!" She stomped toward me with her index finger extended. "Where were you?"

"My apologies, my lady. I was having a meal in the dining hall." I curtsied awkwardly, feeling slightly off-kilter. Was it hot in here?

"A meal? During the middle of your *shift*?" Her eyes narrowed to slits, while her face screwed up. "What is wrong with your skin?"

I frowned. "Excuse me?"

"Your face..." She gestured toward me with an open palm in a sweeping motion. "It's covered in a thousand tiny red dots and uglier than normal."

Her words barely registered. A slight burning sensation had spread along my wrists, and my stomach rocked with a queasy sensation.

"I think I need to sit down," I said, ambling toward the only high-backed chair that was still upright. Nope, I needed to find a bucket, and fast.

Bianca stepped in front of me, cutting me off. "Don't you dare sit in that chair. What if you have the plague or—"

My stomach heaved, and I doubled over, emptying the contents of my lunch on Bianca's dress and satin slippers.

She screamed, which only made me retch again, this time on the colorful wool rug.

"My gods!" She pressed her hand to her mouth, horror and

disgust flashing in her eyes. "Someone get her out of here before she gives me the plague!"

Katherine grabbed my arm as my eyes started swelling shut.

"Get her to the infirmary," someone shouted.

I smiled inwardly as my stomach contorted in pain. *I'm coming for you, Belle.*

Ten minutes later, I was sitting on a bed covered in a crisp white sheet, clutching my stomach as my guts tried to throttle me from the inside. Pip huddled in my pocket.

A short man with a twisted, hawklike nose moved into my blurry vision and handed me a small porcelain cup. "Drink this tea. It'll help with the belly cramps." Judging by his linen tunic and trousers, he was a nurse.

"Thank you." I took a sip of citrus peppermint brew. It had a medicinal flavor that I couldn't quite place. "Is it normally this quiet in here?"

A dozen cots filled the room, but besides the one I was in, only two of them were occupied.

The man shot me an inquisitive glance as he pressed the back of his hand to the forehead of one of the sleeping patients. "Thankfully, you caught us at a quiet time, but things are bound to pick up soon with the wave of new hires."

"Oh?" A shooting pain lanced my stomach, and I grimaced. "Why is that?"

He crossed over to me and touched my forehead as he inspected my eyes. "New hires equal fresh meat. There are sometimes unfortunate accidents."

I swallowed hard as my stomach undulated again, this time for an altogether different reason.

I craned my neck to look around. "My sister, Belle, had an

accident out hunting. She's here with a broken leg. Do you suppose I might see her?"

His eyes narrowed. "She's in the healing room, but that's off-limits to the infirm."

"I'm not contagious."

"And how would an ignorant farm girl know that? You look hellish enough to have the plague." He whisked his tray of things away. "Rules are rules for a reason." I glared at him, but it did nothing to soften his resistance. "Stay put. Doctor LaMazi will be with you shortly."

As soon as he left, I placed my empty cup on the small bedside table and slipped off the cot. The tea had eased the cramps and nausea somewhat, but my face still felt hot and stingy, and itchy welts had bloomed across my arms.

I'd be damned if those were going to stop me from finding Belle.

I moved quietly past the two patients who were fast asleep, one snoring softly, and peeked around the linen divider. More cots filled a broad room, but all were empty. "Where are you, Belle?"

I hurried to the door at the far end and cracked it open. A long hall opened into several rooms. Another nurse in a white uniform stepped out of the nearest one, her attention focused on the silver tray she was carrying. I ducked down behind a cot, and she walked right past. As soon as she was gone, I raced down the hall, checking all the rooms with open doors, but none of the patients were my sister.

"Ella?"

22

———

Ella

My heart leapt at the familiar voice coming from the room to my right. I wheeled around, and there she was, wide-eyed and laid up in bed with a busted leg. I instantly forgot my pain and nausea as my heart filled with irrepressible sunlight.

My sister.

I all but fell into Belle's arms, breathing in her familiar scent. A thousand fears and worries collapsed into nothing. We were together again. Pip peeked out of my pocket to give her a friendly sniff, then ducked back in.

"What, by the Fates, are you doing here?" she asked, worry lining her eyes.

"Looking for you, of course."

She'd lost a lot of weight, and her skin had a waxen look, but more troubling still was her leg, which was bound in bandages that emitted a soft blue glow.

Belle grabbed my arm. "Are you insane? It's not safe in the castle. You shouldn't be here."

"I work here now."

"You have no idea what you've gotten yourself mixed up in."

She pushed the hair out of my face. "And you look terrible. What happened? Did they do this to you?"

I winced. "I did it to myself. It was the only way they'd let me in. But don't worry, it's not contagious." I glanced back at the door, then leaned in and lowered my voice. "Stepmother told me everything. I got a job in the castle so that I could find you. Why didn't you tell me about…about the family business?"

Shock flitted across her face, but then it was gone, replaced with the determination that I knew so well. "I didn't want to put you in danger, Ella. You don't know what you're getting mixed up in. You need to run."

"I'm not leaving. I'm part of it now, and finding you was just the start. Let me help."

She frowned. "You're not going to let me talk you out of this, are you?"

"No. Not now. Not with what I know."

Belle bit her lip and looked around. "Fine. I can't get a message out. Can you?"

I nodded and showed her the bracelets on my wrist.

"Good." She adjusted herself in the bed. "Breaking my leg wasn't all bad. I've learned a lot since I've been cooped up here. The infirmary staff are very chatty, particularly when they think you're sleeping. Do you know about the magic?"

"Like the floating lights in the ballroom and the speaking animals?"

Belle frowned. "I haven't come across many animals here, but yes, those lights and many other things." She rubbed the dressings on her leg. "Even this. It's supposed to heal my leg, but it feels like there's an ant hive under there."

"The priests claim magic was destroyed in the Uprising."

Her gaze darted cautiously toward the door. "There are a lot of things the immortals don't want us to know about, but magic is real—it's just been repressed *outside of the castle*. It poses a threat to the immortals if wielded by the wrong people."

My mouth grew dry. "Repressed? How?"

"They've stolen it," she whispered. "To get these bandages, they had to send someone to the royal wing of the castle. One of the attendants said something that makes me think they have mages imprisoned there—they didn't say it outright, but it matches a rumor I've heard before about a secret part of the castle that is beyond the royal tower."

"Human mages?"

"There are *only* human mages, at least in the histories of the Uprising. The immortals can't wield magic."

My eyes widened.

She clasped my hand. "You mustn't share this with anyone else. The immortals have spies everywhere. Do not trust anyone. *Anyone.* I'm serious. If they even suspected what we knew, we'd be killed on the spot."

A door snicked shut, and a voice echoed down the hall.

"There's not much time," she said quickly. "There's an old woman who lives in a cottage in the woods who can help. Her name is Siggy. I trust her, and you can, too. Follow the red cobble trail into the woods until you hear the waterfall. Go right and follow a game trail until you see a tall—"

"What are you doing in here?" a middle-aged woman with a head of curly raven hair asked pointedly. "The healing quarter is off-limits to ill patients."

Until I saw a tall what? I stared at Belle, trying to will the rest of her instructions out of her mind, but her face was unreadable. She smiled at the woman in the doorway. "Hello, Doctor LaMazi. This is my sister, Ella. She was just stopping by to check on me."

The woman grabbed me brusquely by the shoulder, escorted

me to the door, and shoved me through. "Bothering your sister is the *worst* thing you could do for her."

My nurse rushed into the hall, his face contorting with surprise, then anger. "I told you to stay put!" When he noticed we were standing by Belle's room, he cursed. "Now, I'll have to quarantine them both to prevent it from spreading to the rest of the cattle."

Doctor LaMazi glared. "What are your symptoms, exactly?"

My mind raced. I couldn't let them quarantine me—too much was at stake. But I couldn't tell them the truth. I glanced down at my feet as I searched for a lie. "One of the dressmakers told me about a special herb that, if eaten, would make my skin beautiful, so I ate it. Turns out, it was tarragon, which I'm allergic to."

The doctor looked at me like I'd sprouted a second head or something. "You foolish girl, you could have poisoned yourself!" The two of them escorted me sternly back to the treatment ward. "While there's no cure for thickheadedness, I have something that will fix the rest of you up."

The gods had a wicked sense of humor. *That*, or Nurse Lanny was intentionally trying to kill me. Clutching a bucket, I glared at him as he busied himself in the infirmary.

He must have sensed me watching him because he looked over cheerfully. "Feeling better?"

"Worse, actually."

"Oh?" The twinkle in his dark eyes told me everything.

I'd spent the past hour retching my guts out after he'd *insisted* that I take a precautionary tonic. "We have to be sure you don't have any lingering toxins in you," he'd said. I was certain he was just paying me back for defying his orders.

When it was all over, I set the bucket aside and climbed off the cot, my head wheeling. "Is there a bathroom I can use to freshen up?"

He pointed toward an adjoining room. "Don't stray. I've got my eye on you."

"Don't worry, Lanny, the only place I'm going after this is back to work."

The thought of having to deal with the evil sisters was enough to make me retch again. On the other hand, the look on Bianca's face when I vomited on her shoes had been priceless. Hopefully, she'd be too afraid of the plague to come anywhere near me.

I rinsed my mouth out with a minty tonic and made quick work of washing my face, then looked at myself in the mirror.

I'd seen better days.

My skin was paler than normal, but the doctor had given me a thick salve that had made most of the itchy red spots disappear. My eyes were still a little puffy, and my hair was only moderately disheveled. It could have been far worse.

Maybe there was something to all the teas and ointments and purgatives they'd given me. I combed my fingers through my hair, then smoothed the front of my uniform. "Here we go," I whispered, preparing myself for the hell storm that would certainly unfold once I returned to the western wing.

Lanny held the door open with a wicked smile. "Take care, now!"

He'd *definitely* given me that tonic so that I'd suffer, but all the gut-wrenching pain and vomiting had been worth it. Not only had I found Belle, but I was on to something big.

Imprisoned mages. A secret wing. An old woman in the woods. My thoughts were racing, and excitement thrummed beneath my skin. My whole world had expanded. I had a purpose now that was bigger than tending to the manor, and—

I slammed into a solid wall of a man as I turned the corner.

No, not a man. The prince.

I stumbled back, but he caught me, gently gripping my upper arms. A tingle ran through me, right down to my center, and I inhaled sharply.

His pupils dilated. "Are you all right?" he asked, his voice strained.

Absolutely not. My skin felt like dancing sparks. The furrow in his brow and the intensity of his stormy eyes made me shiver, and the way his thumb traced over my skin...

I glanced down at his hand. His fingers were iron, yet his touch was tender, thrilling and soothing in the same breath. It was scrambling my brain.

"Ella," he said sharply, his voice deep and commanding. "What is wrong with you?"

"Huh?"

Why was he down here, and why in the gods was he talking to me? *And touching me?*

His jaw clenched. "You were in the infirmary. You weren't hurt, were you?"

How had he known I was there? Moreover, *why* did he care?

My breathing quickened with my rising panic, and I gently slipped away from his grasp.

"What is it? What's wrong?" He leaned forward protectively, as if he couldn't help himself.

"Nothing," I managed breathlessly. "I just need a little space. You're sucking up all the air."

A subtle frown ghosted his lips before he seemingly regained control. He stepped back, impossibly poised once again. "Better?"

"A little."

"What happened? If Bianca—" His fist knotted.

"It wasn't that," I said quickly. "I ate something that didn't agree with me. But I'm fine now."

An emotion I couldn't quite place flickered across his face. Worry? "You don't look fine. I'll have the royal doctor look at you again."

Although he didn't move, although he was three paces away from me, there was a ferocious possessiveness to his stance that made my stomach do somersaults. My chest felt tighter, and the walls of the corridor pressed in.

"I'm better now, Your Royal Highness. I promise. Doctor LaMazi took excellent care of me." I backed away. "I need to return to work."

I spun and fled in the other direction before he had chance to object. I could feel his gaze on me, though, following me until I turned the corner.

My mind sprinted as fast as my footsteps.

I was a servant. I wasn't supposed to be noticed. I wasn't supposed to be seen. Yet when the prince looked at me, it felt as if he'd never looked anywhere else. It was intense and all-consuming.

There was no doubt left in my mind that I'd caught his eye. But what that meant, I wasn't ready to find out.

23

———

Ella

Cara hurried over as soon as I returned to the women's residence. "I'm so glad you're okay!" She started to embrace me but hesitated. "You are okay, aren't you? From the rumors, everyone thought you had the plague."

I looked around, then pitched my voice low. "I made myself sick so I could get into the infirmary and see my sister."

Her eyes rounded. "You cunning wench! Did it work?"

I gave her a few of the details. I was tempted to tell her everything—about the prince, the magic, and the old woman in the woods—but I didn't dare. That kind of information could get her killed, and she had become too good of a friend to put in harm's way.

She was really all I had in here.

As soon as I had a moment alone, I scratched out a note to my stepmother on a scrap of parchment from the kitchens. I didn't want to implicate Belle by mentioning her name or condition, just in case it was intercepted, so I settled on six words: *Found her. She's okay. Investigating leads.*

I didn't mention magic or imprisoned mages. For one, that

kind of information would probably instigate a castle-wide investigation if the bird were caught and wind up as a death warrant for anyone who was even a suspect. Second, I needed to verify the information. My stepmother might brush it off as nonsense, but she hadn't seen Belle's face. She *believed*.

That meant I did, too. If I found the old woman in the woods, I'd understand more.

After sending the bird off with my message, I went about my duties, hoping for an opportunity to sneak away. Apart from our first day on the job, first-year staff weren't generally allowed out of the castle. Perhaps I could slip out during my shift in the stables, but there was no way on earth I was venturing into the woods at night.

Luckily, Bianca's ruined shoes and dress provided me with the perfect excuse to leave.

"There's a woman in town who can get the stains and smell out of anything," I calmly explained to the fuming Bianca later that night. "I can take them to her, but I'd need to leave the castle during the day."

I kept my face placid, but my insides were churning. Would she buy the ruse?

Bianca glared at me from ten paces away, still too afraid to come anywhere near me and my virulent disease. It was the only thing protecting me from the beating of my life. "I don't care if you have to take it to the devil himself. Just fix it, or I will turn your backside into my next pair of heels."

Armed with an official pass from Her Ladyship, the *Mistress of Ceremonies*, I headed out the next morning at dawn and dropped off the clothes. Fortunately, I hadn't been lying about the washerwoman. I was tempted to head back home and speak with my stepmother, but our manor was on the far side of town. I'd lose hours, and there was no telling how long it would take to find the old woman's cottage. Plus, I didn't know anything concrete yet about the magic or imprisoned mages—nothing my stepmother would believe, at least.

Getting an explanation from the old woman in the woods was the priority.

The red cobblestone trail Belle had described was a well-known forest access. I followed it until I heard the sound of a waterfall. After searching about, I found a heavily worn game trail and took the right branch. That was where my luck began to run out. After an hour of tromping along the thinning trail, I'd found no sign of a particularly tall *anything*. Just trees and more trees.

My best option would be to head up to the ridgeline, but that would take hours, and I didn't dare linger in the woods past dusk. I'd grown up with rumors of monsters stalking the forest at night, and they were scary enough that I would heed them. Not to mention that if the sisters discovered me missing come nightfall, there would be hell to pay.

My shoulders slumped. I'd have to give up soon and find a way to try again another day. I scanned the forest around me, hoping an old woman would just pop out of the brush. The only signs of life were a few redstarts, flitting from branch to branch. I eyed the birds. We weren't in the castle anymore, but...

I stepped closer. "Hello. Can you understand me?"

It felt *absolutely* insane to ask, but I lived in a castle full of insane people, and it was probably rubbing off. I was willing to cut myself a little slack.

None of the birds responded outright, but a little male flitted down to a closer branch and bobbed at me as if to say hello. He was a beautiful bird, with a big bittersweet red breast, black throat, and gray cap.

I narrowed my eyes. I hadn't heard his voice in my head like with the horses, but I was almost certain he could understand.

I took a step closer to his new perch, but he didn't fly away.

"Hey, there, handsome. I'm looking for a house out here in the forest. An old woman lives there. Have you seen it?"

He bobbed again and then warbled at me before flitting to a branch a little further away.

"I should follow you?"

The bright redstart gave a soft melodic trill, then flew further on.

Could it be possible? I would have thought myself mad for even trying to follow the bird, but after what the other birds had done for me in the stables, I wasn't above it.

I followed, fighting through the thick brush. Once I drew near, the little redstart flew another thirty feet forward and warbled to encourage me on. Step by step, he led me further into the woods. We found another trail, and he began moving faster along it. Confidence growing, I hurried to keep up. Eventually, the trees thinned, revealing a sunlit clearing—and in the middle of it, a ramshackle cottage.

There was no doubt about it now. The forest around the castle was filled with magical creatures—ones that were happy to help. A smile broke across my lips. The magic wasn't trapped, like I'd imagined, but rather all around me.

I grinned in delight at the bright redstart. "Thanks for your help, little guy."

He dipped his head, then with a flutter of wings, disappeared into the trees.

I approached the edge of the clearing cautiously. The cottage seemed like it had been cobbled together by a handful of different builders, all with their own contrary opinions about how a cottage should look. Part stone and part woodwork, it had a second floor much larger than the first—so much so that it seemed like it was ready to pour off the top of the house. A large porch wrapped around two sides of the building, and three chimneys poked out of the slate roof, though only one was going. The smoke carried scents of herbs and animal fat. Apparently, whoever lived here had an early start on dinner.

I approached the cottage, leaving the edge of the clearing, which was populated with shrubs and wildflowers, and entering the eclectic garden that surrounded the house. Patches of gaudy flowers tangled with rambling blackberry vines and the green tufts of root vegetables.

The deafening crack of a musket split the easy silence. I dropped to the ground as the little redstart burst into the air and flew off over the top of the clearing.

"Who's there?" a woman shouted, followed by the slamming of a door. "Show yourself if you mean no harm!"

What in the Fates...? Had she been shooting *at me*?

Heart hammering against my ribs, I slowly raised one hand. "Please, don't shoot! I mean no harm."

"I'll be the judge of that," the craggy voice said. "Stand up!"

Could this really be the helpful old woman my sister had told me about?

I slowly stood. "Are you Siggy? Belle sent me."

The old woman stood on the porch, musket raised and pointed—rather unsteadily—at me. Her hair was streaked with black, white, and gray, and she wore a patch over one eye. "Aye, I'm Siggy. How do you know Belle?"

"She's my sister. We've got the same eyes, if you want proof."

"I can't see that from here, but I doubt anyone else would be as foolhardy as that girl to go wandering about in these woods," Siggy grumbled as she descended the porch stairs and stalked closer.

The barrel of the gun danced back and forth unsteadily, and I prayed she had a light trigger finger.

The old woman paused ten feet away from me and lowered the gun. "Well, the eyes match, if not the hair. Where's your sister, then?"

I lowered my hands as well. "She's got a broken leg, and she's locked up in the castle infirmary."

"That's a stroke of bad luck." Siggy's face fell. "Why on earth did she send you this far out alone? How did you even find your way?"

There was whiskey on her breath, but her good eye looked at me with an intensity that threatened to burn the hair off my skin. I certainly wasn't going to say I followed a bird.

"Belle said you could help. I have questions about magic and the castle."

"Well, you came this far. You'd better come in." The old woman slung the musket over her shoulder and headed back to the cottage.

The stairs creaked as I followed her onto the porch and inside. Sunlight streamed through the windows, illuminating a messy kitchen that adjoined an open sitting room. Every available surface was covered with bits and bobs and old bottles. Dozens of bundles of dried herbs hung from the ceiling and filled the space with a pungent scent.

"You've strayed a long way from the village." She leaned the musket precariously in a corner. "Would you like a cup of tea?"

"Yes, please," I said, folding my hands and looking around. There was a pot simmering on the hearth, the source of the aroma I'd picked up outside.

"It's Ella, isn't it?"

"Yes." I didn't know if I should be relieved or worried that she knew my name.

"I'm afraid I don't have visitors often—which is how I like it." She gave me a stern glance to set my expectations about the depth and breadth of her hospitality, then grabbed a kettle and headed for the hearth.

"How do you know my sister?" I asked.

"I met her gathering medicine in the wood many years ago."

The hesitation in her voice told me it wasn't the whole truth. "What happened to her?"

"Hunting accident. She was brought back to the castle by one of the lords, but she refused to drink his blood."

"Terrible pity. That will be a long recovery." She removed the simmering soup and replaced it with the kettle, then looked up at me. "Do you live in the castle?"

"I just started working there after Belle went missing. I applied because I wanted to find her."

"Ah." Her tone was unreadable. "And how do you find it?"

It was my turn to hesitate. How open could I be with her? "It's a horrible place. Unbelievable wealth clutched in the hands of some very bitter people."

Apparently, very open.

She turned and began fidgeting with some things on the counter. "Once you have wealth and power, it consumes you. That's why I like to lead a simple life and not get too caught up in material things."

I raised my brows. There were possibly more material things crammed into this one room than we had in our entire manor— stacks of mugs, bins of bird feathers, a pile of candle stubs, more books than I'd ever seen, and a very fat, very surprised looking stuffed owl in the corner. I turned my back on the mangy bird with a shudder and watched the old woman work. She was grinding quite a lot of things with a pestle, and I became increasingly nervous about the nature of the tea she'd offered.

She caught me looking but just kept on with her work, smashing up some kind of flower bulb. "You said you wanted to know something about magic. What?"

I bit my lip. If Belle trusted her, I was certain I could, too— but I wasn't sure where to start. I wanted to know everything.

"Until I arrived at the castle, I didn't believe magic was real.

And, well, it was rather a shock. Floating lights. Talking animals. Even hot running water, if you can believe it."

"You were willing to accept that your land is ruled by immortals but didn't believe in magic?" She chuckled as she bustled about.

It wasn't as easy as that. They'd been around forever, and just because we'd never seen one die of old age didn't mean they couldn't.

"My stepmother always told me that there was no magic left in the world and not to hold my breath for miracles," I said, realization making my heart sink. She would've known what Belle knew—that the rumors of magic in the castle were real. It was another lie to keep me safe.

"What an unfortunate thing to tell a child." The woman's eyes twinkled. "I would hate to live in a world without miracles."

She waved her hand, and the kettle rose up off its hook and wobbled through the air toward us. She held out two cups in front of it, and the kettle carefully filled them with steaming water.

My eyes rounded. I would never get used to this.

The kettle returned itself to a spot on the counter as the old woman handed me a cup of tea. "Don't stand there with your jaw flapping in the wind. Have a seat."

24

———————

I cleared away the pile of old socks that were draped over a chair, then sat, warily eying the tea. "Are you a witch?"

"Heavens, no." She laughed and poured a heavy-handed splash of brown liquor into her cup. "I don't have that kind of magic—not that I would turn my nose up if I came into the power."

There were plenty of fairy tales about witches, none of them good. The village priest had spoken of them as women possessed by demons, intent on corrupting the blood and minds of others. I hadn't ever believed a word of it, but my shoulders relaxed involuntarily.

Siggy offered the bottle to me, and I sniffed it. I scrunched up my nose at the pungent scent of whiskey but added it to the tea anyway. Whatever explanation was coming, I was going to need it. "I've never met anyone with magic before."

The old lady laughed. "You've probably met a handful—the immortals haven't been able to entirely breed it out of the human stock. You have it yourself, of course."

The cup stalled partway to my lips. "What are you talking about?"

But I knew, deep in the secret corners of my heart.

"Talked to any horses lately?" A broad grin spread across her face, and she leaned forward conspiratorially. "I guarantee no one else in the castle has."

I hadn't dared ask any of the other staff, afraid I'd sound like either a lunatic or a fool. So, how did she know?

I shook my head, not quite able to believe. "I thought that was part of the castle's magic. I'm not...I don't...I'm not special like that."

Siggy sighed and set down her tea. "They really did a number on you, didn't they, kid? Anyone with two eyes can see you're special."

I couldn't help but stare back at her single eye.

She gave me a foxlike grin. "Having one eye means that it has to see twice as much, and I see you, young Ella. I see you for what you are—a *whisperer*."

The hair on my arms prickled. It felt like I was falling into her gaze, like it was burning away all the walls I'd built around myself, like she was seeing through me.

"What's a whisperer?" I asked softly.

"It's someone whose voice has power," she said as she stood. "More than most."

I took a drink of the bitter tea and coughed slightly, the alcohol stinging the back of my throat. When had I ever had power?

Siggy paced over to the fire and stirred the coals. "A witch's power comes from what they are—it comes from within. But your magic comes from *who* you are."

"I don't understand."

"A whisperer hears what others don't, listens when others

won't, and speaks for those who can't. She gives when she has nothing left to give." She glanced back at me with a fierce expression. "And if I'm right about you, I bet you've never stopped giving."

I swallowed.

"Wild magic is all around us, waiting for someone with the strength to ask for help," she said. "And when a whisperer asks, the world will rise up and respond." The old woman plucked the half-drunk tea from my hands and deposited it in the kitchen. Then she headed to the door and waved her hands. "Come along. I'll show you what I mean."

I rose and followed her out in a daze.

"You've probably been using your magic for some time. Have you received aid from animals? You said horses talked to you."

I cleared my throat. "Well, not so much *talked*, but I thought I heard their voices in my mind...though that sounds crazy when I say it out loud."

"Well, of course they talk to you in your head. Otherwise, everyone else would hear—and I doubt they'd want that. What else?"

I blinked. "When I was in over my head, a bunch of dogs, birds, and horses helped me clean the stables."

She nodded. "Excellent."

"And a redstart led me here," I said, hesitating as other memories flickered to life. "Now that I think of it, a flock of crows protected me when one of the immortals attacked me in the woods. It was before I got to the castle, though...I didn't notice anything before that."

"Oh, I'm quite certain that was your magic," she said with confidence as if she'd seen it herself. "What about plants?"

"Plants?"

She sighed. "That's the problem with the way people are raised these days. Surrounded by an enchanted forest, and they think the only ones with souls are the animals. It's a very myopic worldview." Siggy gestured to a rosebush dotted with little buds. "It's been like this for too long. See if you can get it to blossom."

I raised my brows.

She waved me forward. "Pretend it's a bird or something you're used to talking to."

I knelt and drew in a big breath, then looked back at her. "I feel silly."

"Imagine how the flower feels. Get on with it."

I gave the rosebush a faint smile and tried to imagine it was Pip. "Hey, there, little bush. I bet you have beautiful flowers. I would love to see one, if you'd show me."

Nothing happened.

I looked back expectantly.

Siggy shooed me on. "You think you're going to get it on the first try? Keep going. Speak from the *heart*."

I closed my eyes, trying to sense the flower in front of me. To feel its presence, just like it was a friend. "Don't hide what you are, little flower," I said, and brushed my fingers over the dark green leaves. "We know what you can be. Let the world see."

My fingers dropped away from the bush, and I stared at the bud. A melancholy weight settled on my shoulders, and I opened my lips to try again. But then the bud moved, bending upward at first, then to the right. The sepals rolled back, and before my eyes, the petals began to unfurl, each springing forth in a vibrant burst of pink. The flower bloomed, full and bright, and as beautiful as I'd ever seen.

"Well, that was a tad self-reflective, but it got the job done," Siggy muttered.

Others around it began to open as well. "It actually works..."

"Of course. The roses knew you wouldn't ask unless it were important."

I knelt there, staring at the glorious bouquet, my thoughts

racing with the implications. "Do you think there are others like me? What about Belle? Is she a whisperer, too?"

Siggy shook her head. "I suspect there are others, and I'm certain your sister is special, but her gifts haven't emerged yet—not like yours."

I looked down at my hands. "Why is this happening to me now?"

She shrugged. "It might be because you started working in the castle. Magic flows freely there, while it's repressed throughout the rest of the Bloodvale by a powerful curse. I expect living at the castle gave your powers a chance to bloom, and now that you know how to tap into them, you can blossom beyond its walls—just like this flower."

A curse that repressed magic—that was similar to what Belle had told me.

"What kind of curse? Did the immortals create it?"

Siggy's expression darkened. "That's what I've been trying to figure out. The problem is, immortals cannot weave magic—it's not one of their gifts—so someone must have done it for them."

My mind raced back to my hurried conversation with Belle. "My sister heard a rumor that there are witches or mages imprisoned within a secret part of the castle, where no one but the royals ever go. Could they be responsible for the magical things in the castle?"

Her brow furrowed. "Perhaps. Did your sister say how she discovered this?"

I shook my head. "She overheard something. We didn't have much time together, but maybe I can find out."

"Be careful, Ella. This land has been cursed for centuries. There's probably a reason no one has discovered what's going on. You don't want to end up imprisoned—or worse."

"I understand."

If I could find a way to return magic to our land, our people might stand a chance. It was worth any risk.

Siggy glanced up at the sky. "Speaking of being careful, it's almost dusk. You'd better get going."

Her tone left the unspoken implication hanging in the air: *and get back in one piece.*

My stomach tightened, but not at the thought of my irate employers or the monsters dwelling in the woods. There was still so much I didn't understand about my gift, and who knew when I'd be able to sneak out again?

"I want to make a difference here," I said as I followed the old woman back inside. "I want to change this place so we don't have to live in fear. But I don't know where to begin. I'm not a witch. I can't fly or cast spells or curse the immortals. What good is speaking with animals and making flowers bloom?"

"Don't underestimate yourself." Siggy paused on the stairs. "Centuries ago, a group of witches and sorcerers tried to overthrow the immortals with magic and brute force—explosions and fireballs and whatnot. They *failed.*"

The Uprising.

"Then what am I supposed to do?" I asked softly.

She put her hand on my shoulder, her expression solemn. "Sometimes, a situation calls for someone who thinks building a better world is more important than killing their enemies. Someone who can make alliances. Someone who listens—not to their anger, but to their heart."

The sudden weight of responsibility pressed down on me. I hadn't been given this gift for play. I had a duty now that went beyond Belle or the resistance. Somehow, I had to find a way to change things for us all.

I just hoped I would be strong enough.

25

Cassius

I strode toward the stables as the sun slipped toward the horizon, adjusting the blades at my side. My long blade, Reaper, was slender and finely balanced—a blade for deflecting goring tusks and for severing tendons as I danced around my prey. The short blade, Fang, was for the killing blow. The beasts of the woods were most dangerous up close, with giant lupine jaws that could crush your head and spikes protruding from their limbs that could easily tear out your throat. However, up close was also where they were most vulnerable. You had to move inside their reach and stab them through the heart. A musket volley wouldn't even slow one of the beasts, let alone kill it—not that firearms had any accuracy. They were the tools of cowards and mortals.

When my father was king, he sent men to do an immortal's work, but men died. Maybe a dozen trained soldiers, working together, could take one of the beasts down, but half would be slaughtered if they were lucky.

It was why I hunted alone—or at times, with Aamon by my side.

Sending men only made the beasts hungrier and would ulti-mately lure more across the border with the promise of easy prey. I rode out each day so that they would know one thing: once they crossed our border, *they* were the prey.

I entered the stables and glanced around. Tenebris wasn't saddled. Since she'd taken over tending to him, Ella had been punctual, and the horse had always been prepped and watered before I arrived. A subtle worry threaded through me. Had she taken ill again? Whatever had affected her the other day had seemed severe.

"Is Ella here?" I asked Albert.

The master of the stables shook his head. "Not yet. I thought perhaps she was taking a sick day, but when I asked one of the guards, he said that she'd gone into the village this morning."

I ordered Albert to saddle my horse, then hurried to the gates and found the captain. "I heard my servant Ella left the castle. On whose authority?"

The captain backed away and grabbed the ledger, fumbling through it. "I'm sorry, Your Royal Highness. It says she left at dawn. She had a note from Lady Bianca."

I clenched my fist around the hilt of my blade. *Damn the sisters, and damn that girl.*

I loomed over the captain. "Make sure your men understand that that girl is *my* servant. She only leaves on *my* authority. Bianca and Lorayna have no say over her anymore."

He dropped to one knee. "Yes, Your Royal Highness. My apologies."

I hurried back into the royal wing and threw open the door to my war room. I crossed to the far wall and unlocked the shut-ters that covered my giant map of the Bloodvale—a creation of the Triad, their only gift I truly valued. The chart had been meticulously illustrated. The castle lay at the center, with all its sprawling wings—save part of one—plotted out. The city and its seven noble keeps spread around it, and beyond the outskirts of Upper Town were the shanty villages and farms, like the one Ella had come from.

Further out were the enchanted woods, and further still the border towers. Each was manned by the second child of one of the noble families, sons and daughters whose duty it was to watch the border and repel the beasts, as I had done when my father and brother ruled. The border lords were the only immortals in our kingdom who understood what was truly at stake. While their siblings and families feasted, they did their duty, as I continued to do mine.

The boundaries of the great spell glowed bright blue on the map—the curse over the woods that repressed its magic. It slowed the spread of the beasts and would prevent another uprising by keeping humans from developing their powers.

We would not be caught flat-footed again.

A hundred small, enchanted lights glowed on the map—most clustered so densely over the castle that it was impossible to tell them apart. A few more meandered about the city. Had she gone to visit her family on the outskirts of town?

"Show me Ella Marquette," I ordered. As the enchanted map honed in on her token, the sea of lights faded, and one turned bright red.

Fear strained the muscles of my neck, and fury lit my blood. "Fucking hell!"

The relentless troublemaker was not in the castle, nor in the town or out among the farms. She was deep in the enchanted wood, and night was falling rapidly. The beasts would come across the border soon, and they would hunt her down and kill her without mercy.

I flew to the stables, an unfamiliar dread pulsing through my veins. I had to get to her.

I had to find her before it was too late.

26

Ella

The last rays of the sun were fading behind the tops of the trees, leaving the sky a deep blue. I was going to be *so* late. I wasn't scheduled for Lorayna's service for a few hours, so hopefully, Albert would cover for me in the stables, and no one would notice.

Even if I were reprimanded, the venture would be worth it. I now knew the truth about my magic and the world around me. Siggy had opened my eyes not just to the curse but to my own potential. That was worth any punishment the monsters in the castle would dole out.

If only I could live up to her belief in me.

A branch snapped behind me. I froze, then looked around. After a few moments, my breathing relaxed. It was nothing.

The small owl leading me back to the castle hooted.

"I know, I know, I'm coming." I repositioned the bag of herbs Siggy had given me for the castle kitchen and tromped on through the brush. The game trail was much harder to follow in the gloom of dusk.

Another branch snapped, and I spun around. "Who's there?"

But there was nothing. The owl hooted again, but I didn't move. The hair on my neck stood on end, and my nerves tingled. Something was out there. A boar? A bear? Something worse? Everything was dark beyond the trunks of the trees.

Then the darkness moved.

My heart constricted in terror as a lumbering form shifted in the twilight. The owl cried out in distress behind me, but I was transfixed.

The beast was something I couldn't have imagined, even in my nightmares. Covered in scales and fur, it moved on two legs, while its clawed hands dragged along the ground. It had the head of a wolf, but with huge tusks and boney spikes that erupted from its spine and along the back of its arms. The thing's eyes were blacker than night.

I couldn't think. I couldn't breathe.

My foot crunched on fallen twigs as I retreated several steps. "Don't come near me."

I was a whisperer, and this was an animal. It might listen, right? The thing paused, and then its jaws opened wide, releasing the stench of carrion breath.

I bolted.

Low brush and branches tore at me as I hurled myself through the woods with no direction in mind. I stumbled and wheeled in the darkness, grasping for thin branches to keep me upright and moving. Trees crashed behind me as the giant thing shoved them down.

This can't be the way I die.

"Let go of me!" I shouted in blind panic as a patch of brambles snagged my dress. The bushes slipped away instantly, and I was running freely again.

A thought glinted through the fog of terror. "Make way!" I shouted at the woods as I charged forward. "Let me through!"

Ever so subtly, the trees and bushes bent away, and my pace

quickened. The hammering in my chest and choking fear couldn't entirely strangle my elation. The forest *listened*.

Wild magic is all around us, waiting for someone with the strength to ask for help.

"Help!" I shouted as I ran. "Help me get away!"

I glanced back and my chest clenched. The huge beast was almost on me, tearing through trees and brush with its massive claws. Suddenly, I heard the sound of splitting wood, and a branch swung down in front of it, blocking its way. The beast tore through it, but other limbs took its place. My heart skipped with a spark of hope. The forest was trying to protect me. Although the creature was stronger and faster, with the help of the trees, I was beginning to gain a little distance.

Then my luck ran out.

I stumbled down into a ravine and came straight up against a jagged rock wall running in both directions, too high to climb. I skidded to a halt and spun. The creature leapt through the air and landed ten paces away with a thud.

The limbs of the trees beside me shook and crossed down protectively around me, but I knew that if the bloodthirsty thing wanted, it could smash through them and devour me in a moment. "Whatever you are, I'm not your enemy or your prey. I'm a whisperer," I said to the creature. "Go home!"

The beast roared, and I trembled. My life was in its hands, and the only thing I had was words to protect me. What could I tell the thing to make it listen? What could it possibly want other than a meal?

Thoughts racing in desperation, I pressed myself against the rock wall, keeping my gaze locked on the monster. "Hey, now, don't be hasty—we're on the same side. There's a curse that represses magic in these woods. I'm magic, and I'm guessing by the look of you that you're a bit magic, too. I'm going to find a way to end the curse, but I can't do that if I'm dinner."

The monstrosity growled low, but I didn't look away. I drilled down, harnessing the strength inside me and summoning my will. *Leave me alone.*

"I have a purpose here." I forced my voice to remain calm. "Don't keep me from it. I can make things better for both of us. *Please.*"

The beast's lips curled back as its jaws opened, but then, as if it had changed its mind, they snapped shut. The creature studied me intently, and then, with one last glare, it turned and shambled away.

I stared after it, still quaking, unable to believe that it was gone—or that it had ever been there at all.

I slid down behind the comforting barrier of branches, trying to take control of my breathing. What the hell *was* that thing?

The rumors of monsters had always kept villagers out of the deep woods, though Belle and I hadn't fully believed them.

Now I did.

I let fear and terror consume me for ten breaths, slowly in, and slowly out. That was all I gave myself because I knew if I hit eleven, I might never get up again.

I stood and squared my shoulders, then straightened my dress. "Okay, Ella, monsters are real. That's no big deal. Magic's real, too, so let's go home."

27

Cassius

Tenebris's hooves tore into the soft earth, kicking up mud and leaves. I pushed him harder as night set in. My fury blazed, consuming my thoughts and fueling something worse, something I wasn't accustomed to—fear.

What the fuck was she doing out there? Was she trying to escape? Had Lorayna and Bianca driven her to flee, or was she trying to get away from me?

The villagers all knew that there was no way through the cursed woods. They'd never risk being out at night—not without a purpose. Suspicion crept into the corners of my scorched mind. Had she been meeting someone? A conspirator? Another immortal? A lover?

I tightened my grip on the reins and pushed Tenebris harder.

We followed a hunter's trail deeper into the forest, and I opened my senses, searching for any sign of her. If I'd taken her blood—a misstep I'd soon remedy—I'd already have pinpointed her trail, but as it was, I had to rely on her scent alone.

I'd searched the section of trees flanking the castle and was about to head into the denser growth when I scented her—lilies and fresh rain, lush and intoxicating, and a godsdamned magnet for attention. My cock stiffened even as I scowled. Any immortal within a league would have been drawn to her.

My shoulders relaxed slightly. There was no scent of blood. She was okay.

Yet there was another scent as well—distant, but enough to chill my blood. One of the beasts. It was out there, hunting.

I hurried forward, turning Tenebris off the trail and pushing him through the dense trees. The low brush would cut him, but I'd treat the wounds with a little of my blood later, as I always did.

Neither of us feared pain or scars.

That damned woman. She was too innocent, too enticing for her own good, and I was the idiot who gave a fuck whether she lived or died. It was unfathomable but undeniable. I would have let the beasts devour any other servant foolish enough to wander into the woods. Why not her?

I pulled the reins, stopping Tenebris as Ella's scent overwhelmed me.

"Are you *sure* the castle is this way?" Her voice penetrated the thick trees. "I'm certain we already passed that tree twice."

My fists clenched. The little mouse *had* met someone. A red haze fell over me, and I spurred Tenebris forward, skirting around the dense growth until I saw her.

Ella's eyes rounded with terror as we burst from the cover of the trees. She stumbled backward, and it was almost as if the branches wrapped around her to steady her. "*You,*" she hissed, her expression flickering from fear to relief to fury.

Her boots were coated in mud, and she was holding up the hem of her tattered dress. My greedy gaze fell to her exposed legs, the skin smooth but lightly scratched, and a hunger like no other rumbled through me, heightening my anger.

I maneuvered Tenebris around the trees, searching for Ella's companion, but there was no one. My mood darkened further. "Who were you talking to?"

She was taken aback by the force of my words, and so was I. "Nobody. I'm alone."

"Don't lie to me, little mouse." I narrowed my eyes at her, suspicion creeping over me. "I heard you speaking to someone. Who was it?"

She lifted her chin even as her fists trembled. "I'm not lying. I was talking to an owl. There is nobody out here besides you and me."

I sniffed the air. I only scented her—the scent of pure fucking delight. No one else.

She was telling the truth.

Ella took a tentative step backward, her eyes darting around like a cornered animal. She was a runner. It didn't help that I was circling her like a predator, but I didn't care. She needed to learn that the woods were dangerous and not a place for maidens.

"Then what are you doing out here after dark, alone?" I growled. "Are you insane or a fool?"

She looked up at me, a vision of defiance and beauty. "What do you care? I'm a servant, not your prisoner."

A low, guttural growl rose in my chest. "Because you're *mine*."

Her eyes rounded with shock, and I instantly regretted the words that had come from instinct. The claim was not something to be said lightly—not for my kind. I cleared my throat. "You're my subject, and if I tell you to stay out of the woods, that is law. Do you understand?"

Some of the tension from my slip of tongue left her. "I grew up in these woods, and I know them better than most."

"Apparently not, if you've resorted to asking *birds* for directions."

She sighed in exasperation, and my attention fell to the rise of her breast and the sheen of sweat on her collarbones. "I have never been in *this* section of the woods, but I'm not naïve about the dangers here."

She was the epitome of naïveté, and it drove me fucking mad that she thought otherwise. "What do you know of the dangers out here?"

"I know enough."

I bared my fangs. "Monsters are not the things of bedtime stories, Ella. They dwell among us, and the sooner you realize that, the safer you'll be."

Her gaze flicked to my mouth, and a wry smile crossed her lips. "Indeed."

Fury blazed across my neck. She had no idea of the danger she'd been in. "If you met one of the things that dwell out there, you wouldn't last a second. I would've been lucky to find a fragment of your corpse."

"I see," she said flatly. "Lucky for me, you arrived in the nick of time."

I gritted my teeth. Her gaze was steady and unwavering, too confident for a farm girl by far, and her words wavered on the knife's edge of sarcasm. I would have cast it off as foolishness or hubris, but there was something more. Something deeply unsettling.

She couldn't know about the beasts in these woods, could she?

Ella crossed her arms. "I've gotten by just fine taking care of myself most of my life, and though I might be weak compared to an immortal, I am neither an idiot nor a silly little girl with her head stuck in the clouds."

I tensed. "That's not what I was implying."

Something flashed in her captivating eyes. "Why are *you* out here, Your Royal Highness? Hunting defenseless animals as usual?"

"Looking for you," I said through clenched teeth. "I am a hunter, Ella, and you…you are the most delicious kind of prey."

The shadow of fear crept onto her face for a moment, but then it was gone, and she lifted her brows. "So, the prince personally goes hunting for all of his wayward servants."

It was not a question but a statement. Irritation rippled through me. "My servants know better than to disobey me."

Defiance burned through her. I wanted her to say some snappy remark that would give me any excuse to toss her over the back of my horse, but she didn't.

She smoothed her features and looked up at me, the defiance repressed and her expression calm once more. "Well, are you going to lead the way back to the castle or just sit there like a pompous prince and bluster?"

Contempt curled my lips. "Actually, I had other things in mind."

28

———————

Cassius's expression hardened with a cold anger. I hadn't meant to call him a pompous prince; it had just slipped out. Fear constricted my throat as his furious gaze fell to the throbbing pulse in my neck, a clear reminder of which one of us was the predator and which the prey.

My pulse quickened, and his pupils dilated. Was he going to leap from his horse and drive his fangs into my neck? The prince was no ravening monster, but something told me that once he'd decided to hunt, he would not be so easily turned away.

Eyes darting around, I searched for an escape. The dense trees would give me an advantage if I ran as before, but I'd be kidding myself if I thought I could outrun him, and using my magic in front of the prince would be too risky.

The dark rider eased his horse forward until he was staring straight down at me. There was no escaping him now. His lip curled as he extended his hand. "You'll ride back with me."

I swallowed. That was mildly better than the other scenarios, but I shook my head. "Absolutely not."

The muscles in his jaw tightened.

"I'll walk. You lead the way." I repositioned the satchel hanging over my shoulder and began heading in what I hoped was the right direction. I already felt like an idiot, and I didn't need to give him any additional reasons to doubt me.

"That wasn't a request," his voice boomed from behind me—not a shout, but with the force to stop me in my tracks.

Panic blossomed. There was no room on the horse. I'd be pressed up against the monster of a man. Maybe that was what Bianca dreamed of, but for me, it was a nightmare. I shivered as I remembered the way his touch had sent tingles along my arm and the way his looming presence addled my thoughts.

When I didn't move, he said, "If you don't come willingly, I'll throw you over the back of Tenebris and tie you down. I promise *that* won't be comfortable."

Neither would riding with him.

I wanted to protest, but his tone told me the arrogant, entitled bastard wasn't going to negotiate. What did he care how I, or any woman, felt?

I grudgingly turned back and took the prince's hand. A shiver slipped over my skin, just as it had the other day. I bit my lip.

He paused for just a fraction of a second. Had he felt it, too?

Without warning, he heaved me upward. Deftly maneuvered by his hands, I dropped into the saddle in front of him with one swift tug.

Oh, Fates.

The rich, earthy scent of leather and vetiver enveloped me, and my breath quickened as liquid heat spread through my body. I stiffened, my back straighter than a board as I inched forward, but his body was large, and there was only so much space in the saddle for the two of us.

"Is this really necessary?" I squeaked.

"It's the fastest way home." The prince leaned forward, his

chest brushing my back. "And if you're late for your shift at the stables, the prince will be very displeased."

"The prince doesn't seem to be the sort who is ever happy," I muttered. "He's as grim as the castle gargoyles."

"Is that what they say?" he asked, his voice rich like honey and laden with threat.

He urged Tenebris into an easy stroll, and the gentle rocking motion made it even more difficult not to lean into him. I shimmied my hips forward.

He growled deep and low. "Stop moving, will you?"

"Well, if you weren't taking up so much space, I wouldn't have to."

He slipped his arm around my waist and drew me back against him with a quick yank. My anger flared, and I struggled, but his hand stayed firm against my belly, pinning me in place. "You are only making this worse for both of us," he rumbled, his voice stiff with irritation. "Not to mention the horse."

His thick thighs cradled mine, and the warm, hard planes of his body pressed into me, including the bulge pushing into my lower back.

Heat spread through me, and I stiffened. Everything about this was so, *so* wrong, yet it felt...thrilling.

I'd imagined he'd be as cold and hard as his exterior, but he was the opposite. The rocking motion of our bodies was driving me to madness, and shame engulfed me even as I savored the warmth and strength and hardness of him. I dug my nails into the pommel and searched for anything that might distract me from the desire that was building at my core.

"You never answered my question." His breath heated my skin, and I swore I felt his lips brush against my neck. "What were you doing out there?"

I pressed my eyes closed, willing myself to get a hold of the shivers that spread in the wake of his touch. "I was looking for medicine to heal my sister, but you wouldn't understand."

"I understand more than you would think." It was like he'd turned to ice. The warmth of his breath was gone, and the arm wrapped around me became nothing more than a cold iron restraint. There was something there beneath his words. Pain. A loss. After a moment, he cleared his throat and continued, his tone different. "Is she the one you were looking for that night I met you?"

His question caught me off guard. "Yes."

"So, you found her?"

"I did. It turned out that she wasn't far."

"Then you are lucky." His voice was distant, and it piqued my curiosity.

"And you? Why were you in the woods that night? Looking for a snack?"

"My brother," he said in a tone laced with ice and sorrow. "He slipped into these woods fifty years ago and never returned. I have no idea if he is alive or dead, or if he even wants to be found."

"I'm sorry," I said softly. "I didn't know." I couldn't imagine the pain of losing Belle and never learning her fate.

"How could you not know?" the prince asked. "Valen was to wear the crown, not me."

Now that I thought about it, I *had* known. His brother had disappeared during my father's youth.

"We're little more than your playthings, so who rules the Bloodvale makes no difference to our kind."

"It should," he rumbled.

Some of the rumors had even suggested Cassius had killed his brother to take the throne—a common path to power for immortals of all ranks—but something in the tone of his voice made me suspect he hadn't. It vibrated with a consuming loss and affection that even his practiced iron exterior couldn't completely conceal.

The disappearance might be ancient history to me, but it seemed still raw to him.

"You miss him."

Cassius growled, shifting against me in irritation. "He abandoned his duty. The throne should be his."

I'd always thought that the immortals were as thirsty for power as they were for blood—Bianca and Lorayna proved the type—but the prince didn't sound happy about the prospect of taking the throne. It made no sense. "Don't you want to be king?"

"What I want doesn't matter. Duty comes before desire."

My anger rose like a swarm of hornets. "You talk of duty like it's a burden. You do realize that you have more wealth than most people can dream of? The power you wield over us...it's not right."

He pulled his arm away, releasing his hold on me. "It *is* a burden," he said sharply. "And wealth and power mean nothing to me."

"That's because you don't know what it means to have *nothing*."

He remained silent, then said grimly, "I do not. But you do not know what it is to rule. My court may enjoy their privilege, but I do not live for myself, and if I do not take the throne, you have no comprehension of the chaos and misery that would ensue. Your life and the lives of those you love hang on the decisions I make, so do not speak to me about things you do not understand."

His tone was biting and cold, and I wondered what kind of chaos and misery *would* unfold if he didn't become king. I imagined Lorayna and Bianca, unchecked in their power, and I swallowed.

It was completely dark now, and the castle lights flickered through the trees. We rode in awkward silence until he finally spoke. "I'm sorry, Ella. That came out harsher than I'd intended."

I wasn't sure what baffled me more, the fact that I was straddled between the prince's thighs or that he'd just apologized to me. "We're from different worlds. I don't understand yours, just like you don't understand mine."

What I really didn't understand was why I was trying to make *him* feel better. He was the enemy. Whether by choice or by duty, he ruled. He was the one responsible for repressing magic and keeping humans like chattel.

And yet, I was beginning to see that he wasn't the cold, murderous, power-hungry bastard I'd imagined. There was something more to him. Maybe it was the way he spoke of duty. Maybe it was that he could recognize our struggle.

Lorayna and Bianca certainly did not. They lived for themselves at every moment.

We exited the woods, and as the prince lightly lifted the reins, Tenebris stopped. Puffy clouds blocked the stars, casting an eerie glow over the valley.

"You are quite the enigma, Ella," he said. "Perhaps that's why I find you so intriguing. But do not take my kindness for granted. If I catch you sneaking into the woods again, I will *not* show you mercy."

Well, that was going to put a damper on things.

With a swift motion, he urged Tenebris into a gallop across the grassy meadow below the rear of the castle. The imposing fortress perched on a high cliff overlooking the river, its walls almost seamless with the sheer rock face. My vision wavered for a second, as if I were looking through heat rising from coals, and for a moment I thought I saw another spire rising into the sky, taller even than the prince's tower.

Then whatever I'd seen was gone. I blinked but all that remained was the castle as it had always been.

I shook my head. *Just a trick of the wind and the darkness.*

My attention was torn away from the castle as Cassius's arm returned to my waist, and we both fell into the rhythmic cadence of the horse's gallop. My eyes watered from the onslaught of the cool wind, but I relished the fresh air and momentary relief from the prince's intoxicating presence.

Charging across the landscape on horseback had always felt freeing, and I wistfully thought of my father's manor. Though it was just around the valley, it felt like a million miles away.

29

─────────

Ella

We rode through the gates twenty minutes later, under the scrutiny of the watchful castle sentries. Whatever peaceful feeling I had slipped away. If the guards gossiped—which I was sure they would—the castle would be rife with rumors by the next evening: *the prince came riding back with a silver-haired serving girl in his lap.*

Fates. The sisters might actually kill me.

The prince lingered as I put away the horses, watching me like a hawk.

"Are you afraid I'm going to run off?" I asked, my voice slightly sharper than intended.

His jaw ticked, and he gave me a look that suggested I just might. "You're not to leave the castle again. Not without *my* express permission."

So I *was* a prisoner then.

Annoyance prickled as I put away the tack. "I have to go into town and get Bianca's clothes from a washerwoman, or she'll have my hide."

"I'll send someone else. You're to go straight to the women's residence, do you understand?"

I kept my eyes on my work, and my back to him. "Yes, *Your Highness.*"

"Good."

There was a long pause, but I didn't look back. Finally, his footsteps departed, and I let out a long, unsteady breath. Thank goodness he was gone. The brute was suffocating. That's why my breath always felt short around him.

I finished my work and headed back to the women's residence, trying to shove the damned prince from my mind, along with his accursed name and his eyes that shone like the winter sky at twilight. I had bigger problems.

By the time I dropped into my bunk, my head was bursting with thoughts like a sack of oats that had gotten wet in the cellar. Monsters were real. Magic was real, and I was a whisperer.

If that wasn't enough to wrap my mind around, someone had placed a curse on the Bloodvale that repressed magic beyond the walls. Now that I knew what to look for, I could sense the change. While the forest and town had been stifling, inside the castle, I felt a low thrum of energy flowing through me.

But who had created the curse?

If Siggy was right and immortals didn't have magic, then that almost guaranteed that there *were* human mages in the castle. Someone had to cast the spells that heated the water and levitated the chandeliers.

And if Belle was right, they were prisoners held in a secret part of the royal wing.

I rubbed my forehead and stared up at the ceiling. This was information that might be able to transform the resistance, but I couldn't tell my stepmother yet. I barely believed what I'd heard and seen myself.

That meant I needed to find proof that the imprisoned mages existed—and I needed to do it without getting killed.

Belle's voice echoed in my mind. *The immortals have spies everywhere. Do not trust anyone. Anyone.*

I could trust Cara, I was certain, but I didn't dare implicate her in my activities. I would have to go it alone.

I woke the next evening just before my shift.

With the masquerade ball only ten days away, the castle had exploded in a flurry of activity. The sisters were almost too busy to harass me—*almost*. Cara was occupied with decorations, while Katherine and I and the other maids prepared every guest room in the castle, cleaning it to Lorayna's impossible standards.

The general hubbub and distracted supervision created the perfect cover to begin asking questions, though I never asked about the imprisoned mages overtly. I asked about rumors instead, or about a dungeon and its prisoners, or about places in the castle no one went—particularly in the royal wing. I tried to keep it casual. Just curiosity or pretending to repeat rumors.

A slow trickle of information began winding my way. At first, it was myths. Ghosts. Treasure. Monsters living in cesspools or dungeons. But then it became interesting.

One of the guards who had taken a fancy to me told me about the prisoners kept in the dungeon. Unfortunately, as far as I could gather, they were all highwaymen and cutpurses. Murderers were executed immediately, of course, as killing townsfolk directly impacted the immortals' food reserves.

An older maid told me that a few of the day staff performed work that no one talked about in the royal wing, and that they had been sworn to an oath of silence. That got my attention, but I made no progress on finding out who they were or what they did. While my schedule meant I didn't cross paths with the day shift, the kitchen staff did, and after much pestering, a plucky redhead told me that she'd heard a rumor that some servants took food to another part of the castle during the day. She didn't know where, though, only that it was at the northern end of the castle, within the royal wing.

While I didn't report on the magic, anything else I learned that would be useful to the resistance, I sent to my stepmother. Requests for additional information began arriving by crow courier every day or two. Names of guards. Timing of work shifts. I investigated as discreetly as I could and sent replies. She wanted plans of the castle, but I couldn't figure out how to attach them. It became overwhelming. There was nothing my stepmother *didn't* want to know—except, of course, how Belle or I were doing.

It didn't surprise me. Words were valuable, and our relationship...well, our relationship hadn't been like that to begin with.

Cassius went riding just once over the next few days. I only saw him in passing, and he never spoke to me. I knew I shouldn't expect anything from the prince of the realm, but his indifference was smothering. I was nothing. I was beneath him.

I reminded myself he didn't care. He'd come for me in the woods because he liked control and didn't want any of his pawns or playthings out of place.

I threw myself into my work to push him from my mind, yet as hard as I labored, I couldn't pry him from my thoughts. Every task was a reminder that the ball was a week away, and dancing at the center of it all was a man with eyes that could take my breath away.

How was I supposed to forget that?

30

Cassius

No matter what I did, I couldn't escape the bloody serving girl. She was always there, haunting my thoughts, even while dueling with Aamon on the fencing room floor.

I pressed my attack as if my obsession was *his* fault, driving him back toward the training room wall. I lunged, but he deftly parried my blade, then flicked his own within an inch of my throat. "You're getting rusty in your old age."

Annoyance flared. I stepped back from the hovering tip and smacked it away with the flat of my blade. "I'm no more rusty than you. My mind was elsewhere."

"Elsewhere," he said dryly as he readied himself for another go. "Let me guess, were you mentally crossing out the eligible maidens from the list I gave you?"

"Eligible?" I shot him a violent glare. "Not a single one fits the criteria I gave you."

"That's what happens when you give me impossible criteria." He raised his blade in challenge. "You were thinking about the silver-haired woman again, weren't you?"

I stepped forward quickly and deflected his sword, beginning the dance. "So what if I was?"

He lifted his brows and shrugged. "I'm not judging you. I also daydream about beautiful women—though I try not to do so when fencing with a live blade." Aamon tested me with two blows. "Or, for that matter, right before I'm supposed to pick another woman to marry."

Another woman? Ella was the only woman I'd thought about since I'd brought her back from the woods three days before. I wasn't used to the knot of frustration that had rooted in my chest since her arrival.

"It's not daydreaming." I pressed the attack, driving him backward across the training room floor. "It's a bloody fucking obsession."

Aamon stalked sideways, avoiding the engagement. Now his interest was piqued. "How so?"

"She's like a godsdamned siren, messing with my mind. I can't do a single thing without thoughts of her creeping in. How do I make it stop?"

He lowered his blade with a smirk. "Seriously?"

I glared at him, my patience paper thin. "Well? Don't just stand there like a fool and tell me you have nothing to say."

"Isn't it obvious? When was the last time you fed from the vein? A century at least?"

"It doesn't suit me." I struck out at him, but he deftly parried.

I hated the idea of some doe-eyed woman offering her neck up to me because I demanded it. I did not want *submission*.

He shook his head. "You've been restricting yourself for too long. It's a wonder you haven't gone on a feeding frenzy like that fucker in the forest."

Disgust coiled in me. That bastard had been the worst of us. Our control was what separated our kind from the monsters that dwelled in the woods. It was the mark of civilization. In part, that was why I'd refused the vein for so long—to prove to myself that I was different from the creeping things I hunted. I forced the attack, blow after blow, backing him up until I had him pinned against the wall. "I've been off the vein for years, and I've never found myself obsessed with a woman like this."

He casually pushed the tip of my blade away from his face with the fingers of his left hand. "That's because you're stronger than most, Cassius. Clearly, it's caught up with you. If it's the silver-haired woman you desire, then take her. Drink from her. Fuck her. You're the prince."

An image rose in my mind of Ella lying on my bed, stripped bare, hunger brimming in her eyes. A dream that had haunted me for days.

I sheathed my blade. "The power we wield over them, it's not right."

Her words. I'd rarely considered the morality of it before she'd called me on it, and she wasn't wrong. The way we treated humans was cruel and far from humane, even if it was law.

Aamon sheathed his sword as well. "Well, if you won't feed *from* her, I could always collect some of her blood for you to drink."

"No," I snapped, my tone harsher than intended. "No one lays a finger on her."

I shoved past him and headed toward the door, Aamon following behind, my overzealous watchdog.

"How do we go about solving this, then?" he said with an insolence I would permit from no one else. "I need your mind sharp and void of dallying thoughts. We have important business to settle beyond the ball. There are alliances to consider and unrest."

I strode down the halls of the castle, feeling like a caged animal. I needed to expunge Ella from my mind like a disease from the body, but the thought of sending her away tortured me for reasons I couldn't fully explain. After everything that had happened in the forest, I *needed* to know where she was, that she was safe.

Expelling her might make the distraction worse. I'd be wondering about her relentlessly.

Aamon caught up with me as I stormed toward Lorayna's and Bianca's quarters in the western wing. "Where are you going?"

"To get Ella to saddle my horse. I need to clear my mind by fighting something that won't talk back and won't pester me with inane questions. One of the beasts should do. I caught the scent of one the other day in the woods."

"Ella," he purred. "You're on a first-name basis, then."

"It's her name. What else should I call her?"

Aamon smirked. "It's just curious, is all."

My friend let me brood as we headed to the sisters' suites. As we approached the corner, there came a loud smack, followed by Bianca's shrill voice. "You stupid little wench!" she shouted. "That was the gown I was planning on wearing this evening. Do you have any idea what this means?"

Bianca loomed over a dark-haired serving girl with her arm raised. A pink handprint had blossomed on the girl's cheek. I halted for a second, and then my chest tightened in recognition.

It was Ella. She'd dyed her hair.

My fangs extended as my hand flew to my sword, but Aamon gripped my arm. "Restrain yourself. You know who her father is."

As long as their family was favored by the Triad, I needed Bianca and Lorayna's father on my side—at least until I secured the support of enough loyal families to wipe their line out.

I pulled free of his grasp. Fuck her father. This was my castle. I strode forward.

Ella's lips had drawn taut. Her eyes were locked on Bianca,

and her own anger was barely restrained. "You requested that it be washed this morning, my lady. It is not yet pressed, but if you insist, you could wear it wrinkled."

Her audacity was impressive.

Bianca lifted her arm to strike again, and I snarled, closing the distance in a breath.

They both looked up in surprise, and then Bianca turned on Ella. "Get out of here! Do not offend the prince with your vulgar presence."

Before I could stop her, she was gone, slipping through the open servants' door, her look of betrayal and shame burned in my mind.

"Your Royal Highness," Bianca said breathlessly as she turned back to me and curtsied. "I wasn't expecting you. How may I be of service?"

I pushed the palm of my hand into the sharp pommel of my blade, focusing my thoughts. *Control yourself, Cassius.* As much as I wanted to send Bianca's head back to her father, control was what separated us from the beasts.

Instead, I pinned her against the wall.

"Your Royal Highness!" she said in a delighted and sultry voice. "Not while Aamon is watching. Not unless you intend for him to—"

I grasped her throat. "Never again. You and your sister will never lay a hand on that girl again."

Bianca's eyes widened. "Of course, Your Royal Highness! She's an insolent thing, but for your sake, I will endure her—"

My hand tightened. "You will endure silence. Ella is off your service, and off your sister's service. As far as you're concerned, she does not exist. She is *mine*."

Bianca struggled. "Yes, Your Royal Highness."

"You understand what *mine* means, don't you?"

She whimpered and nodded. "Of course."

I released her and stepped away. "Tell your sister. Make it clear—if either one of you touches her again, I'll break *your* hand. And if anything happens to the girl, I will end you both."

She curtsied, then fled toward Lorayna's chambers.

Aamon lifted his brows. "Was that wise?"

"Of course not," I said as I walked away. "But I needed a new maid."

31

Ella

I hurried down the darkened passage, bumping into a man and muttering a quick apology, not bothering to stop. My cheek stung, but it paled compared to the tight ache in my chest.

Why was I so upset?

I was used to getting scolded and beaten by the sisters, but for some reason, this time was different. This time, he'd seen.

The shame of it burned me almost as much as my anger did. He'd just stood there, judging me like I was nothing but a foolish, insubordinate servant girl, and he'd done *nothing*.

I pushed through an unassuming doorway and stepped onto the narrow balcony overlooking the kitchen's herb garden. I'd discovered it the night before while scouting the castle, and though it was overgrown with ivy, it was quiet and private, and seemingly forgotten.

The fresh air cooled my heated cheek but did little to temper my rising anger.

What did I expect? He was the embodiment of this cursed kingdom, after all. He'd never spared an ounce of pity for his subjects, let alone servants, so why would he now?

Because, for a moment, I'd thought I'd seen something different in him.

I'd been wrong.

With a deep sigh, I tipped my head back and gazed up at the stars. "I need to stop thinking about him."

He'd filled my thoughts for days, a constant distraction. He didn't matter. What mattered was finding the truth of what was going on in this place, and that meant keeping a low profile and taking whatever they threw at me. I'd endure until Belle was free, and the imprisoned mages, too—if they were here at all.

I gave the night sky one last look, then headed inside. Katherine caught me as I was heading into the laundry room. "The sisters are looking for you."

By her expression, I knew it was going to be bad, but there was no point in running or delaying. If I wanted to make a difference, I had to face them head-on.

The twin devils were waiting for me when I entered Lorayna's chambers.

Bianca craned her head around, her cheeks red and puffy. "You evil little snitch! You spoke to him, didn't you?" She stomped toward me, her finger extended like a dagger. "Told him lies so that he'd take you off our service."

The blood drained from my face, and my skin felt tight. "Wait, what? No."

"Liar!" Bianca shrieked.

Lorayna pushed her sister away like she was an insolent child, which wasn't far from the truth. "Shut up, Bi. You heard what the prince said. While I'd be delighted if he peeled the skin from your back, it would only make my time here worse than it already is."

My mind reeled. Had the prince threatened Bianca for hitting me? The fury in his expression took on a new light.

Lorayna loomed over me, the rich scent of her magnolia

perfume burning my nose. "You might think you're being smart, but you've just dug your own grave."

I swallowed the lump in my throat. "I'm not sure I understand what you're saying, my lady. This must be a misunderstanding because I didn't tell the prince anything."

Bianca scoffed as she tore shreds of fabric from the wrinkled dress I'd washed for her. "No, you just made sure to provoke me while he was watching so that he'd take you *off our service*."

Oh, hell. Was I being fired? I still had important work I needed to do here. "I didn't know—"

"Stop speaking," Lorayna snapped. "You're on his service now, so you're his problem. I don't have to listen to your incessant bleating anymore."

"You mean I'm not dismissed? I'll work for the prince now?"

"As his whore." Lorayna's lips curled up in a cruel smile as my eyes widened in shock. She gripped my chin, her perfectly manicured nails digging into my skin. "You are nothing more than a plaything to the prince. Do you understand that? A meaningless toy." She released her grip and shoved me back.

"That's right." Bianca smirked. "You don't have any bite marks yet, but you will. As soon as he's done fucking you and draining you dry, he'll discard you. You're *trash*."

Panic ignited my senses.

"Aww," Lorayna said with pity. "Does that hurt? Did you think the prince wanted you on his service because he likes you?"

Bianca shrieked with laughter.

My head spun. Surely the prince wouldn't do those things, would he? Rumors were that he never drank from the vein and seldom took mistresses. He had a will of iron and stood aloof from the debauchery of the castle.

For a moment, I thought of the man portrayed on the ceiling of the ballroom, drenched with blood and wrapped in a carnal embrace. The male in that painting—that wasn't him. Everything about Cassius screamed *coiled restraint*. He would never lay a hand on me, not unless I allowed it.

My breathing quickened. But what if he asked? What would I say? A million thoughts raced through my head.

Lorayna circled me like a vulture. "While the prince has insisted that you continue your work at the stables, you should remember that accidents happen all the time around dumb animals."

Bianca had stopped her howling and watched gleefully as her sister taunted me.

"A horse goes wild, your foot slips in shit, a saddle strap comes undone..." Lorayna continued with a hint of amusement. "I hope you don't end up crippled. Or dead. Considering the dangers of the job, I give you less than a week."

"In case you don't understand what Lorayna's saying," Bianca added, gesturing between herself and her sister, "we have the power to end you at a moment's notice."

Yeah. I got that.

How in the Fates was I going to keep them from murdering me in my sleep or tormenting me every chance they got?

My eyes flicked from one to the next. "Perhaps there's a way that I can make this arrangement beneficial to you."

Bianca frowned, but Lorayna paused thoughtfully. "Go on."

"Well," I said calmly, "he must be considering you both to be the next queen. Perhaps I'll overhear something of value or rumors about your competitors."

"So, you'll spy to keep us from snapping your neck?"

I was already doing it for the resistance. I could feed them other tidbits or just lie.

Lorayna's hazel eyes glittered. "I want more than just information about any potential suitors. I want to know his whereabouts and who he talks to."

Of course she did.

"I don't care *who* he talks to if it's not to *me*," Bianca said.

I had to stop myself from rolling my eyes. "I could even put in a good word about you two. Subtly, of course."

Bianca perked at that. "Yes, you could tell him about my hobbies."

Her sister glared back at her. "You have no hobbies, fool sister. Besides, the prince has no interest in you."

Bianca swooped up the trinkets on the coffee table and began lobbing them at Lorayna. "He does, too! You have no idea the secrets we've shared."

I dodged a porcelain figurine that almost took my eye out, while Lorayna caught a painted gold egg. "Enough, Bianca! I don't have time for your endless tantrums." She turned to me, her expression stern. "You have your orders, girl. Spy on the prince. Tell us everything you learn, and do not get caught."

"Yes, my lady. I will do as I'm told."

"Good. And I expect daily updates on your progress."

That would prove troublesome, but I nodded.

I made my way toward the door, weaving around the destruction caused by Bianca, when the destructor herself added, "And don't forget to put in a good word for me."

Oh, I absolutely would not.

My mind was spinning as I hurried out of the room, excitement thrumming under my skin. Not only was I about to be free of the sisters, but this was my way into the royal tower. It was a chance to spy and search for the imprisoned mages—to finally get the answers I was looking for.

32

─────────

Ella

Lord Aamon escorted me to the prince's chambers himself. The royal wing in the high tower was protected by sentries at every exit, and despite the prince's own counsel as my escort, they regarded me with suspicion. The royal tower was off-limits to most servants, and I would never have gotten in on my own. If nothing else came of my reassignment, I'd finally be able to draw a complete plan of the castle.

The royal wing was far more opulent than the rest of Silver-thorn, but in a more muted and appealing way. Everything was meticulously organized and clean, and the graphic scenes on the ceilings of the ballroom were replaced by the royal insignia, patterns of twisting roses. Paintings of rustic landscapes adorned the hallways, and along with the vases of freshly cut wildflowers, they were bittersweet reminders of what our kingdom might have been, if not ruled by monsters.

We circled higher and higher through the tower until, at last, Lord Aamon opened a set of elaborately carved wooden doors for me. "You may begin in here," he said with a twisted smile. "I'm sure you'll be quite suited to the work."

I stepped inside the dimly lit room, and my eyes zeroed in on the oversized canopy bed. "But this is...his bedchamber."

The lord lifted one eyebrow. "Yes. Does it displease you?"

Infinitely.

"Of course not," I answered. "I'm happy to serve."

"Good. Then you can get started on..." He paused and swept his gaze across the immaculate space before turning back on me. "Do you know how to prepare a fire?"

"Of course I do."

The question should have been whether I could prepare a *bonfire.* The brick fireplace was large enough for me to stand in, and I estimated that if I contorted my shoulders, I'd be able to climb up the flue to expunge the ashes. Hopefully, they had pages for that.

"Excellent. Afterward, I suppose you can busy yourself with whatever else you see fit." He paused in the doorway, halfway out. "Best of luck, Ella."

His tone suggested I'd need it.

I stared at the doors as they clicked shut.

I was a spy, alone in the prince's most private quarters. The potential of it gave me butterflies. Whatever happened, whatever the prince expected, I couldn't mess this up. It was an opportunity my stepmother would have never dreamed of.

Pip scurried out from the folds of my dress and began inspecting the room. "Don't stray too far," I warned him.

Several logs were already neatly stacked along two iron bars in the fireplace, each bar welded to an intricately wrought dragon that stared back at me with empty eyes. I arranged tinder and kindling beneath them, opened the damper, and lit them with a match from a silver box on the mantel. It wasn't long before flames licked through the eyes and mouths of the winged beasts and smoke spiraled up the chimney. The royal emblem of the prince's house was a rose, but I recalled from my father's teachings that an ancient line had borne a dragon insignia.

A shiver raced down my spine. If magic was real, perhaps dragons were, too.

Pip darted across a thick rug toward the bed, which was neatly made with plush pillows and a giant fur coverlet, and was big enough to sleep three or four people. Did the prince entertain his mistresses there? I imagined him coiled in the arms of two women, sighing with pleasure. My mouth tightened with an emotion I didn't want to admit. What did I care who he bedded?

Just as long as it's not me.

Crossing toward the heavy drapes, I flung them open, revealing a set of windowed doors that opened onto a private balcony. "What I would give to have a view like that," I murmured.

Doubts began to creep in as I continued my assessment of the flawless room. I brushed the pad of my thumb over the swooping wooden backrest of the settee. Not a single speck of dust. Who'd cleaned this place before me? Everything was neat, edging on militaristic. There were no discarded piles of clothes or empty glasses like in the sisters' rooms. No rumpled, blood-stained sheets like the ones Katherine and I had to change in the guest rooms. What was I even supposed to do?

I glanced at the bed again, then pointedly looked away and explored the rest of his chambers. Two adjoining rooms flanked the main quarters, a glass-domed lounge that offered a sprawling view of the night sky, and the largest and most impressive bathroom I'd ever seen.

"Sweet Fates," I whispered as I stepped into the bathroom.

Soft light flickered from sconces, casting the space in a warm, sensual glow. A lavish clawfoot tub with a swooping faucet sat in the center of the room, framed by black decorative tiles, while a spacious vanity with dual sinks and mirrors took up an entire wall.

I smiled to myself. Perhaps I'd take a bath one night while the prince was out riding.

I checked the tub. Pristine. Did he even live here?

On my way out, I paused by a strange fixture in the corner of the room. It was like a large, marble-tiled closet with a spout in the ceiling. I'd never seen anything like it and couldn't imagine the point.

I headed into the lounge with the glass ceiling, and a writing desk at the far corner caught my eye. A black and gold fountain pen lay alongside an inkwell and a stack of blank paper. The sheets were smooth and silky and probably worth a fortune. I peered at the doors, then slowly opened the top drawer and shuffled through a pile of loose papers. An invitation to a luncheon held by the Duke and Duchess of Eparnay. Another to a state dinner held by House Cavney.

This had potential.

I delicately paged through the countless invitations to social gatherings. They probably weren't important documents by royal standards, but they might prove useful to the resistance.

This is the opportunity I've been waiting for.

With a quick glance over my shoulder, I took an empty sheet, dipped the nib of the pen in the ink, and began transcribing names, dates, and the family signets—at least, when I could discern them in the broken wax seals.

It was strange that I didn't recognize any of them. I didn't frequent the village often, but I was familiar with the names of most of the immortal nobles who lived in the Bloodvale. Whoever had written these invitations didn't live around here.

A chill worked down my back. How many other villages or kingdoms existed beyond the Bloodvale? I'd heard rumors of people living past the haunted forest, but I'd never seen evidence of it until now.

The immortals were keeping secrets from us.

I tensed as voices sounded in the corridor outside. Setting aside the pen and inkwell, I quickly straightened the papers and put them back in the drawer, but the voices outside quieted. I waited for a minute but heard nothing.

Oh, what the hell?

I peeked into the second drawer, my mouth souring at what appeared to be a thick dossier of eligible brides. The topmost woman, who was obviously an immortal, was Lady Marbury of House Darr—beautiful beyond words, judging from the miniature painted portrait. Dark raven hair like the prince's, sweeping cheekbones, and oval green eyes...

The double doorknobs rattled.

I shut the drawer and shoved my transcribed notes down the front of my dress, barely ducking beneath the table before someone strode through the heavy doors. I pressed my eyes shut and shook my head. Why was I hiding? This would look even more suspicious if I were caught.

The footsteps paused for a moment, then slowly angled toward the desk under which I was crouching. "What are you doing beneath my desk?" The prince's face appeared before me, his thick voice grazing my adrenaline-flushed skin.

Panic hit me. "I was desperately looking for something to clean in this mausoleum of a room. Apparently, you don't actually live here, or someone has already beaten me to the job."

"Nobody but you has been in my bedchamber."

Did he mean today or this past week?

He extended his hand toward me. I stared at it for a moment, then took it, letting him pull me to my feet. His skin was warm and calloused, and something about that made bubbles alight in my belly.

He watched me carefully, his stormy eyes a shade paler tonight. "Do I still frighten you?"

My heart raced, and I felt a little breathless from the adrenaline. I stepped around the table, putting some distance between us. "You're the future king of the Bloodvale, and you've murdered more humans in your lifetime than I could probably count. So, yes, you frighten me a little."

He circled the large desk, his long legs quickly closing the distance between us. "Why did you dye your hair?"

My breathing quickened. He must have been out riding or hunting because the sleeves on his soiled shirt were rolled up and sweat glistened on his thick forearms.

"I was tired of standing out. I was drawing unnecessary attention, and I thought I'd try something new."

More accurately, Bianca had given me the option of dying it brown like hers or shaving it off. She'd seemed to prefer the second option and had generously offered to do it herself, implying she might like to lick the blood from the razor.

The prince paused. "I liked your natural color. It reminded me how singular you are, and to never take anything about you for granted."

I swallowed hard. "Oh?"

He stepped close, and the rich leather scent of him enveloped me, making my stomach flip and head spin.

"For instance"—he leaned across the desk, his face at the level of my breasts, and readjusted the inkwell and pen—"your job is to clean my quarters."

My stomach dropped. Oh, hell.

His gaze scoured me, and I wanted to die. "Can I trust you to respect my privacy?"

"I'm sorry, I bumped the desk and tried to put it all back."

He watched me intently. "For future reference, my desk does

not need to be cleaned, nor the area beneath it. I will tend to it myself."

"*Nothing* in here needs to be cleaned," I protested, hoping my feigned anger would mask my guilt. "Why was I assigned to your quarters, Your Royal Highness?"

"My name is Cassius."

Something about the rough tone in his voice sent a shiver of pleasure down my back, and I blushed. "I don't think I should be using the prince's first name."

"I'd prefer it when we are alone."

Like a dirty little secret.

I swallowed. I didn't dare refuse him, did I?

"Yes, Your High—I mean..." I cleared my throat and whispered. "Cassius."

"Say it again." His gravelly voice grated over my tender skin in the most delightful way, and I pressed my thighs together.

"What?" I asked, head suddenly spinning.

"Say it again."

My breath caught. He was only one step away.

"Cassius." His name slipped off my lips in a sultry breath, and hunger blazed in his steel eyes.

It was too much. I backed off, putting the desk between us. "Why *am* I in your bedchamber, Cassius? There seems to be no work for me to do here."

The muscles in his jaw tensed, and something heated flashed in his eyes. "I value your talent with my horses. Assigning you to Lorayna and Bianca was a mistake."

Bullshit.

I didn't want to jeopardize my good fortune by questioning his decision, but I also needed to have his expectations laid out crystal clear. There were some lines I wasn't willing to cross.

At least, I thought there were.

"Why not assign me permanently to the stables, then?" I

placed my hands on my hips, instantly regretting it as his pale eyes tracked the motion.

Cassius moved around the front of the desk, his gaze locked on me like a predator to his prey. "The stables fall within Lorayna's purview, and she would still consider you her thing to torment. I don't want either of them to have anything to do with you. This way, it is clear that you are *mine*."

"What do you mean, I'm *yours*?" I matched his movement, slowly circling the desk, maintaining the distance between us. The prince had a way of sucking up all the air when he was close, and I wasn't going to make that mistake again.

"You're my servant, with all the protections that go with the role."

That wasn't the way he'd used the word. It had verged on possessive. Almost guttural. My palms grew sweaty as Bianca's warning dashed through my mind: *As soon as he's done fucking you and draining you dry, he'll discard you.*

"Do you plan to have your way with me, then?" I asked. "Or am I here to pay the tithe?"

Surprise flashed in his eyes, and his pupils dilated. "No. I haven't fed on another for centuries, and I don't plan to start now."

The tension left my shoulders as a mixture of relief, curiosity, and—*disappointment?*—fell over me. "Well, good."

Of course, there were other routes by which he could have his way with me...

He stepped forward, and suddenly, his chest was only inches away, rising and falling in a heavy cadence. I saw the desire in his eyes, restrained but burning still. I felt its reflection in my core, flickering flames of curiosity and need.

He reached up to touch my face, then dropped his arm, fist clenched. "Don't worry. I will never feed on you without your permission." His voice was thick as honey. "Nor take anything else you do not freely give."

Anything else...as in a kiss? Or my maidenhood?

I inclined my head. "Why? You're practically the king. You can take whatever you want."

He leaned closer, his intoxicating male scent heightening the treacherous desire building inside me. His eyes focused on my mouth. "Can I? Take whatever I want?"

Fates save me.

His sharp teeth grazed his lower lip in a seductive motion that nearly undid me.

I knew right then that he was telling the truth. He wanted me, but he'd never touch me without permission. I could feel his almost violent restraint. He vibrated like a bowstring pulled taut, the arrow mine to release.

The power was intoxicating. *Enthralling.* I had the prince of the Bloodvale hanging on my word—and I wanted to give it. It was a dangerous desire, and it called to me the way the candle flame begged you to touch it.

It didn't matter that I despised what he represented, because the truth was that I'd wanted him since I'd first seen him silhouetted on the back of his horse. Since he'd thrown himself between me and certain death. Since he'd first looked at me with those stormy eyes.

"You can have anything, Cassius," I said, my lungs starved of breath.

His pupils dilated again. He cradled my chin, his fingertips rough but pleasant, tipping my head back so my mouth was in line with his. "That is a dangerous thing to say to a male who has murdered countless souls like you."

I should have been frightened, but I wasn't. My core ached, and I wanted so badly for him to kiss me. As if sensing it, his lips pulled into a sinful grin, and he leaned in—

Strong fists banged against the doors.

The prince released me, and the moment shattered. The fire was banked, and I no longer held him in my grasp.

He gave me one quick, heated glance, then strode toward the door, fists clenched. "What is it?" he growled, flinging open the doors.

A red-haired female dressed in a black leather cuirass and military insignia peered in, her eyes rounding at the sight of me. "Apologies, Your Highness. You've been summoned by—" She hesitated. "You've been summoned."

"Of course, Commander." The prince strode out of the bedroom without sparing me a parting glance.

She narrowed her eyes at me suspiciously, then disappeared after him.

33

Ella

"Get a grip of yourself, Ella," I muttered, opening the doors that led onto the prince's balcony.

My thoughts exactly, Pip said as he scuttled out from beneath the bed. *He looked like he was going to eat you.*

That wasn't too far from the truth.

I breathed in the cool night air, letting it clear my racing thoughts.

The prince had nearly kissed me. Hell, I'd openly begged him for it. His scent, his power, the way he *looked* at me—they were as intoxicating as late-harvest wine. It was like being looked at for the first time by anyone, ever.

I dragged my hands over my tired face. "I'm in over my head, aren't I?"

Pip began cleaning his whiskers with his tiny feet. *Definitely. He's like a big house cat luring you into a trap. I'd be more careful if I were you.*

"He's hardly like a big house cat," I said, shaking my head. More like a six-and-a-half-foot tall, gorgeous mistake.

They eat you.

"It's not eating, not really…"

He's the predator, and you're the prey. Go into the jaws of death if you want, but I'm keeping my distance.

I shivered. He *was* a predator. He had the power to take whatever he wanted, and whomever he wanted. According to the stories in the village, he did. Ruthlessly.

But those stories no longer matched the man I was coming to know.

I sighed and rested my forearms against the stone railing. The balcony looked like it wrapped around the entire tower, and the view was beyond anything I'd ever imagined. The prince's tower was positioned at the northern end of the castle, perched atop the sheer cliff face. I heard the roar of the river below, though I couldn't see it. Instead, I looked out over the lights of the town that shone like twinkling stars.

What did he see when he looked out? Did he appreciate the beauty? Did he think of the people he ruled? Did he even care?

My gaze dropped to the old walls that bounded the servants' garden below. I hadn't considered it before, but now that I saw them from above, a section of the outer walls was different than the rest. The battlements were all crenelated and topped with iron spikes—a popular place for impaling criminals. Each of the walls had a wide walkway for guards *except* for a section of the north wall, right above the staff garden. It had crenelations, but no wall-walk or stairs to the top.

I'd never given it much thought. Perhaps sentries weren't needed on that wall because it overlooked the cliff. Still, it was curious. The longer I stared at the architecture, the more certain I became that something about the northern end of the castle just didn't make sense. My intuition prickled. Belle had mentioned rumors about a part of the castle beyond the royal tower—but nothing was there. Just a plunge to the river below.

Perhaps rumors were all that they were.

Letting the frustrating thoughts drift away, I idly picked a dried tendril of ivy that clung lifelessly to the stone. I followed the tendril, finding more along the outer face of the balcony. "Poor thing, what happened to you?"

I lit one of the lanterns and inspected the enormous balcony. Several large pots of withered plants decorated the large outdoor space, but they were in the wrong places. The roses and miniature fruit trees needed more light, while the begonias needed less. All of them needed watering and pruning.

"Either the prince wasn't blessed with a green thumb or his gardener has abandoned him," I said to the withered begonias.

Or the prince ate him, Pip added as he leapt onto the railing. *Because that's what they do. Like cats.*

I found a porcelain pitcher and filled it with water, then returned to Pip. He'd already nipped the dead buds off the roses and was digging around in the begonias.

We spent the next hour tending to the dilapidated balcony garden by lanternlight and practicing my magic. I spoke to the flowers, trying to coax them back to life with mixed results. Brushing the soil from my hands, I stood and appraised our work. The ivy might not make it, but the roses and begonias had a good fighting chance. "I think our work here is done, Pip. Should we get something to eat?"

He climbed onto the railing and nodded eagerly.

Soft wings beat against the air, and Pip froze, eyes wide and staring at the sky.

A shadow cut through lanternlight.

I lurched forward and scooped up the little rat as a large barn owl plummeted down from the sky. "Oh, no, you don't, sir!"

The bird landed a few paces away. It tilted its head to the side and blinked twice. *That was my dinner*, it said in a dejected male voice.

"I should hope not. This is Pip, my *friend*. He is definitely not dinner."

The owl blinked again and eyed Pip. *You're a whisperer. How delightful. I wouldn't eat the friend of a whisperer, even one that was so plump and mouthwateringly scrumptious.*

I held Pip a little further away. "I'd appreciate that, and I promise that I'll bring you something from the kitchen tomorrow night."

Perhaps a bit of chicken or duck. I do love the way they prepare it here, the owl said matter-of-factly.

I frowned as I pet Pip, whose heart was still racing. "I didn't think owls ate cooked food, but sure."

I have quite refined tastes. He eyed Pip again, who darted up my arm and burrowed into my dress. *There are many tasty morsels here in the castle, though most do not scurry so invitingly.*

I glanced out at the darkened courtyard. "You have such keen vision—you must know the castle grounds very well."

The owl stretched his wings, his creamy white feathers a stark contrast to the night sky. *Of course I do. This is my home. I know every window, tower, courtyard, and garden, as well as the fields and forests around it.*

Hope sparked at the opportunity. I'd searched the castle inside and out, but never from above. "My, you are an accomplished explorer," I said, doing my best to butter up the pompous birdie. "Is there anything beyond the northern wall? A hidden part of the castle, or something perched on the cliff face?"

The owl opened its beak and appeared to yawn. *You mean the fancy garden with the golden pavilion?*

My breath stilled as I looked out across the castle below. "There's another garden?"

Near the very big tower.

I nodded. "So, it's near this tower. This is the largest tower in the castle."

The owl looked at me with an expression that suggested he was tapping into his last reserves of patience. *No. The big tower.*

I looked out across the courtyard again. "I don't see anything. There's just the cliff."

That is because you are on the wrong side of the wall, he said, as if I was a silly child. *You can't see it from this side.*

My thoughts stumbled. What he said made no sense. "I can't see it from this side of the wall—but I could from the other side? How is that possible?"

I could show you—for a price, of course.

I was already supposed to bring the greedy bird cooked duck, but this was too important to haggle over. I sighed. "Whatever it is you desire, I'll fetch it for you." The bird's giant eyes flicked to Pip, poking out of the top of my apron, and I shook my head. "Except that."

I will require roasted pheasant, and perhaps some quail eggs.

I raised my eyebrows. How did he know they had quail eggs? It was going to be damned hard to get a hold of them, but maybe Sylvester could help me, especially since I'd given him all the herbs Siggy had sent with me. "It might take a couple days for me to get it."

He spread his wings. *I will check for you each morning just before dawn in the vegetable garden, the one where all the juicy mice live. I'll show you where to cross the wall—though you'll have to climb.*

"Deal," I said. I was about to hurry back inside when an idea tugged at the back of my mind. I pulled the crumpled notes from my bodice. "Can you deliver this note to someone for me? I'll bring you some pheasant again next week."

The owl blinked. *I'm intrigued.*

"Do you know of the small manor in the fields to the west? The one with pink rose bushes that blossom nearly year round?"

The owl ruffled his feathers. *I've seen it a few times on my hunts. It's quite a long way.*

I quickly folded the sheet a dozen times so that it resembled a small tube, just big enough to fit in the owl's talons. "Bring this to the grouchy woman who lives there, and I'll make it worth your while."

Well, then, I'd better go if I'm to make it back before morning. Bring me your offerings in the little garden.

I stepped forward and awkwardly handed the owl the rolled-up paper, which he clutched with one foot.

"If I can't get it by dawn, check for me the next day."

That is suitable. He crouched and opened his wings, ready to take flight, then paused and looked back at me. *Don't get caught scurrying out in the open, little rat. There are hungry creatures all around.*

With that, his wings beat heavily as he lifted into the air.

Had he meant that warning for Pip or for me?

34

Cassius

I avoided Ella as best I could for the next two days, throwing myself into preparations for the ball, organizing the border patrols, and even, when I grew desperate, narrowing down Aamon's lists of brides.

But always, my mind was on her. I couldn't help it. She was all-consuming. I could still feel the warmth of her lips mere inches from mine. I cursed myself that I hadn't kissed her, and I cursed myself for letting it get that far.

If you fall in love, the woman you choose will destroy everything your father built.

But I was not in love, not with a serving girl. It was impossible. She was simply a distraction—though a distraction could be enough to put my kingdom in danger. Perhaps this was what the old woman had been trying to warn me about.

I redoubled my efforts to ignore her, yet I couldn't stay away. Her absence was like a lingering wound, scabbed over but still aching.

Shortly after sunset, I found her in the stables. Unable to help myself, I paused at the door and watched. She stood with her back to me, stroking the muzzle of a brown mare and speaking to it in hushed tones.

I inclined my head, lengthening my senses. First came her scent, and I forced myself to take only one deep inhalation. Too much, and my long-repressed blood lust would rise. Instead, I focused on the sounds of the stable until they roared to life in a deafening storm.

"Do you know what lies beyond the Bloodvale, or were you born in this valley, too?" she whispered to the mare. There was a short pause, and then she said, "I've never been out, either, though I've always wanted to know what was on the other side. Maybe we'll go someday, you and me."

My brow furrowed. What lay beyond was danger, but also beauty—worlds she probably could never imagine. An unfamiliar pang of guilt tore at me.

Maybe her kind deserved better.

She deserved better.

I'd never felt anything for humans. My relationship with them was transactional. We ruled, they served. We protected them from the monsters, and they fed us with their blood.

But something about that made me hesitate. Perhaps it was the way Ella looked at the world with clear eyes and an open heart. It was why I should stay the hell away. I would only corrupt her.

And yet, I was a selfish bastard, and I wanted her for my own.

I cleared my throat as I approached.

Ella spun. "Your Highness." She dropped into a low curtsy, cheeks flushed. "I didn't hear you come in."

"Do you always speak to animals?"

She froze as if I'd caught her robbing the treasury, then quickly looked away. She plucked a carrot from a sack at her feet and fed it to the brown mare, who ate it eagerly. "Of course. I find them to be far better company than most people, immortals included."

A thin smile crossed my lips. I couldn't agree more.

When I headed to Tenebris's stall, I found he was already saddled. The irascible warhorse nickered as I led him out and inspected the straps under his belly, all secured as they should be. His coat had also been recently brushed. I glanced over at Ella. "You seem to have the same knack with flowers as you do with animals."

Her eyes widened, shock on her face. "What do you mean."

Did my presence really frighten her that much?

"You somehow managed to bring the flowers on my balcony back to life."

"Oh, those." She released a relieved breath, as if what I'd said hadn't been what she'd expected. "They were never dead," she continued, looking at me over Tenebris's shoulder. "Just dormant. You never watered them, *ever*. It's amazing how a garden will flourish when the gardener actually pays attention."

My expression darkened. "Are you implying something?"

"Certainly not, Your Highness. I wouldn't question why the prince must go hunting every day and leave the castle in the hands of his underlings." She reached up and scratched the area behind Tenebris's ear, just the way he liked it.

How did she know to do that already?

"You're bold for a serving girl."

She looked me straight in the eyes with breathtaking tenacity. "Does that threaten you?"

"Not at all."

The fucking opposite. Her unabashed assertiveness made my cock hard, and nobody had done that in a long time.

I wrapped my fingers around the hilt of my blade. Coming to the stables hadn't only been an excuse to see her. I'd planned to ride to the border and check for signs of the beasts, who'd grown bolder over the last weeks. I'd thought a kill would clear my mind, but I was certain now that it wouldn't. It would just remind me of our ride through the forest and the danger she'd been in.

How different our lives were. I could ride unafraid, but she could never enter the woods at night without putting her life in jeopardy. She'd never have the chance to smell the night-blooming flowers or see the beauty hidden beneath the hungering darkness.

"Can you ride?" I asked.

She eyed me suspiciously. "Of course."

"Good." I nodded to Chastity, the mare she'd been tending. "Take that horse and follow me."

When I didn't hear her move, I looked back. She stood there, lips pressed together and hands on her hips. "Why would you want *me* to ride with *you*?"

"Do I need a reason? Will you ride or not?"

"I'm not going to watch you murder creatures for sport."

"I don't murder for sport," I said in a tone that would have my courtiers drop to their knees and piss themselves.

But she simply narrowed her eyes at me, calculating, then collected the horse's tack and began to saddle her.

Did she think that just because we'd nearly kissed, she could defy the prince of the Bloodvale?

Audacious.

She led the brown mare out, and I realized she wasn't properly dressed for riding. The notion of her straddling a horse in trousers was suddenly all I could think about. I cleared my throat. "Perhaps you should change your clothes first."

"I can manage," she said as she calmly continued her work. "I don't own the kind of clothes Bianca wears."

Of course she didn't. That was a problem I was going to have to remedy.

I mounted Tenebris and watched as Ella adjusted her own saddle with the ease of someone who'd spent years around horses. Then, hiking up the hem of her dress, she hooked one boot in the stirrup, offering me a quick glance at her smooth calves before pulling herself effortlessly into the saddle. Desire pulsed through me as I imagined how soft the skin of her thighs might be.

She glanced over at me as she guided her horse forward. "Is something wrong? You look bothered."

Bothered was one way to put it. "Let's see if you can ride." I lightly tugged on the reins, and Tenebris broke into an easy canter. "Keep up, if you can manage."

As soon as we cleared the back gate, Tenebris exploded into a gallop, as eager as I was to be free of the heavy confines of the castle. The forest was where I belonged, standing watch in one of the tall towers on the ridge, not pampering myself in the suffocating confines of the court.

We tore across an open field that had turned ruddy in the waning light, the horses' hooves digging into the ground in a rhythmic melody. I eased up on the reins to let Ella catch up. After all, the brown mare was no match for Tenebris. But instead of falling into pace beside me, the unlikely pair bolted by us, heading straight for the woods. Ella whooped as she passed me, the skirt of her dress billowing, her dark hair a wild flag whipping behind her. *It should be silver.*

Who was this hellion of a woman?

Tenebris wasn't one to be shown up. He hurtled forward, racing after the two like a hound scenting blood. The thrill of the chase coursed through my body, and I grinned at my mark.

I had almost caught up to her when she looked over her shoulder, locking her gaze on Tenebris. Oddly enough, he started to fall back. I spurred him on, but his pace didn't accelerate. "Are you really going to let them beat us?"

Ella and the brown mare reached the thick tree line and circled around so that she was facing me as I approached. Her skin was flushed from the ride, and tendrils of her disheveled hair kissed her cheeks. She beamed at me, defiant in her beauty. "It looks like we beat you after all, Your Highness."

"Apparently so," I said grimly, but I couldn't help the strange warmth that was spreading in my chest. "What did you do to my horse?"

"Me?" She winked at Tenebris. "Perhaps you just miscalculated Chastity's cunning and speed."

"Unlikely." I eyed Ella suspiciously. "Where did you learn to ride like that?"

"My father. He used to take me out in the fields around our manor each morning, and we'd race back."

I sensed the love and pain she carried. "Used to?"

"He disappeared when I was twelve."

Disappeared. Like Valen. The familiar numbness spread through me. "I'm sorry."

She glanced at the woods as if it contained the answers she sought. "I sometimes imagine that he might still return, but I know he won't. It's a fool's dream."

A fool's dream we shared.

The forested valley pressed in around me as I scanned the distant tree line, silver touching the darkening sky. Valen would never return. I had to accept it. I had to move on.

Without a word, I guided Tenebris up the trail and into the shadowed woods.

Ella was silent as I led her along the single track that wound deep into the forest, each of us lost in our own reflections. It was a comfortable silence, the type that I couldn't even share with Aamon.

Eventually, the sound of rushing water filtered through the trees, pulling me from my reverie. I pulled Tenebris to a halt as we entered the clearing at the base of the thundering falls. They roared out of a gap in the cliff face high above, crashing down into a deep pond at the base in a cloud of mist. The thin crescent moon reflected in the ripples at the edge of the pool and made the stones sparkle like diamonds.

"My gods," Ella whispered as she pulled up alongside me. "It's beautiful."

I watched her as her eyes drank in the space. She was so full of wonder, it left me with a feeling of emptiness. What would it be like to see this place as she did?

"We could go closer, if you'd like," I offered. "There is a path of stones across the water."

She nodded and slipped off the back of her horse. "Why did you bring me here?" she asked, her gaze still on the falls.

I dropped down beside her and tied off Tenebris's reins. "Because it's beautiful, even to me. It's the only one in the valley and not far, yet I rarely visit."

She kept her eyes trained on the falls, but she couldn't hide the change in her posture. "So, there are others beyond the Bloodvale?"

The question seemed innocent, but she knew exactly what she was asking: *what lands lie beyond our borders?*

"You should direct less energy to things that are forbidden to you," I said dismissively.

"Forbidden," she said solemnly. "Everything is forbidden. We're just your little toys to keep and to hoard like a greedy child."

She began picking a path along the round river stones toward the pool's edge. Irritation burned under my skin. This woman had no sense of her place in the world, and the irreverent way she addressed me was maddening. It stoked a fire in me, a heat I hadn't felt in ages.

"You do realize that I could lock you up or have you flogged for the way you speak to me? You have no respect."

She stopped a few paces from the pool and looked back, the flames of accusation in her eyes. "Respect? The truth is you have too much power and too little respect for your subjects. Do you really expect us to live in ignorance? To go about our lives confined in this small valley without questioning what exists beyond? To live like animals in the pen you've built?"

"You don't know the danger that lies beyond those borders," I snapped back. "We protect *you*, and you serve *us*."

The justification felt strangely hollow as it left my mouth.

She dropped down to unlace her shoes, as if her challenge were mere conversation. "If you think your rule is fair, you're sorely deceived, Cassius."

"Am I?" I asked, the threat thrumming in my voice. Her directness crossed every line, but I could barely think beyond the way her lips formed my name. It conjured all sorts of tantalizing images.

She slipped off her shoes. "You claim that you protect us, but you forbid us to have guns. Perhaps we could protect ourselves. Perhaps things are not as equitable as you suggest."

"You go too far," I growled, hoping my tone would frighten some sense into her. "If you spoke like this in the castle, you would be accused of treason."

As if my warning were nothing out of the ordinary, she simply lifted the hem of her dress and stepped into the shallows of the pool. She gave me a placid look, but her voice was sharp as my blade. "Then I suppose I must thank you again for not executing me, Your Highness."

35

———

"I would never hurt you," Cassius said, the words almost exploding from his lungs, like he'd taken a blow to his chest.

For a fleeting second, I thought I saw anguish flash across his face, but it made no sense.

I waded through the icy water, just beyond his reach. "It's not me I'm worried about. It's the rest of my people. Will you extend them the same courtesy?" He said nothing, so I turned to face him. "You'll stop Bianca from beating me—but what about the others?"

"You're different," he whispered. "I—"

Anger flashed in my chest. "I thought *you* were different," I said, unable to hide the bitterness from my voice. "But of course you aren't. We're nothing but cattle."

Cassius looked like I'd driven a stake through his heart. I tried to keep my expression even, but my thoughts were racing. Was that guilt? Regret? A flicker of conscience?

"There are some things I cannot change." He stalked forward over the river stones. "Even when I'm king."

Did that mean he wanted to change things? Could he

possibly believe humans deserved better? It was more than I'd hoped for, but not enough. Wanting it didn't matter, not if he did nothing with his power.

"*There are things I cannot change* is the favorite excuse of all men who enjoy power. It's the oath of cowards."

The prince growled, and with lightning speed, he'd pinned my arms to my sides. He glared down at me, a bonfire of emotion in his eyes. "I'd be more careful with what you say, little mouse."

I knew I was playing a dangerous game, but I couldn't shake Siggy's words. *A whisperer speaks for those who can't*—and unlike any other human, I seemed to have gained the ear of the prince. "What if I can't? What if I have things to say that you need to hear?"

"When you question my authority and push back against me..." His broad chest rose and fell rapidly, his eyes darkening. "It makes me want to do things to you."

The prince held me firmly, his grip unyielding but not painful. The moonlight brushed his cheekbones, accentuating the strong contours of his face. He was breathtaking and terrifying, and his body practically vibrated with fury. That should have been a warning, but for some reason, it only made me want to push him further.

"Do *things* to me?" I glared up at him, challenging him. "Will you be teaching me a lesson now?"

Cassius's pupils dilated as longing and something far more dangerous burned in his eyes. "What do you want me to say?" His rough voice grazed over my skin, leaving heat in its wake. "That I don't know if I want to bed you or exile you for treason?"

The admission stole the breath from my lips.

I should hate him. *Despise* him. But though he was a monster, the thought of him taking me sent desire racing through my core. There was an attraction between us that I couldn't explain or deny.

"Does it matter what I say? Doesn't a prince do what he wants?"

I was tempting him, pushing him, trying to see how far he would go—looking for proof that he was a monster like all the others, not the man he appeared to be.

"No," he ground out with difficulty. His eyes burned with need, held back by iron will.

A surge of fear and something close to excitement caught my breath, and the yearning at my center became almost unbearable. I met his eyes. "Well, he should."

The prince froze.

Then, in a swift movement, he pulled me forward, and his lips crashed against mine. Heat enveloped me, along with the intoxicating scent of his skin, his soap, his desire.

By principle, I wanted to protest, but instead, I met his hungry kisses with equal ferocity.

One of his hands clutched the back of my head, while the other circled my waist, catching me as I slipped on a river stone and pulling me against his hardness. My anger from earlier morphed into molten heat, and I melted into him, my soft curves meeting the strong contours of his body like we were meant to fit together.

I'd never been with a man before, yet somehow, my body knew exactly how to respond to his touch. I trembled with need, but...but this was wrong.

I tore my mouth free and sucked in a breath. "Cassius."

His kisses traced along my neck, leaving a delicious trail of gooseflesh in their wake. I felt alive, vibrating with energy and delirious desire. Gods, I wanted him so badly it hurt, but I couldn't. I didn't dare. He was to become king of the Bloodvale, and I was part of the resistance, sworn to help overthrow him and his kind. We had no future. It was madness.

"Cassius, stop."

The prince broke off the kiss, concern in his eyes. "What is it?"

My heart raced, desire still a liquid fire in my veins. "We can't do this. I...I can't do this with you."

Frustration flickered, and the passion I'd seen in his face vanished, replaced by a mask of cold stone. He stepped back. "I will do nothing against your will, no matter how much I want it."

I stared at him. He *was* different than the other immortals. They were self-absorbed vipers who served only themselves, but Cassius had honor and a sense of duty. I saw it in the way he talked about his duty to the crown and the respect that he showed me. Why couldn't he impart the same respect and courtesy to the rest of the kingdom?

He slipped away from me, his posture stiff and formal. "I apologize if I was too forward or took liberties you did not want."

"I do want you to take them," I said around the lump that had formed in my throat. "I mean, I did, but..." For once, I was at a loss for words. "We should get back to the castle."

He measured me for a beat, his expression unreadable. "Of course."

I looked away, disappointment searing a hole through me as I donned my socks and boots. Gods, I wanted him.

Cassius's gaze burned into me as I picked my way back to shore. When I looked up, one of the water-rounded boulders I'd stepped on rolled under my weight, and I tilted sideways. His arms were suddenly around me, lifting me like I weighed nothing as he carried me to the waiting horses. His eyes fell to my lips for a heartbeat before he gently set me down beside Chastity. "I don't understand you."

A vein of hope threaded through me. "How so?"

"You make me feel things I haven't felt in a long time. I've trained myself mercilessly to control my emotions, but around you..." His jaw clenched. "It is as difficult as anything I've had to do."

A fist tightened around my heart. "I've been told that I have a way of provoking people."

The ghost of a smile tugged at the corner of his mouth. "*Provoking* would be an understatement. You're like a tiny cinder that sets the forest ablaze."

Downplaying the warmth that spread through me at his words, I swung up into Chastity's saddle. "That might be the nicest thing anybody has ever said to me. I hope I don't trouble you too much."

He mounted Tenebris in a fluid motion, then glanced over at me with a glint in his eyes. "You trouble me immensely, but for reasons you wouldn't understand."

I wanted to press him on what those reasons were, but he was already heading into the forest.

An hour later, we were back at the stables. Relief washed over me when he left the horses to my care. I watched him walk away, once again tall and cold and completely iron. There was more to him beneath that frosty exterior. I knew that now for certain.

My head and heart were still spinning over everything that had happened. The words we'd had. The passionate kiss we'd shared.

Fates, I'd accused him of being a bad ruler.

I brushed Tenebris's coat more vigorously than necessary.

Did I even know what I wanted anymore? I was a spy. He was my enemy. A vampire. A bloodsucker. But the term felt wrong on him now. He was different, and the thought conjured fear and something even more treacherous in my heart—hope.

If he could care about what happened to me or what I wanted, perhaps he could see the value in my people.

Siggy had said, *When a whisperer asks, the world will rise up and respond.*

Maybe the world wouldn't listen, but might he?

It was preposterous. A desperate fabrication to justify my growing feelings for him. A delusion. He'd said he couldn't change things. I should take him at his word.

Cloak pulled around me, I wove among the servants bustling through the castle. There was a storm of activity—everyone frantically polishing windows, scrubbing the floors, setting out flowers to get ready for the ball. It was only five days away.

The reality of my situation crashed down on me. I couldn't let myself get close to Cassius. Whatever had happened between us, in a matter of days, the prince would choose a bride.

What would that make me? His mistress? A dalliance? The other woman?

I frowned. He'd probably put me out of his mind. He certainly wouldn't listen. That was a fool's dream.

I couldn't lose sight of my true purpose. I had to find the mages, if they existed at all. If anyone had the power to change things, it would be them. With their strength, my people might finally have a fighting chance.

36

———————

Ella

The next morning, I slipped into the servants' garden as twilight inched toward dawn. The night staff was all settling in, while the gardeners and the rest of the day staff hadn't begun their shift yet. It was the perfect time to poke around—dark enough to hide me but light enough to see.

I set down the small bundle of food I'd gotten from Sylvester after a relentless round of haggling and begging. It wasn't everything the owl had asked for, but hopefully, it was enough. Cupping my hands around my mouth, I gave a soft hoot. Moments later, the owl landed on the edge of a raised bed.

He cocked his head. *You do not sound like an owl at all. At least not a pretty one. Maybe the type with weird ears.*

Weird ears? I reached up to touch my own self-consciously, but my fingers only found the plain scarf I'd wrapped around my hair, as was the fashion among the household girls.

You have my delicacies? He peered at my bundle.

I spread out the fare I'd brought for him and waited while he greedily consumed each bit, gobbling strips of pheasant down his gullet. It was somewhat unsettling, and I was glad I hadn't brought Pip.

A half dozen crows, noticing the feast, hopped down and began inching forward. *Treat?*

I tossed them some of the bread I'd brought for myself, and they fluttered about, eating almost as greedily as the owl.

As the birds feasted, I studied the northern wall. The owl had claimed that behind it lay a garden with a golden pavilion and tall tower on the far side, but that you couldn't see it from the castle grounds. Was it just a trick to get a free meal, or was there really a hidden portion of the castle?

The sky was just beginning to brighten, and I started to grow nervous. "Can you show me where I need to go to find the garden with the golden pavilion? It's almost sunrise."

Just over that wall, the owl said, swallowing a strip of meat.

Annoyance pricked at me. "I'm going to check it out. Join me when you finish."

The crows hopped around, pecking at things, and one looked straight at me. *Need help?*

I nodded, glad to have some allies that weren't quite so mercenary. "Can you be my sentries? Alert me if you see anyone coming into the garden or if anyone on the battlements turns toward me."

Another pecked at the first. *Yes, yes! We'll chase them off. Very brave.*

A laughing smile broke across my face. "Yes, you're very brave. All of you."

He pecked his friend again just to make sure I realized that he was the bravest of them all.

With a quick glance at the castle towers, I stole toward the far end of the garden, keeping to the deep shadows. The back wall was lined with low flowerbeds and covered with ornamental ivy. I quickly searched the vines for a hidden door, pushing the leaves out of the way and digging my fingers in the cracks of the wall.

Eventually, I stepped back, my hands on my hips. Nothing.

There was a soft flutter of wings, and the little owl landed on the path beside me. *You're on the wrong side.*

"I get that. I'm guessing you can't pick me up and fly me over."

The owl cocked its head and blinked at me like I was an idiot. Apparently, sarcasm was not a universal language.

I turned back to the wall with a sigh and tugged gently on the ivy. "I don't suppose you could help me out and grow over the top."

The vine moved in my hand, and I jumped back with a soft yelp. The dark green tendrils began snaking their way up the wall. Leaves sprouted along their lengths, and small rootlets latched onto the stone.

My skin prickled, and I gaped at the rising wave of green. It was magic—*my magic.* And it was getting stronger.

The implications hit me like a lightning bolt, and I spun around, scanning the courtyard. If anyone had witnessed what I'd just done, the game would be up. But no one was stirring in the courtyard or on the battlements, and my sentries were busy at work, circling the sky above.

I breathed a deep sigh of relief. Clearly, I needed to double-check my surroundings *before* I started asking plants for personal favors. It hadn't been anything more than a joke, but now...I tugged on the matted vines. Could I actually climb up and over? Was I mad?

It seemed likely.

The creeping ivy slowly wrapped around the iron spikes that topped the crenelated wall. The garden staff would probably begin work in half an hour. I needed to hurry.

Now or never.

I grasped a bundle of ivy strands in each hand, then heaved myself up and climbed hand over hand, using the thick vines as a makeshift rope and the stones as a ladder.

Scaling the wall was brutal work, and fear clenched my chest each time the vines strained and swayed as their rootlets tore away from the wall, but they held at the top. Finally, I pulled myself partway up so I could peek over the wall.

There was absolutely nothing on the other side—just a few trees and the steep cliff that protected the flank of the castle.

I closed my eyes for a bitter second, trying to settle my stomach.

The owl alighted on the top of the wall beside me. *Almost there.*

I glared at him, disappointment filling me as I avoided looking at the endless drop below. "What are you talking about? There's nothing here, and I'm completely exposed!"

He rustled his feathers. *You're still on the wrong side.*

I glanced back at the courtyard, and my stomach knotted. *Completely exposed* didn't begin to describe my situation. The tower guards had a clean line of sight on me, as did the two figures who'd just entered the far end of the gardens. If any of them looked my way...

I had two options. Give up and drop back down or flip over the other side and find my way back in through the main gate.

Hurry! the owl said. It spread its wings and hopped off the top of the wall—

And disappeared.

My heart skipped a beat. There'd been a ripple in the air, and then he was gone. Had someone shot him down? Or...

Grasping the iron spikes, I quickly heaved myself over the top of the wall. My dress caught, then tore as I yanked myself free. The world around me shifted, and my skin tingled as I clung to the wall on the other side.

I glanced down, and my breath stilled. Everything had changed.

Where there'd been a cliff, there was now a pleasure garden enclosed on three sides by a colonnaded hall with a golden-roofed pavilion at its center, half covered by the shadow of a tall tower.

A *tower*.

Clinging to an iron spike with one hand, I glanced up, blocking out the rising sun with my free hand. Although the elegant tower soared twice as tall as the prince's own, I'd never seen it before. It was absolutely impossible. That, or magical.

Grasping the vines with both hands, I skidded down the face of the wall. The ivy stopped ten feet above the ground, so I dropped the rest of the way, landing on my backside behind a fragrant bush.

I froze and held my breath, listening. My heart felt like it was going to gallop out of my chest, but when there were no immediate shouts of alarm or ringing bells, my shoulders relaxed.

The tower and its garden had been hidden by some kind of spell—of that much I was certain. I'd felt it prickling my skin as I'd crossed over the top of the wall. But why? Could it be a prison for the mages that Belle had mentioned?

I frowned. If it was as easy to get out as it was to get in, it wouldn't make a very secure prison—at least not for someone with magic.

My surroundings further complicated the matter. The lush garden with its exotic flowers, the marble fountain, and the golden pavilion were ostentatious displays of wealth that surpassed even the excesses of the castle. If the interior of the tower matched, it would probably put the prince's residence to shame.

I craned my neck to look at the impossible tower again. Supported by graceful flying buttresses, it was far more imposing than anything in the main section of the castle. Perhaps this was the prince's secret refuge. That would explain why his chambers were always so clean.

But why keep it a secret?

Could it be because the mages were here? What if they were locked inside the tower? It would explain why the only servants allowed to enter this area were on the day shift and sworn to silence.

I was growing more and more convinced that just like the castle, the prince wasn't what he seemed to be. Perhaps he'd forced the mages to cast a spell to hide the tower and garden, concealing their own prison. The bitter irony of it knotted my fists.

There had to be a way to free them.

Unfortunately, time wasn't on my side. Golden light was already creeping into the garden.

Keeping low, I stole toward the nearest colonnade, taking cover behind a bush with bright orange flowers. I checked the walls and grounds again, and then a third time.

There were no guards posted anywhere. The only sign of life was the owl perched on the peak of a roof and my crows circling above.

It didn't feel right. There should be some kind of guard.

I surveyed the garden. The air was heavy with a floral perfume I didn't recognize, likely from one of the unfamiliar plants or diminutive fruit trees. I could make out the backs of several golden chairs beneath the pavilion and possibly the glint of gemstones.

Staying as low as I could, I darted forward through a gap in the colonnade and crouched behind the half-wall that fronted the garden. The adjoining building had large windows and several doors. Checking both directions, I scooted across the colonnade and peeked in. The windows were foggy, but I could just make out a large pool of steaming water and the shadowed forms of two young women. *Naked* women.

I blinked in surprise. What in the Fates?

One of the crow sentries I'd stationed cried out. *Someone's coming!*

I ducked back into the garden, taking refuge behind a large, woody bush with fragrant white blossoms, then peeked through the branches. Two men and a woman emerged from a door at the base of the tower and strode into the garden, heading toward the pavilion...

And toward me.

They had the timeless look of immortals about them, neither young nor old, and all three were dressed in bright robes crafted from shimmering cloth. High nobles of a sort?

I shifted position slightly as they ascended the marble dais so I could get a better view. The woman wore gold and emerald earrings and a matching necklace, while the grim man in black robes on her right was no less adorned, with a heavy pendant and rings on his fingers. He dropped down into one of the golden chairs beneath the pavilion. "Let's not make this take any longer than it needs to. I don't want to keep the girls waiting."

The woman gave him a condescending sneer as she took her seat. "So much fuss over something that will only last a minute. Your priorities are so *mundane*, Horace. The ritual of the tithe is the only thing worth savoring."

"Maybe you're too old to appreciate the pleasure of the flesh, Thalindra, but I'm not. The tithe makes it impossible for me to think of anything else, so get any politics out of the way first."

She leaned back, letting the rising sun illuminate her face. "You know nothing of how to pleasure a woman's flesh. Don't pretend you do."

My breath stilled. They were sitting and talking in direct sunlight as if they didn't mind it at all. Hell, she looked like she was savoring the warmth. They couldn't be immortals. They didn't even have fangs.

Could these lords be human?

Before I could sort out my thoughts, a door opened at the end of the far colonnade, and a soldier stepped in.

I ducked and pushed my back against the low wall.

The butt of a spear cracked against the stone three times. "His Royal Highness, Prince Cassius!"

37

Ella

My stomach plummeted. I shifted back to my vantage behind the woody bush, hoping its fragrant white flowers would conceal my scent. I knew I shouldn't risk looking, but I had to see.

Cassius strode briskly down the colonnade and stepped out into the garden. He grimaced as the sunlight cut across him, but then the expression was gone, replaced by unyielding iron. The prince stopped on the bottom step of the dais, waiting. His expression was stoic, but the severe line of his mouth made it clear he despised all three of the people on the dais. There was something aloof and rigid about his stance that reminded me of how he regarded Bianca and Lorayna. He never betrayed his hate, but it was there just the same, simmering inside.

"Good morning, Your Highness," Thalindra said luxuriously.

Cassius stared her down for a second, then bent slightly forward in acknowledgement. "Triad."

My breath stilled. It hadn't been much, but his slight bow had signaled deference. Who on earth would expect the Prince of the Bloodvale to bow to them? I pushed the branches down, trying to get a better view.

The woman motioned him forward. "Do join us."

Cassius grudgingly ascended the dais but didn't sit.

The man with the bejeweled rings leaned back and gave the prince an appraising look. "Rumor has it you've ridden out hunting every day for the past week. Finding yourself bored with your position?"

Cassius glared at him. "The woods are more restless than I've ever seen them. I've had three kills this week."

Thalindra dismissed the comment with a wave of her hand. "I wish you'd send Aamon and a party of outriders if you don't think he's up to it alone. I don't like you risking yourself needlessly."

Cassius's hand flexed, and he clasped it behind his back. "It's not needless. It's my duty to this kingdom, and Aamon doesn't know the woods like I do."

"Not many heads hanging on your wall," Horace chuckled.

The prince sneered openly at the black-robed man, his face contorted with disgust. "I don't take trophies. Unlike you."

A cruel shadow crossed Horace's face. "I like to remember the things I've enjoyed."

The woman pursed her lips. "I wonder if all this hunting is simply to avoid your other duty—choosing a bride."

"That will be done soon enough," Cassius said.

Her mouth curled up in a self-satisfied smile. "We'll attend the masquerade ball, of course. We all eagerly await your decision."

The other man, whose name I hadn't learned, leaned forward. Dressed in shades of green, he was tall and thin, with hawklike features. "You understand why we are so concerned, do you not? Your grandfather was merciless, but your bloodline has grown weak. Your brother was not strong enough to bear the burden of rule, and we have our doubts about you."

"I doubt you have fond memories of my grandfather," Cassius said flatly. "Few humans would."

My breath stilled. They *were* humans, as I expected—but how could mere humans hold power over an immortal?

More problematically, how could they have known the prince's grandfather? He'd been dead hundreds of years. They couldn't have lived that long—they didn't look a day over fifty.

The man in green robes drummed his fingers in agitation on the arm of his chair. "The point is, you need to pick a strong queen so that your heir will be strong. Choose someone with an ancient bloodline, and we will be very much appeased."

The prince bared his fangs and took a step forward. "The choice is mine, is it not? Or have you already decided that as well?"

Thalindra stood and raised her hands. "Let's not fight. We all want the same thing—what's best for the kingdom."

Cassius released a bitter laugh as he rolled up his shirt sleeves. "Don't pretend you care about this kingdom. All you want is my blood, so take it. Let's get this done with so I can end my day in peace."

His blood?

A deep, unsettling dread welled inside of me, curdling my stomach.

"Look what you've done, Malthus," Thalindra said, giving the man a dirty look. "You've upset our prince."

She twisted her hand in the air, and light began streaming from her fingers. The prickling sensation of magic danced over my skin, and then my breath caught as she shaped the dancing lights into a golden chalice and set it on the table.

It was magic.

The truth dawned. *They* were the mages I'd heard about in

the rumors. They had to be the ones who'd created the floating fountains and lights and hidden the secret garden and its tower.

They weren't prisoners. They were *in charge.*

Before the full implications could sink in, Cassius slipped a long knife from the sheath at his side. He extended his arm and drew the blade across it. Crimson welled up, and I had to stop myself from crying out in surprise. I watched, stunned, as he let the blood run down his arm and drip into the goblet. My guts churned violently, but I couldn't look away. The three mages, on the other hand, observed passively, as if they'd witnessed it happen a hundred times. Horace's face was the only one I saw fully, but there was an eager hunger in his eyes.

The mages were going to drink the prince's blood. An *immortal's* blood.

The cawing of crows tore me out of my stunned reverie. I whipped my head around. A servant with a silver tray was coming through the same door Cassius had used.

My stomach knotted. I was hidden from the pavilion but in clear view from the colonnade.

I dropped and scrambled out of sight behind the low wall of the colonnade, but my foot scuffed against a loose stone.

"Is someone else in the garden?" Cassius asked.

Damn the bloodsuckers and their keen hearing. My chest was tight and pulse thundering. Would the prince be able to hear it?

Someone sniffed like a hunting hound.

No, no. no.

"What is it, Cassius?" Thalindra asked.

"It's..." The prince abruptly paused. "Never mind. It's nothing."

His tone had changed. His voice had lowered and sounded almost strangled.

The footsteps approached down the corridor, and I

scrunched myself as close to the base of the wall as possible. It was a terrible hiding place. If they didn't turn away, they'd spot me in a matter of seconds.

"I don't like this," Horace said. "Something isn't right."

There was the sound of a chair scraping back, then two sets of footsteps coming down the dais.

With a flutter of wings, the crow that had raised the alarm alighted on the wall right above me and cocked its head. I pleaded at it with my eyes. *Please help.*

Footsteps closed in on my position from both sides.

The crow squawked and burst into the air, and a second later, something metal clattered to the ground.

"The chalice!" Thalindra screamed. "There is blood everywhere! My dress is fucking ruined! Someone, bring me a towel!"

The footsteps in the garden stopped suddenly, but the ones in the corridor sped up. They'd be on me in a second. With any luck, the mages were distracted by the spilled blood. This was my chance.

With no time to think, I darted forward into the colonnade, upending the servant with the tray. He cried out and collapsed against the wall, sending the silver platter and its contents clattering across the ground. I raced toward the far door. Pandemonium broke loose in the garden, and the door at the end of the hall burst open.

Two guards appeared. I slowed half a step, but there was a flurry of black wings as my sentries dove beneath the roof of the colonnade and attacked. The soldiers shouted as they threw up their arms to protect their eyes from the assault of beaks and claws.

I was on them in two strides. I shoved one guard into the other then darted through the closing door as they collapsed to the ground behind me.

I charged down the halls of the castle as fast as I could run. I recognized them from my brief time in the royal wing, though I'd had no idea where they led. I just had to get to one of the servants' passages. I was nearly to the end of the hall when the door behind me burst open. I glanced back as the prince and a cadre of soldiers charged through.

Despair crashed over me. I'd never outrun him.

I darted right into a long corridor lined with doors. I chose the third on the left and burst into a large sitting room. I was alone—but that was where my luck stopped. The stained glass windows wouldn't open, and there weren't any other exits, not even a servants' door. A pair of chairs with carved backs flanked an enormous hearth with a broad stone mantel. I could have squeezed beneath one of them, but I'd still be exposed.

That left me with one insanely desperate option.

I stepped into the wide hearth and looked up into the flue. I could just make out the blackened iron rungs set into the stone, installed so chimneysweeps could climb up and dislodge caked soot.

Voices shouted in the hall, and the sound of the doors slamming open reverberated through the wall. They'd be here any second.

I reached up and seized the first rung, then heaved myself into the cramped flue. While I wasn't an eight-year-old boy, I was slightly built and just able to wedge my shoulders inside. Soot burned my lungs, and I clenched my chest to keep from coughing. Hand over hand, I pulled myself up another set of rungs.

The door flung open. I wrenched my legs up, praying that my feet weren't dangling out.

"I thought I saw them go in here," a male said. Heavy boots rang against the floor as the men searched the room. Holding my breath, I pressed myself against the wall as hard as I could to keep still. My heart hammered so loudly against my chest, I had no doubt the prince would be able to hear it. Hell, maybe even the human guards could.

I was a dead girl.

A set of footsteps paused just below me. I tightened my sweaty hands on the rung. If they were going to take me, they'd have to haul me out kicking and screaming.

But the grasping hands didn't come.

"There's no one here," the prince said.

I nearly choked in fright. He had to be less than two feet from me, standing right in front of the hearth.

Fates. Don't cough now.

"I'll check the rest of the rooms in this hall," the prince said. "You four, run and search the corridors ahead. Recruit any guards you find to help and send a runner to the captain. I want this castle turned upside down. We can't let the spy get away. A pouch of gold to whoever finds *him*."

"Yes, Your Highness," a man said, and the footsteps fled out into the hall.

Had the prince gone with them? The door clicked shut, but I didn't move a muscle. I didn't dare breathe. Soot stung my eyes and burned my lungs, but I bit my tongue and held on for dear life.

I waited a minute. Then two. My heartbeat began to slow. Did I really get away with it?

I released a slow breath.

"You can come out now, Ella," the prince said, sending my heart flying into my throat. "They're gone."

38

Cassius

A thin dusting of ash drifted down from the hearth, but Ella didn't come out. Fury rippled through me. Did she really think she could hide, even now?

I pounded on the stonework. "I know you're in there. Come out before I drag you."

There was a moment of silence, followed by a resigned, "*Damn it.*"

A plume of cinders and ashes billowed out, and I stepped aside as an absolutely filthy woman dropped into the hearth. Her face and uniform were coated with soot, and the rag wrapped around her dark hair was a disheveled mess. I barely recognized her.

"What the hell were you thinking, breaking into that garden?" I rumbled.

Rather than answer, she glared silently back at me with her teeth bared, like some sort of vengeful fire sprite summoned from the hearth—beautiful yet vicious, and likely to leave you burned. There was something so spirited yet pathetic about her.

I'd never seen a more miserable creature. My rage slipped from my grasp.

She squared her shoulders and matched my steely gaze. "To find out what was so important that you had to conceal it in a magically warded tower."

Unbridled anger coursed through me. "Are you insane? Your recklessness may have cost you your life."

I tasted her fear as her heart quickened. There was more to this story than she was letting on, and I'd get to the bottom of it —but not here, not now.

"How did you know it was me?" she asked.

How could I not? The soot and ash couldn't cover the sweet scent of her skin, like lilies after a morning rain. It was intoxicating and beguiling—not to mention the rapid flutter of her heartbeat, which I'd heard the moment I stepped into the room.

I moved closer, unable to stay away. "I'm a predator. I'd scent you anywhere."

She swallowed, and my gaze tracked the way her throat moved. I hadn't fed from the source in over a century, but by the Fates, it was all I could do not to sink my fangs into her every time she drew near.

She slipped away from my touch and took a step back toward the door. "If you knew it was me, then why did you send your men away? Why did you tell them to search for *him*?"

Because I was a fool. An idiot, drunk on her beauty. And her fire.

I should have executed her on the spot or let my soldiers drag her back to the Triad kicking and screaming—though the truth was, had any of them laid a finger on her, I would have ripped out their throats.

Clearly, the woman had made me insane.

"I like to have options, and if any of those soldiers or the Triad had seen you, I would have been obligated to execute you." She opened her mouth, but I silenced her with my finger. "No more questions. You're not out of this yet, so if you want to live to the end of the day, do exactly as I say."

She nodded.

Fucking Fates. What the hell was I going to do with her?

I grabbed an embroidered blanket off the back of the sofa and wrapped her in it. "You're a dust cloud. Try to keep covered. And be still."

With a single motion, I heaved her over my shoulder like a sack. She gasped, then tried to wriggle free. I slapped my hand on her ass, forcing myself not to linger. "Settle down. If any guards see us, they'll assume I'm playing some kind of game with my prey."

"A sick game," she muttered, not an ounce of fear in her voice.

I shrugged. Maybe, but the idea of playing games with her made heat rise within me. I shoved the thought aside.

I opened the door and checked the hall. My guards had followed my orders, and the corridor was clear for the moment.

"Well, get on with it," she whispered. "It's not comfortable up here."

Fates be damned, the fool girl actually *trusted* me. Was that what had stopped me from revealing her location? Or was it that I actually felt something for the mortal?

Impossible. A gorgeous woman could make a fool of any man, and by all evidence, I was that fool.

"Let's go—and keep it quiet."

As I headed to the right, she wiggled frantically and whispered, "That's back the way I came."

Apparently, she wasn't completely trusting. Good.

"If I were going to hand you over, I would have hauled you back to the Triad by your hair. There's a faster route to my chambers this way. Now be quiet and keep your face covered by the blanket. This isn't a flawless plan." If someone saw us and my out-of-character behavior drew suspicion, I didn't want them knowing the identity of the woman over my shoulder.

I strode silently through the castle, listening carefully before turning any corners. By the time we neared my chambers, my frustration had reached a boiling point. Right before reaching the corridor to my quarters, I stashed her in a small closet. "Stay here while I get rid of the guards at my door."

She nodded, and I retreated, rounding the corner and striding up to the posted guards. "There's been an intruder, and I need everyone at the ready. Report to the captain and see what you can do to help with the search. Send word the moment there's a lead."

They saluted and hurried off. As soon as they disappeared down the hall, I summoned Ella forward and shoved her into my room.

She let out an unsteady breath and burst into a fit of coughing as soon as the door clicked shut. Once she'd recovered her breath, she turned to me, her expression melting into relief. "Thank y—"

"Have you lost your mind?" I snarled, stalking toward her. "What were you thinking?"

Her eyes widened, and she backed away. "I—" she stammered. "I told you. I was just exploring."

"Liar." I crowded her back against the wall. The thrum of her heart was undeniable, and it took everything I had to keep my gaze from the soft curve of her neck. "What gave you the idea to go sneaking in there? How did you even know how to get in?"

"There are stories," she whispered, her voice depleted of oxygen.

"What stories?"

She resisted my question, but I stared her down until she finally broke. "I heard that there were mages imprisoned here."

A bitter laugh escaped my throat. The bloody irony of it. I leaned closer, the sweet scent of her muddling my mind and awakening inexplicable urges. "And do you believe such fairy-tales, Ella?"

"I believe what I saw, which was three humans with magic being kept in an off-limits and magically fortified wing of your castle."

"You have no clue what you saw," I snarled. "And that doesn't explain how you knew to look there. That area is invisible. How did you find it?"

Her heart quickened, but her tone remained steady, as if she weren't terrified of the monster before her. "It didn't add up. The northern wall is unlike all the other walls in the castle. When I went to investigate why, I noticed a bird disappear out of thin air. That's how I knew."

She was smarter than most, but fuck, if she'd come to these conclusions, others might, too. "I should execute you for setting foot in there."

Her expression hardened, and she raised her chin. "Will you? Because if so, get it over with."

"Fuck." I turned away, taking a spot by the window. "I told you I would never hurt you. I keep my word." The very idea was repellant.

"If what I've done is so bad, why spare me?"

I glanced back at her. I couldn't tell her the truth. Hell, I couldn't accept it myself.

I chose a more palatable explanation. "Because it would fuck me over. I've clearly favored you and even made you my personal attendant. If they'd caught you there, it would've cast suspicion on *me*. The Triad would have assumed you were spying on my behalf."

It was the truth, but it wasn't the real reason, the *unspeakable* reason that gnawed at my heart.

A little of the brightness faded from her eyes. Good. Let her think I was a selfish bastard.

"Who *are* the Triad?" Ella asked.

I cursed myself again. How much of a fool was I? I should've never mentioned their name—not in front of a mortal. "They're none of your business. If you want to keep that pretty head of yours, you'll forget everything you saw. You'll forget their name. You'll forget everything that happened in that garden."

She dropped the blanket from her shoulders and walked toward me, undeterred. "Are they mages?"

Anger and concern for her dueled inside, each pushing me closer to the edge. "Didn't you hear a word I said?" Mortals were forbidden to know about them. Even among my kind, the Triad were no more than a rumor. Only the most powerful knew the truth.

"Are they your prisoners?" she pressed. "Are you stealing their magic?"

"Did they look like fucking prisoners?" I growled.

She met my gaze head-on. "Why did they drink your blood? Are they sick? The woman said it was the blood tithe, but I thought the tithe was meant for humans."

My jaw strained.

"Who are they, Cassius?"

I closed the distance between us and gripped her chin, needing her to understand the magnitude of the shitstorm she was in. "They're people with the power to kill you. They won't stop until they find out who was spying on them. Do you understand? You're still in danger, even now. Even here in this room."

Her eyes flicked across my face as if trying to peel back the mask I wore. "Then what am I going to do?"

For all her relentless determination, fear and desperation thrummed in her voice. It was buried but there. She was terrified, and I wasn't helping matters.

"Go hide in my fireplace. You're already dressed for it, and they won't be able to scent you out."

She gaped at me, and then the corner of her mouth turned up in a half smile at the feeble joke. "I think I'll pass. As it is, I'll be hacking up soot and cinders for a month."

I foolishly wiped a smudge of ash from her cheek. "I should start calling you Cinders if you're going to keep climbing up chimneys. Better yet, Cinderella. I like the ring of that."

My hand dropped away as I studied her, as if seeing her anew. It had been another joke, but there was something delightful about the way it rolled off my tongue. *Cinderella.* Somehow, with her fine features and hair, it suited her. Ella was a farm girl. A scullery maid. But Cinderella—there was almost a timeless elegance to it.

She shook her head and looked away. "Ella is just fine."

"Ella or Cinderella, you need to clean up. Use my bath. And wash that hideous dye out of your hair. If anyone caught a glimpse of you, they'll be looking for someone with dark hair." I preferred it silver, but I didn't mention that.

She looked back at the bathing chamber, then raised her eyebrows. "Your bath? With hot water?"

"I assume even peasant girls know how to bathe. You're filthy, and you need to wash."

The thought of bathing her myself instantly stiffened me. I'd always preferred the shower, but the image of her bare in my tub, dipping beneath the water, might make me change my mind.

I had to stop thinking this way. The seer's prophecy wasn't to be ignored.

She crossed her arms. "Are you implying that I smell?"

The corner of my lips turned up, and I leaned close. "Your scent is intoxicating and unforgettable, and it drives me wild. That's what I meant."

Her eyes widened, and her confident demeanor wavered as her pulse quickened. "Oh. Um, what about my clothes? They aren't exactly fresh."

"I'll find you something else to wear—something suitable to your station." Needing to put some distance between us before I did something I'd regret later, I turned her toward the bath and gave her a little shove. "Hurry now, little Cinderella. My guards may return with a message, and I don't need a sooty servant standing in the middle of my chambers."

She headed to the washroom but paused at the door and looked back. "Don't come in."

I lifted my eyebrows. "What kind of prince do you think I am?"

"One who's used to taking what he wants."

I dug my fingers into my palm. Fates be damned, I wanted her, even sweaty and covered with soot. I wanted to bathe her luxurious skin and show her what true pleasure was like. She was right, I could take whatever I wanted. Normally, I did. But with her, I didn't dare. That was a disaster waiting to happen. The headstrong woman had already caused me a world of trouble, and I suspected the fallout was only beginning.

"I'm leaving," I said, my voice thick with restrained desire. "I'll lock the door behind me."

"Is that to keep others out or to keep me in?"

"Both."

39

————

Ella

Clouds of steam wafted lazily around me as I stared at the soot-stained woman in the mirror. Apart from my telltale eyes, I hardly recognized myself. My hands were trembling from the shock of everything I'd seen.

The mages were real. Rather than prisoners, they had some kind of bargain with the prince. They seemed petty and cruel, far from the saviors I'd been suspecting, and now they were hunting me.

Why was the prince covering for me? His reasons didn't add up.

Was it desire? We'd kissed before, and his eyes had smoldered when he spoke of my scent. I absently brushed my fingertips across my lips. Did he know that his scent had the same effect on me?

I couldn't deny it. Not now, not after everything that had happened. The woods. Our ride together. The kiss at the falls. Covering my escape.

I desperately wanted him, and I knew he wanted me. But

true or not, it was a dangerous path—one that could only lead to dark places.

Just get cleaned up and put him out of your mind. You have enough things to worry about.

The marble floors of the bath chamber warmed the soles of my feet. The chamber was even more extraordinary than Lorayna's. It had to be magic. I still wasn't sure what the tall, rectangular glass room in the corner was for, but its mosaic interior looked like a tapestry of the night sky.

Hot water gushed from a sweeping spout into the oversized copper tub. I'd dumped a generous helping of rose-scented bathing soap in the water, and bubbles crept precariously close to the tub's curved lip.

Glancing one more time at the closed door, I dropped my soiled clothes in a pile near the sink, then slowly lowered myself into the hot water with a sigh.

Luckily, most of the soot had stayed on my clothes, so the water wasn't instantly filthy. My aching muscles cried out in relief as I leaned back and dipped my shoulders under the suds.

Gods, this is divine.

What would make it even *more* divine were if the prince returned to bring me a towel. I peeked one eye open and spied the neat stack of fresh towels on the shelf. Okay, not a towel. Perhaps if I lingered in the bath too long, he'd come to check on me.

I sank beneath the water, relishing this brief moment of respite.

Yes, that was it. He'd step inside, feigning concern for my wellbeing, only to find me perfectly fine. He'd cross to the bath and kneel, and then, picking up the washcloth, he'd say, *You've missed a few spots.* He'd wet the washcloth and gently brush it along my collarbone, bringing it down between my breasts, then lower over my belly, dipping under the water until he found...

My eyes flew open, and I pressed my legs together, shame and surprise—and something I didn't want to name—burning through me.

It was madness. Maybe it was shock, or being saved, or maybe I'd hit my head climbing out of the chimney. It didn't matter. I couldn't permit myself such ludicrous and treacherous thoughts.

The kiss we'd shared had already been one too many.

I grabbed the washcloth that was neatly folded by the faucet and began vigorously scrubbing my arms with the lavender bath soap. After I erased all traces of soot, I turned to my hair and more pressing matters.

The mages.

Who were they? The prince had called them the Triad, and their authority seemed greater than his. Was that because he wasn't the king yet or because they really were more powerful? More troubling still, they said they'd known his grandfather. They couldn't be that old, could they? Immortal blood healed wounds, but could it also prolong life? Could they possibly be older than Cassius?

A deep unease settled over me as my father's history lessons came creeping back. The Uprising had been led by three mages...

It was impossible. They'd been captured and executed, so they couldn't be the same as the ones I'd seen in the garden. Besides, the stories had said that the mages had been on *our* side, and one thing I knew without having to be told was that the three I'd seen were not. Frankly, I doubted that they were on anyone's side but their own.

My head began to throb. I dipped beneath the bubbles, hoping the water would drown out the world and clear my mind, but it did neither. I scrubbed my head vigorously, washing out the dark dye Bianca had forced me to use. If only my troubles washed away so easily.

Halfway through my rinse, a door closed in the other room, and I froze. Had Cassius returned? Excitement thrummed down my spine.

I sat up and listened but heard nothing. Minutes passed, but the prince didn't appear, and so I finished rinsing the dye from my hair and unplugged the tub. The dark water swirled down the drain as I climbed out and dried off, then wrapped myself in a plush robe hanging on the opposite wall.

What would I have even done if the prince had strolled in?

"Don't be a fool, Ella," I muttered to myself in the mirror, combing my fingers through my damp hair. Silver once more. It was nice to look like myself again, and hopefully, this would protect me from the mages finding me. Thank the Fates that my hair had been a different color.

A small pang of disappointment fluttered in my chest when I stepped into the bedchamber and found it empty. Was I meant to strut around the castle in a bathrobe?

The answer lay on the bed.

Someone had arranged a crimson satin gown over the foot of the mattress. It had a heart-shaped neckline and delicate black lace embroidery along the bodice and full skirt. I strolled over, noticing a black silk chemise beside it.

My heart quickened as I inspected the chemise. The evil sisters had garments like this, but I couldn't imagine most people actually wore them.

Courtesans did.

The implications of that thought both terrified and thrilled me.

Checking that the doors were locked, I dropped my robe and slipped the scandalous chemise on. It was surprisingly comfortable, and…I paused when I caught my reflection in the mirror. Risqué.

Had the prince chosen this himself?

Heat flushed my skin. This had to be part of his grand plan. Obviously.

"Fates," I whispered, lifting the gorgeous gown and spinning toward the mirror. It looked to be my size, but I'd never worn anything so luxurious or heavy. The fabric alone would have supported the manor for a winter.

It was a wonder I was able to get into the gown on my own with how fitted the waist and hips were. A dozen eyelet clasps secured the bodice down the center, emphasizing my bust and cinching my waist.

For the second time, I didn't recognize myself in the mirror. My silver hair hung in damp curls over my shoulders and contrasted strikingly with the deep crimson gown. It clung to me, accentuating my curves and flowing like water every time I moved.

I looked like a royal courtesan.

A knock sounded at the door, and I jumped.

"Are you decent?" The prince's deep voice sent shivers over my skin.

That depended on what I was dressed for.

"Yes," I said, suddenly feeling lightheaded. I blamed it on the gown.

The lock clicked, and the prince stepped in, pausing when he caught sight of me. His gaze tracked over my body, his eyes darkening the way the sky did right before a storm.

I swallowed, uncertain what he was thinking. "I assume this was for me." I gestured down at the gown. "I hope it's suitable."

"Yes." The prince's voice was strained, and he cleared his throat. "It will do."

I narrowed my eyes at him. Had he been standing at the door, listening to me dressing? His timing had been too perfect.

"You were gone for quite a while," I said, fiddling with the trail of lace stitched along my waist. The prince seemed fixated on the movement, so I stopped.

His stormy eyes met mine. "I was cleaning up your mess—figuratively and literally. If the Triad knew what I'd done, they'd bring down hell on me."

"Are they still searching?"

He took a few steps toward me, but then, as if thinking better of it, stopped. "They'll turn this place upside down until they're certain they've caught the spy. They're going to question everyone."

I retreated a step inadvertently, trying not to think about the way his strong thighs moved beneath his fitted trousers. "I've never seen nor heard of them before today."

"They ensure that it stays that way." He stepped closer, his movements graceful as a leopard's. "Their servants are cursed with a spell to bind their tongues."

My backside bumped against the foot of the bed. "How long have they been here?"

In an instant, he consumed the distance between us and stood just inches away. His body was tauter than a bowstring, tension simmering just below the surface. "You must stop worrying about who they are," he said roughly. "And worry more about what they're going to ask you."

My heart drummed against my chest. "Me?"

"I'll try to implicate another of the staff, but if they don't catch someone, they're liable to interrogate the entire castle."

The thought of Cara or Belle being interrogated because of what I'd done made my heart ache. "No," I said sharply. "Don't implicate anyone else. I don't want anyone's blood on my hands."

His stern expression didn't waver. "Then you're ready to face their questions?"

"I'll have to be, won't I?"

"How long were you lurking out there? Would the rest of the staff notice you weren't in your bed? Did anyone see you leave?"

I stood before him, panic rising.

"Fuck," Cassius said, my silence telling him everything he needed to know. Dragging a hand through his dark hair, he turned and started pacing the room. "Okay. We can fix this. You'll tell anyone who asks that you were here with me. Everyone already thinks I've chosen you as my mistress."

"Not everyone," I said, causing him to stop and fix me with a deadly gaze. "The sisters know you're not feeding from me."

Something violent flashed in his eyes. "How?"

Was he really that dense? "How do you think? They didn't see any bite marks, and they assumed. I didn't even need to tell them."

Cassius released an almost feral snarl and stalked toward the balcony. His fists closed, and he seemed seconds away from breaking something. When he turned back and looked at me, his steel visage had been replaced by a savage rage. "I warned them to keep their hands off you."

His sudden protectiveness, both terrifying and exhilarating, sent flutters through my belly. Did he really care so much for the fate of a simple serving girl?

"If—*when*—the Triad comes asking questions, tell them about kissing me in the forest. Tell them that the only reason I put you on my service is that I wanted you, and that I liked the way you taste."

It was a lie, of course, but part of me wished it were true. "Do you think they'll buy it? It's rumored that you don't feed from the vein."

His expression darkened. "Then we'll give them proof that I do."

40

———

Cassius

It was fucking madness.

After a century of abstaining, I couldn't believe I was entertaining the idea of feeding from her. I'd broken myself of the thirst, finding strength in self-denial. And yet, for all the will I possessed, there was no way I could resist her—not for much longer. She'd reawakened primal desires that would not be silenced.

But if I were to give in at last, at least it would serve a purpose. There'd be no question of where she'd been—or what we'd been doing.

Whatever excuse I had to give myself.

"What kind of proof do we need?" Ella asked, her voice tight with apprehension.

She stood at the foot of my bed, a vision of innocence and all that was pure despite the seductive red dress. *But not that innocent.* She'd broken into the Triad's garden and wasn't telling the truth as to why. Whether she knew it or not, she now had the power to end me.

"I'll be your alibi," I said. "I'll claim that I've made you my mistress, and that before I entered the garden, I was feeding from you. It'll confirm what everyone expects already—that I've taken an interest in you."

Her breath hitched, and she glanced up at me through lidded eyes. "And have you?"

It was too obvious for her not to know. Her interest in me was clear as day. Hell, every one of my senses had detected it from the moment we'd met. The way her skin heated under my touch, the way her scent grew rich with undertones of lilies whenever I was near. Her attraction toward me was undeniable and dangerous. But what point would there be in giving her false hope?

"Does it matter?" I said coldly. "They just need to believe that I have."

I watched the hurt flash in her beautiful lavender eyes and hated myself for it. "If the Triad's going to believe our charade, then they'll need to see for themselves that I've fed from you," I continued. "They'll need to see the marks."

Her throat moved in a sensuous way as she swallowed. "Then you mean to take the blood tithe from me."

"Yes."

She stood impossibly still, a perfect statue draped in bloodred silk. "Do I have a choice?"

I paused, measuring her determination. "Of course. I told you I'd never touch you without your permission. If you prefer, I'll claim that I was just fucking you—though there'd be no proof we could offer of that other than damp sheets."

Heat poured through me as wicked images flashed in my mind. It would be more than just fucking her. Once I'd been inside her—*tasted* her—there'd be no turning back, no letting go. She'd be mine for real, and I'd burn this kingdom to the ground if anyone stood in my way of keeping her.

Ella and I were an impossible match, and the truth of it

stung. I could taste her, but I could never have her—not in the way I truly needed.

She silently weighed the options.

I moved toward her, unable to stay away. "If neither of those appeals to you, I could help you run. I'll give you a horse and money and send you over the border."

As soon as the words left my mouth, I knew it was a lie. I couldn't let her go.

"I won't run. This is my home." She fixed me with a steady gaze, then angled her head, exposing the long curve of her neck, as if giving her blood were a simple transaction. "Take your tithe, Cassius."

The gods were fools to put something so beautiful, so delicious, in my path.

"Are you certain this is what you want?"

Her voice was brave, but I saw her trembling and could hear the drum of her rising pulse. She was frightened, but a trace of a smile pulled at the corner of her perfect mouth. "I'd be lying if I said I wasn't curious about what it'd be like."

I bent low, my hungry lips grazing the shell of her ear. "It won't be unpleasant for you, I promise."

"Then what are you waiting for?"

Cradling her head with one hand, I dragged my thumb down the side of her neck, the rhythmic pulsing of her blood becoming the sweetest of siren's calls. "I haven't fed like this in over a century. I'm savoring the moment."

"Do it," she whispered. Her chest rose and fell rapidly, and I scented both her desire and trepidation.

"So eager." I lowered my mouth to the crevice at the base of her throat and pressed a kiss to her silky skin. "If I am to do this properly, then you cannot be afraid."

"I'm not afraid."

I smiled wickedly against her skin, dragging my lips across the sensitive flesh of her neck. "You're a terrible liar."

The scent of her body and sweet taste of her perfect skin stoked a raging fire within me, and it took every ounce of control not to drink from her then and there. But I had made myself into iron over the years, and now that I knew I could taste her—and nothing more—I'd bide my time. I'd do it right.

I drew my lips across hers, coaxing her mouth open, then kissed her slowly and deeply. My tongue caressed hers, eliciting a soft moan from her throat that went straight to my cock. Her fingers sank into my hair, pulling me closer as I reveled in the way she tasted, the way she felt. She was as hungry as I was, and by the Fates, I wanted more.

I stepped back, and she reached for me. "Why are you stopping?"

"Making things more accessible." I grasped the clasps that secured her bodice and ripped them apart.

The heavy fabric tore easily, the metal closures flying free and exposing her breasts. Her pink nipples strained against the sheer black lace of her chemise, begging to be worshipped.

"Fucking hell." I said, my voice like gravel as I glided the sleeves down, allowing the silky ribbing to fall to her waist.

Embarrassment flashed in her eyes, and she raised her arms to cover herself.

"Don't," I said, gently taking her hands. "You're beautiful, and I want to see you."

"I've never...never been with a man before."

Never been bitten. Never been another man's. It was intoxicating, and my trousers strained further against me, but as much as I wanted to lay claim to this woman, I couldn't. My kingdom be damned, she was too pure, too good.

I pulled her close, savoring the warmth of her breasts against my chest, then kissed her softly. "I would never claim what isn't mine to take."

"And if I asked you to?"

She was dizzy with lust and not thinking straight.

"I'd decline." It was a lie. I wasn't a decent man. If she begged me then and there, I'd take her innocence without a second thought. "But that doesn't mean I can't show you pleasure."

But she hadn't begged me, only looked up at me with romance in her eyes. The poor girl didn't know that I didn't have an ounce of romance in me.

She gasped in delight as I swiftly lifted her onto my bed and lay beside her, one arm bracing me. I grazed my thumb over her nipple, causing the supple skin to pucker, begging me to lick and nip and suck.

"Yes," she sighed, arching her back.

The scent of her desire nearly undid me. It had been over a century since I'd last been with a woman, and never had I felt such need. The sensation was so foreign, it made it more acute. I took her nipple in my mouth, sucking on it as I palmed the other.

"More," she moaned as she melted in the furs sprawled beneath her. She was a vision I'd never forget. Her luscious breasts peeking out of the lace, her silver hair and skirts sprawled around her like a fallen angel. *One begging to be corrupted.*

Bracing my weight, I leaned over her and claimed her mouth with mine, my free hand pulling up the fabric around her legs until my fingers met warm flesh. Her thighs parted as if on command, hungry for my touch. I was eager to oblige. I drew a small circle over her clit with my thumb, eliciting a soft mewl from her throat. Slipping my middle finger into position, I parted her flesh with one long stroke.

She was so fucking wet.

I groaned when I sank my finger into her heat, my cock straining for release.

And so fucking tight.

Her hips arched against me, and before long, her body was trembling, her hand fisting the fur blanket as she moved against my hand.

"That's right, my Cinderella," I purred. "I want you to come undone for me."

I watched as she pressed her eyes closed, a silent moan parting her bruised lips as she quivered at the precipice of release.

Now.

I sank my fangs into her supple neck, bringing her across the threshold in a wave of ecstasy. The moment her blood touched my tongue, her desire became mine.

Her body arched as the orgasm rocked through her in waves, heightened by the effects of the bite. My hunger was insatiable, and the taste of her was like nectar, sweet and intoxicating, flooding my body with pleasure and heightening my senses to a fever pitch. I became attuned to every note of her scent, to the pulsing roar of blood through her veins, to the harsh exhalation of her breath, to the way her skin pebbled under my touch...I was spiraling into a dream.

I lifted my head, a flash of guilt shattering the dizzying flood of stimuli. I hadn't been prepared for how powerful drinking from the source would be. No, not just from the source—how powerful drinking from *her* would be.

Ella collapsed languidly beneath me, her chest rising and falling rapidly as the aftershocks of her desire rippled through her. Like a raging river in spring, her lifeblood coursed through me, filling me with an overwhelming sense of vitality and power that I hadn't felt in years.

She opened her eyes and looked up at me through heavy lashes. "Is that what it's always like when you feed on a human?"

It had never been like that.

I brushed the back of my hand across my mouth, still stunned by the intensity of her taste. "Nothing has ever been like feeding from you."

I was so attuned to her senses that I could barely separate my own experience from hers. I felt linked to her. This was only supposed to happen when a human fed from an immortal, not the other way around.

"Well," she said lazily, "you certainly did it properly."

I sat up, staring at the two crimson marks that tainted the smooth skin of her neck. The overwhelming contentment and peace I felt drained away, replaced at first by fierce possessiveness, and then a flicker of guilt.

I had marked her. Corrupted her. I'd given in to primal instincts that had lain dormant for a century and awoken something dangerous.

What had I done?

41

———————

Ella

I lazily brushed my fingers across my swollen lips as I lay dreamlessly on the prince's fur coverlet, enraptured by the after-effects of the exquisite things he'd just done. The rumors about the blood tithe had been wrong. It wasn't just pleasurable—it had been far, far more.

The prince climbed off the bed, something unreadable on his face, and the warm, bubbly haze that had settled over me dissipated. "What's wrong?"

Before he could answer, two hard knocks sounded at the door. Suddenly, I was on full alert, my heart racing. Had they come for me? I bolted up to hide, but Cassius gently restrained my shoulder, his eyes serious. He shook his head once before dipping his mouth to my ear. "It's best if they see you here," he whispered, sending shivers of heat down my tender neck as he pulled the coverlet over my exposed skin. "We must keep up the ruse."

Right. Because that's all this was.

Cold rushed over me.

He traced his lips down my neck, then was up and striding toward the door, leaving my skin pebbled and wanting.

"Yes?" he asked as he threw the door open, wide enough for the visitor to catch a glimpse of me on the bed. His hair was tousled and shirt undone, and the way he stood there, cocky and relaxed, made him look just the part—a prince who'd just bedded and fed on his mistress.

Anger rose within me, alongside something heavy in my chest.

The visitor wore crisp military attire, a uniform I didn't recognize. In addition to the royal insignia, he had a silver knot pinned to his shoulder. He stepped across the threshold of the room, and his searching gaze found me immediately.

I instinctively pulled the fur to my chest.

"Well?" the prince demanded, his tone imperious. "What is it? As you can see, I'm presently occupied."

The man didn't flinch. Instead, his scrutinizing eyes zeroed in on the bloody marks on my neck. Cassius's arm shot out, blocking the man from getting any closer.

The man—an immortal, I was certain—met the prince's gaze without an ounce of trepidation. Who was he? Did he work for the Triad?

"Just checking on you, my lord," the man said placidly, though there was a subtle undertone of suspicion.

"I'm feeding, as you can see, and not quite finished yet." Cassius's voice was even, but each word was laced with threat.

"It's been a long time since you've fed on a human," the man said, but the marks on my neck were undeniable proof.

Turning toward me, Cassius's gaze raked over me slowly, and he grinned. "I've made an exception for this one."

This one.

I knew he was just putting on a show, but it felt slimy all the same.

The man exposed a fang as he eyed me.

Cassius turned back in time to catch the newcomer's expression, and a muscle in the prince's jaw tightened. Protectiveness echoed in his voice when he growled, "Keep your gaze away from her, or I'll have your eyes."

The slimy feeling disappeared. There was only so much Cassius was willing to tolerate, it seemed.

The man swallowed hard and nodded, averting his gaze.

"What of your duties?" Cassius asked. "Has the intruder been found?"

"Not yet. But we'll find him. Or her." I didn't miss the emphasis on *her*, nor the way his eyes flashed to me again. "It's a strange time to feed, Your Highness. With a spy on the loose."

The prince gripped the man by the throat and thrust him against the wall. "I was interrupted earlier, and now you've interrupted me a second time. If you don't have any news for me, I suggest you continue your search."

Face pale and eyes wide, the officer struggled against the prince's grip, barely choking out an apology. Cassius dropped him, and he scurried away.

As he was leaving, a boy in a servant's uniform appeared at the door, obviously terrified. "Your Highness," he stuttered, bowing low and holding out a folded purple garment with trembling hands. "The dress you requested."

The prince took the dress, then shut the door.

"Here," he said, tossing me the purple dress. "You should be seen. It's best if as many people know about us as possible."

About our lie.

Climbing off the bed, I took the dress and pressed it to my chest, wishing I could rub away the ache there. "That was quite the show you put on."

"Hopefully, it works."

It seemed he wasn't going to give me any privacy, so I set the purple dress on the bed and began shimmying out of the red and black gown. "Who was he?" I asked over my shoulder. "You gave him more leeway than you would a normal guard."

"That impudent fucker is the head of the Triad's personal guard. He owes allegiance to them, not me—a sticking point in our relationship. I shouldn't have been so aggressive with him, but... "

The prince's voice cut off as I dropped the red gown to the floor. Suddenly, he was behind me, tracing his fingers across my bare shoulders. I shivered, his rich scent making that ache in my belly return.

"Still thirsty?" I asked, my voice low and shaking a little with the thought.

His hands traced down my sides, leaving fire in their wake. "It's almost noon. You should go. You have a part to play."

"Just like that, you're done with me?" I knew he was right, but I also wanted to stay—I wanted *him* to want me to stay.

The prince growled, and his lips grazed the sensitive skin below my ear. "You could give me a century, and I wouldn't be done with you. You taste like nothing I ever imagined."

When he said things like that, I wanted to believe that this *had* been more than creating an alibi. But if so, where would that leave us?

His hands grasped my hips, and he pulled me against him. "Go back to the servants' quarters wearing that dress, and the rumors will spread like wildfire."

His words said *go*, but his body...

I squeezed my eyes shut. "I'm never going to live this down."

"That you're the prince's blood mistress?" He slowly kissed the span of my neck, each touch of his lips prickling my skin and sending a shiver along my back. "Yes. I think that's going to stick with you."

What would the servants think of me? That I'd given in? Or

was feeding so common here in the castle that it wasn't looked down on like in the village?

"My mark will protect you," he said as if reading my thoughts.

Or get me killed.

I leaned back into him, savoring how broad and strong and safe he felt. He was supposed to be my enemy. I despised the immortals—so why did the thought of him trying to protect me fill my belly with warmth?

Because I'm inches from the hangman's noose.

Cassius's tongue brushed over the tender puncture wounds, sending a silent promise down my spine. This man—this immortal—was quickly unraveling me.

Breaking free from his grasp, I stepped into the purple dress and faced him. "*Will* you protect me? Can you, even?"

It was clear the Triad had some power over him, and I was a servant girl, not a queen. Hell, he was going to be king, and I was living a lie.

His stance hardened, and the man who'd seduced me was gone, replaced by cold iron. His perpetually stormy eyes turned dark. "I can, and I will. I'll get you out of here, right now, if that's what you wish."

I *should* run. I *should* flee this place with its cutthroat court and secret rulers. What I knew was certain to get me killed—what I *was* could get me killed. There were lands beyond the Bloodvale—I'd seen them documented in his desk. He could get me there, couldn't he?

But I couldn't abandon my sister or Cara, or the rest of the townsfolk. They had so little hope to live on, and even less truth. If I could find some way to help them, then the risk would be worth it.

There were other reasons as well. This relationship of ours was supposed to be nothing more than an alibi—but that intention was quickly becoming more and more a distant memory.

I placed my palm against his chest, feeling his corded muscles beneath the layers of fabric. "I'm not running. I want to stay."

Relief and concern flashed in his eyes. "You have work to do, then. If anyone asks—and they will—you slipped out at dawn to join me, and I drank from you twice. There's a salve you could use to quickly heal the bite marks, but I think you should leave them and let the rumor mill do the rest. By the end of the night, I expect I'll hear tales that we were together for days without sleeping."

The blood rushed from my face. If the sisters heard, I wouldn't have to worry about the Triad. They'd rip me to pieces between them. "So much for my reputation."

"Your reputation comes second to your safety. Every time someone repeats the rumor that you were with me today, it makes you that much safer."

That's all he and I were—a lie to ensure that I kept my life and he kept his throne.

The prince gently lifted my chin so that my eyes met his. All the tenderness he'd shown earlier was gone. "You need to be careful, Ella. The Triad are perilous. They will interrogate everyone in the castle until they find their spy or determine that he can't be found. When it's your turn to be questioned, choose every word cautiously." His thumb traced along the side of my cheek. "Do not let them see who you really are."

A flicker of guilt squeezed my chest. Did he suspect I was working for the resistance? He couldn't, or I would've already been hung from the castle walls. Could he sense I had magic? I was almost certain he hadn't bought my story about exploring, yet he hadn't asked again. Why turn a blind eye, and more importantly, what did he suspect?

My breath came a little quicker. "And who am I, really?"

A traitor and a liar.

The prince leaned in and brushed his lips across mine. "You're someone who is brave and kind and beautiful. Someone who's far more than she seems."

My stomach fluttered, and I pushed back against the emotion. Lying to the prince wasn't supposed to be this hard, and he wasn't supposed to say things like that to me. I was working against him. Although I didn't move an inch, it felt like I was plunging down the face of a cliff.

Cassius kissed me softly and gently, then stepped back. "Whatever you do, don't let them see how strong you are. Make them underestimate you. Only then will you be safe."

It was just past noon by the time I reached the servants' hall, and everyone was awake. The murmurs started the moment I stepped in. Some of the girls stopped and stared at me, while others leaned close and whispered to each other. My neck heated, but I strode forward, wearing my dress proudly. People had whispered about me my whole life. My hair. My eyes. Now the dress and the marks on my neck.

To hell with them all. Why should I hide?

The bleary eyed headmistress turned to me and raised her brow. "That's not the traditional staff uniform, Miss DuPonte."

I angled my head slightly, exposing the bright red bite marks on my neck. "My other one got damaged. I'm afraid I'll need a replacement."

She shook her head and gave me a sad smile. "Oh, lass, you've gone in deep now. Careful with yourself."

Her words weren't judging or unkind, and when she brought

me a new uniform, her typically stern disposition had thawed. "It's a very nice dress, but I'd appreciate it if you'd wear this while at mess and when going about your, well, less intimate duties."

Would they all assume I was sleeping with him as well as paying the tithe? Considering how his bite had pushed me over the edge, it wasn't much of a stretch.

I blushed and took the clothes, then nearly bumped into Cara as I headed into the women's residence. "What is that gorgeous thing you're wearing?" She stepped back, and her eyes widened. "Oh, gods, Ella, your *neck*! Who—"

"The prince," I said, flatly. Loudly.

The room around us slipped into a shocked silence, and my neck heated as everyone turned to stare at me. For a moment, no one said a word, and then Annie snorted. "You're full of shit. He hasn't fed in *centuries*."

I raised my chin. "Well, he has now."

"But *you?*" she said incredulously.

Had the Fates made us bunk mates just to torture me?

Whatever shyness I'd felt earlier melted away. I would own this. I gave her a withering look. "He didn't just drink."

Annie's eyes rounded.

Cara pulled me aside, and we headed into the washroom, away from the prying ears and eyes. "*The prince.* Are you serious? I can't believe it!"

"I can't either, really," I said, voice low. "It just sort of happened."

Her expression clouded. "Are you okay? You always said you wouldn't let one of them feed on you. He didn't force you, did he?"

I shook my head and gave her a guilty smile. "He had my full consent."

She grinned and plucked at the sleeve of my dress. "In all

fairness, I think I'd let him bite me anywhere for a dress like this."

"They bite other places than the neck?"

Cara's mouth opened, then snapped shut.

"She means they stick their head between your thighs and lap it up," someone shouted from the toilets in the back.

Cara winced. "I mean, there are other places, too. Like your wrist. Not just, um, down there." She coughed. "Though there are big blood vessels in that spot."

I nodded as my mind came to terms with the idea of Cassius's mouth dragging across the soft flesh of my inner thigh. Goosebumps rippled along my skin, and suddenly, the dress felt very, very constricting.

Cara cocked her head to the side. "Wait a minute, are you serious about what you said to Annie? You two didn't—"

I coughed loudly. "We found a variety of ways to engage ourselves, thank you very much."

I had to establish an alibi, but that didn't necessarily mean airing all my dirty laundry for everyone to see. I didn't think I was strong enough for that level of public scrutiny. However, Cara looked at me expectantly with wide and eager eyes, like a puppy waiting joyfully for table scraps. "So, I guess you were with him *all* day, then?"

"I joined him right after dawn," I said loudly enough for my voice to carry to the back of the washroom. Hopefully, it would be common knowledge in an hour. "We didn't get much sleep."

"Then you have no idea what's been going on?"

"What?" I asked, a pang of guilt prodding at me. I hated not telling Cara the truth, but it was safer for all of us this way.

"Something crazy happened in the castle. We were all sleeping, and then there was a commotion in the halls. Guards burst in, asking the headmistress for her list of names—that's when everyone noticed you were gone. They were searching the servants' halls, the kitchens, everywhere."

"Searching for what?"

"We don't know. I've heard a dozen rumors ranging from someone robbed the treasury, to a prisoner escaped, to there was an assassination attempt on the prince himself."

My stomach twisted at the thought of one of his rivals coming after him, and that left me unsettled. Now I was worrying about him? Not only could he take care of himself, but I should hate the bastard. His kindness toward me couldn't erase the evils he'd stood for and committed. Had I gone completely daft?

My fingers traced the bite mark on my neck. Yes, I probably had.

I lifted my brows in what I hoped looked like shock. "Well, I can verify the last one didn't happen. The prince was alive and well when I left him."

"Whatever happened, it was big," Cara said. "They've been taking the staff away and interviewing us, one by one. No one has ever heard of them doing that before."

The low weight of dread settled in my stomach, and I rested my back against the wall as my doubts began piling up. "What did they ask about?"

"That's the crazy thing. No one will say. I even tried bribing some of the girls with extra dessert or free sewing, but they wouldn't come clean. They were scared silent. Practically terrified." She flopped back against the wall beside me. "Whatever it is, I hope they catch whoever is responsible before my turn comes. I don't want anything to do with it."

"Yeah," I said weakly, as I let my treacherous head clunk back against the wall. "Me, neither."

42

———

Ella

The interrogations disrupted everything. Few of us got any sleep. Only essential workers and those who'd completed interviews were allowed to leave the servants' residence. The thing that haunted me most wasn't my own fate but Belle's. Hopefully, since she was laid up with a broken leg, they wouldn't even bother asking her questions.

She's smart enough to keep her mouth shut.

I would've been a bundle of nerves if it hadn't been for Cara. While everyone else was on pins and needles, she was in an irrepressibly good mood, whispering with bright eyes about what *exactly* could have caused all the uproar. She also kept wheedling me for more tidbits about my time with the prince. With plenty of eager ears listening in, I reluctantly told her what I dared. The rumor mill did its work, and before long, half the girls in the room were convinced they'd seen the prince carry me off to his bedroom to himself.

Despite the lingering glare of the headmistress, I didn't change out of my dress. It was one more part of my alibi. I had to look the part—a simple girl, marked by the prince.

His blood mistress.

It was nearing sundown by the time the guards finally called my name. "Ella DuPonte."

Exchanging a look with Cara, I rose and turned to face them, relieved that Cassius had not shared my real name with anyone else.

"You're to come with us," the guard ordered, his voice like stone.

I took a deep breath. My turn.

"You'll be fine," Cara whispered, and gave me a wink.

I wove between the beds and fell in line behind the guards. The headmistress was giving them the evil eye, obviously resentful of having self-important *men* marching in and out of her private kingdom.

The guards led me to a tower I hadn't yet visited. We waited in the hall for five minutes before a door opened and one of the other serving girls walked out. Her face was pale, and her hands shook like she'd just seen a ghost.

Whatever lies in the room, that girl is who I have to be. Not a whisperer. Not a spy. Just a simple girl who caught the eye of the prince.

The guard shoved me brusquely, and I stumbled through the open door into a posh room with bookshelves, weapons mounted on the walls, and a black desk with ornate scrollwork.

"This is Ella DuPonte, Lord Horace. A serving girl, recently hired." The guard shut the door behind me, sealing me in with the grim man who dominated the room.

Dressed in ebony robes trimmed with gold, he had a pinched face that contrasted harshly with a pair of cruel lips and thick-lidded eyes that watched me relentlessly. His power vibrated in the room, a low thrum that pulsed out from him like waves lapping the shore of a lake.

My chest tightened. He was one of *them*. The Triad. I'd seen him hours before in the garden, taking the cup from the prince.

Lord Horace reclined idly in his low-backed chair, but he was no more at rest than a cat pretending to sleep as it watched a mouse. He was a predator, lethal and vicious in a way that even the immortals were not. They hunted for food. I sensed that this man killed for fun.

Lord Horace gestured to an empty chair in front of the desk with his ring-laden fingers. "Do delight me, Ella, and sit for a while."

The slick insincerity in his voice made my ears itch. Every instinct told me to run, but I forced myself to curtsy low before him. "Thank you, my lord."

As I tucked my dress and sat, his lips twisted up in a wicked grin. "So, you're the prince's new whore."

I stiffened with shock. I wanted to lash out at him with my tongue or hurl the inkwell at him, but of course, a simple farm girl wouldn't do that. She'd be awed and terrified.

I shrank back in my chair, trying to look meek. "I'm honored to serve the prince—should he wish to feed from me or desire something else."

Lord Horace grunted, his eyes drifting to my chest and the curve of my breasts. Suddenly, the beautiful purple dress Cassius had given me began to feel garish and too exposing. "I see why the prince is taken with you. Silver hair. A welcoming form. And those lavender eyes." He leaned forward, his gaze thick and rancid. "I don't think I've ever seen their like."

"Thank you, sir," I said, looking away, as if in some other world, his words were a glowing compliment. "How can I serve you?"

He smirked. "I can think of several ways."

I wouldn't give him the satisfaction of letting him watch me squirm. I simply held my chin up and focused on the flowers lining the balcony behind him.

"Of course, I don't think His Royal Highness would appreciate that." Lord Horace sighed and traced his fingers back and forth over the papers on his desk. "Why you? He's not fed in a century. What's so special about you that he would *break* his fast?"

I shrugged, not entirely certain myself. "I don't know. Perhaps because I look different? Or perhaps it's because I'm a virgin and we taste different. I'm not an immortal and wouldn't know. I'm just a girl from a small manor."

His eyes narrowed in a catlike way, and I couldn't ignore the way he'd shifted when I said *virgin*. Gross.

"Apparently, you've been asking a lot of strange questions for a farm girl."

I felt the cold, iron jaws of his trap closing around me. What all had I asked? What did he know? My breathing quickened slightly, despite every effort to keep it calm. "The castle is very daunting, and I'd never met an immortal before I came here. There were so many things I didn't understand, so I've had to ask a lot of questions."

He pursed his lips. "I'm sure it was quite overwhelming."

I nodded. "Yes, my lord."

He leaned forward on his elbows, drumming the tips of his fingers together. "What interests me is why an overwhelmed servant girl would be asking so many questions about the northern end of the castle. It's forbidden to all but a few select servants, yet you were *very* interested in them and where they were going."

Terror sank its tendrils into my thoughts, and my mind went as blank as a crisp sheet of parchment. Could he hear heartbeats like the immortals could? If so, my hammering chest would give my guilt away.

What the hell was I going to do?

If he knew all this, he probably knew I'd also been asking after Belle. It was risky, but I could use that. I licked my lips. "I was looking for my sister when I first arrived. She'd disappeared, but I've since learned she was in the infirmary."

"Yes..." he said with a voice that could have melted steel. "But if you found her, why were you asking so many questions so *very* recently?"

The walls pressed in, and the door behind me began to feel infinitely far away. My palms and brow moistened. How could I explain snooping around? Anything I said would betray me. I would end up on a spike, and probably Belle as well.

I opened my eyes wide. "Is it real? Are the rumors true?"

I knew it was a feeble attempt to lead him off.

"Why would you wish to know?" Horace asked, his voice vibrating with anticipation.

My skin tingled, and I felt the subtle urge to speak freely, to tell the *kind man* everything I knew. *He's coaxing me with his magic.* I dug the nail of my thumb into the tip of my finger, trying to control my churning nerves. Whatever spell he was trying to weave over me, I would be stronger.

I closed my eyes, forcing myself to remember who I was supposed be. Not Ella, the spy. If I were her, I'd be doomed. I needed to be what the bastard expected—a pretty girl without brains. I'd be a ladder-climbing mistress, obsessed with the prince and nothing else. An innocent girl, too naïve and foolish to find a way through a magical barrier. Why would *that* girl be asking after a hidden wing?

A desperate ruse shaped itself in my mind. It was a one-in-a-hundred shot, but considering Horace thought I was little more than the prince's plaything, it just might work. I'd use his expectations against him.

"Is that where *he* goes?" I asked, lacing my tone with venom.

"He's always disappearing at strange times, especially during the day."

Lord Horace's brow furrowed. "Who are you talking about?"

"The prince, of course!" I clenched my hands around the end of the armchair and forced my face into a mask of jealousy. "Is he hiding another mistress from me?"

The predatory grin slipped from the lord's lips. "Another mistress? What are you talking about?"

Although I'd spent most of my life on the manor, I wasn't entirely sheltered. I'd seen enough jilted women at the tavern or the fair to know how to play the part.

"Who is she?" I hissed. "Where is she? The prince is *mine*. He chose *me*."

Lord Horace looked at me like I was a glop of slime mold. "You're worried about another lover? You realize the prince is about to marry, don't you, silly girl?"

If I was going to convince him I was nothing more than a snooping lover, *silly girl* wasn't enough. I had to be more convincing. I had to be possessive and petty and at the edge of crazy. I had to be...

Oh, Fates. I had to be *Bianca*.

Steeling myself for the performance of my life, I burst from my seat and wheeled on the mage, clutching my fists dramatically. "Silly girl? That shows you what you know. The prince will never love anyone like he loves *me*."

Horace's expression fell into a state of shock.

I wiped my eyes for effect. "He said I was *beautiful*. He can't have another mistress hidden away, can he? He wouldn't do that to me. He said I was the only one, he said I was *special*."

Horace leaned back, his faced twisted in revulsion. "I doubt that assessment very much."

I sniffled and rubbed my nose as obnoxiously as I could. "The prince said he hadn't drunk from the source for three centuries, but *I* convinced him to drink from *me*. He wasn't lying about that, was he?"

According to Cassius, it had been about a hundred years, so hopefully, the discrepancy would make me look even more naïve.

"I don't give a damn what happens between you and the prince," Horace said, slamming his palm on the desk. "I want to know how you knew to ask about a hidden part of the castle."

"I'd heard rumors about it, that's all," I burbled. "I thought that maybe he'd hidden another woman away. There's lots of rumors everywhere. Like the giant white dragon-lizard that swims in the sewers beneath the castle and guards the prince's treasure. Is that real, too?"

He sighed with frustration and began shifting through the lists of names on his desk. "And who did you hear these rumors from?"

I blinked. "Why, everyone, of course. They're *rumors*."

Lord Horace gave a low growl of frustration and waved his hand at me. "And you've never gone seeking the forbidden wing?"

His magic flared, rippling through the air around me. I plopped down in my chair, bracing against his will. I was stronger. I wouldn't tell him what he wanted. My voice was my own.

Yet I could feel him squeezing the truth out of me, like pressing the whey from the curd.

"How would I even find it?" I asked, sticking to the truth but evading his question. "Would I ask an owl where to look? I'd have better luck finding the dragon-lizard's gold in the sewers."

Lord Horace regarded me with utter disdain, drumming a pen against the papers on his desk. At last, he said, "You're a pretty girl, but you've got the brains of a goat. I almost pity you. The new queen is going to eat you alive."

I touched my chest in feigned horror. "The prince would never let anything happen to me."

"Of course he wouldn't," Lord Horace said sarcastically as he waved me away. "Now, get out of here."

Relief flooded my chest as I rose. He thought I was nothing but a dim-witted strumpet clutching at rumors. I couldn't believe the chauvinistic bastard had bought it.

It was the first time in my life I was glad to be underestimated by a man.

He sighed as I headed toward the door. "Thank you for reminding me why we let them prey on you."

I bit my tongue. Nothing he said mattered. I'd gotten away with it. I'd found the hidden wing and learned that the mages were complete assholes, and I'd be able to get word to Belle and my stepmother. My job here was almost done.

I placed my hand on the knob and started to turn it, but his words cut through the air. "But there is just one more thing."

My veins iced, and I turned back, heart pounding faster and faster. Had he been playing with me like a cat? Had he known I was lying?

Lord Horace raised his hand, and his eyes went black as night. "You will never speak of me or what was said in here. You'll never mention Lord Malthus or Lady Thalindra, or the name of the Triad to anyone."

A stream of light spiraled from his finger and lanced my chest. My head kicked back from the jolt of magic, and I staggered into the door as his spell poured though me. Power crackled in my bones, threatening to yank my ribs apart.

Lord Horace's condescending smirk became a vicious snarl. "You will never speak of our magic, and you will not seek out the hidden wing of the castle. You will deny its existence to others, and if you ever hear rumors of who infiltrated our garden, you will tell the prince immediately."

The magic circled my throat like a noose, then raced over my lips, prickling them like they were being stitched together.

"May this curse bind you for the rest of your days," he barked, and then the magic stream cut off. I collapsed, bracing myself against the door as I took a deep, agonized breath.

Lord Horace glared at me. "Get out of my sight—and tell anyone you wish what an idiot girl you are."

I didn't dare let him see the relief surging through me. With a look of what I hoped was terror, I fled the room, wiping my eyes with the back of my wrist for effect—praying I looked as afraid as the girl who'd left just before me.

If Horace's curse held, my plan was ruined. I wouldn't be able to tell Belle or the resistance about the mages or the secret wing they lived in. But at the moment, it didn't seem to matter so much. I was alive, and *that* was what counted. As for what I'd learned, I'd find another way to share it.

I had to, for the sake of the resistance. For the sake of my family.

43

Cassius

I paced the royal rose garden in the twilight of day, fuming as I waited for Ella's interrogation to finish. I'd hoped Horace would have me there, but they'd cut me out. I'd have to rely on Ella to know exactly what was going on.

Damn that girl. Now that I had my head straight and wasn't dizzy with lust and an overwhelming desire to protect her, I needed answers.

What the hell had she been doing in the Triad's garden? Was she spying? If so, for whom? She seemed too unfamiliar with immortals and the ways of the court to be a mole for one of the great houses. What about for the humans, then? She was passionate about the plight of her people. Was she a revolutionary?

I paused by the spot where I'd found her sneaking among my roses the other night. She'd been tense. I'd thought it had simply been because I caught her out of place, but now...now I had to decide what to do with her.

My father would have executed her at the mere inkling of suspicion. So would any other member of the court. But I couldn't. Every instinct told me to protect her, and after centuries of defending the border, I'd learned to trust my instincts.

Did I have the strength to trust them now?

The scent of lilies and fresh rain carried on the midnight breeze, and my blood heated. I turned as my guard escorted Ella into my rose garden.

She's all right. Relief washed over me, but I buried it beneath an exterior of steel. I gave her a curt nod as she approached, then addressed her escort. "Give us some privacy. I want the garden cleared, and we're not to be disturbed, save by Aamon or the Triad themselves."

"Yes, Your Highness!" He saluted and left, leaving us mercifully alone.

The purple dress I'd given her made the lavender of her eyes even more brilliant. The neckline dipped low, revealing the soft rise of her breasts and the inviting length of her throat. Desire flared at the sight of the two marks on her neck—they'd protect her better than anything, proof that she was *mine.*

I crossed to her and touched the length of her silver hair. It had to look as though I was smitten with her, after all. It wasn't a hardship.

"You're okay." My voice was rougher than I expected.

She lifted one eyebrow as if mocking me. "I'm the prince's trollop and of no threat to anyone. Why wouldn't I be?"

I scowled. Now was not the time for levity. "Walk with me."

"Of course, *Your Highness.*"

We wandered the path that led between the roses, now in full bloom. Bloodred, ivory, pink, and yellow—the castle garden had become a riot of color. Had the gardener done something different? I'd never seen it so full or resplendent.

Or perhaps it had always been this way, and I'd just never noticed before.

We lingered in silence until eventually she said, "The roses are beautiful."

"They're the symbol of my house," I responded absently. *She* was more beautiful by far. Even in the sea of color, she drew the eye—a perfect silver rose that put all others to shame. She was a bloom like no other, and I stiffened at the thought of how sweet her nectar would taste.

She glanced over, suspicion in her bright eyes. "Why do you keep looking at me that way?"

I tore my covetous gaze away and focused on the path ahead. "I was just thinking that dress suits you."

"Lord Horace seemed to think the same."

Horace. The lecherous bastard. I'd witnessed the results of his *interest* on several occasions. My vision tunneled into darkness, and I couldn't stifle the growl that tore from my throat. "Did he touch you?"

Her lips parted in shock at the ferocity of my tone. "Fates, no. I'd never let that bastard get close enough to touch me."

Like she could stop him. My knuckles cracked as I strained to control my anger.

The Triad were all cruel in their own ways. Thalindra was vicious and conniving, while Malthus was ruthless and cold. But I despised Horace more than the others combined. He wore golden rings and expensive robes, but he was still the same wretch he'd always been—an abusive bastard who worshipped nothing but power and gold.

I'd put him in the ground if I could, and the rest of them as well.

Unfortunately, an outright attack was doomed to fail. While I was stronger and faster, their magic was far too powerful, and I doubted I could take on one of them, let alone three. Worse, they'd been drinking my blood for centuries. It not only prolonged their lives and youth but also gave them the ability to heal from almost any wound within a matter of heartbeats. I'd considered trying to poison the blood, but the Triad provided their own enchanted goblet and blade and insisted that I bleed while they watched. Clearly, they suspected betrayal.

The bitter irony of it burned through me. My kingdom was under the heel of three sociopaths, and it was my own blood that kept them in power.

I'll find a way to overthrow them, one way or another.

Until then, I had more pressing concerns. Ella.

I forced my hands to relax but I couldn't meet her eyes. "What did Horace ask you?"

"He—" She clasped her throat, voice suddenly stifled by a spell of silence. My smoldering fury reignited, even though I'd known to expect it.

"Stop," I commanded. "Don't try to answer."

Her eyes dilated, and she drew her lips back in a snarl as she fought against the curse.

I grasped her shoulders. "Don't fight it. You cannot win. They mute all those who serve them."

Her eyes flashed with anger. "I *don't* serve them. That bastard took my voice."

I shook my head. "It is for the best. If you can't speak of the Triad or what happened, then you can no longer be a danger to them, and thus, not to yourself."

Rather than soothe her, my words seemed to anger her. She pulled free of my grasp, and her expression twisted with fury. "This is so wrong. You should have warned me."

"And if I had, you likely would have resisted or fled and gotten yourself killed."

I wasn't blind. Ella was no innocent serving girl, and she'd been in the hidden garden for a purpose. Although I didn't know why yet, I was certain she wouldn't let her hard-won discoveries be taken from her.

Horace's curse of silence protected her and me both.

"Who are they? *What* are they, and why do you tolerate them?"

"Like I said before, they are none of your concern," I said coldly, then turned and started walking away. "No more questions. No more investigating. Let it go."

She grasped my arm and stepped in front of me, forcing me to stop. "What power do they have over you?"

A muscle in my jaw twitched. "How are you asking me these things? Didn't Lord Horace's curse silence you?"

Determination flashed in her eyes. "Just from speaking about them. He didn't say anything about asking questions."

Suspicion crept over me. Why leave her the ability to ask questions? It had to be intentional. While I'd certainly let my guard down around her, the Triad were different. They never stopped scheming. What did Horace stand to gain?

I narrowed my eyes at her. "Did Lord Horace order you to bring him information?"

She bit the bottom of her lip, then pointed to me.

"You're to bring it to me?" I frowned. Either Horace trusted me blindly or planned to test me. Either way, it was a bad sign, and a deep unease settled over me. "This conversation is over."

I continued on, but I couldn't free myself of the troublesome woman or her inquiries.

"If I can't speak, what's the harm in telling me?" she pressed as she hurried after.

I spun on her, my fear for her safety fueling my anger. "Were you born without any common sense? The Triad is none of your business. Why should I tell you anything?"

She straightened and glared. "Because those people just screwed with my head."

"You're lucky you still have one."

She pivoted in front of me, cutting me off in a brazen challenge, with her hands on her hips. "Clearly, whatever this kingdom is, it's a lie. *You* are a lie."

I froze, her words crushing my chest like a war hammer.

She stepped closer, until we were inches apart. "I don't know what's going on, but I can tell you hate it. Don't you wish there were someone you could tell? Someone you knew who would never speak the truth?"

I set my jaw. The poor girl believed the truth would set us all free, but the reality was that our entire kingdom depended on the lie. It depended on *them*.

She raised her eyebrows expectantly. "You want to tell me, so *do it*. I'm forbidden to speak what I know, so there's no risk."

The words ached to be free, but I was a fucking fool for even considering it. She was a spy. *If you fall in love, the woman you choose will destroy everything your father built.*

I couldn't possibly love the girl—I didn't have the capacity—but the warning was germane, all the same. I'd been playing with fire, and I had to stop.

"Of course there's risk. Everything has risk." I stepped around her and continued walking.

"Then take one," she challenged.

I turned and glared. "I did that already when I saved your life. That's risk enough."

"Is it?" she asked, but I walked away, leaving her standing among the roses. A beautiful siren promising release but doing nothing more than calling me to my doom.

I vowed to resist her as long as I could, but the gods knew I couldn't stay away.

I avoided Ella the rest of the night, but I couldn't shake her from my thoughts. She'd become a specter of need and worry that haunted my mind.

Although I'd sent her back to her duties, she was far from safe. Whether they knew it or not, the Triad were hunting her, and they would not stop until they discovered the truth. I spread what disinformation I could, but I knew it wouldn't be enough. Protecting her might call for something more drastic.

The castle walls pressed in on me, and the dank air grew suffocating and claustrophobic. It felt like every conversation echoed too loudly but was muffled and indistinct. Around every corner was another preening idiot who'd bow and scrape and flatter me as if my power mattered. The Triad constantly meddled with the politics of the court and were a check against every decision I made, living handcuffs that fed off my strength.

The bitterness of it galled me. The crown I would soon claim would be as much a lie as my marriage.

By the next evening, the need to be with Ella had become almost maddening. Aamon and Cassandra peppered me with questions about the frontier and the beasts and the ball and alliances, but I barely listened.

I loosened the neck of my shirt. I had to get out of the castle. I needed to get away from them all—the court, the Triad, the simpering fools. I had to be alone.

No. Not alone.

With *her*.

For all the trouble she'd caused, for all the danger and distraction she presented, she promised release. I dismissed my advisers and sent word for Ella to immediately meet me at the stables.

She made me wait, which only stoked my incendiary mood, and I was pacing in agitation by the time she arrived. She'd abandoned the purple dress, returning to the blue and gray uniform that all the house staff wore, but rather than cool my desire, it only fanned the flames. The plump curves of her breasts and their perky nipples were hidden, but I'd sampled them and had to resist the urge to rip the neckline down so that I could taste them again. Her silver hair was pulled back, exposing her neck and the slowly healing marks I'd left for all to see—the marks that reminded everyone that she was *mine*.

The hunger ignited within me. I wanted to hike up the plain cloth of her dress and plunge myself between her legs, then drive my teeth into the sweet flesh of her neck. I didn't care if it was up against the wall of the stable or if anyone saw. Let them all watch me claim what was mine. What I *wanted* to be mine.

What I didn't dare take.

The girl didn't deserve to be corrupted by the likes of me.

I crushed the railing of the stall beneath my grip, and she looked over. "Is something the matter, Your Highness?"

"Saddle Chastity. You're riding out with me," I ordered more harshly than I'd intended.

We didn't speak as she prepared the mare, but I watched her relentlessly. She was so skilled and gentle with the beasts, it was no wonder she'd found a way to tame me and bend me to her will—for Fates' sake, the woman had gotten the godsdamned prince of the Bloodvale to lie for her and hide her treachery.

Either I was fool or she was a siren. Or both.

Ella must have sensed I was in a mood because instead of badgering me with relentless questions as we rode, she stayed uncommonly silent, letting me brood. It only made things worse. Her words continued to claw at me, slowly corroding the iron around my heart. *Clearly, whatever this kingdom is, it's a lie. You are a lie.*

My chest felt like it was going to crack, bursting with repressed desire and long-hidden secrets I was desperate to speak. That truth had been something I'd always lived with, but it felt more like a burden than ever. A mad part of me longed to tell her everything, regardless of what she was, informant or revolutionary or spy.

All I knew was that whatever her true motives for being in the castle were, she had a good heart, better than any I'd known. I saw the signs everywhere she went—the compassion she showed animals, the love she had for her people, and the strength with which she suffered the slights and abuses of the sisters.

She made me want to be better. She made me feel like I *could* be better.

I could barely stand it.

We crested a rise and paused, looking out over the tree-lined slopes toward the river and the castle high above. As I stared at the white towers of my home, all the emotion inside of me became a sea of bitterness, and like floodwaters battering a dike, my will finally broke.

"The kingdom is a lie," I whispered, not taking my eyes from the castle. "You were right."

Her breath stilled. "How so?"

A simple question that had dangerous answers. I was a fool for even speaking the words, but she had cracked my foundation to the core. I couldn't resist telling her any more than I could resist the sweet taste of her blood.

"You asked for the truth," I said, meeting her impossibly enchanting eyes. "The truth is that we lost the war, and your kind won."

44

Ella

I stared back at Cassius in stunned silence. He couldn't be serious. "What are you talking about? Immortals rule, and we serve. We *lost*."

He shook his head. "Maybe I should have said we *all* lost."

Anger flushed my skin. The sheer *arrogance* of it.

I turned Chastity about and brought her alongside Tenebris so I could face the prince directly. "Are you serious? We *all* lost? You live in a castle with wonders like hot running water, limitless wealth, and dozens of servants ready to tend to your every need. You didn't lose—*we* did, the poor bastards digging in the dirt and scraping by on the scraps from your table. The Uprising failed."

Cassius looked at me, his eyes dark and cold. "It's not that simple."

What could be simpler? It was all I could do not to scream. "Are you blind? We're little more than your slaves. The ceiling of your great hall is covered in pictures of my people being slaughtered. The history books—"

"*Tell the stories we want them to tell.*" His voice was a winter wind, cold and violent, and despite my fury, I stilled. His broad frame trembled with barely restrained anger. "It's all a lie. The books, the murals, the priests—they only tell part of the story. It's true that your kind were slaughtered by the thousands, but while one of us can fight off ten men or twenty, we can't fight a hundred at once. We were fewer then, outnumbered, and overwhelmed. What the murals don't show is that we lost in the end."

Shock and disbelief swept over me like a tremor in the earth, but his eyes didn't lie. They burned with an intensity that told me he believed what he was saying.

I shook my head. "That doesn't make any sense."

"Only because you believe in heroes. There are no heroes, Ella." Cassius looked out across the valley, his mood dark and somber. "Tell me what you know of the Uprising. *Not* what they teach, but what is whispered among friends and in the dark corners of taverns."

That it was still alive.

If that's what he wanted me to confess, I wouldn't. "What's there to tell? They say our people united, but we were defeated in the end."

"What else?"

"That there were those who could wield magic, but after we lost, they were all executed, and magic hasn't returned since. Or at least I thought it hadn't until I came here."

He gave a low growl of displeasure. "Magic is alive and well, I'm afraid. Your Uprising was led by three powerful mages, but they didn't give a damn about the rest of you. To them, the farmers and laborers and craftsmen who bled for the cause were chaff, readily sacrificed at the altar of war. The mages incited the revolution to get what they wanted, and once they had it, they tossed the rest of your kind away."

His words piled up one by one, the bricks of a house

collapsing on top of me. Three mages. It couldn't be, and yet, hadn't I suspected it as much, deep in my heart?

My throat grew taut as the horrid truth dawned, but I couldn't accept it until I heard him say it. I had to see the truth in his eyes. "What did the mages want?"

"You already know what they wanted." The prince looked down at his hand and flexed it slowly. "Our blood—the secret to defying death. It was the one thing their magic could not give them. Immortality."

My stomach plummeted.

Seeing my comprehension, he gave me a grim smile. "Yes, *the Triad*. Horace was one of the leaders of the Uprising three centuries ago. He and his allies sold you out. There were many mages like them once. The Triad convinced the others to let them channel their power to defeat us—but instead of just borrowing it, they stole it. And once they'd won, they had us execute their rivals."

Everything I'd come to believe about our history came raining down like a scorched pile of cinder and ash.

"There's a sick poetry in it, I suppose," Cassius said bitterly. "You serve us, and we serve them. You pay us the blood tithe, and I pay it to them. The Triad drink royal blood—my father's, and then my brother's, and now mine. It's the reason they're so invested in ensuring my line continues. Without it, they'll wither and age, and their powers will fade."

"If that is true, then why do you serve them? Why don't you fight back?"

His shoulders and hands knotted, and for a second, I thought Cassius was going to lash out. Instead, a deep hollowness came over him. The emotion drained from his face. "Because they're far more powerful than I am—than anyone. They can call lightning and fire down from the skies and force you to speak and bow against your will."

He looked back at the castle, his eyes trained on the place where their invisible tower should be. "If they wanted, they could chain me up and tap me at their leisure like a barrel of wine. In some ways, that would be easier. I wouldn't be party to their crimes. But instead, I keep my freedom and resist them from within. It's one of the reasons I haven't fed from the source for a century. I'd hoped it would weaken them, even if it weakened me, too."

Were the Triad truly so powerful they could make all the immortals bow before them? My stomach twisted as I imagined the prince hung like a cow at the butcher's, bled from the neck while the Triad fed off him.

"What if you just left?" I whispered. "Flee the Bloodvale and go somewhere they could never find you."

"Like my brother did?" The pain and betrayal in his voice lanced through me, and I touched the mark on my neck, my heart aching.

I knew it was dangerous territory, but I licked my lips and pushed on. "With you both gone, they would no longer have access to the royal blood. Perhaps they'd grow old and die, and in time, you could return to claim your throne."

His expression didn't waver. Hard. Cold. Relentless. "I've considered it," he said with hesitation. "But I doubt it would work. While the Triad demands royal blood, it might only be a symbol of their dominion over our house. Even if it's the blood of our line that they require, I have cousins they could put on the throne." His back straightened as if he'd reached a decision. "No. Even if it would weaken them, I won't abandon my people to their rule—or yours. Imagine what this place would be like if Lorayna and Bianca and their family claimed the throne. They're loyal to the Triad, and the next most powerful house."

My guts clenched at the thought. It would be chaos. Slaughter and debauchery and unrelenting cruelty, the ceiling of the great hall brought to life. We would truly become no more than slaves and cattle.

He shook his head. "My brother abandoned his duties. I will not do the same."

His voice ached with betrayal and loss. He must have loved Valen as much as I loved Belle.

"I'm sorry, Cassius. I really am."

Cassius sank into a silence I didn't dare break. I watched him staring off into the darkness, admiring the hard line of his jaw and the ferocity in his expression. He was a severe man, but my instincts about him had been right. He *was* different. The prince had a sense of duty unlike any of the immortals I'd met or heard about. It seemed relentless, almost selfless—and it wasn't just to his house, but to the Bloodvale. To his people and mine. Even though Cassius seemed to despise the crown, I sensed he wanted to be a good king.

Could that be an opportunity? Was there a chance that he would change things if I showed him the value of human life? He'd stood up to Bianca for me. Maybe, in time, he could be a king who stood up for all of us.

I placed my hand on his arm. "I'm glad it's you on the throne and not your brother. The Bloodvale needs someone who stands for its people and protects them. Not someone who abandons them and runs."

He scowled and shook his head. "*Abandoned* is the wrong word—it's just half a century of bitterness speaking. Valen would have been a good king, a better king. I think the Triad sensed that and drove him mad to get rid of him."

My eyes widened. "You think he tried to resist them?"

"At first, I thought that our father's death or the burden of rule got to him, but now, I'm not so sure. Maybe he didn't like being used as a puppet any more than I do. Maybe he fought back, and the Triad taught him a lesson. I don't know. I lived at one of the border keeps then, and I wasn't part of the court or its machinations." He glanced over, his jaw set and expression stern. "I've never told anyone my suspicions. I shouldn't be telling you."

Doubt prickled my mind. Shouldn't I tell my stepmother or Siggy? Even if I was gagged by Horace's spell, there had to be something I could tell them, yet the thought of doing so and betraying his trust made me sick.

"I won't speak a word to anyone," I promised, my chest tightening. For whatever reason, the oath felt even stronger than Horace's spell.

Cassius's stormy eyes slipped into sadness, and his mouth became a mournful smile. "But you *will* speak if the Triad demands it. They'll use their magic to squeeze every word out of you."

My breathing became shallow. I had way too many secrets burning in my heart. The resistance. My magic. And everything Cassius had shared. Those secrets could doom everyone I cared about. Belle. Cara. My stepmother and her allies. The old woman in the woods.

And him.

My head spun, and I thought I might be sick. "If they can make me speak, why tell me all of this?"

He backed Tenebris away from me. "Because I'm a selfish bastard. Because I couldn't keep the truth trapped inside of me any longer—even if it damns me. I don't care. I was never meant to belong to those bastards or the throne."

The prince suddenly seemed more alone than I'd ever seen any man. Trapped in his palace, forced to rule by duty and obliged to serve by force. He hadn't even been given the luxury of marrying for love. It was another obligation. Another trap.

No wonder he fled the castle on horseback each day—it was because he couldn't flee for good.

"We should go," Cassius said, and turned his stallion to head back the way we'd come.

"What if there was something I could do?" I called after him as I spurred Chastity to follow.

He gently pulled Tenebris to a halt. "And what would you do, little spy? What could you or the people you work for possibly do?"

The people I work for? I stared at him, aghast. He knew? He knew, and yet he'd told me all of this.

He narrowed his eyes at me, his expression glacial. "I'm no fool, Cinderella, and neither are you. Unless you work for three mages equal in power to the Triad, then there is nothing any of us can do."

Cassius urged Tenebris forward again, down the trail. We rode in silence as I replayed everything he'd said, over and over. Did he know I worked for the resistance, or had it been a guess? Had everything he told me been the truth, or was it a ploy?

I wanted to trust him, perhaps tell him everything, but that was a foolish instinct. What would it gain me? How would we ever change things, faced with mages powerful enough to defeat a kingdom of immortals and to kill all their rivals?

There was still too much I didn't know—most importantly, about the curse.

"Why is magic repressed beyond the castle walls?" I asked.

He glanced back and shook his head. "There will never be enough answers for you, will there?"

"I seriously doubt it. I'm the inquisitive sort."

"So I've noticed," he muttered.

"I already know enough to damn you and get myself killed, so why hold anything back?"

Cassius shook his head and turned to the path ahead. It seemed he'd say no more, but a few minutes later, he spoke. "The Triad cursed the Bloodvale after they took power. I don't pretend to understand how, but they created a spell that drains the magic beyond the castle and fuels their own power. It's like a whirlpool that pulls in magic. That's why there are no mages or witches left to lead your people, or to help us against the Triad. They've all been stifled."

Stifled.

Was that how I felt? Siggy had called it repressed.

I closed my eyes, searching for the difference between the way the world felt within the castle and the forest. It wasn't so much the presence of a spell, but an absence—a hollowness, draining the magic within me and drawing it into the darkness of the woods. I felt it slipping away in subtle waves, almost like a heartbeat.

Everything Siggy had told me began to make sense, but the magic wasn't repressed as she'd imagined it. It was being taken from us both. The Triad's curse wasn't stifling or repressing us, but rather draining our magic, just like the immortals drained our blood. That's why our powers were weak beyond the wall.

Weak, but not nonexistent.

Siggy had levitated a kettle, and I'd called trees to my defense against the beast. Repressed or drained or stifled, I had power. That meant there was hope.

"Do you really think there's no one with magic left?" I asked, keeping my voice casual, like an offhand remark.

"It's unlikely."

I locked my eyes on the path, not daring to look at him. "And what would you do if you discovered a mortal with magic?"

"Hunt them down," the prince said.

My shoulders tightened. "So, you'd just hand them over to the Triad?"

"No." He grunted and looked back. "If they were strong, I'd beg them for help."

Beg? I raised my eyebrows in surprise. "And if they weren't?"

Cassius's expression turned back to stone. "I'd tell them to run, to get out of this place and never come back, because sooner or later, the Triad would find them and steal their power—just like they've done to every other poor soul unlucky enough to be born a witch."

The ramifications of his words sent my thoughts spiraling all over again. "Then there've been others?" Cassius's eyes narrowed sharply with suspicion, and my heart skipped a beat as I scrambled to cover for my slip. "Others like those in the revolution, I mean."

For a long moment, the prince's interrogating gaze rested on me, but then he turned back to the trail. "Don't get your hopes up, little mouse. Witches are killed as soon as they're discovered—each and every one."

45

Ella

We didn't speak during the rest of the ride. Cassius drew inward, his mood dark and brooding, while my own thoughts were as tangled as the briars in the undergrowth. It only worsened as we neared the castle.

"May I have permission to visit my sister?" I asked, breaking the unnerving silence. "Doctor LaMazi has very strict rules."

He looked over at me, as if not truly seeing me. Perhaps he was thinking of his brother. "Of course. I'll send word to the doctor."

After that, he lapsed into silence again.

As soon as we rode through the gates, Aamon intercepted Cassius and pulled him away on urgent business. The prince's friend shot me a suspicious look as they departed, and I wondered if the urgent business had simply been to get Cassius away from me.

It was a relief, in all honesty. As much as I coveted the prince's presence, I could barely think around him, and I desperately needed to get my head straight. I set to work grooming the horses and cleaning the tack. The rhythm of the familiar work and the scent of the stables began to clear my mind.

In the last twenty-four hours, I'd probably received more information than the resistance could hope to learn in a hundred years. The problem was, I was cursed to never repeat anything about the Triad or their magic, and the rest of what I'd learned barely made sense without it.

What would my stepmother say if I'd told her that the immortals had lost the revolution and didn't really rule? She'd call me crazy and a fool. She'd say I was just making up things to sound self-important—or to cover for the fact that I'd learned nothing at all.

Hell, with what I could repeat, Belle probably wouldn't buy it, either. I'd barely believed Cassius's story myself.

I finished my duties to the animals and headed back to the women's residence to wash up. But before I made it to the servants' hall, two shapes appeared out of the shadows. I stepped back quickly, but Bianca lunged forward and dug her nails into my arm. "You little whore!"

I tried to jerk away from her inhumanly strong grip, but she wasn't alone. Lorayna grabbed my hair and yanked my head to the side. "So, it's true. He finally broke his fast."

"I told you she was a filthy hussy," Bianca moaned. "She's trying to steal the prince from me!"

"Let go!" I grunted as I struggled, but their strength was like iron. My breathing quickened as panic set in. We'd all heard stories about the immortals' strength, and given the murderous look in their eyes, it was entirely possible they intended to rip me limb from limb.

Lorayna's fingers tightened, pulling the roots of my hair. "Didn't Bianca order you to dye this repulsive mess?"

"The prince ordered me to wash it out. I've only done what he asked."

"And have you done what *we* asked?" Her voice dripped with threat. "What information have you discovered?"

The darkest secrets of this kingdom.

But the wicked sisters only cared for power and the ball, and there were a dozen meaningless things I could feed them without compromising the prince's agenda or mine. I rattled off empty tidbits—his preferences for his privacy, snippets of information I'd learned about his appointments, names I'd heard mentioned, and a few from the papers—but the more I said, the more I realized it wouldn't be enough. They'd wanted me to find something that would help them draw his eye, but the only thing that seemed to captivate the prince's attention was me.

"You're useless," Lorayna declared.

Bianca's face loomed over me, her eyes wild with hatred. "More than useless. She's a traitorous little *wench*. She was never going to help us. She planned to seduce him and steal him for herself. But I don't think he'll have much use for a corpse." She feigned a pitying expression. "They're so much less interesting to play with."

Darkness clouded the corners of my vision as my resolve strengthened. They were bullies, and submission would never get them to leave me alone. I was tired of it, and I refused to play the docile servant any longer.

I spat in Bianca's face and kicked her, my foot slamming into her shin. "Go ahead. Do what you want, you crazy bitch. But when they find my body, who do you think the prince will blame for murdering his concubine, the only woman he's wished to feed from in a hundred years? You—and I assure you, he will *not* be pleased."

Bianca screamed with rage as she wiped the spittle off her face, but Lorayna only smiled. "I guess we'll find out."

A harsh laugh escaped from my throat. "I've told him everything about you two. He knows *everything* you've done to me. He will fall on you like a thunderstorm."

Lorayna smirked, unfazed by my threat. "You've overplayed your hand, foolish girl. He needs us, but he doesn't need you."

"He needs *me*," Bianca insisted.

"For three more days," I said, giving her a wicked grin. "What purpose will you serve after the ball? To announce to the court every time he walks through the door? You're essentially useless, Bianca. Easily disposed of."

She slapped me across the face. Braced between them, my head kicked back hard, pain flaring in my cheek.

"What about you, Lorayna?" I continued. "If Cassius thinks you harmed me, he might just as well tell his new queen she can pick another chamberlain who will be loyal. She'll obviously want to make a mark here, and the quickest way to do that will be to get rid of you both, particularly if her new husband thinks it's for the best."

"Cassius?" Bianca shrieked. "You're a serving girl. You dare use his name?"

"You've fooled yourself if you think he cares for you," Lorayna said, false pity thick in her voice.

Her words stung harsher than the welt on my face.

Bianca grabbed my chin. "He's going to marry me. *I* will be the new queen."

I twisted my head free. "Not in a thousand years. He despises you."

"That's not true," the pretty sociopath wailed.

"It is. He's not going to marry either of you. It's already decided."

Lorayna's expression grew dark. "Then tell me, *girl*, what use are you to us? Because if we're both going to lose our place at court, there's no reason not to rip your throat out and lap the blood from your neck right now."

She clenched her hand around my throat and squeezed. I kicked and gasped. There was no doubt she was willing to do me in, and as much as I wanted to defy them, I also very much wanted to live.

"There's—a—list," I choked.

She eased her grasp. "What did you say?"

I sucked in a deep breath, my lungs burning. "He keeps papers on all the potential brides. I think he has a short list. I can bring it to you."

"What use is a list if my name is not on it?" Bianca hissed, looking over her sister's shoulder.

"You can make alliances with the potential queens before they arrive. If he chooses a foreign bride, she'll need friends in the castle. Why not you? Save your position, or hell, bargain for more power."

Bianca screeched, then stormed away. "Gods, kill her already Lorayna! I want to see why His Highness thinks she tastes *socoo* good."

But Lorayna didn't waver. "Bargain what? The information you've given us so far is *useless*."

"The list itself," I rasped under her tightening fist. "I doubt the new queen will want any rivals. She'll want to know what other women caught her husband's eye, and I'm sure the new queen would be eternally grateful if you helped secure her power in the court."

There was a flicker of hesitation in Lorayna's eyes, but it betrayed everything. There was no negotiating with a madwoman like Bianca, but Lorayna was cunning, and you could bargain with cunning.

I had her on the hook. Now all I had to do was reel her in. "Think of what you could do if you were in sole possession of the prince's list. If there were women you might want eliminated or banished from court, you could even write their name down. The new queen would see them as rivals, too."

Lorayna released me, and I collapsed, gasping, on the floor.

"Why are you letting her go? I want to bleed her dry!" Bianca shouted, but Lorayna held up a hand, silencing her sister.

I rose and straightened my dress. "The key, of course, is to gain her trust early, and you can't do that if you don't know who the real candidates are."

Lorayna crossed her arms. "Then you have twenty-four hours. Bring me the list by this time tomorrow or I will hunt you down and kill you myself."

"Yes!" Bianca said, glancing between me and her sister, only just coming up to speed. "Bring *us* the list, or I'm going to peel your skin off one piece at time, like picking petals from a daisy. *Then I'm going to eat them.*"

As if I had any doubt, she slowly mimed the process, licking her fingers and smacking her lips together delightedly at the end. I backed away in horror from the two bloodthirsty lunatics and tried to keep my thoughts straight. "What stops you from killing me once I hand it over?"

Lorayna's mouth twisted in a vicious smile. "You're a clever little girl. You'll think of something, I'm sure."

46

———

Ella

I got the shaking under control by the time I got back to the women's residence. I'd bought myself time, but after tomorrow, I was going to have to find a way to *never leave the prince's side again*, because if I did, I was a dead woman.

A very vocal part of me wanted to flee and get away from the homicidal sisters and the brutal inequity of the castle forever. But just as Cassius couldn't abandon his kingdom, I couldn't abandon my duty. There was too much at stake now, and too many questions still burned in the back of my mind.

And then there was *him*.

I was a moth drawn to the flame, a mink caught in the hunter's snare. There was something about him that pulled me in—a relentless magnetism that I couldn't shake, no matter how much I tried.

It wasn't just the scent of his body or the taste of his lips. It wasn't the electric way my body responded to his bite or the thunderous waves of ecstasy and desire he'd sent through me. It wasn't even the safety that I felt around him or the familiar comfort that had grown between us. There was something *more*

—a deep thrum of purpose that I couldn't put my finger on. I needed to be here, near him.

I shook my head as I changed into my nightgown—or day gown, as it was. What I needed was to turn off my brain and get some sleep.

Annie snorted contemptuously as I crawled into bed. "I thought you were too good for us, but I guess you're still sleeping in the shit with the rest of the scum."

I laid down, and Pip cuddled up beside me, thankfully without asking any questions.

I didn't sleep well, and the next evening, when the first bell sounded, I dragged myself out of bed and went through the motions of getting ready. I was half asleep until partway through breakfast, when one of the girls burst into the servants' mess. "Matthew's dead!"

My head cleared instantly, and I sat up. The head gardener?

The headmistress grabbed the girl by the arm and started to pull her away. "Quiet, now, or you'll make a scene. Come outside and we'll talk about what's happened."

"They've hung him in the servants' garden," the girl blubbered. "From the north wall!"

We were all out of our seats before the headmistress could stop us, running in a jumble through the servants' halls. We tumbled out of the corridor and into the garden, and stared in stunned silence across the expanse of plants.

Matthew hung from the wall, his body bloody and contorted. They'd impaled him on a spike driven into the stone, his head hung back with an open mouth, as if releasing a silent scream.

My stomach plunged like a rotten ferryboat finally slipping beneath a lake.

That was the wall that I'd climbed over to investigate the hidden wing. The vines I'd grown lay in a pile at the base beneath his corpse, cut from their roots. In the drama of the interrogation and everything I'd learned, I'd forgotten all about them. The Triad would have noticed, of course, and now Matthew had taken the blame.

His death was my fault.

"There's a message on him," one of the girls said. "Who can read?"

Most probably could, but no one wanted to step any closer. He stank of death, a crystal-clear reminder that we served—and died—at the pleasure of our masters.

I pushed through the crowd and lifted the note. The words felt like a noose around my throat, but I read them aloud anyway, hand shaking. "*Behold the end of a traitor. Behold the result of neglecting your duty. Do not cross this wall, or you and all those you love will beg for the mercy of the gardener's end.*"

"Fates," one girl said. Then all their voices came in a rush, like winter winds driving the waves of the lake on shore.

"Why him? What did he ever do?"

"Maybe he helped the thieves? That must be it!"

"What about his family? I wonder if the immortals killed them, too?"

"Do you think they'd really kill us all?"

I stared in horror at his face, his dead eyes bulging and staring at the sky. I'd never been so close to a dead man before. His wounds whispered that death hadn't been gentle or swift.

And I'd done it to him just as surely as if I'd beaten him to death myself. I wanted to vomit, but I steeled myself and wrapped my arms around my chest, digging my fingers into my skin.

Had this been the Triad? Or had it been Cassius? Had he killed Matthew to protect me and throw the Triad off my scent?

I glanced up at the prince's high tower, and the dark implications sank in. Cassius had killed to protect me before, that night in the woods when we'd first met. But this was different. Matthew wasn't a bloodthirsty immortal. He was an innocent bystander. A man who delighted in pruning roses and who'd never hurt a soul.

The walls of the castle pressed in around me. As soon as I could get away from the commotion, I hurried through the halls to the prince's chambers, but he wasn't there. I found him in his study, with a pair of soldiers stationed at the door. One of the guards held up his hand as I tried to enter. "I wasn't aware His Highness had requested your presence."

"I need to speak to him. Now." I tried to slip past the guard, but he simply shifted his bulk to block my way. I crossed my arms and cocked my head expectantly. The guard measured my determination for a moment, then sighed and knocked.

"What?" the prince asked, his voice muffled by the door but his irritation evident.

The guard cracked it open and leaned inside. "The serving girl, Your Highness."

The condescending jerk didn't even bother using my name.

There was a short delay, and then Cassius appeared. He wore a trim black military uniform that screamed *all business*.

"What are you doing here? I didn't send for you," he said, distracted and annoyed.

"Oh, yes," I said, accusingly. "*You very much did.*"

He glared at me for an eternal breath, then finally recanted. "Come in."

Aamon stood by the window and raised one eyebrow as I entered. "I wasn't informed we'd be receiving the ambassador from the scullery kingdom today, Your Royal Highness."

My neck heated, and Cassius gave his consul a pained look. "Will you give us the room for a minute?"

Aamon bowed quickly to him, and then bent long and low to me, a sly grin on his face.

As soon as the door clicked shut, Cassius asked, "What is it?"

"There's an innocent man hanging from the wall of the servants' garden." I spoke quietly, stepping close. The guards probably couldn't hear through the door, but Aamon was an immortal and blessed with acute hearing. If he was lurking within earshot, I was afraid a whisper might even be too loud.

Cassius pulled me to the far side of the room. "I am well aware. I am also sorry the gardener turned out to be a traitor."

The word turned my mouth sour. He *knew* the only traitor was me. I wanted to scream, but I couldn't. The way he'd chosen his words probably meant people could be eavesdropping.

"Was it you?" I asked. "Or was it the—" My throat seized up as I tried to speak their name.

His lips became a thin line of displeasure. "Do not speak of things you *shouldn't know*. The gardener's dead. It doesn't matter who was responsible."

"He was an *innocent* man," I hissed.

The prince lifted an eyebrow. "Was he? He let the vines grow over the wall. If he hadn't, the intruder wouldn't have been able to get in."

The intruder.

Me.

Cassius sat down in the leather chair behind his large, ornate writing desk. "His neglect played a part in what happened, and he was punished accordingly. That's the end of this conversation."

Matthew hadn't neglected anything. *I'd* grown the vines, and *I'd* left them there—but I couldn't tell Cassius that. I didn't dare reveal my magic. Not now, not without a purpose. Matthew was dead, and there was nothing I could do to change it.

I shook my head in disbelief, and Cassius rubbed his brow. "The man died trying to escape. He was the intruder or an accomplice. Either way, as he was not able to testify before his death, the affair seems settled."

Meaning, his death bought my life.

The prince was so cold, so unaffected by the murder of an innocent man. Was this who he really was?

He glanced at the door, then leaned forward, fixing me with a cold stare. "I understand you're upset, but this should be a timely reminder to *every* member of the staff. They should not go exploring the castle. They're to stay where they *belong*."

To stay where we belonged? In the cramped servants' quarters or the shitty hovels of Lower Town? In menial jobs, sweating and breaking our backs, while his court and the Triad grew fat off our labor?

The anger inside me whipped into a firestorm.

We were slaves and cattle. We should know our place. We shouldn't ask questions. And most of all, when one of our kind was killed for no reason, we shouldn't raise our voices. We should look away and accept it all, like the beatings the sisters loved to dole out.

I glared at him, sitting there behind a desk that was worth more than my year's wages, really seeing him for the first time. Why had I thought he was any different? Why had I been such a fool? He might care for his kingdom, he might care for me, but he'd never see my kind as anything more than livestock.

With a last accusing look, I turned and headed toward the door.

He half rose from his seat. "Ella, where are you going?"

I wrenched the door open. "The servants' quarters. Back to where I belong."

He stared, but he didn't stop me.

Of course he wouldn't, because underneath it all, he was one of them.

47

Cassius

The door shut behind Ella, and the room grew cold, like the heat of summer had slipped into winter. I relaxed at last, glad to breathe more easily.

Once, it had been torment while she was away. Now, I could barely stand having her near. The scent of her body, the drum of her pulse, the way her lips danced when she spoke—they threatened to drive me to madness.

I loved her fire and anger and the casual way she defied me. She was unlike all the others, with no sense of decorum or propriety, and it had been all I could do not to shove her up against the wall and sink my teeth into her neck, to plunge myself into her and savor her warmth. She was a vicious reminder that in another life, there might have been a different path for me. One where I didn't have to wear a crown and serve a kingdom. One where I could have served myself and all my desires.

Unfortunately, that path was long gone, while the road ahead was dark and full of trouble—trouble that began with her and everything I'd said.

I'd been a fool to tell her about the mages and the revolution. It went far beyond what was safe, even with the curse sealing her lips. It was like I was tempting fate and the Triad to come down on her at once.

Yet, *pathetically*, I hadn't been able to help myself. There was an earnestness to the way she looked at me that made me want to confess. She deserved the truth. All her kind did.

But that was madness.

Perhaps I'd been drunk on desire. Courtesans and mistresses always made good informants because men love confiding in a pretty face. They shared their secrets and worries and doubts, thinking that they'd found a dark hole they could spill their troubles into. I was no different—a fool running my tongue, like any other.

Aamon let himself back in unannounced. "Your new toy looked rather flushed when she left. A quick bite for lunch?"

"No."

"What was so urgent?" he asked, idly looking out at the dark courtyard below the window—though there was nothing idle in the question. His mind was always going, which was one reason I kept him so close.

I waved my hand dismissively. "Nothing. She was upset about the gardener—as were all the staff. However, *she* has the prince's ear."

"Then the message was received as intended."

I nodded. It had been brutally handled, but it had to be done. The moment the Triad had learned of the vines, the gardener's fate had been sealed. They would have tortured him until he'd divulged everything he knew, and if he had seen Ella...

I shoved that thought away.

His lips were sealed forever, and I could pass it off as him dying while trying to escape. If it protected Ella, the rest didn't matter. Still, Aamon's theatrical display had pushed things too far.

I was lucky I didn't have a riot of servants on my hands.

Aamon flopped down into the seat across from me. "What *is* your intention for that woman, anyway?"

I slumped back in my chair. *What, indeed?*

When I didn't respond, he pressed. "Clearly, you care for her,"

"I do not." My words came too sharp, too quick to be anything but a lie.

He laughed in that good-natured way of his, one I could never echo. "You can't be serious, Cassius. Everyone in the castle knows you're fascinated with the creature, from the scullery maids to the lords of your court. Hell, the Triad themselves probably know."

Oh, they knew—which put Ella in danger. I had no reason to protect a random serving girl, but if they suspected I truly felt anything for her, or that she affected me so profoundly, they might reconsider dismissing her quite so quickly.

I brushed the question away. "She's nothing to me. A fleeting distraction."

He scoffed. "She's the first one you've fed on in a hundred years. She's the opposite of nothing."

"Once I'm married, I'll be expected to dine with my new bride. I wasn't sure if I would lose control. This way, there will be no surprises."

"Maybe not for you, but what about the girl? What do you think your new bride will do to her once your contract is signed? Welcome her new husband's lover into the bedroom on your wedding night?"

I glared at him.

Aamon crossed his arms. "Chances are, that girl will be drained dry or suffer a terrible accident before the first week is up. If you truly feel nothing for her—which I absolutely doubt —then do nothing. Otherwise, pay her off and send her on her way before she gets hurt."

A black rage ignited inside of me like gunpower, and I slammed my hand on the desk. "I won't let that happen. Who am I if I cannot protect even *one* of my subjects?" I jumped to my feet and paced to the window, looking out over the cursed woods. "I spend half my time in that forest, hunting and killing monsters that would make my court piss itself, yet here in the castle? What am I?" Letting my gaze drift down to the iron spikes atop the walls, I muttered, "The court plots and schemes and does whatever they wish when they think my back is turned. Perhaps I need to hang a few more immortals from the battlements."

Aamon leaned back and folded his hands behind his head, unperturbed by my outburst or suggestion. "Once you've consolidated your power, you can stake whomever you wish. There are several heads I'll help you mount myself. Until then, you need to play the game."

"I cannot stand any of it. The negotiations. The promises and double-speak. My brother was the politician, not me."

"Which is why you need to send the girl away. She is a *distraction*. You need to be focused on your duty to this entire kingdom, not a simple farm girl."

But she wasn't so simple, was she?

"What was it the old woman said?" Aamon continued. "If you fall in love, the woman you choose will destroy everything your father built?"

"Don't be ridiculous. I haven't fallen in love with the serving girl."

I couldn't love anyone.

Aamon lifted his brow, unconvinced, then asked, "How better to destroy a dynasty than to distract you when you're supposed to be making the most momentous decision of your reign?"

My blood simmered, but his words weren't entirely lost on me. "This kingdom will not rise or fall on the choice of a queen."

"Your father didn't build a kingdom. He built an alliance with the Triad, and if they should decide that someone else better suits their purpose..."

They'd put a puppet in my stead. There would be no one to hold back the bloodthirsty houses or guard the border. It would become a nightmare, just as I'd warned Ella on our ride.

My fists clenched. "I won't leave the fate of the Bloodvale in another's hands."

"Then do your duty. The masquerade is two days away. There will be a dozen houses represented there. If you make a strategic match and bend a few others to your will, you will have enough influence beyond the Bloodvale to get rid of the sisters and their family. If that isn't motivation enough, I don't know what is."

I shoved aside my map of the Bloodvale and flipped open the hated folder on my desk. A stack of lifeless papers that held nothing for me. Dozens of women, and on the top, a short list of names. Six. I skimmed them but felt nothing.

There was only one woman I was interested in, and she could never be queen. As for the rest of the names, they were just a jumble of meaningless letters. But if I chose the wrong one, my people would pay the price, just as the old seer had warned.

The truth was, I needed to focus—and there was no way I could with Ella nearby. The scent of her blood and the sound of her heart made my desire almost unbearable. I could have controlled myself before I'd drunk from her, but now, all bets were off. And if Aamon was right: if my new bride tried to have Ella killed, chances were that I'd take the queen's head myself.

No. Ella wasn't just a distraction. She was a dangerous obsession. She'd be far safer away from me and the court and the Triad, especially after everything I'd told her. That knowledge was tantamount to a death sentence.

I'd been a fool before, but that ended now. I threw the list of names back in the folder and shut it. "I'll send Ella away tonight."

I had her wellbeing and that of the kingdom to consider, let alone my own sanity.

Aamon slapped me on my shoulder. "Good. It's better to break her heart now than to watch her pay the price."

48

———————

Ella

I went to see my sister as soon as I left the prince's study. I was shaking with frustration, and Belle always had a way of calming me. While Doctor LaMazi had received Cassius's orders, she only permitted me five minutes, and she watched me like a hawk the entire time.

Considering my previous stunt, I probably deserved it.

Unfortunately, with the doctor hovering over my shoulder, there wasn't much we could say. Belle had overcome her fever and weakness, and was now moving about on crutches, agitated by her confinement. Luckily, as she'd been under strict observation, she hadn't been questioned during the uproar.

Some of the weight pressing on me lifted at this news, but a small part of me was disappointed. If she'd been questioned, Horace would have silenced her like me, and she'd realize the mages were not on our side. As it was, everything was still a mystery to her.

When she saw my neck, the lines of her face grew taut with anger. "Who did this to you?"

"The prince. I was with him during all the commotion."

Her eyes widened, and she opened her mouth, then shut it as she realized the implications. "Oh, Ella. I'm so sorry."

"I'm not."

I leaned in to whisper in her ear, but Doctor LaMazi put a restraining hand on me. "Your sister has had enough excitement for one day and needs her rest. Visiting hours are over—for a week."

She and Lanny ushered me out before I could say another word.

Feeling no better, I headed to the stables and set to work grooming the horses, though they didn't need it. I was desperate to do anything to keep me busy and keep my mind off all that had happened.

I was brushing Tenebris's thick, silky hair, when he nickered softly. A cold shiver danced down my spine, and I glanced over my shoulder.

Cassius stood in the doorway, masked in shadows. "I've been looking for you."

The tone of his voice was off. Something was the matter.

"I visited the infirmary to check on Belle," I said, aiming for casual.

His body grew tense, and though I couldn't see his face in the shadows, I understood his silence: *You didn't tell her anything, did you?*

"I said nothing," I whispered.

I hadn't divulged what the prince had told me in the woods with Doctor LaMazi hanging on every word. Even if she hadn't been there, the information was too dangerous to speak inside the castle walls, and I didn't dare put my sister at any more risk than necessary. Beyond that, Cassius had revealed a part of himself that he kept hidden from the world. He'd trusted me with that, when he'd probably known he shouldn't. He should be my enemy, but after everything he'd done, didn't he deserve my discretion? How could I betray his trust?

The bitter truth sank in. Whatever my original intentions had been, I'd fallen under his spell.

"How is your sister?" he asked softly.

"She's healing well. The doctor even said that she might be able to leave next week if she's lucky."

"Good." His tone was clipped, and none of the tension in his broad frame had eased. He met my eyes with a gaze as cold as the winter sky. "Due to present circumstances, it's time for you to leave, too."

My breath stilled, and my mind went blank. The temperature in the stables had plummeted, and the soft breeze blowing through the door had grown frigid. "Leave?" I said, my voice tottering. "As in now, or next week?"

"Now. The sooner, the better, in fact." His voice was ice. Compassionless. Devoid of emotion, just as it'd been when we first met.

It was the voice of someone who would not be defied.

Panic seeped in like frost around the edge of a window. I couldn't leave the castle *now*, not with everything I'd just learned, not without some way to reveal the truth of who the Triad were and what they were doing. Not when he and I had grown so close.

"No," I said, forcing the storm of emotions from my voice. "Please, no."

He stepped into the golden lamplight, the sharpness of his expression matching his words. "The ball is nearly here. I need to focus on my new queen, not some farm girl intent on destroying me."

His words plunged deep like the tip of a pike. I set my jaw as I drew close, unable to fight the magnetic pull he had over me. "Is that all I am to you? A stupid farm girl?"

His eyes were dark and tired, his hair disheveled like he'd raked his fingers through it too many times. "You're not safe here," he said violently, releasing a fraction of his tightly coiled tension. "You need to go home to your manor and never look back."

But I couldn't leave. I needed to find a way to break the Triad's spell over the woods as well as their hold over him. If not that, I needed to at least find evidence that I could bring to my stepmother—a clue that could reveal the truth I couldn't speak.

"I know it isn't safe. I don't care. Just let me stay through the ball," I pressed, willing to beg on my knees if necessary. "Let me leave with Belle."

A muscle in his jaw clenched, all patience gone. "You're leaving now."

He grasped my arm and towed me toward the doorway. I dug my heels into the ground, trying to break free of his hold, but his mind was set, and I was no match for his strength.

"Cassius, please. This is a mistake."

"The only mistake was letting you get so close." He didn't look at me, just took me outside and gestured to the two waiting guards. The servants and soldiers in the courtyard all stopped what they were doing and stared.

My throat tightened as all my ambitions fell away. I wasn't just losing a chance to help the resistance. I was losing him.

I pulled free. "I'm not a mistake. We could fix—"

"We can fix nothing." He looked down at me then, a tempest in his beautiful gray eyes. "This was always bound to end badly. I was a fool to let it go on so long."

I saw it then, the flicker of sorrow on his face. Perhaps he didn't want this. Perhaps he was just following his duty to the throne, to the Triad, to the whole bloody kingdom, or even just keeping our secret safe, as he'd promised to do.

Or perhaps he just felt guilty, casting me away like I was a crust of moldy bread.

I pressed my palm to his chest, searching for any indication that his heart was breaking like mine was. "Don't lie to yourself. You and I—"

"There is no you and I." Cassius stepped back and let my hand slip away, a pitying expression cutting his face. "I'm the prince, and you were nothing but a distraction. You believed what you wanted to believe. A fairytale. That's all there ever was."

I heard the guards snicker and felt the judging eyes of the crowd searing my back. My chest ached with anger and shame, but I refused to give them the pleasure of seeing me crack. "That's not true, and you know it."

He opened his palm. "I need your token."

I needed to get word to Belle, and I couldn't leave without Pip. "I need to collect my belongings."

"They're being collected as we speak."

I could forgive him for sending me away, but not like this. I wasn't naïve. I knew it couldn't last. But he didn't have to publicly shame me at the castle gates. I pulled the bronze token from around my neck, and it glinted in the torchlight as I pressed it into his palm. "You're a bastard, you know that, right?"

"I never pretended to be otherwise," he said coldly, without an ounce of remorse—or any emotion—in his voice. Then he turned to the guards. "Escort her home. See to it that she makes it there unharmed."

The guards fell in beside me, an armed escort like I was a convict, not to be trusted. It was over. No more spying. No more negotiation. No more waiting to feel his lips trace over my skin.

It was done.

"Will you tell Belle that I'm gone?" I asked softly, though there was no way to disguise the hurt or humiliation in my voice.

The prince nodded, like he couldn't be bothered to waste his breath, then reached into his coat, pulled out a velvet pouch, and tossed it to me. "For your service to the Crown."

My service to the Crown. My skin heated with anger.

The weight of the pouch told me there were far more coins in there than I was owed. The gesture should have been kind, but instead felt like I was being paid off and carted away for my dirty deeds.

And they *had* been dirty. I'd fallen for the enemy, let him feed on me and seduce me. My stepmother—hell, everyone in the resistance—would be shocked if they knew what I'd done. I'd seen the horror on my own sister's face.

"Come now, miss," one of the guards said.

I didn't put up a fight. There was no point. The prince wanted me gone, and that was that. I would be gone, and he would marry his queen.

My heart splintered at the thought. Not just for myself, but for him. His brother's abdication had condemned him to spending an eternity with a woman he didn't love or desire. Like all of us in the Bloodvale, the prince was trapped.

I tore free of my escort's light grasp and spun to face Cassius one last time. He met my glare with an unyielding gaze.

"Marry Lady Marbury," I said earnestly. I'd read about her in his stack of papers.

The prince's stone expression wavered in surprise.

"She's your best option for queen. She's well-connected but not so much as to be a burden. She likes horses, and rumor has it she's kind to her servants. She'd be good for the kingdom, and she'd make a good match."

My information for the resistance might not change anything, but perhaps if Lady Marbury were queen, then our lives would be a little less grim.

The prince's brow furrowed, something unreadable there.

Regret? His lips parted as if to say something, but then he turned and walked away.

The prince's men marched me toward the gate, forcing me to endure the silent judgement from a handful of staff who'd gathered to watch from the steps.

Shame and frustration churned my gut. I hated leaving without saying goodbye to Cara. I was sure that there'd be a dozen new rumors about what had happened to me, and I didn't want her to think the worst. But even if I managed to slip away from the guards, I couldn't enter the castle without my token.

Worse was leaving Pip. How was I going to get him home?

I struggled, but the soldiers' grip on my arms tightened. "Don't make this any more difficult than it has to be, miss."

The wicked sisters emerged on Bianca's balcony. Even from a distance, I could discern the triumphant grin on Lorayna's face.

"Your time is up, it seems," Lorayna's voice echoed from above. "What a pity. I was looking forward to seeing what the new queen would do to you."

Bianca's beady eyes danced in delight. "Don't worry, we'll tell her all about you and where you live. I'm sure she'd love to visit your little pigsty. Maybe you could even give her a pointer on how to *whore* for the prince."

Anger burned through me, but I held my tongue and looked away, refusing to show them any emotion. One of these days, those two would get their just deserts.

I reached the gate, and Cara's voice carried across the courtyard. I turned to see her running toward me with my satchel and a bundle in her arms. "Ella! Wait!"

I slipped around the guards and met her halfway, wrapping her in a hug. "I'm so glad to see you."

Her warmth burned through the despair and betrayal weighing me down, and for a moment, my heart felt light again. Of course she'd come. She was a rock.

"I heard you were dismissed, and I came as fast as I could."

I released her and stepped back as guilt tugged at me. "You shouldn't be seen at my side. You don't need my reputation following you—I'm poison."

"I'll always be on your side." She handed me my satchel, and relief fell over me at the flash of white and brown fur that moved under the leather flap. *Pip.*

"Thank you," I whispered, unable to find the words to express my gratitude, and not daring to say anything more with the guards so near.

She pressed the bundle she was carrying into my arms. "This is your mother's dress. I wanted to make sure you didn't leave it behind."

Something twinged in my chest. I tried to speak, but instead, my eyes welled up.

Cara smiled knowingly. "I fixed it a while back, but when you became the prince's mistress...well, I fancied it up a bit as a surprise. I'm afraid it's not what you would wear around a manor house, though."

I pulled her into a hug again. "Thank you, Cara. You were always the best thing about this place. I'm going to miss you."

"Fates, the castle is going to be lonely without you."

"I hope you get to see the masquerade. You've worked so hard for it."

She smiled at me, eyes forlorn. "We seldom get what we want, do we?"

"That's life in the Bloodvale." I looked up at the prince's tower, swearing there had been someone standing in the window.

I threw my sack over my shoulder, made Cara promise to be safe, and let the soldiers march me out.

49

———————

I retreated to my tower the moment I left Ella's side. Despite my immortal speed, the guards were already marching her out the gate by the time I reached the balcony. My heart pulled against my chest, as if caught by a ship's anchor.

I watched, arms tightly crossed, until she left the winding royal carriageway and disappeared behind the houses of Upper Town. The ache in my chest should have eased, but it seemed to worsen by the second. A deep, relentless melancholy stretched over my thoughts like shadows consuming the day.

I slammed the doors to my balcony shut behind me as I stormed inside. What I felt and wanted didn't matter. She was gone, and it was for the best. I'd be free to do my duty, as much as I despised it, and she'd be safe from the Triad and the new queen.

I turned my attention to the wretched stack of papers I'd been avoiding since Aamon had delivered them. Shuffling through the loose sheets, I found my quarry.

Lady Marbury from House Darr in Turmoor. Beautiful and obedient, the lady hails from an old bloodline with relations across the

Alyrian Sea. No established political ties in the Bloodvale. Said to be of even temperament and kind to her people and staff. A keen rider and lover of horses.

"Well, fuck." I shook my head in disbelief as I skimmed the rest and set the sheet down.

The more I read, the more certain I was that Ella had to have read the dossier. The castle was awash with gossip about the potential suitors, but Marbury had neither visited nor formally written, so it was unlikely that her name was part of the rumor mill.

I fisted the papers on my desk as a consuming anger blossomed. I'd always suspected, hadn't I? The first day she'd come to work for me, I'd caught her under my desk. She hadn't been cleaning but rather snooping through my belongings. She'd read through Aamon's notes and put them back carefully. Almost perfectly, but not quite. The inkwell had been moved.

I'd known—I just hadn't wanted to believe it.

Like a fool playing with fire, I'd enabled her at every step. I'd given her free rein of my quarters. When she'd broken into the Triad's garden, I'd protected her instead of punishing her. And when she'd pressed me for information, I'd poured it out recklessly like a drunkard pouring himself a glass of wine.

And I'd do it all again.

I hurled my desk against the wall, the wood and plaster buckling and splintering under the force. It did little to lighten my dark mood.

I leaned against the archway leading to my balcony, staring out at the night. Ella was gone, and soon, she'd be a memory— one I'd probably cherish and curse for the rest of my days.

But the question remained: who was she working for?

Not the sisters. While Lorayna and Bianca's father, Lord Perrault, had been trying to unseat my brother for years, their torment of Ella had been real. They lacked subtlety, and they weren't clever enough to pull off a charade.

My eyes fell upon the crumpled sheet with the painting of Lady Marbury on it. She was the image of sweetness. Perhaps she'd recruited Ella to drive me toward her. Perhaps that was the reason for Ella's final tortuous words.

She'd be good for the kingdom, and she'd make a good match.

Could Marbury have been behind it all?

There was a knock on the door, and I wrenched it open, revealing Aamon, who looked satisfied. "Impressive, Cassius. I doubted you had the balls to get rid of her. Either you came to your senses or you actually feel something for that girl."

I didn't know what I felt. Anger. Frustration. Longing. It didn't matter.

"What's done is done." I shut the door as he stepped in.

"You're pacing like a madman. Did something happen?"

"The sisters or others might try to find a way to torment her now that she's beyond the castle walls. I want it known throughout the castle that if anything happens to Ella, there will be hell to pay—and it starts with both their heads."

He nodded, then glanced at my broken desk and papers scattered across the floor. "Should I be worried?"

I had the urge to tell him everything, but instead, I found myself protecting the little spy once again. "I'm fine. Just tired of being trapped."

If Aamon suspected she was a spy, he'd have her killed without question. Then I'd have to kill him. I didn't want any of that.

He toed the splintered remains of one of the desk's legs. "Oh. I thought it might be a ploy to request a new maid."

I ignored the smirking bastard and knelt to gather up the papers. "What do you know of Lady Marbury? Besides the scribble of notes you left."

Aamon's eyes brightened the way they usually did after he'd murdered somebody. "She'd be a fine match, Your Royal Highness."

I slapped the pile of papers down on a side table. "So I've been told. But what makes you so sure?"

He immediately began leafing through them. "Her family has ruled their lands for two centuries without serious bloodshed. They govern with a strong but fair hand. Lady Marbury is the eldest of the three daughters, and she has held a minor but not insignificant role in administering their titled lands. She has done so fairly, neither squeezing the peasants for taxes nor ignoring the needs of their house." He slipped Lady Marbury's portrait out of the stack. "She is also very pretty, is she not?"

Long raven hair. Emerald eyes. High cheeks and ruby lips. She was strikingly beautiful.

But she isn't Ella.

"Having a pretty face is the least of my concerns," I said.

Aamon raised his brows. "Unless that pretty face has lavender eyes and silver hair, right?"

I kept my expression placid. Ella was gone. I couldn't let myself think of her. That affair was over.

"Are you certain that Lady Marbury doesn't have any political motives for becoming Queen of the Bloodvale? No hidden alliances with any of the high lords?"

Aamon laughed when he realized I was serious. "I highly doubt it. Look, Cassius, I handpicked each of those suitors. You can rest assured that I've pored over every detail of their lives, including their social and political connections, as well as their deepest secrets. No one is going to be perfect, but Lady Marbury would be as close as you could get. I don't know why I didn't see it myself."

He hadn't, but Ella had. Somehow, her instincts for what I

needed had been better than those of my closest friend and advisor.

I withdrew the paper from the stack and read the profile again with bittersweet attention. I grew more and more certain as I read that Ella had not been ordered to whisper Marbury's name in my ear. It had been a parting gift—the one name that might bring peace to the kingdom, and perhaps a little peace for me: Lady Marbury.

I wished that the name had been Ella's.

The thought was sheer madness. She was a human and a spy, likely for the resistance, if it did exist. And yet, my heart called to her.

If you fall in love, the woman you choose will destroy everything your father built. And if she ever takes the throne, she will make your people pay the price of their thirst.

My jaw tightened. Had this been what the old woman meant?

Perhaps.

The weight of duty felt heavy on my shoulders as I looked at the paper again. No matter my desires, my kingdom came first. Lady Marbury was a woman who wasn't part of the court or a murderous lunatic. She shared an interest in horses and could make a strong ally. And most importantly, she was a woman I could never love because she'd always remind me of the one I might have had, had my life been my own.

That was what my duty demanded. I picked up Marbury's creased profile and handed it to Aamon with a nod. "I think Lady Marbury may be the one."

50

Ella

Two hours after I was unceremoniously evicted from the castle, I pushed through the front door of the manor, my feet tired from the walk and my heart aching. The guards who'd escorted me home waited until I was inside, then departed— taking with them the knowledge of where I lived.

A deep unease fell over me as I looked back toward the spires of the castle in the far distance. Would the sisters come to exact their revenge? Or perhaps the new queen might stop by to eliminate her rival for the prince's attention.

I quickly locked the door and bolted it—not that that would do anything against the strength of an immortal—then dropped my bundle of things on the table. "We're home, Pip."

The little rat peeped his head out, then let out a sharp squeak and disappeared as my stepmother swept around the corner in her nightgown. "Ella! I didn't think you could visit. This is excellent timing."

I shook my head, suddenly feeling too weary for the conversation that I knew was about to unfold. "I'm not visiting. They ended my service."

He'd ended it. Maybe it had been to protect me, or maybe it was to protect his own interests. It didn't matter—he'd tossed me out like rubbish.

My stepmother froze, her expression drawn tight. "What? Why?"

Because I'd learned too much. Because the new queen would kill me. Because I'd pressed my luck one too many times.

I angled my neck so she could see the evidence of that fateful morning. The one that had changed me, for better or worse. "At first, the prince was interested. Then he wasn't."

It wasn't far from the truth.

The blood drained from her face. "You let him feed off you? Do you have any sense in that thick skull of yours?"

I hesitated. I wanted to say, *He was protecting me.* But then she would ask me why, and I wouldn't be able to speak. It would only create more questions and confusion and suspicion.

"I was poking around and needed the cover," I said at last. I'd find a way to explain the truth once I had my head straight.

"Foolish girl," she said, her face pinched. "Your job wasn't to *poke around*. It was to keep a low profile and wait for instructions."

Too tired for this, my patience evaporated. "I didn't hear you complain about any of the information I sent. I was doing everything I could."

"And now you're fired. I should have known better than to trust you with this."

Her words stung like a slap across the face. After all I'd done, after everything I'd endured and risked, this was the reception I got?

But a part of me feared she was right.

She turned and headed into her study, and I followed. "You're acting like this is my fault," I said.

She spun and gripped my shoulders, her fingers digging

painfully into my skin. "Of course it's your fault, or you wouldn't have been relieved of your position. We needed you *inside* the castle, now more than ever."

"Why?"

"Because we need to know what is happening at that ball! And now our eyes and ears inside the castle went and got herself expelled because she never learned her place."

Hadn't Cassius said as much as well? Hadn't everyone said that?

Bile burned the back of my throat. "What do you know about it? Since I walked through the castle gates, I've been beaten, hounded, humiliated, chased, and fed from. I kept my head down and endured it all to help *you* and the resistance."

"Wonderful," she said bitterly as she dropped down into the chair behind her desk. "How does that help us now?"

No matter what she believed, I was still worth something. I straightened my spine and stared her down, refusing to let her make me feel small. "You want to know what's going on with the ball? I can tell you everything. I know the staff assignments, the schedule, the menu, what the decorations are going to be, who's invited, who's been snubbed—anything you want to know."

She closed her eyes and rubbed her brow. "Maybe there's something we can salvage."

My nails dug into my palms. She was no different than she'd always been. My best was never good enough.

She pulled a stack of parchment from her desk and set a pen and inkpot on top of it. "I need you to write down everything you know about the preparations for the ball, the staff duties, and who's attending. And I need it by tomorrow morning."

I took the writing materials, and stared down at them, exhausted. "Why so soon?"

She scowled. "Because the ball is in two nights, so next week will be too late."

"I meant why is the ball so impor—"

"Because I asked for it, that's why! Your job isn't to question every single request. It's to follow orders. Do you understand?"

I held my tongue, reminding myself that this wasn't for her, but for the resistance. "I'll get right on it."

She nodded. "I also want maps of the castle as far as you know it. Every floor you've visited, with the servants' passages marked and labeled."

"By tomorrow morning as well?"

Her mouth sharpened into a razor-thin line. "Yes, before it slips out of your scatter-brained head."

Ignoring her words, I shoved down my exhaustion and hunger and the lingering disappointment of the day, and took a seat at the dining table, resolved. I'd prove my value and show her that it hadn't been a mistake to send me. I'd fill her with more information about the castle than she could dream of.

I worked tirelessly into the night, writing and drawing by dim candlelight, until my neck ached and my hand cramped. The work was, in many ways, a mercy. With everything that had happened, I doubted that I could have slept. Pouring out my knowledge kept me from thinking about *him*, even if I couldn't shake the sharp ache in my chest that felt like it might swallow me whole.

Eventually, Pip scampered up the curtain and dropped down on the table. *You should eat.*

My hand froze, mid-stroke above the paper, and I lifted my gaze to the rat. "What did you say?"

I'm starving, and your stomach has been rumbling for hours. Loudly.

I opened my mouth and then closed it. I could hear Pip's voice beyond the castle walls. Was our connection strengthening? Wonder threaded through me. "How is this possible? I couldn't hear you before."

Pip scratched his ear. *Maybe your magic's getting stronger? Let's steal some food while the evil woman is asleep.*

He bounded off the table and scurried down the hall. Shaking my head, I rose, my body protesting as I followed him into the larder.

I retrieved a little ale and hard cheese, which delighted Pip and improved my condition greatly. By my second mug of ale, Pip was asleep on the settee, and my pen was flowing across the page as I relived each step and detail of the castle.

After completing my notes about the kitchens, I pulled a blank sheet of paper from the pile and paused, my pen hovering above it. As much as my stepmother wanted it, everything I'd written didn't truly matter. What I desperately needed to tell her about was the mages and the truth of what they were: immortal traitors and the dark power behind the throne.

I had to try.

There are three mages in the castle, I thought as I dipped the pen and pressed it to the paper. The muscles in my hand clenched, and as I tried to force the words out, the nib scratched a jagged line across the paper.

Gritting my teeth, I carved the words on the parchment letter by letter. A jolt ran up my arm, and my bicep seized. I jerked back, then stared down at the paper, frozen.

Seven jagged letters stared back at me. *SILENCE.*

A shiver ran down my spine. "Holy Fates."

Whatever knowledge I had was going to die with me. Maybe there was a way around the mages' curse, but it wasn't going to come to me tonight.

I crumpled up the parchment and threw it in the fireplace, then pulled a new sheet and rubbed my aching hand. I might not be able to reveal the truth about the mages, but there was still plenty to do, and I set to work in feverish defiance of all I could not say.

Sometime later, my body was rolled to the side with a shove. "What are you still doing here?"

I sat up with a jerk, shielding my eyes from the light streaming through the windows. The shape of my stepmother formed in front of me. "You're a mess," she decreed.

Pip was nowhere to be seen, and my notes were strewn across the table. Crisp, neat handwriting covered the first sheets I'd filled, but it became progressively looser, and the final sheets were jammed with cramped and barely legible text.

I swallowed. It looked like the work of a madwoman.

My stepmother eyed the half-finished mug of ale with a scowl. "You were drinking?"

"Yes, I was." I scooped up the papers in order, along with my maps, and shoved them into her hands. I was too tired to put up with her snide remarks and incessant orders. "This is everything you asked for. I'm going to bed."

"What about breakfast?"

I paused by the stairs. "You've survived without me this long. I think you can manage."

Ignoring her protests, I dragged myself up the stairs and collapsed into the warm comfort of my own bed, delighting in the luxurious folds of the blankets.

For better or worse, I was free of the sisters and the prince. I wasn't going to be anyone's servant anymore.

51

Ella

Mercifully, my stepmother didn't disturb me, and I slept through the day and next night, waking at dawn at the crow of a rooster. I pulled the pillow over my head. *I miss the castle bells.*

And I missed him.

I went through the morning routines in a daze. My old chores felt like an echo from a dream. I even mucked the stables, which Tarran seemed to have neglected. This time, I didn't ask the birds for help. The few stalls in our barn were nothing compared to the work I'd grown used to, and I'd wanted to sweat and lose myself in the work. I wanted to forget that tonight was the ball and that soon Cassius would select his new bride. Perhaps in another month, there'd be a wedding, and he'd be lost to me forever.

I threw the pitchfork against the wall. Who was I kidding? I'd already lost him. Hell, I'd never truly had him, had I?

Except for a moment.

Stepping outside, I closed my eyes and let my head fall back. "Could I have had at least one more night like that?"

I didn't want to spend my life as another man's mistress, yet I couldn't deny the fact that his presence had made me feel bold and powerful and alive in a way I'd never felt before—different even than when I'd used my magic.

The noon sunlight warmed my face and skin, and I imagined it was his touch, his kisses brushing along my neck. I traced my fingers over the fading scars there and the memories they carried.

"Ella!"

My eyes shot open as my stepmother burst out onto the porch. "Why in the name of the gods are you standing about and staring at the sky? I've been calling your name. We have visitors."

Could it be him? My heart leapt at the ridiculous thought.

I splashed some water on my face and hurried up the stairs and through the back door as my stepmother shook her head. The butcher and seamstress were waiting in my stepmother's study, my notes and plans scattered about on the desk and side table, and I tried not to reveal my disappointment.

"We've been looking over your work," the seamstress said. "It's incredibly detailed."

The butcher nodded in agreement. "We're very impressed. It was a damn shame you were let go."

I stood in the doorway, knotting my hands. "Not my intention. I got unlucky."

The seamstress raised her eyebrows. "We heard that...well, that you had *dealings* with the prince."

My cheeks heated. "I took care of his horses and his chambers." I touched the marks on my neck. "And of course, there was also this."

The butcher's face reddened with anger, and the seamstress shook her head sympathetically. "I'm so sorry you were subjected to that. I pray that one day, no one will ever have to pay their blood tithe again."

What could I say to that? That I'd do it again in a heartbeat? That I couldn't stop thinking about his kiss and his bite and the delicious ways that he'd touched me? They'd label me a traitor for sure. Instead, I shifted and said, "I knew the risks going in."

My stepmother crossed her arms and leaned back against the wall. "I'm sure Ella doesn't appreciate reliving the humiliation of the past, and neither do I, so let's get on with this."

The butcher stood. "Our plan was to have you inside the castle tonight, but considering the wealth of information you've discovered, it may be lucky we have you here." He pulled the maps out. "It will be very helpful if you could clarify some details for us."

A sick feeling threaded through me. "What plan?" I asked.

"We're breaking in. The masquerade ball is a perfect cover, as there will be many unfamiliar servants and people. Everyone will be too busy to notice a few extras."

My mind began to race. Breaking in would be insanely risky. "They make all the humans in the castle carry tokens, some kind of magical pass. You can't get through the gates without them."

"We know, which is why we've already procured four for our team."

The hair on my neck stood as a deep unease spread down my spine. "How?"

He shrugged. "Their owners were detained early this morning. With any luck, they won't be missed until this is all over."

The resistance had abducted some of the castle's servants? My thoughts flew to Cara and Katherine.

"Until *what* is all over?" I pressed.

A grin broke across the butcher's face. "We're going to give the bloodsuckers a night to remember."

"You're going to attack?" Fear constricted my throat, and my voice came out strained. "With only four people?"

The butcher's grin broadened.

"This is none of your business," my stepmother interrupted. "You're to answer questions, not to ask them."

I ignored her, shaking my head. "If you think you can attack the castle from within, you're *insane*. There will be more immortals present than ever."

"More witnesses," he said with the supreme confidence of the uninformed. "We'll show them that humans will not bow forever—a lesson that won't be forgotten."

"We appreciate your expertise and instinct for caution," the seamstress added. "But trust me, we have thought this through long and hard. It's been months in the planning. We just need you to confirm the movements of the guards and the layout of the servants' passages. You've already provided us with more information than we'd thought we'd have."

My breath quickened. Whatever they were planning was suicide, and everyone the plan touched would bear the cost. The servants they'd taken the tokens from were as good as dead, as was anyone who entered the castle under pretext. "Even if your men can get in, they won't be able to smuggle weapons through the gates. Everyone who isn't an immortal is searched, including the staff."

The butcher patted his pocket confidently. "There are plenty of weapons in the armory, and you gave us the key."

The key I retrieved from the garden.

I shook my head as anxiety made my skin itch. "No matter how many men you send or how well armed they are, they won't last a second in there. *Trust me.* The immortals are five times as strong as any human and unimaginably fast. The moment blood is spilled, they will tear your men apart. It's suicide."

"Of course it is," the seamstress said, her face suddenly pinched hard in anger. "Our operatives have chosen to give their lives to make a difference rather than spend the rest of their days bowing and scraping beneath the heels of tyrants. It's the choice we all made when we swore on the book."

My thoughts flashed to my interrogation with Horace. "But it's not just them," I said. "They have ways of making you speak. If even one of your operatives is caught, they'll expose you and the entire resistance. Is that really worth killing a handful of immortals—if you even get that lucky?"

"Not a handful of immortals," the butcher said, his eyes glinting with a malicious light. "Just one—and his death will shake this kingdom to its core."

The room swayed as everything came into sickening focus. "You're going to kill the prince," I whispered, unable to repress my horror.

The butcher rocked back on his heals, clearly proud of himself. "We're sending a message to the immortals that will never be forgotten: *rule at your own peril.*"

My stomach tumbled as the truth sank in. *I'd* made this possible. All the information I'd delivered. Every task my stepmother had given me, from sending the key to making maps. It had all been leading to the assassination of the prince—the man I'd come to know and care for. The man who'd shown me kindness like no other immortal had. He wasn't the villain they thought he was—that I'd once assumed he was.

My stepmother's face flushed with concern. "We shouldn't be telling her this. She doesn't need to know the details."

I looked from one to the other as panic churned through me. "Don't try this."

The butcher ignored me, turning to my stepmother. "I thought she was a soldier, Lucille. Is she going to be a problem?"

"No, she won't. This conversation is over. We have enough to go on."

My stepmother grabbed my arm, aiming to tow me out the room, but I pulled away. "Killing the prince isn't the solution. There are so many worse than him—immortals who actually deserve to die. It won't solve anything."

My stepmother spun on me, but the butcher held out his hand to forestall her and approached me slowly, suspicion burning in his eyes. "Why, exactly, are you so adamant about this?"

I knew what he was thinking, but I couldn't back down. Things would have been simple if I could have told them about the Triad or their curse on the woods and the power they wielded over the immortals—but I couldn't because of Horace's spell. I had to find another way to change their minds, and fast. Otherwise, they'd find out themselves the hard way.

"The prince isn't the problem. I've seen how the court works, and he'll only be replaced by someone worse—someone far worse. Killing him will tear this kingdom apart, and all of us with it."

The butcher's expression darkened. "Will it? Or do you have another stake in this? Have you turned on us, Ella?"

"Of course not! I'm trying to stop you from making a foolish mistake. There's a power—"

My voice strangled as Horace's spell wrapped around my throat, an invisible vise cutting off the words I so desperately needed to speak. The harder I fought against it, the tighter it drew, and I bent double, choking and gasping.

Panic flashed across my stepmother's face. "What's the matter with you?"

"Magic," I gritted through my teeth, though even that word scorched my throat.

"She's been compelled to silence," the butcher said, his voice ringing with awe. "The prince must have made her his thrall after he took her blood, and he's forbidden her to speak."

I shook my head, but the seamstress rose, her face pale. "That's why she doesn't want us to kill him."

I wrenched myself free of my stepmother's grasp and backed away from them. I couldn't tell them about the Triad, but I could tell the truth about him. "I'm not the prince's thrall, but I've seen the truth behind the throne. He's a good man at his core, and he knows that what the immortals are doing is wrong—"

"Listen to her!" the butcher growled as he glared at my step-mother. "What more proof do you need than that? She's a thrall, and she's probably told him all about us and our plans."

Her expression melted into dread. "Is it true? Did you reveal us to the prince?"

My back bumped against the wall. "No! I'm not his thrall, and I'd never betray the resistance. I didn't even know about the assassination until you told me just now!"

Her judging gaze pinned me in place, boring into me as if it could peel away the layers of my skin, one by one. I raised my chin, defying her to doubt my word.

After three eternal breaths, her lips turned down. "She speaks the truth. I can always tell when she's lying."

The butcher put his hand on my stepmother's shoulder. "Lying or not, it doesn't matter. We can't trust her anymore. She's clearly under his influence."

My neck flushed with anger. "How does *telling the truth* not matter?"

"Because you've shown us where your true allegiance lies: with the immortals and with *him*. You've betrayed your vows to *us*." The butcher's expression took on an ominous cast. Suddenly, he was no longer the friendly man from the market. He was a man willing to die for his cause—and to kill for it.

He stepped forward, but before I could bolt, my stepmother

moved between us, her arms wide like a mother goose protecting her young. "You'll not harm her. She may be a foolish girl and blind, but she's served us well. Better than any operative ever has."

He loomed over her. "Whatever service she's provided, she's no longer on our side. She'll betray us if we give her the chance."

My stepmother didn't waver. "Then we'll lock her away until this is over."

He released a bitter laugh. "Once this is over, the chances are that we'll all be dead—you, me, and her. It's better—"

"No," my stepmother growled with a ferocity I'd never witnessed from her.

The butcher's jaw set. "Fine. We'll lock her up."

The hell they would.

I threw myself past my stepmother's outstretched arms and rushed toward the kitchen door. The brute shoved her out of the way and was on top of me in a second. We crashed through the door and into the side of the kitchen counter. Pain burst through my side.

"Let go of her!" my stepmother shouted as she rushed in.

I clawed at the butcher, but he just grunted and pulled one of my hands behind my back. "She ran! She was going to warn them!"

With a shout, I raked my heel down his shin, and when he tried to cover my mouth with his hand, I bit down hard. Blood trickled across my lips, and he bellowed in rage, but his grip only tightened.

Then the seamstress was there, restraining my arms and helping him pin me against the wall. "Help us, Lucille! Your daughter is out of control!"

"Stop fighting, Ella!" my stepmother shouted. "I won't let them hurt you."

It wasn't me I was worried about. I twisted to face her,

restrained by their hands. "If you kill the prince, they'll find out the truth. They'll massacre everyone in the resistance! Maybe everyone in the village! They'll kill Belle!"

My stepmother's eyes flickered with a moment of doubt, and then... then it was gone. Her features turned to iron, burying the sadness I'd seen there. "That's the risk—but we aren't doing this for ourselves. We're doing it for the generations to come. We can give them hope—that the immortals can be defeated. All of us might die, but the resistance will rise again, stronger than ever."

"No," I said, spitting a bit of the butcher's blood. "It will be stamped out forever."

"That's enough!" The seamstress shoved a wadded kitchen rag in my mouth. "Help us, Lucille!"

I roared at my stepmother through the gag, and tears broke from her eyes. "I'm sorry, Ella. This is for the best."

My heart shattered. I kicked and struggled, but I couldn't hold all three of them off. They bound my wrists, then hauled me out the back door, fighting like a wild horse.

"Gently!" my stepmother implored as they manhandled me down the cellar stairs—as if that would do anything to make up for her betrayal.

The butcher shoved me hard, and I stumbled forward and toppled onto the dusty cellar floor. My skull cracked against the cobbles, and my shoulder strained as I rolled to the side, my vision swimming.

My stepmother was a blurred silhouette against the light streaming down the stairs. "I'm sorry, Ella, but we can't have you endangering yourself or this operation."

"Let's go." The butcher wiped his hands on his trousers. "We've got more important things to deal with than a blood traitor."

"She's not," my stepmother snapped. "She's afraid and lost her way."

He clomped up the stairs with the seamstress. "Whatever you need to tell yourself, Lucille. This is on you."

My stomach twisted. Did he really think that I was a traitor to my kind? I was trying to save them and Belle and everything they'd fought for. They were going to throw it all away, and along with it, perhaps kill the one person with the power to change things.

I bit down on the gag as my heart hardened with a certainty I'd never known. The prince *was* different than all the others. He would help if he could. If he were free of the Triad. If he could learn to see our worth.

He'd seen mine.

My stepmother lingered. I summoned every drop of resentment and bitterness I could, concentrating it in my glare. She was the only traitor here.

She walked downstairs and knelt beside me. "This is the best shot we've had in decades. Killing an immortal or two would do nothing, but killing the prince will show everyone that the kingdom itself can be defeated. That's why it must be during the ball—there will be too many witnesses to cover it up. We'll claim credit for the resistance immediately after. It will give the people hope like they've never had."

And then the immortals would kill us all.

"Belle!" I screamed in outrage through the gag. "*Belle!*"

She stiffened, and I knew she could understand the muffled word. She wiped her eyes. "We all swore on the book to give our lives for the resistance. I doubt any of us are going to survive the night, but what we've done will live on. It will be passed down to the next generation, and our people will rise again."

I kicked and squirmed, trying to loosen the gag.

There'd be no next generation. We'd relive the massacre on the ceiling of the great hall, but this time, there would be no end. Not until every soul in the village was dead.

My stepmother retreated to the cellar stairs and glanced back at me. "This is just the beginning. You'll see."

Then she left. The thick doors shut, blocking out the light. A lock clicked, and then there was the sound of something heavy being dragged across the wood.

I screamed into the gag.

It wasn't the beginning of anything. It would be the end.

52

———————

Ella

I flopped back against the floor, breathing hard in the pitch-black darkness.

The resistance thought they were going to be martyrs for their people, but they'd doomed us all. Cassius and Aamon were the hand of civilization holding back the bloodthirsty monsters that stalked their court—monsters like Lorayna and Bianca, who cared nothing for our kind. If the prince died and their family came to power, they'd probably kill half the humans in the city out of revenge. Then they'd go slaving in the outer world and find new cattle to fill the empty, blood-splattered homes.

I began working my arms back and forth, but rather than loosen the ropes binding my hands, it only made my wrists raw. I groaned in frustration as doubt hammered away at me. I should have told them about my magic and Siggy. I should have shown them.

But what good was talking to birds and mice and sprouting flowers? Would it have changed anything? They were set on revenge and could see nothing else. They would've locked me up either way.

I eased my head back against the cold stone and tried to gain control of my ragged breathing, stifled by the gag. Suddenly, something scampered up my arm, and I jerked upright with a muffled scream. Pip gave an outraged squeak, and relief flooded through me.

"Sorry," I mumbled through the rag.

He chittered and hopped down. *Hang on.*

I closed my eyes against the darkness as my heart swelled. I wasn't on my own. I still had my rat and my magic. The rage and despair that had strangled me were torn away by hope.

A minute later, a scuttling chorus of squeaks rose in the darkness, and a stampede of tiny little clawed feet scampered over me.

Hold still! Pip commanded with an irritated squeak, and I braced myself against the assault of ticklish claws and whiskers brushing my skin. Warm little bodies clustered on my neck and arms, followed by the sound of gnawing. Tiny claws and teeth pulled the wadded gag free from my mouth, and I drew in a gasping breath of the dank cellar air. "Thank you. Thank you all!"

Hold still, we're not finished! Pip chittered at me.

Finally, the ropes parted, and I pulled my numb and tingling arms free. A chorus of distressed squeaks rose from around me as little feet ran across my clothes. *Don't squish us!*

"I won't." Moving very slowly, I carefully stood and moved to the side of the cellar. I felt around until I found the old, shuttered window and opened it quietly. It was too narrow to squeeze through, but it allowed a little light in.

My saviors huddled in an expectant cluster in the beam of light—four mice and two brawny rats. And Pip.

I knelt beside them and brushed my fingers over the top of Pip's fuzzy head. "My heroes."

Some of us are girls! one of the burly rats squeaked.

"My heroes *and heroines*," I whispered, then went over to the sealed cupboard and pulled out a small wheel of cheese, which I laid before the wide-eyed rodents. "I cannot thank you enough."

They tore greedily at the rind before tucking into the golden cheese below. *This is a good start*, the burly female rat squeaked, her mouth full.

I shook my head with wonder. It wasn't just Pip. I could understand them all. I *was* getting stronger, or at least more attuned. But how could I use it to get out? Little rats could bite through rope, but unlocking the cellar door was another thing.

Was there a chance Tarran would come by to pick up his wages? Could I get word to him?

I hurried to the far corner of the cellar beneath the kitchen, then closed my eyes and strained my ears. Muffled voices reverberated through the floorboards. I couldn't make out what they were saying, but I could place the voices—the butcher, the seamstress, my stepmother, and someone else. They were hurried and agitated.

The arrival of additional conspirators was a bad sign. If I tried to break out now, they'd hear me and probably silence me forever, over my stepmother's objections or not. Clearly, they considered all our lives forfeit after tonight. They wanted to be martyrs.

I crouched in the corner, monitoring the voices and watching the rodents gnawing happily away. It was time for patience and a plan. I had to warn the prince—but I had to do so without getting my stepmother or anyone else killed in the blowback.

More problematically, I had to get into the castle, and he'd taken my token.

Could I get Cara a note? I had no doubt she'd lend me her token to get in, but if I were discovered, it would be the end for her. I couldn't do that to my friend.

I froze as footsteps headed in my direction and rang on the kitchen floorboards above me. "I'll saddle Clorinda and join you outside," my stepmother said.

My stomach leapt. They were leaving.

Footsteps descended the stairs and crunched on the dirt and gravel of the barnyard, moving away. I stood motionless, waiting for more noise from above.

When I was certain they'd all left the house, I peeked through the narrow slit of the window. My stepmother emerged from the barn, leading a saddled Clorinda. She mounted up, and with a sharp jab of her heels, they were off and out of sight.

I breathed a heavy sigh of relief and leaned back against the wall. Hopefully, all the conspirators had gone with my stepmother, because if they hadn't—well, they were about to get a show.

"Pip," I said, letting in a little more light from the window, "I need you to get Thisbe and the goats. Tell them I'm trapped in here and that I need them to break me out."

Thisbe? Pip squeaked apprehensively.

I scooped him up and held him to the windowsill. "I know she hates me, but tell her my stepmother is in danger and might be killed if I don't do something about it."

I'll see what I can do, he chittered anxiously, then scampered across the barnyard, with his crew not far behind.

At least my stepmother had taken Clorinda. That mare was right wicked.

I waited for what felt like an eternity, but suddenly, there was a crash from the barn, and Thisbe emerged into her pen. The irascible mare took a run, then vaulted the fence in an arcing leap and landed in the middle of the barnyard.

"Thisbe!" I shouted from the cellar.

She walked over slowly, looking around warily.

"Lucille is in trouble. I need to save her and Belle, but I'm trapped in here."

The mare dipped her head to the low window and huffed. *Is this a trick?*

"No," I insisted with all the earnestness I could muster. "When have I ever lied to you? I know we don't see eye to eye, but this is important."

The goats joined her side, looking around curiously. She sniffed at them, then turned back to me. *What do we need to do?*

I couldn't keep the triumphant grin from my face. "Kick the cellar door in."

She nickered. *Stand back.*

The animals moved out of sight, and then the cellar shuddered as three sets of hooves slammed into the door, over and over, sending dust swirling in the air. The pounding blows reverberated through the small cellar like a hammer in a smithy, and I covered my ears. Finally, splinters sprayed through the room as one of the doors ripped off its hinges and crashed down the stairs.

I scrambled out into the bright sunlight, then looked back at the manor house and exhaled slowly. No one had come out. I was in the clear.

I scratched the goats on the head, then wrapped my arms around Thisbe's neck. "Thank you all."

She shook her head and pulled free. *We don't do this. We aren't friends. This is about saving Lucille.*

I looked up at the sun. It was probably three o'clock, which meant I had four hours of daylight left before sunset and the beginning of the ball. I turned back to the mare and crossed my arms. "You're not going to like this, but if you're serious about saving Lucille, I'm going to need a ride."

She narrowed her eyes and pulled her lips back. *Why am I not surprised?*

53

An hour later, I plunged down the forest path on Thisbe's back, my saddlebag stuffed with Pip and the things I might need for the break-in. A grudging accomplice, the mare tried to *accidently* rub me off on the passing branches every chance she got.

"Work with me, here," I pleaded as I gently pulled on the reins. "We're almost there."

You're terrible in the saddle. The horse snorted. *Absolutely graceless.*

Like a spoiled child, she'd adopted my stepmother's worst tendencies.

As hard as it was to remember, there was good in my stepmother. The sting of her betrayal lingered, but I knew that she was trying to restore hope to our people, even if it cost her life.

But it wouldn't just be her life. It would be scores of lives, if not the life of every human in the city.

And Cassius's life.

The trees thinned, and Siggy's ramshackle cottage came into sight. Thisbe slowed as we rode into the clearing. Siggy was sitting on the front porch at a small table with two chairs and two tall glasses of what looked like ale.

I dismounted and tucked the reins. Typically, I would have tied Thisbe off or hobbled her, but I was a *whisperer*, for Fates' sake. I'd convinced the prince's warhorse to lose a race with a glance. I could deal with Thisbe. "Stay here," I said.

She huffed. *You're not my owner.*

"Just—" I sighed. "For Lucille's sake, please stay. I won't be long."

I headed up the steps and onto the porch before the horse could respond.

Siggy beamed at me and raised her beer glass, a far more pleasant greeting than being shot at. "Ella, what a surprise! I thought you'd be busy at the ball tonight."

The corner of my mouth quirked up in a half smile. "That's what I came to talk to you about—but seeing as you've set out a couple of drinks, it seems you might have been expecting someone. Me, perchance?"

Her smile morphed into a foxlike grin. "Expectations and reality are two very different things, at least for most people."

"But not you?"

She shrugged and motioned to the chair beside the table. "You never know when someone important will stop by, so it's best to be ready. Now sit and have a drink, and tell me what's on your mind."

I glanced wistfully at the welcoming chair. "I'm sorry, but I can't stay long. I've got some trouble and not a lot of time to fix it."

She stood and put the glass of beer in my hand. "What's the problem?"

The problem was I couldn't tell anyone about the damned Triad, and I had no idea how to convince them I wasn't crazy without that information. I took a long swig of the ale. Sweet and malty and surprisingly cold, it reminded me of how parched I was.

"I got let go from the castle."

Siggy snorted. "Fools. The immortals wouldn't know a good thing if it hit them in the mouth."

"And I need to get back inside tonight."

She raised her bushy brows. "Why?"

I hesitated for a second. "I can't tell you half of it, so I'm going to need you to trust me."

"Of course. I'll help however I can—just tell me what you're able."

Sadness tore through me at her warmth and instant acceptance. Shouldn't my stepmother have offered those? Then again, I hadn't ever asked her to trust me, had I? At least, not outright, not in those words. I'd grown so used to fighting over the years, I'd assumed she never would. Now, I'd never know. That bridge was burned.

I took another long drink and set the glass down. "There's a plot to kill the prince, and I need to save him."

Siggy sighed and shook her head. "That's princes for you, always in need of saving. You'd think they'd show a little initiative every once in a while and save themselves."

Her expression danced with light, and I narrowed my eyes. "Why does every conversation with you feel like it's part of some kind of inside joke, which I am neither part of nor meant to be?"

"That's because it is, honey." She drained her glass and wiped her mouth. "You need to learn to laugh when the world gives you the chance, or else things get a little dark."

I crossed my arms. "Things are going to be *very* dark if I can't stop the assassins. The immortals will retaliate, and I think the court will burn the town down."

"Likely," she mused. "Is this your stepmother's work?"

I gaped. I *knew* she had the gift of sight, but her uncanny intuition startled me every time.

"Don't look so surprised, honey dear. My job is to know things—and I know that protecting your village isn't the only reason you want to save him."

My cheeks flushed. "I think he could change things if he became king."

"The way you're trying to?"

"Yes. I believe he's more than what he seems. He's different than the rest."

Siggy nodded thoughtfully. "Well, that makes two of us. His father was a shit, and his brother a rake, but he's a far better man than either. Do you know what he's doing out here, riding the forests every day?"

I shrugged. "Escaping the palace?"

"Hunting."

"For his brother."

Siggy shook her head and looked out toward the woods. "For all kinds of monsters. Anything that slips across the border that could threaten this kingdom and the people in it—and he kills them. It's the only reason I can live this far out, or that the Bloodvale knows any kind of peace."

"That's what he was doing the day he met me—hunting a feral immortal."

Siggy released a dismissive grunt. "There's far worse things out there."

I shivered, thinking of the beast I'd faced in the woods, with its razor-sharp teeth and savage tusks and horns. How would a man, even an immortal, fight a monster like that and live?

"He never mentioned it," I said, trying to think back on all the times I'd saddled his horse. "He'd just ride off into the woods alone. Said he was going hunting, but never what *for*."

She waved her hand dismissively. "Some men hunt for glory

or for the thrill of the kill and then brag about it later. He doesn't care about any of that. All he cares about is protecting this kingdom." Siggy looked at me pointedly. "You two have that in common."

There was something heavy in her gaze, as if she were placing an unseen burden on my shoulders. Perhaps it was the burden of finding a way to make peace and have someone on the throne who thought of us as people instead of cattle.

The ceilings of the castle recorded the path of war. Somehow, we had to find a path toward peace.

"I think he would make a good king if his hands were free," I said.

If the Triad were gone and his bloodthirsty court were on a leash.

"Then what do you need to do?"

I released a heavy breath. "Well, I have to break into the castle and stop the assassins. If I can't do that, I have to warn the prince."

Siggy's expression darkened. "You know this could be a one-way trip, don't you?"

I straightened my back and met her eyes. "People I love could die. I'll take the risk."

She crossed her arms and glanced at Thisbe. "Then what's your plan to get in? Charge in on your mighty mare like a knight out of legend?"

Grimacing, I replied, "I was hoping you might have an idea."

She chuckled. "No, you weren't. Otherwise, you wouldn't have brought that big saddle pack with you. You've got something up your sleeve, and you want me to tell you which of your near-suicidal ideas is going to work."

I narrowed my eyes. "No one plays cards with you, do they?"

"Not if they've played me before. Let's hear your plan."

54

Ella

My plan?

My plan was going to get me killed.

"I thought about sending a raven to warn the prince, but then I wouldn't be able to control his reaction, and I can't risk exposing the resistance."

"So, what do you propose?"

I met her single eye apprehensively. "I disguise myself as one of the immortals and try to go through the main gate. It's a masquerade, so I might not be recognized, but I don't have an invitation or a token to get in, and even if I did, no one is going to buy that I'm a high lady if I show up without a carriage and groomsmen. But I don't have either of those things—which is why I'm here."

The old woman gulped down the final dregs of her beer and leaned forward. "Let's concentrate on the positive. What *do* you have?"

I glanced back to where Thisbe stood. "I have a horse and a dress."

My mother's dress hadn't ever been a ball gown, but Cara had said she'd fancied it up, so I hoped it was a start.

Siggy motioned encouragingly to me. "The dress is always the hardest part. Let's see it."

I retrieved the bundle Cara had given me from Thisbe's saddlebag and laid it on the table, loosening the ties around it. The cloth fell away, revealing the rich blue of my mother's dress. My eyes widened as I lifted it. A waterfall of blue and silver unfolded before me, and I sucked in a sharp breath. I recognized the original blue satin fabric, but it had otherwise been transformed. Delicate silver embroidery decorated the sweeping bodice and hips, forming a patchwork of flowers and vines. Additional layers of silk had been added to the skirt to make it fuller.

"Wherever did you come by that?" Siggy asked, her voice tinged with wonder.

I stared, astonished. "It was my mother's, but my friend Cara —" I looked up at Siggy. "Maybe she has magic, too."

"An artist, to say the least." Siggy nodded. "Let's see how it looks, though I might suggest scrubbing a bit before you put it on."

I glanced down at myself. My hair was tangled from the ride, I was sweaty, and my clothes were filthy from lying on the dirty cellar floor and mucking the stables. I definitely stank.

She pointed to the back of the cottage. "There's a stream with a deep pool at the edge of the clearing where I like to bathe. Let's go get you cleaned up."

Siggy's stream was little more than meltwater. Each second I scrubbed sent numbing cold shooting through me.

"Gods, that was brutal." I staggered out of the pool and grabbed my towel from the tree. My teeth chattered as I pulled it around me, too cold to even dry off.

"Nothing like a brisk bath to give a woman the power to face the day," Siggy chirped from her spot on a fallen log, where she was busy whittling away at something. "I take one every morning."

Madwoman.

I dried off and shimmied into the silky black chemise the prince had given me, as there was no way I was putting my old one back on. It felt like it would be an insult to Cara's dress.

"You could always just go like that," Siggy mused as we headed back to her porch. "I'm sure no one would stop you."

"Not funny."

She helped me into the dress, pulling the laces a little tighter than necessary. "Need to breathe," I wheezed.

"You'll be fine." She gave another tug, then tidied the last of the folds and fetched a mirror.

My heart stilled as I inspected myself. The delicate lace of the sleeves hung softly below my shoulders, inviting others to gaze at the sweeping expanse of my neckline and chest. The gown hugged me perfectly, emphasizing each curve, while the soft layers of the skirt draped around my legs in a blue cascade. I felt it wasn't just the dress that had been transformed, but me as well. Turning sideways, I admired the way the satin laces of the bodice peeked out from my loose silver curls.

"It's incredible," I said softly, marveling at the way the silver embroidery caught the light.

"You can say that again." Siggy put her hands on her hips. "Now all you need is a mask—a big one."

"Do you know how to make one?" I asked.

"Don't look to me to solve all your problems. You're a whisperer. Just ask the forest for help." She shot me with a loaded look. "The forest will always be there when you need it."

I raised my eyebrows doubtfully.

She shooed me toward the edge of the porch. "Go on. You might as well try."

I grimaced and turned to the woods. A few songbirds flitted down to the lower branches and looked at me almost expectantly.

This was awkward.

"Hey, there, uh...woods in general. I'm going to a ball, and I need a mask—something that will obscure my face but not my mouth or eyes. Can you help me?"

There was a moment of agitated chittering, and then the birds burst into the air and flew away.

I turned back to Siggy. "Okay, maybe we try something else."

A moment later, one of the little redstarts flitted back down and laid a long, supple twig on the porch. Then another arrived, and another. I stepped back as dozens of birds overtook the porch, squabbling and harassing each other. I could barely see what they were doing. More twigs arrived, along with thin vines, sprigs of grass, and flowers in every shade of blue.

The excited chatter rose to deafening levels, and then, with a burst of feathers, the flock disappeared. Where they had been lay a mask woven from the forest itself.

I picked it up in wonder, turning the delicate thing over in my hands. They'd intertwined twigs and vines to create a base, lined it with soft moss, and threaded the stems of flowers throughout, creating a mask that was as full and vibrant as a bouquet.

"It's amazing," I whispered.

Siggy held up the mirror. "Try it on."

I secured the loop of vines around the back of my head, then pulled the mask over my face and stared at my reflection. The various shades of blue and gray complemented my eyes, and the feathers that had been neatly tucked into the sides swept up my cheeks and over my ears. A train of woven leaves draped down the back, concealing my hair.

My heart fluttered with excitement and awe. "I look like a goddess of the forest."

Siggy smiled at me. "You are, my dear."

I stepped back to admire myself at a distance. The tapestry of flowers and moss that shielded my face accentuated the rich blue fabric and silver embroidery of the dress, like the two had been crafted together.

A bittersweet smile broke across my lips. It was the most beautiful outfit I could have ever dreamed of. It also might be the last one I ever wore.

It's one hell of a way to go out.

"I'm really doing this, aren't I?" I whispered.

"You're going to stun them!" Siggy put the mirror down and held up the pair of fangs she'd whittled. "Open wide. It's time for the pièce de résistance."

"The...what?"

She dabbed a little wax on each of the fake fangs, and when I opened my mouth, she wiggled them over my upper incisors. "If they fall out, just squish them back into place."

I gingerly touched them with my tongue. "Are these wood?"

She shrugged. "Sure."

"They're not...are they..."

They'd definitely been part of some creature.

"You'll also need this." She stepped behind me and held up a silver necklace with a sapphire-blue pendant. I lifted my hair, and she secured it around my neck. "This is your ticket into the castle."

A token. I touched the cool gemstone. "Does it have magic?"

"Yes. It'll get you inside." Siggy lifted the soft folds of my gown and clucked at my bare feet. "I almost forgot—and before you say it, no, those riding boots you brought won't work. Maybe if this were a Western, but... no. They just won't do."

Western? Where was she from?

"I have the flats that I wore in the castle in my bag," I said, the new fangs garbling my words slightly.

I adjusted the left one a smidge as Siggy shook her head. "Honey, I'm just an old woman who lives in the woods, and even I know flats are wrong. You need *real* shoes."

She grabbed the pair of dirty beer glasses from the table and emptied them, then dunked them in the rain barrel. She handed them to me. "Put these on your feet."

I screwed up my face apprehensively. Was she kidding?

"Just do it."

With a shake of my head, I set the glasses on the porch, then wedged my feet into them one by one. "This is ridiculous. I can't possibly walk in these."

Siggy nodded. "Well, it's certainly stretching the limits of how much I *should* be meddling, but this is an *extreme* case. A dress is nothing without the proper pair of shoes. I think the Fates will let me get away with this one." She grabbed a fly swatter off the table and pointed it at my feet. "Huzzah!"

My skin tingled as the air stirred, and then a stream of crackling blue light leapt from the swatter and into the pair of glasses. They glowed and grew warm as the glass wavered and molded over my toes. It was almost like the glass was melting, though not as hot. I stared in astonishment as glass flowed into shape around my feet, then pooled beneath my heels, lifting them higher and higher. The blue light faded, and the glass cooled, leaving my feet enclosed in a pair of shimmering heels.

"Fates," I whispered.

The old woman waved her hand to quiet me. "Hush, now, and don't use their name so much. It draws their attention, and this is our little secret."

I nodded without comprehension, still too stunned by my new pair of glass shoes. "They're beautiful," I said, my voice hushed and reverent. I took a step and wobbled. "A little rough to walk in."

"Shoes like those can practically walk themselves," Siggy said, then looked at the sky. "And it's about five, so you've got a little while to practice."

I took a few more steps, trying to balance. "Do you think they'll let me just ride in on Thisbe? What about a carriage or groomsmen?"

Siggy glanced at her garden, then shook her head. "No, that's preposterous. I'm afraid we're just going to have to steal them instead."

"Steal them? From whom?"

She grinned in delight. "From someone who stands no chance of winning the prince's heart."

55

———————

Ella

A couple of hours later, I found myself crouched beside Siggy, lurking at the edge of the woods like a highwayman—that was, if highwaymen wore blue ball gowns. Dusk had settled over the sky. While the spreading darkness would hide me among the bushes, the setting sun also meant time was running out.

I peered through a branch at the deserted road. "Do you really think this will work?"

"I hope so," Siggy whispered. "You should be more confident, though. It was your idea, after all."

"This was *your* idea."

"I might have been the inspiration, but only a whisperer could come up with a hairbrained scheme like this. I might have tried the damsel in distress card, myself, but to each their own."

"Then why didn't you propose that an hour ago?"

"Not my plan, not my story," she muttered.

My palms grew sweaty. As if sensing my rising panic, she reached over and patted me on the back. "There, there, it will all go fine. Just trust yourself and your magic. I'm only teasing."

Zero extra confidence—that's how much her pep talk gave

me. I knew she could see bits of the future, but where her gift ended and sheer audacity began, I wasn't so sure.

"Probability of success?" I asked as I fiddled with my left fang for the third time.

She shrugged. "I don't like math, but we'll find out soon enough."

The sound of hooves and wheels split the silence. My heartbeat quickened, and a minute later, a team of horses came into view, followed by a black coach decorated with the crest of a house I didn't recognize—a heron swallowing a snake that was wrapped around its neck.

A high lady headed to the ball to win the prince's hand.

Not if I can help it.

My limbs tingled with anticipation, but my stomach was swimming. Siggy and I had practiced our plan twice, but our success would depend as much on luck as on magic, so I didn't dare get my hopes up.

"Whoa!" the driver called, and the coach and horses slowed, coming to a stop in front of a large tree that had fallen across the road.

"Arms out, and keep your wits about you, boys!" the coachman shouted to the footmen riding on the back, then pulled a flintlock pistol out and scanned the woods.

They weren't entirely fools, it seemed.

The footmen hopped off the back of the coach, their pistols drawn as well.

"What's the problem?" a woman shouted from inside. I could barely make her out through the glass windows of the carriage.

"There's a tree down across the road, my lady," the coachman said. "It could be highwaymen."

The glass window opened, and a woman poked her head out. Her hair was bound up in golden ringlets, and her features were pinched with anger. "We're running late as it is. If it's highwaymen, let them come, and I'll tear them limb from limb myself!"

She cursed, ducking back inside.

The coachman, not entirely placated, swept the tree line again, then holstered his pistol and leapt down. "You heard Lady de Montague. Let's get this tree out of the way."

The three footmen braced and strained against the massive trunk, but it didn't budge. Siggy nodded next to me, but still, I didn't make my move.

The men grunted and cursed, and finally, the far door of the carriage opened. "What is taking so long, you bloody fools? I have a date with the *godsdamned prince*, and I'm going to be late!"

My heart hammered against my chest. I just needed her to step away from the carriage...

The coachman stood and wiped his brow. "I'm sorry, my lady, but the tree is too large. There's no chance the three of us can push it alone."

And there it was—the only solution if she wanted to get to the ball.

The high lady cursed as she climbed out. "Do I have to do everything myself? If I ruin my dress, I'll drain you dry and leave your corpses for your family to find."

Fates, was she related to Lorayna?

The immortal woman strode over with furious purpose, her elaborate golden gown swishing around her legs. The men stepped back as she pressed her hands against the massive trunk, and with an unladylike grunt, shoved. The tree shuddered and moved a fraction of an inch.

"Don't just stand there! Help me, you useless dolts!"

The three dim humans hurried to her side, and soon, all four were straining against the massive tree.

My stomach lurched as the trunk moved again. *Showtime.*

Siggy squeezed my hand. "Good luck, honey."

"Thank you for everything," I whispered, and squeezed it back, then slung my bag over my shoulder and addressed the bushes. "Let me through as quietly as you can."

They parted before me, and hitching up my gown, I carefully and silently picked my way toward the carriage, barefoot.

The horses looked in my direction and nickered as I emerged from the brush at the side of the road. One started to back away nervously, so I raised my hand and whispered, "Please don't be frightened. I desperately need your help...and a ride."

The gelding, clearly the lead animal, shook his mane. *Why?*

Ahead, the heavy tree shifted another foot. All four were still bent to their labors, and hopefully wouldn't hear me.

I crept quietly to the gelding's side and brushed my hand over his brown coat. "Because I need to save a lot of people from people like *her*."

He tossed his head. *Get in.*

"Thanks," I said, then stepped lightly up onto the runners of the coach. "Once the tree is clear, make a break for it. I assume you don't need a coachman to find the way to the castle."

Of course not. The horse nickered. *They're just for decoration.*

The woman had left the carriage door unlocked, so I quietly opened it and eased myself into the seat. Thankfully, the noblewoman hadn't been travelling with a handmaid.

I set down my satchel and quietly locked both doors, then I peeked out the far window. The woman and her three servants were still struggling with the massive tree, but they'd actually moved it much further than I'd expected—about a quarter of the way clear. She had to be impressively strong, even for an immortal. That meant she'd be fast, too. Could she outrun a horse?

Not in those shoes.

I took three deep breaths, then stuck my head out of the window. "Clear the trunk!"

The two massive oaks at the side of the road shook themselves to life and bent down like ancient, weathered giants, shoving the fallen tree out of the way with their thick branches. The trunk tumbled across the road in a shower of leaves and bark.

The high lady screamed and stumbled to the far side of the road as her henchmen dropped to the ground beside her.

"Go now!" I shouted to the horses, then waved to Siggy, still hiding in the woods.

The horses reared in fright but gathered their wits quickly and charged forward. The coach lurched, and we were rolling toward the gap in the road.

I pulled the curtain covering the rear window aside and stared out the back. The woman in the gold dress was gaping at me in astonishment as her men picked themselves off the ground. Her face contorted with rage, and then she kicked off her shoes and began to run.

Oh, no. Even in her giant gown, she was impossibly fast.

"As quickly as you can!" I called to the horses, and the coach shook as they accelerated. A cloud of dust and gravel sprayed up behind us, but it wasn't enough. The immortal in the golden dress gained on us with every stride.

I flung myself to the window and called out to the trees, "Block her path!"

The forest stirred like grass in the wind, then began to swipe and bat at my pursuer with their lithe limbs. Birds rose up from the darkness and dove at her, screeching and cawing.

The immortal screamed as the living forest closed in, driving her to the ground. Soon, she was far behind, and my heart swelled with thanks.

I slumped back against the seat. "I can't believe that worked."

Pip scampered out of my bag. *Neither can I. Does she have any food in here?*

Her footmen had probably been both escorts *and* snacks, but I looked around anyway. The woman had left her handbag. With a quick glance over my shoulder to make sure she'd been left completely in the dust, I popped it open. The bag held a letter, some coins, a jeweled folding hand mirror, and a number of small bottles. "Sorry, no cheese, but there should be some in my pack."

I ate that while we were waiting. Pip began investigating things on his own.

I unfolded the letter and drew my eyes across the elegant writing—an invitation to the ball, and at the bottom, the prince's signature.

My mouth turned sour.

"Apparently, I'll be playing the part of Lady Eva de Montague tonight," I said, and tucked the letter back into the little golden purse. "Hopefully, no one has any idea what she looks like."

I rummaged through the bottles. A few seemed to be some kind of alcoholic tincture or medicine, and I set those aside. There was a rather large spray bottle of perfume, which I tested. Citrus and rose. "Not unpleasant," I mused.

The rest of the items were all cosmetics, a selection of paints and powders to whiten the complexion and redden the lips. I dabbed a touch of bright rouge on my lips, doubtful I had the skill to apply the rest in a rumbling carriage. Rouge was illegal for our kind to wear. Bloodred lips were the mark of an immortal, after all.

I rubbed my lips together as I'd seen some of the noble-women do and held the mirror up to examine my work. My lips were a luscious cherry red, almost the shade of fresh blood.

I pursed them, loving the color.

The coach lurched, and a livid face appeared in the mirror.

I screamed and spun around. The lady in the golden dress was glaring at me through the back window of the carriage.

"I'm going to wear your entrails as a stole, you treacherous wench!" She flung herself around the side of the coach. The door jerked, and when it didn't open, she punched her hand through the glass, sending shards raining down across the seat.

I scrambled to the opposite side as she dove at me, flailing with her bloody arms.

Holy fates, was she going to crawl through the broken window?

I turned and kicked at her wildly. My bare foot swept her arm out of the way, and the next kick connected sharply with her jaw.

She froze in surprise, and then her face contorted into a vicious leer. "You're a human. A filthy, weak *human!*"

The immortal lunged partway through the window and seized my ankle. My body jerked forward, and she grinned. "I'm going to feast on your flesh, then let the prince lick your blood from my lips. What a fine gift you will be!"

"He's already had me," I snarled, then drove my free heel into her nose.

Her grip on my leg released, but she laughed as blood streamed from her face. "Now this is what I call a party!"

She pulled back and grabbed for the door lock.

I seized the perfume and spritzed it in her eyes. Twice.

She screamed and let go of the handle, clawing at her face. "You little bitch!"

I threw myself across the seat and slammed my shoulder into her. She yelped as she slipped backward and barely caught the windowsill with her hand. Blood welled up where the broken glass cut her fingers.

Panic and anger threaded through me as I smashed the large

perfume bottle down on her knuckles again and again. Her grip slipped, and she disappeared into the darkness. The coach rocked to the side as it rolled over something, and the immortal let out an agonized howl.

I crouched at the window with the bloody perfume bottle raised, my chest heaving, but she didn't return.

Are you okay? Pip asked, appearing on the seat.

My heart was pounding as fast as the hooves outside. "Yeah. I think so."

Is she?

I glanced out the back window, then sat back down and swallowed bile. "Nope."

Will she come after us?

"Not if she needs her legs to run," I said weakly, then looked at the little rat. "Immortals heal, right? Like, after *really* bad stuff?"

He looked at me blankly.

My stomach turned. She was probably a bloodthirsty tyrant, judging from the few minutes I'd known her, but I still felt bad. I'd just planned to borrow her coach. It had been a nice, bloodless plan, one in which nobody got hurt.

Something told me there was going to be a lot more blood before the night finished.

I looked around the ruined interior of the coach. "How am I going to clean this up?"

I'll help, Pip said as he ripped a little stuffing from the bottom of the seat.

Miraculously, my dress was almost unscathed. No rips or tears from the glass, just a light splattering of blood on my arms, which I suspected was reasonably common for immortals. Dinner could get messy, so it probably added a touch of authenticity.

I grabbed my satchel from the corner and breathed a sigh of

relief. My glass shoes and delicately packed mask hadn't been crushed.

Using spit and tufts of stuffing, I began wiping the blood and glass off the seat, and by the time the castle came into view, Pip and I had the interior of the coach as tidy as it could get—minus one window.

As the brightly lit spires of the castle loomed overhead, a shudder raced down my spine. The mages, the sisters, and the assassins were all inside, along with the prince and scores of other bloodsuckers, all vying for his heart.

"Stop at the gate," I told the horses as I tucked my feet into my glass heels. I quickly tied my hair in a loose bun and pulled on the delicate mask of flowers. With the veil of woven leaves hanging over my hair, hopefully no one would notice the telltale glints of silver.

I checked myself in the mirror one last time and practiced baring my fake fangs. "I'm a bloodthirsty immortal. I'll eat you for breakfast, you weak little human."

There was a bit of rouge stuck to the pesky left tooth, and I rubbed it off with a curse as the carriage rolled to a stop. The tricky part was going to be explaining where my footmen were, not to mention the driver.

A pair of heavily armed guards approached, and my chest tightened. This was it. No going back.

Time to crash the ball.

56

―――――――

Ella

The pair of sentries appeared at the open window of my carriage, their spears raised in salute.

I lifted my chin and straightened my back. If I were going to be Lady de Montague, I had to be above them. They were not men but prey, and barely worth acknowledging. Cattle standing by the edge of a pen.

I looked down with a high lady's disdain. "Let me through. I'm here for the ball."

Of course I was.

The captain's eyes flicked to the empty driver's seat and then back to me. "Where is your coachman?"

I bared my fangs. "Does it look like I need a coachman? The horses do as I say, and so will *you*. Now let me through, as I believe I'm late."

The captain swallowed and glanced toward the rear of the carriage, clearly unsettled. "But you have no footmen, either. It's highly irregular."

I tilted my head in the way that Bianca always did when she

was close to losing her shit. "Thank you for enquiring, but I already ate and didn't want to haul the *dead* weight along."

He paled. "Yes, mistress—"

"You may call me 'High Lady Eva de Montague' or 'my lady.' Anything else, and I will take out your throat."

He flinched but remained stoic. "Do you have your invitation?"

I pulled it from the little golden purse and flicked it out to him. "Here. As you can see, it's signed by my future husband. I suggest you don't keep either of us waiting any longer."

He checked it, then handed it back with a bow. "I'm sorry for the delay, my lady. Do you need us to guide your coach—"

"Take me to the front steps of the castle, and look sharp about it!" I shouted to the horses.

Assuming I was speaking to him, the sentry moved to comply, but the coach lurched ahead as the team began high-stepping through the courtyard. I glanced back with a wicked smile at the guards as they gaped, watching the carriage circle around on its own to the grand entrance.

Pip scurried over and placed his paw on my leg. *Please be careful.*

With a lump in my throat, I gave him a scratch, then handed him the warning I'd prepared for Belle. "*You* be careful, Pip. And for Fates' sake, watch out for cats—I couldn't bear it if anything happened to you."

He took the note in his little claws. *Don't worry, the cats and I have an understanding here. I'm a whisperer's chief companion, so I'm off the menu. I think they'd let me ride them straight to the infirmary if I asked.*

I raised my brows in surprise. I'd never considered that our association might give him an elevated status among other animals. "You're more than my chief companion, Pip. You're my best friend."

As the coach pulled to a stop, I tightened my fists and relaxed them, over and over, trying to get my nerves under control. "Please look after Belle."

Don't worry. I'll make sure your sister gets out safely. The door rattled, and he scampered to his hiding spot behind the pillow. He gave me a last parting look. *You're going to amaze them all.*

Then he disappeared.

I unlocked the door and sat up proudly as a footman in formal livery swung it wide. He bowed and proffered his hand with a graceful sweep of his arm. "Good evening, my lady. Welcome to the Bloodvale."

A shiver of fear steeled my spine. I tucked my dress and took the footman's hand, then carefully eased out the door.

My breath caught.

In the two short days I'd been gone, the castle had been transformed. An array of twinkling lights hung high above the courtyard like a cloud of fireflies, while strings of jasmine flowers had been draped over the walls, perfuming the air with a heady sweetness and hiding the bloodstains that tarnished the stones.

My momentary euphoria died at the memory of Matthew's lifeless body hanging in the servants' garden—a chilling reminder of the danger I was walking into.

A crimson carpet spilled over the front steps of the castle, mercifully sparing my glass heels from the cobblestones. I climbed the stairs, and the doormen opened the grand doors.

Fates, I hope Siggy's enchanted necklace works.

I said a silent prayer and crossed the threshold, the gem around my neck warming against the magic that guarded the castle. The clock had officially started. *One hour to warn the prince and get out of here.*

"Welcome to Castle Silverthorn," said a man dressed in a formal black uniform embroidered with crimson roses. He bowed deep, then opened a large book and looked up expectantly. "May I have your name, my lady?"

"High Lady Eva de Montague." I made my tone sharp, hoping it disguised my fear.

Fake it until you make it, Belle would say.

He ran his index finger down a page of the guestbook and tapped it twice, frowning. "I'm afraid your name is not on the list."

My heart drummed under my ribs.

Giving my best impression of Bianca, I stepped forward and snarled, hoping the tips of my false fangs showed. "You must be mistaken."

The host paled, a sheen of sweat lining his brow when he met my gaze. "You're right, my lady. I am mistaken. I do see your name here under M, not D." He extended his arm toward the entry hall. "Please enjoy your evening."

After a cursory search for weapons, an usher guided me down the hall toward the symphony of music ahead.

Like the courtyard, the servants had transformed the interior of the castle. Bursting bouquets of white and red roses perched on every available surface, garlands and streamers hung from the walls, and gently sparkling fountains of light illuminated the ceiling.

I slowed as I approached the grand ballroom. Its towering doors were shut, with two footmen standing guard at either side —attendants from the royal wing. I touched the train of leaves dangling from my mask, praying it concealed my telltale silver hair.

The usher whispered something to one of the footmen, who swung the doors open so that I could step through.

"High Lady Eva de Montague," bellowed the man at my side.

My stomach knotted, and I wanted to duck under a table.

Would the courtiers who knew the real Eva recognize me as an impostor?

Fates, don't let anyone speak to me.

I forced myself to keep walking, and my fears faded as, apart from a few whispers, no one took much notice. Moments later, I was swept up by the crowd and left adrift in wonder. For all that I had seen, nothing had prepared me for the grand ballroom and its arching glass ceiling. Lit by floating spiral chandeliers that moved to the music, it was a magical wonderland filled with dancing colors and a symphony of sounds.

Hundreds of immortals filled the opulent space, their murmurs and whispers overshadowed by the soft melody of an orchestra I couldn't spot through the crowd. The males wore extravagantly embroidered frock coats and waistcoats in rich hues. The women were even more mesmerizing, their sumptuous gowns of silk and lace whispering across the marble floors as they glided like ethereal creatures of the night. All wore elaborate masks adorned with filigree, feathers, and silk. Some even resembled strange mythic creatures with horns.

There were more immortals than I'd ever imagined in one place. Most were already drunk on wine, but all still thirsted for blood and power.

I straightened my back. Lady Eva de Montague would not be frightened or awed. She would be here for one purpose and one purpose alone: the prince.

So was I.

Placing one glass slipper ahead of the other, I strode confidently through the crowd, searching. Were my stepmother's assassins here already? Between the crush of mingling bodies and whirling couples on the dance floor, it was nearly impossible to see. I needed a higher vantage point.

I beelined toward the second-level balconies but halted as icy fingers snaked down my wrist.

"You smell divine," the male said, his accent thick and unrecognizable.

I froze. What would Lady de Montague say to this feral beast of a man?

I pulled my arm free and glared at him. "Of course I smell divine. I *am* divine."

I was certain he was going to see right past my charade, but instead, he bowed. "A goddess of nature, to be sure," he murmured. "For all the masquerades I have attended, I've never seen a mask as striking as yours. If your face is as beautiful, then you will be the belle of the ball."

I made to move around him, but he stepped in front of me, his honey eyes glittering behind a bejeweled purple mask. "Please, my lady, grace me with your name so that I might call on you for a dance."

I didn't want to spend another second cornered by the vermin, but then again, I might need an excuse to get on the dance floor. "Lady de Montague." I gave him my most beguiling smile. "But I will be dancing with the prince tonight, and *only* the prince."

"We'll see about that, my beautiful goddess," he said, a veiled threat in his tone. He took my hand and pressed a soft kiss to it. His tongue traced against my skin, and my stomach curdled.

I yanked my fingers free and spun away. Hurrying to the stairs before I was accosted again, I passed a dim alcove. An immortal in an emerald mask braced a woman against the wall, her skirts bunched up and his arm clutching her bare thigh.

Grabbing my own skirt, I hurried up the swooping stairs, my heart drumming in my ears. A dozen balconies jutted over the ballroom, most filled with guests who were either watching the spectacle below or engaged in lewd acts. My thoughts turned to the orgy painted on the ceilings of the great hall. Was that where the ball was headed? A feast of flesh and blood?

I skirted past a group of women, their dark eyes tracking me behind frozen porcelain masks. Their murmurs filtered toward me through the din. "Who is she?"

I watched them for a breath too long, and one bared her fangs at me. I was surrounded by vicious, blood-drinking monsters...and they were growing suspicious. I was in way over my head.

Chest growing tighter by the minute, I rushed toward the nearest open balcony and braced myself against the stone railing, trying to calm my breathing.

Get a hold of yourself. There's too much at stake.

I fought down my moment of panic and scanned the room. The crystal chandeliers cast an effervescent glow over the shifting bodies below. From my current vantage, I had a clear view of the whole ballroom, save for the adjoining hidden alcoves and hallways. The music had ebbed, and guests loitered around the edges of the dance floor.

Dozens of servants moved seamlessly through the room, offering refreshments or flirting with the guests. My stepmother's assassins had to be among them somewhere. The problem was, I didn't recognize any of them, and none looked suspicious. They were all part of a clockwork machine, creating order among the chaotic throng of immortals.

I glanced at the silver clock on the far wall. *Thirty-eight minutes left.*

If I couldn't identify the assassins, then I'd have to find Cassius and warn him.

I caught sight of a large, gilded balcony at the far end of the room. A curtain of semi-opaque black lace concealed the occupants, but I felt eyes behind the darkness, watching us all relentlessly. My skin prickled.

The Triad.

I shuddered. No question. Now that I was concentrating, I

could feel the sick vibrations of their power shrouding the room, an unseen specter that belied the laugher and music below.

I started to turn away, but a sudden hush fell over the room. The crowd below the veiled balcony parted as a couple strode forward. My mouth went dry.

Cassius.

He wore a tailored midnight suit that somehow both concealed and accentuated his tall, broad frame and chiseled physique. His matching velvet frock coat was adorned with roses embroidered with a silver thread that almost glowed under the soft light. It was the mask, however, that captured his true mystique. Crafted of black lacquered metal, it was decorated with silver filagree that matched his coat, the edges sweeping upward along his cheekbones, ending in delicate wing-like shapes.

A prince of darkness. Soon to be king.

A tight, burning sensation spread through me as he guided a woman toward the dance floor. Her raven hair matched his, and though her crimson gown and silver mask were subdued in comparison, she was beautiful. I couldn't see her face, but I knew she was Lady Marbury.

Had he actually considered my advice?

The elegant pair stepped onto the empty dance floor, and a dagger twisted in my chest. I should have been flattered that he'd listened, but instead, my heart ached.

A lone violinist began a slow, romantic melody. The couple took their positions, the prince extending his hand toward her, palm up in a formal invitation to dance. When she accepted, he brushed his lips over her knuckles, and then, eyes locked on hers, he guided her to the center of the floor, one hand taking her waist as he led her in a series of slow, sweeping steps that matched the violin's dark, mournful melody. The tempo of the music picked up, joined by a cello and bass, and their steps grew quicker and more elaborate, their bodies moving in effortless harmony as if they'd practiced the steps a hundred times over.

They were perfect together. Breathtaking, even.

My illusions crashed in, windows shattered by a storm. Although I'd dreamt of his lips and hands and kiss, I'd never been any match for the prince, nor worthy of him. Compared to the statuesque beauty in his arms, I was nothing.

His words from the other day rose in my mind: *I need to focus on my new queen, not some farm girl intent on destroying me.*

The truth was, he'd been right. He deserved a woman like Marbury—elegant, graceful, and perfect.

But while I was just a farm girl, I could do one thing that the flawless lady could not: save his life, and perhaps the human half of his kingdom.

The music swelled, and other couples joined the dance, their movements also executed with effortless grace as they spun and dipped. More immortals left their conversations and pressed in around the dance floor, a masked throng of riotous color.

My gaze landed on a single waiter carrying an empty tray, making his way against the flow. He moved without the graceful clockwork of the other staff and was pushing toward the prince.

My stomach fell with the weight of certainty. The assassins were here, and they were hunting. I checked the time again. Only thirty minutes remained.

57

———————

Cassius

The song reached its crescendo, and I did my part, whisking Lady Marbury across the dance floor. Our movements mirrored the intensity and passion of the music, yet I felt neither.

I should've been captivated by the woman looking up at me. By every assessment, she was perfect. Beautiful. Poised. Well-mannered. A clever tongue to match her clever mind. I should be enraptured, hanging on her every word and subtle gesture, but I could barely focus.

My thoughts and gaze wandered through the room as we danced. Countless others watched as I led her in a series of turns—the men intrigued, the women waiting their turn to sink their claws into me.

The song ended and Lady Marbury looked coyly up at me. "You are quite the dancer, my prince. I'm afraid I came ill prepared."

Her voice was breathless and inviting, and I had no doubt she'd practiced the line a dozen times. Her fingers traced provocatively along my arm, not with desire but rather precision. She fluttered her eyes, trying to lure me in. She was a hunter, just like all the others.

Like me, and I respected it.

I pressed a kiss to her hand, my actions equally rehearsed. "Nonsense. You are perfect."

And it was true. There was no flaw in her. The flaw was in me and had always been.

The orchestra launched into another song, and the queue of noblewomen pushed forward like hungry vultures.

As if raising a shield against them, I lifted her hand in invitation. "I know I shouldn't be fixated on one woman so early in the night, but you're irresistible. Might I have another dance?"

Her expression flickered in triumph. "Of course, Your Highness. I would be delighted."

Couples swarmed the floor around us, their ridiculous outfits and masks doing little to conceal their true identities. Arrogant, conniving lords and ladies scrabbling to dip their golden-clad fingers into the royal coffers. Everyone's attention was on us—prospective queens, Aamon, the Triad.

Gazing down into Marbury's pleasant emerald eyes as we danced, I knew I would never—could never—love her. By the old woman's warning, that made her the perfect choice for a queen.

The beautiful lady spoke, and I responded, though our conversation was mechanical. I hardly registered the words. I doted on her, playing the part of a besotted idiot, little more than a marionette.

And then, something in the air changed.

The hair on my neck rose, and my senses flared. The woman in my arms became crystal clear, my attention sharp and drilled into the moment.

Something's wrong.

I scanned the room, no longer pretending to partake in conversation, my attention rapt.

There was a flash of color, and then it was gone. I dipped Marbury as I followed the dance, searching the crowd as we spun away. What was it?

Then I saw her—a woman drifting behind the sea of faces, drawing my attention like a siren luring a sailor. She was draped in a blue gown that skimmed her soft curves, the silver embroidery along her bodice shimmering in the candlelight. Her mask was unlike any I'd ever seen, a whimsical masterpiece of flowers and foliage that added to her devasting allure.

She was magnetic, pulling me like a burning beacon, and an impossible inkling gripped me. The wheeling dance brought us within a few yards of her, and the woman glanced my way. For a second, I saw a flash of lavender eyes and caught her tantalizing scent, hidden beneath perfume. Realization snapped through me like lightning, searing me from the inside out.

Then she was gone, lost among the churn as the dance carried on.

It couldn't be. Not her. Not here.

Marbury gasped as I spun her away, now moving against the current of the dance. I had to see. I had to be certain. I searched wildly, ignoring Marbury's protestations.

Even with the mask, I knew it was Ella. I could sense her with every inch of my flesh. The sweet scent of her skin, the taste of her blood, the drum of her heart, the short, rapid breaths slipping past those full lips...her presence thundered over the din of the room.

Then she was there again, standing at the edge of the crowd like a vision, one foot on the dance floor as if she were going to stride right out.

The song wasn't over, but I stopped in my tracks as the rest of the world spun by.

"What's wrong, my prince?" Concern flickered in Lady Marbury's eyes as some of the dancers stared at us.

"I'm sorry, but there's a problem I must attend to. We shall dance again later." I tugged her toward the edge of the dance floor and passed her off to Aamon in one quick movement.

"What the hell?" Aamon protested, but I was already stalking toward Ella. She was exposed and out of place.

I took her by the wrist and stepped close. "You need to leave."

Her lavender eyes flared behind the mask, and the delicate blue flowers outlining the eye holes only made them more mysterious and captivating. "Not until we talk."

Fucking hell. Everyone was watching. And listening.

I grabbed her waist and pulled her onto the dance floor, slipping into the throng of dancers.

"What are you doing?" Ella blurted, looking around wildly as the orchestra began a new song.

"Dancing, like everyone else," I growled, her lilies and rain scent igniting something deep and primal in me. "Now talk."

If she was going to dress the part, then she would play it.

She winced as she stepped on my foot, her body stiff and lacking any sense of rhythm. "I don't know how to dance!"

Impatience burned through me. "I can tell. Let me lead." I spun her around before tilting her in a low dip, my gaze level with her breasts. Blood pumping. Fear rising. A sheen of sweat feathering the plump curves of bare skin. "Couldn't this have waited?"

"Obviously not," she seethed as I lifted her, pulling her toward me until her chest was flush against mine.

She stepped on me twice more before the tension in her finally eased up, and she let me guide her across the crowded floor. I glanced over my shoulder. Aamon was dancing with Lady Marbury, whispering in her ear as he glared at me over her shoulder, hopefully repairing the damage I'd just done in spurning my future queen in front of the entire court.

His expression drew taut. Did he have any idea who was in my arms?

Taking Ella's waist, I lifted her into the air, mirroring the movements of the other dancers but subtly moving us away from him and my potential bride.

Her lips parted on a silent gasp, revealing the ivory tips of fangs.

I set her down. "False teeth? Are you serious?"

She bit her lower lip, the action exposing the tip of one ivory fang pressing dangerously into the rosy flesh. It shouldn't have been tantalizing, but it was. The vision of Ella with fangs sent heat straight to my cock.

I twirled her away, then pulled her back. "What in the name of all the gods did you hope to gain by this ruse?"

"I didn't have a choice. You're in danger!" She arched into me, her arms looping around my neck.

My breath caught as desire pulsed through me. The power the little vixen had over me was unnerving.

"No, my darling, you're the one who's in danger." I peeled her off me and guided her in a series of sweeping turns before pulling her back. "The Triad has been asking about you. We have to get you out of here before they unmask you and—"

"I don't have much time so shut up and listen," she snapped, anger flushing her cheeks. Her eyes darted like a caged animal's, terrified and ready to fight. "There's going to be an attempt on your life tonight. You need to leave the ball, *now*."

The intensity of her words lanced through me like a white-hot iron.

She was telling the truth, or at least what she believed to be the truth. I could see it in her eyes and feel it in her racing heart-beat. "You're serious..."

"Yes."

"Who?"

I had a dozen rivals, but the immortal who thought they could take me on was about to learn a very dark lesson.

Ella shook her head. "People who don't know the truth and think that removing you will solve all our problems."

"How do you know?" I asked, unable to steal my gaze from her perfect mouth. "Are these the same people you've been funneling information to?"

Her breath hitched, and she tripped over my feet. Her look betrayed everything, and my mood became dark.

"I knew you were a spy, but tell me, *Cinderella*, was everything a lie?"

"It's not what you think! I didn't know this was happening until I overheard it a few hours ago, but I can assure you, this is real, and you must leave immediately." She leaned closer, the urgency in her voice and the panic in her eyes sending a cascade of alarm signals through me. "The assassins are posed as servants. They're already here, and they're armed."

Humans? Did they really think they stood a chance?

"Impossible," I muttered.

"I need you to trust me," Ella whispered, the urgency in her voice on the verge of panic. "We can fix this."

The song had ended, and another began, but my attention was solely on her and the madness she was spewing.

Could I trust her? The Fates knew I shouldn't.

I scanned the room, reevaluating every face, immortal and human alike.

"Please, don't take revenge on my people. They're just desperate for hope." Her lavender eyes had deepened, the pale streaks of blue and red in them a chaotic frenzy, like oil paint splashed across a canvas. "I'm warning you because I believe in you. Because I know you're different."

"You know nothing," I snarled.

Ella's body tensed, her gaze locked on something beside us. Before I could turn, she threw her weight against me, catching me off guard and mid-step.

A dark shape whizzed through the space I'd just occupied, grazing Ella's shoulder.

The crossbow bolt ripped through the throat of the lord dancing beside us, and blood splattered against my cheek. The woman in his arms screamed as he gurgled, then tumbled to the ground. The clockwork of the dance collapsed into chaos.

Within the span of two heartbeats, I'd identified my attacker on the far side of the dance floor, dressed in servant's attire and loading a second quarrel into a small hand crossbow.

In one more beat, I crossed the distance and grabbed his throat. I rammed my fist into his chest, shattering bones and tearing skin, then yanked out his beating heart and dropped his twitching body to the floor.

His blood painted the marble.

My gaze locked on Ella, her masked face etched in horror as she saw me for what I really was—a murderous monster. Her sleeve was torn, blood dampening the scraped flesh of her shoulder, tempting me like some sweet, forbidden elixir, yet driving me into a rage.

The orchestra was still playing, and although the screams and shouts were rising, half the revelers still hadn't noticed.

Movement to my right.

I spun as a pair of servants lunged forward from the opposite side, twin blades plunging toward my heart. I ducked back and seized the hand of one of my assailants, then drove his knife into the eye of his friend.

The blinded man screamed and stumbled back, straight into the arms of Aamon. My friend grabbed the assassin by the chin and ripped his head off, sending a torrent of blood spraying across the rabid crowd.

I impaled the man in my arms on his own blade, ripping him across the belly and letting his viscera spill onto the floor.

The scent of fresh blood spread through the air, pungent and intoxicating. It took only another breath for the ballroom to descend into pandemonium, lords and ladies of the noblest houses morphing into their basest forms, hungry and blood-crazed and senseless. They turned on the remaining servants in the room, plucking them from the crush of bodies like ears of corn.

Fear coursed through me as I searched for Ella. She was isolated on the dance floor, spinning around, her face pale with terror as the bloody scene unfolded before her eyes. Her gaze caught mine, and she screamed, "Save the servants!"

I only cared about her, yet I leapt onto the platform where the orchestra had been set up, abandoned instruments now strewn hastily across the stage. "Stop!" I roared, projecting the full weight of my power into my voice.

It ripped through the crowd like a wave, and the violence halted. Utter silence crashed over the room, save for the shrieks of fleeing servants.

"Not another human dies," I growled. "And I will eviscerate the first person to defy me." Every immortal hung on my words. Marionette or not, I was not without power. Our line ruled for a reason.

The sheer curtain on the balcony above wrenched open, revealing the Triad—demons that watched over us in the place of angels. Horace strode forward, Thalindra at his side. His eyes scanned the room and settled on Ella, and he pointed at her. "Seize that woman! She tried to kill the prince!"

My blood iced, protective rage a wildfire in my blood. I wouldn't let them have her.

Aamon and the royal guard shoved forward, circling Ella like wolves closing in on a trapped deer. She looked around wildly, her panicked gaze catching mine.

"Stop!" I roared.

Horace's face went livid. "The prince has been deceived. She's an assassin. Take her now!"

Fuck him. I rushed forward, no thought in mind for what I was doing, only that I had to protect her.

She backed away and spun toward the window. "Help me!"

Her voice lanced through my heart, but to my surprise, it wasn't me she was calling to. I followed her gaze to the windows above.

There was an explosion of glass, followed by the woosh of what sounded like hundreds of beating wings. Broken glass cascaded from above, bouncing across the marble floor in a deafening peal.

I stopped short, my boots skidding on glass shards, as I stared up at the gaping hole in the towering windows. A billowing murder of crows descended upon the ballroom, a black thunderstorm, shrieking and cawing like banshees.

They circled Ella as a funnel cloud, swooping down and attacking anyone who drew near her. Immortals plunged to the floor as dozens of birds descended on them, pecking and clawing at the faces of anyone foolish enough to approach.

I froze, my limbs feeling like solid steel. What was happening?

"She's a whisperer!" Thalindra's voice rose above the discord. "A witch!"

She couldn't be.

Memories rose like steam from the sun-scorched earth after a hard rain. Ella's uncanny abilities with animals. The times I'd caught her speaking to herself in the forest or the stables. The way she'd nurtured my garden back to health.

Thalindra was right, and I was a godsdamned fool for not seeing it before. I'd fallen into her trap.

What would you do if you discovered a mortal with magic? Ella had asked me once.

I caught sight of her behind the storm of wings, regret and sadness filling her eyes. Then she turned and ran, the crows driving a path through the crowd. Her mask and its veil of leaves had been torn free in the chaos, and her hair cascaded down her back in loose waves like flashes of moonlight.

"Kill her now, you idiots!" Thalindra shrieked. "She's escaping!"

My sentries took up the cry and sprang forward.

Fucking meddling mages.

I grabbed Cassandra as she hurried toward me. "Take the royal guard and get the Triad to safety. There may be assassins coming for them."

Hopefully, the confusion would waylay both the guards and Triad and buy Ella some time.

Before Cassandra could respond, I flung myself across the stage and charged after Aamon. He'd made it out of the ballroom and down the great hall before I seized him. "Do not touch her!"

Aamon spun on me, grasping my jacket, and shoved me back. "She's trying to kill you!"

Anger scorched through me, searing my patience and pushing me past the brink of violence. I threw Aamon into the wall, plaster falling as I strode forward and gripped him by the throat. "She *warned* me, you asshole. She's the reason I still have my head."

"I watched her maneuver you and shove you right into position. It's a miracle you don't have a crossbow bolt in your neck." He bared his fangs as he pushed back against me. "She's a *witch*. This was *her plan*, and I won't stand by while she plays you."

Could it be?

The lying. The fake name. The spying. Hell, the hidden powers.

I fought against the notion even as the hairline cracks of doubt spread through my chest, splintering into aching fissures.

Aamon gripped my shoulder, the fire in his tone replaced with something bordering on remorse. "The rumors I've dug up say the leader of the resistance was once married to a silver-haired woman."

My voice scraped over my throat like sandpaper. "And what happened to him?"

"No one knows."

I'd asked her once about her father. *He disappeared*, she'd said.

I'd suspected she was working for them, but had she been more? What was I to believe?

I released my stalwart friend, and he met my eyes. "What is your command, my lord?"

I cast off my mask as I strode toward the door. "Get Cassandra and make sure no one else leaves or dies. I'm going to hunt Ella down. Alone."

The beautiful siren would answer to me, one way or another, before the night was through—but it would be my judgement, and mine alone.

58

———

Ella

The thundering of wings drowned out all sound, even my hammering heart, yet I could still hear my saviors speaking frantically in my head.

Keep moving!

They're coming.

We'll get you out of here.

All I could see were black feathers everywhere and the marble floor passing as I sprinted through the castle, guided by the frenzy of birds.

"I need to get to the stables," I said, my lungs straining for air.

A loud bang of a door, followed by a short scream, filtered through the chaos. The storm of birds parted as I emerged from the castle and into the courtyard.

The heel of my glass slipper lodged itself in a crack between the stone steps, and I stumbled. My foot slipped free, and I rolled across the ground, ankle throbbing as guards rushed from the castle. I kicked off my other shoe as the cloud of crows split, half diving at my attackers, while the others swooped around me.

Dragging myself to my feet, I half-hobbled, half-ran toward the stables, my ankle screaming and heart hammering.

"Chastity!" I yelled as I burst through the doors. "I need to get away! Can you help?"

The mare kicked open the door to her stall. *Climb up. No time for a saddle. Hold tight.*

I dragged a stool next to her and mounted. I'd only ridden bareback a couple times when I was a girl, and never in a gown.

Where are we going? she asked.

"As far away as we can." I turned to the other horses, which were watching, wide-eyed and agitated. "The immortals want to kill me. Please don't lead them my way."

They whinnied, and two or three reared in support. My eyes fell on Tenebris. He watched me suspiciously, clearly torn between helping and duty. He nickered. *Be careful, Ella.*

Chastity charged out of the stables as Horace rushed toward me, his face beet red. Guards swarmed the gates as he extended his arm. "Run, little witch! You'll have no power in our woods. We'll hunt you down and burn you at the stake for all to see!"

An explosion of purple-white light pierced the air in front of us. Chastity flinched and dodged the blast, nearly sending me flying before she evaded the soldiers and bolted through the castle gates. The iron portcullis rattled and fell behind us, nearly grazing her rump as it slammed into the ground.

Hugging Chastity for dear life, I glanced back. Cassius skidded to a halt behind the portcullis, anger and betrayal cutting his face as he shouted for the soldiers to raise it.

If he hadn't been a prince, if the Triad had never existed, then perhaps things could have been different.

But they weren't.

We galloped through the nearly deserted streets of town,

sending the few bystanders diving for cover. I glanced over my shoulder as the castle gates receded in the distance. Torches glinted in the night, but there were no signs of riders. Not yet, at least.

I closed my eyes and offered a brief prayer of thanks.

I didn't dare head back to the manor, so I turned Chasity toward the cursed woods, following the same route I'd taken with Cassius.

Do you have a plan? she asked as we plunged into the shadow of the trees. *Where will we go?*

"I'm not sure yet," I admitted. "We need to put as much distance between us and the castle as possible. Then we can decide."

Chastity snorted and tossed her mane. *Not many can keep up with me, except for Tenebris.*

My stomach knotted as thoughts drummed numbly against my skull. Would Cassius follow? Did I want him to?

Yes. To both.

I wanted desperately to explain everything and to beg him to protect my people, but a part of me worried he wasn't the man I thought he'd been.

Did he realize I'd been trying to save him? Or did he think I was one of the assassins as well?

I rubbed my palm against the deep ache in my chest. *He's not going to save you now.*

The Triad was coming, which meant I couldn't rely on him or anyone. I had to find my own way out of this mess. If they got their hands on me, I had no doubt they could force me to betray Cassius, my stepmother, and the resistance—anyone and everyone who'd ever helped me.

First order of business: don't get caught.

As Chastity followed the hunting trail deeper into the woods, the canopy thickened, filtering the starlight and forcing her to slow her pace. At least the path was familiar to her, and her steps remained sure, if not as quick.

"How well do you know the forest?" I asked.

There are plenty of game trails out here, she said with a tired huff. *We can take one and lose them...unless they bring hunting dogs, of course.*

I closed my eyes and strained my ears, listening for the baying of hounds in the distance, but all I could hear was the drumming of Chastity's hooves and the beating of my own heart.

That was something, at least.

My throat tightened as waves of sorrow crashed over me. I'd saved Cassius's life, but I hadn't been able to stop the assassins from revealing themselves and the resistance, and I hadn't had time to get Belle or Cara to safety. The bloodsuckers could very well murder the entire castle staff for this.

Guilt stabbed me, but as I replayed the events of the day over and over in my mind, a simmering fury took hold. My plan had failed, but the fallout was my stepmother's fault—hers, and the leaders of the resistance. They'd put our town at risk.

If they'd only listened...

I hardened my heart. It didn't matter. They hadn't listened, and there was no changing the past. I had to find a way forward. I had to find a way to fix things and protect the people I loved.

I'd thought Cassius would be the one to save us, but it had to be me.

I glanced at the trail ahead. The further we got from the castle, the deeper my dread grew. My options were limited. My first instinct was to go to Siggy, but I couldn't put her at risk. If the Triad found her, I was certain they'd execute her on the spot, not just for helping me but for what she was—the last sliver of hope for our people. She had to survive.

That left me with two options—take my chances in the

cursed woods and cross the border or stay here in the Bloodvale and hide. The first option held a high probability of death, but the second was guaranteed suicide.

Since I didn't have any reins, I gently patted Chastity's shoulder. "Stop."

She slowly came to a stop. *What is it?*

"I need to think."

I closed my eyes, feeling the Triad's curse over the forest more clearly than ever—a deep, thundering absence of magic. It thrummed in my bones like a low, silent pulse, and now that I knew what to look for, I swore I could almost feel it drawing my magic out, feeding on it like the immortals fed on blood.

A slow, seething rage crested in me. How many girls were like me, born with magical gifts they never knew they had, cursed to have their power leeched away without their knowledge? I'd lived like that my whole life, only discovering something was wrong when I stepped into the castle.

My fists tightened, and I opened my eyes. As much as I wanted to flee, I couldn't run. I was the only mortal who knew the truth, and I couldn't share it. That meant finding a solution rested on my shoulders, and mine alone.

The dark woods pressed in, a cavern formed of stately trunks and branches, black and inhospitable around me—and yet, there was something comforting to the claustrophobic presence. I didn't fully understand the connection I shared with the wild, but I knew that as long as I was in the woods, I'd never be alone.

I was a whisperer.

The forest will always be there when you need it, Siggy had said.

A nervous hope budded in my heart, flickering to life like a sputtering candle. The trees had helped me before. Would they listen now?

I looked into the deep darkness and lifted my voice to

address the trees. "I can feel the curse over this place with every beat of my heart. Can you feel it, too?"

The leaves stirred in the still night air. There were no words in my mind, but I understood the meaning of the sign. *Yes.*

I released a shuddering breath as a desperate plan began to take shape in the shadows of my thoughts. Cassius had told me the spell was like a whirlpool, drawing magic down into its heart. If the curse had a source or point of origin, perhaps I could destroy it.

"Can you guide me to where the curse is strongest? The source of its power?" I asked the trees.

I waited, a nervous sweat dotting my brow. The branches began to creak and groan. My breathing quickened as ancient limbs arched upward and the dense brush pulled back, creating a dark tunnel through the woods—a black hole beckoning me forward.

They'd listened.

Maybe it was my imagination, but I could almost swear the throbbing pulse of the curse was stronger now that the path was open, an inaudible beat echoing down the dark corridor ahead.

Chastity pulled away with a warning huff. *Bad place.*

I gently stroked her neck, soothing the agitated mare. "I know. I don't like it, either, but I'm afraid that's where I've got to go. I owe you my life for bringing me this far, and I won't ask anything more of you. You've risked enough."

I prepared to dismount, but she snorted and shifted. *Not alone. We'll go together, if we must.*

"Are you sure?"

The mare stepped off the trail and into the dark tunnel formed by the trees. I released a sigh of relief and stroked her neck. "Thank you."

Hopefully, I wasn't marching us to our deaths.

I twisted, looking back at the trail we'd left, then searching the trees on either side. "Can you hide our passing? I'm being hunted, and I don't want anyone to follow."

The bushes behind us stirred. Their branches swept the ground where we'd passed, obscuring Chastity's hoofprints, then stretched out and settled across the trail, hiding it from view. The forest closed in behind us, creating an impenetrable curtain of foliage.

My skin tingled. I was in a wild place with only one way out—forward.

"Okay, let's do this."

Chastity picked her way slowly at first. The arching limbs blocked out the starlight, leaving us only faint glints of silver to navigate by, but the woods provided us a safe path. In places where gnarled roots poked up dangerously from the forest floor, they flattened themselves as we passed and pushed unstable rocks from our way. The bushes bent to let us through, then folded back behind us, obscuring our passing.

It was like riding a wave, with the dark tunnel opening just ahead of us and closing behind. Chastity began moving faster as her confidence grew, and soon, we were trotting through the darkness.

The deep, inaudible pulse of corruption intensified with every stride, and the tiny hairs on my neck rose. The weight of the curse pressed down on me, a stifling presence. After a while, when I spoke to Chastity to reassure her, she no longer replied with words in my mind—just a nervous whinny.

My power was slipping away.

I gritted my teeth, clinging to the sensation of our connection. A cold sweat beaded on my forehead, but I pushed her on, and the trees still parted before us.

After what must have been an hour, the forest began to thin. The moon had long since risen, and the woods became a bright mosaic of silver light and shadow.

The black shape of a structure loomed ahead, and soon, the outlines of a spire emerged above the tops of the trees. Chastity slowed to a stop. The darkened building was a dilapidated church, abandoned in an overgrown clearing.

The repressive power of the curse was stronger than ever, hanging in the air like a choking cloud. The deep thrum of the spell they'd cast pulsed steadily from the sinister church ahead, an ethereal heartbeat that boomed through my chest and limbs. No longer a malicious sense of absence, it was a hungry presence, and I could feel it tugging away at my magic with every beat.

Whatever the mages had done, they'd done it here.

I swung my leg over Chastity's back and slid to the ground. Leaves crunched beneath my bare feet, suddenly focusing my attention on how still the woods had become. It was deeper than the simple silence of night.

This was a haunted place. A forbidden one.

I hitched up my gown and delicately picked a path into the clearing, then across the old cobblestone pavement that had been hidden by the dry grass. I stopped in front of the low iron fence that ringed the building. Someone had boarded up the windows, and heavy beams had been nailed across the door to seal it shut. Traces of red and white suggested it had once been brightly painted, but now all that was left was rotting wood and overgrown stone walls.

"What is this place?" I craned my head up.

A branch snapped behind me, followed by a sinister chuckle. "It's the place you're going to die."

I spun around as the dark form of a man emerged from the tree line like a specter. Starlight traced the pinched features of his face and glinted on the rings covering his fingers.

Horace.

He grinned. "This is where your story ends, little whisperer."

59

———————

Ella

My stomach leapt into my throat, and I shuffled back, my heart racing. I grabbed a broken branch and held it in front of me like a spear—as if it would do anything against the powerful mage. "Stay back."

Horace stalked toward me, his dark eyes brimming with the promise of vengeance. "Surprised to see me?"

I kept my gaze trained on him as I backed away, forcing down my rising panic. The rest of the Triad were bound to be here soon, but if I could stall him for a few seconds, maybe I could reach Chastity.

"How did you find me?" I rasped, my throat so tight I could barely speak.

Horace reached into his cloak and pulled out my glass slipper—the one I'd kicked off on the castle stairs. "You left a trail."

Confusion rocked me. "My shoe?"

He turned the glistening slipper idly in his hand with a bitter smirk. "Objects know their owners, and like a faithful dog, they want to be reunited. The connection is even stronger for magical objects. It's how our tokens work—they're linked to you by the invisible thread of fate."

He hurled the slipper at my feet, and the tip of the heel shattered against one of the overturned cobblestones.

"Your slipper led me straight to you—and now, like a lost shoe, you're going to lead me to *your* owner." His expression turned savage. "Who do you work for, little witch?"

I was only four strides from Chastity. *So close.*

Breath shaking, I took another step back. "I work for no one. I am my own."

Horace barked out a laugh. "I think not. You're a puppet. Someone is pulling your strings, or you would never have found this place. Is it the resistance? Or the prince?" His eyes became pure ice. "Or is it one of the others?"

The others?

My thoughts stumbled over themselves. Did he mean the rest of the Triad? Did Horace think one of them was working against him?

Maybe I could use that to buy me time.

"You don't know what you're dealing with, Horace. When—" I cut off my words and reached for my throat, imitating the effects of his own spell of silence.

He froze, eyeing me like a viper. Then a sickening smile spread across his face as he saw my charade. "Clever try, but you won't play me for a fool a second time. I'm going to rip the truth from you—your entire story, scream by scream."

My stomach plummeted. I had no doubt he could do it. I'd implicate everyone who'd protected me and everyone I cared about. No matter what happened to me, I couldn't put them in any more danger.

Desperation rising, I hitched up my gown and hurled myself toward Chasity.

Horace threw up his hand, and a burst of purple light split

the night. Pain erupted across my ribs as I flew sideways into the trunk of an oak. The wind exploded from my chest, and I collapsed at its base, unable to pull air into my lungs.

Chastity reared and pawed the air with her hooves, but a second blast sent her reeling.

"Run!" I wheezed as I rolled to the side, my chest aching. "Get away!"

The mare whinnied in protest but took cover among the trees as Horace's magic tore through the air around her.

The mage crouched down in front of me, tiny sparks of purple lightning dancing between his raised fingers. "Alone at last—and this time, I will have the truth out of you."

A warm trickle of blood ran from the corner of my mouth, but I raised my chin defiantly. "Over my dead body."

Horace's gaze didn't waver. "Oh, yes, I'm going to kill you. But how you die is up to you. Swift and painless, or after days of agony. I can teach you suffering like you've never known."

His breath stank, and I grimaced. "I'm good at suffering."

I tried to rise, but he lunged forward and wrapped his hand around my neck. "How did you find this place?"

I grasped at his fingers, trying to peel them away as I croaked, "I don't even know where I am!"

He tightened his grip, and I squirmed as my throat constricted. "No more lies."

"It's the truth," I said, my voice a ragged whisper. "Why is this place so important? Were you an altar boy here once?"

He yanked me forward and slammed me back against the trunk, driving the breath from my lungs. "You think you can mock me? This is the heart of our power—the place where you are weakest and I am strongest. Sooner or later, it will take everything you have, little witch, and I will have what I want."

I kicked at him, but an avalanche of magic poured through

his hand, pinning me in place against the tree. It felt like searing iron bands wrapping around me, tighter and tighter.

He grinned. "I can bind your body with my magic just as easily as I can bind your words."

I tried to resist, but his power over me was effortless. The hungering pulse that emanated from the church dragged at my strength and magic, leaving me weak and helpless before him.

"You will give me names," he said in a whisper that could have made stones tremble.

I closed my eyes against his demand, futilely searching for some hidden reserve of inner strength but finding little. Yet, in the dark hollow where my own power had been, I felt something else in its absence—something far greater than myself lingering at the edge of perception.

The cursed woods.

Their magic had a whisper of its own, and I felt it calling to me—a vast reservoir of strength, just beyond my grasp.

Let us help.

Horace's demands faded away as I reached out with my soul, desperately seeking a connection. *I'm here.*

I strained, trying to pull their strength into me but not knowing how to. Despair shuddered through me, and I cried out, "Help me!"

The world around me shifted.

A myriad of sensations that weren't my own flooded through me—birds bursting into the sky and the cold night air rustling the leaves above. I felt the grass in the clearing stir and the roots burrowing beneath the earth.

A thousand connections came to life, entwining me with the magic of this place, and the truth of my power dawned like the sun breaking the horizon.

I didn't have to whisper, or ask, or command. The forest had awakened within me, and suddenly, we were one.

My breathing steadied and my heartbeat slowed as Horace's shouting came back into focus. "I command you to tell me the truth!"

I opened my eyes, and my lips turned up. "You want to know who I work for? I work for this land. And I'm going to cleanse it of your filth."

"Insolent bitch." Horace's hand cracked across my face, but I barely noticed it. I was lost to myself. Instead, I felt the limbs of the tree above me like they were my arms and its branches as if they were my fingers. I flexed them as I would my own hand. Wood groaned, and fragments of bark rained down.

Horace looked up in a single, beautiful moment of surprise. Then I seized full control of the oak and swept one of its limbs straight into his chest. He flew into the air and crashed to the ground ten yards away, twisting in pain.

The spell pinning me to the earth dissipated, and I staggered to my feet.

Horace started to rise, so I reached through the ground, joining with the tree beside him. I brought a heavy branch down like a hammer, stomping him into the dirt.

"You're a thief, Horace. *I* am a whisperer, and I have the strength of an entire forest in the palm of my hand." I seized control of another oak and slammed the mage across the clearing. "And the forest is angry."

Horace's body tumbled like a rag doll's until he crashed into the iron fence enclosing the churchyard. I strode toward him, my expression dark.

A cruel grin cut his face, and he yanked a splinter of wood from his bare neck. Blood spurted, and dread coursed through me as the wound closed. "You think you can hurt me, Ella? I've been drinking the blood of immortals for centuries. You can't kill me or overpower me, and there is nothing you possess that I can't take away."

"We'll see about that." I poured my magic into the tree beside him and swung, but Horace flipped up his hands and unleashed a blast of purple lightning. The limb exploded in a shower of bark and splinters.

I threw up my arm to shield my face as they raked across me, tearing through my skin and gown like knives through warm butter.

A second bolt ripped into its trunk, and it split with a deafening crack. My connection to it vanished, leaving a dull absence in my chest where our bond had been. Rage exploded through me at the sudden loss.

I called the forest down upon him, but Horace danced around the edge of the clearing, dodging limbs as gracefully as the courtiers twirled at the ball. A crackling storm of lightning bolts ripped through their grasping limbs. He extinguished the trees one by one until none remained that could reach him.

Burning cinders drifted down, covering the clearing and the dead trees with a rain of ash. Horace grinned. "The trees may obey you, little whisperer, but I will teach you the true meaning of obedience!"

He whipped his hand up, and a burst of magic yanked me to my knees. I reached for the power of the forest, but he'd killed every tree that could strike. I gasped and fought against it, but the chains of his magic held me firm.

Horace's eyes flared with a cruel light as he approached. "Do you wonder now why the immortals bow before us? Because they are nothing compared to our power. *You* are nothing."

He stopped in front of me, inches from my grasp but impossibly far away. "We taught the immortals what it meant to submit, and I'll teach you the same lesson. I'll make you beg for death, even as you serve me in every way I demand. You will debase yourself for me and learn the true price of *defiance*."

Panic flared. I strained against the prison of his magic, but the harder I pushed, the tighter the bonds grew. My heartbeat hammered against my chest, threatening to drive all sense from my mind. Then there was another beat, shuddering through the ground beneath me. Thunderous and violent, it grew louder and louder until it became the earthshaking cadence I knew all too well.

My eyes rose as Tenebris exploded into the clearing. And upon his back was the dark rider.

My breath stilled as Cassius leapt, becoming a black angel against the sky. He seemed to float there for a second, his cape fluttering in the air. Then he slammed into Horace in a blur of fury and darkness.

60

Cassius

I rammed my shoulder into Horace's chest and sent him rolling across the forest floor. Rage blinded me to everything but protecting Ella. I drew my sword and lunged in for the kill, striking like a viper. "I'm going to carve out your fucking heart!"

Lightning ripped across my body, flinging me backward, searing flesh and clothes alike. I collided with a shattered tree trunk, then hurled myself sideways as a second flash shot toward me. It detonated behind me, and my vision danced with spots, my ears ringing. I took cover behind a tree and shook my head to clear it.

I fucking *hated* fighting mages.

While my kind were stronger and faster, speed and precision weren't enough to dodge lightning bolts and fireballs, and our heightened senses were little more than a skull-splitting liability. You had to think three steps ahead if you wanted to win. I'd learned that the hard way during the Uprising.

I leapt over a fallen log as a sparking bolt of magic clipped my blade. The sword burst from my grip, clattering across the ground, and I shook my singed hand.

Apparently, after three hundred years, I was a little rusty.

"What do you think you're doing, Cassius?" Horace roared.

"You shouldn't have fucking touched her," I growled. "You're a dead man."

Horace went red in the face, and I gave him a *come and get me* gesture as I slipped deeper into the woods, taking refuge behind another tree. If I could lure him away from Ella, she could reach Tenebris and escape.

A lightning bolt lanced the trunk I'd used for cover, cracking it in half in a shower of sparks.

"You can't be serious." The corrupt mage laughed as he stalked toward me. "You'd dare challenge me over that witch? You're more fool than I ever imagined."

I ducked through the trees, my movements precise and silent and as swift as an arrow. In two breaths, I was standing directly behind him.

"The foolish thing was not killing you centuries ago." I seized the bastard and hurled him against a tree, his face ricocheting off the bark with a grunt. I was on him in another heartbeat, driving blows into his kidneys and splitting his jaw.

Horace slammed his hand against my chest, and molten pain tore through me as a burst of magic flung me into the air. My ribs and forearm cracked when I hit the ground, and my spine groaned, a hair's breadth from snapping.

Somewhere, Ella screamed.

As my broken bones and torn tendons began to knit together, I flipped over and searched the woods for her.

Please don't follow.

She darted out from under the cover of the trees toward Horace. Dread cleared the throbbing pain from my mind. I could take this punishment, but she was mortal. Getting her free was all that mattered.

"Run!" I roared.

Yet Ella didn't heed my words.

Horace stumbled to his feet as she rushed forward. She swung her fist through the air—and then, to my astonishment, the forest itself moved. The tree beside her slammed one of its limbs into Horace's back.

I watched in shock as his body rose into the air and crashed to the ground in a hail of bark. She struck with her hand again, and a second tree brought its heavy branches down.

By the gods.

It wasn't just animals. She could command the trees themselves.

Astonishment dulled my senses, and I stared in awe.

The hesitation cost me everything. By the time I grabbed my sword and climbed to my feet, I was too late. Horace released an unrelenting cascade of power and light into her body.

Terror ignited inside me like gunpowder, and I charged forward, lunging for his heart with a feral roar. Horace turned. The tip of my sword skimmed across his chest, then sank into it, a little too low for the heart.

He gasped in surprise, and I kicked him back to free my blade. I raised it for the killing blow, but a wave of power lifted me off my feet. A second later, I crashed into the dirt, a relentless pressure crushing the wind from my lungs. Invisible chains wrapped around me, and as I fought to rise, my limbs barely moved.

"Get out of here, Ella!" I said, using the last of my air. But she didn't answer.

Horace staggered upright, clutching his chest as trails of crimson ran from the wound and dribbled from the corner of his mouth. "You fucking fool," he rasped. "You could have had it all."

Not all. Not her.

I pushed against his magic, fear for Ella driving me to the

edge of madness, but the spell didn't yield. It was like an invisible iron cage had been crushed around me.

"Did you really think you could defeat me?" He lurched closer, hand pressed over his wound. "This is why your kind serves *us*."

I spat. The die had been cast long before.

He pulled his palm from his chest and looked down as thickening blood drained out. He chuckled. "You got closer than most, I'll give you that. But seeing as you gave me your blood this morning, this scratch will be an old scar in minutes."

Bitterness twisted my gut. My kind's blood would save him and doom Ella in the same moment. The Fates were fucking cruel.

Horace twisted his hand, and suddenly, the pressure choking my throat eased slightly. "Tell me who that witch is."

"She's mine," I growled, unable to keep the beast from my voice.

Horace glanced at the crumpled blue shape lying in the clearing, and a sadistic smile crossed his lips. "She belongs to no one now, save the maggots and the flies."

My chest crushed inward. It couldn't be. She was stronger than his magic. *She had to be.*

Until she'd appeared, I'd been a ghost haunting the halls of a castle I didn't want. She'd restored me to life, and now I'd ended hers by choosing the shackles of my duty over my heart. I should've taken Ella and fled like my brother had.

My mouth turned bitter. What was I fighting to protect each day when I rode into the hills? Not her people, and certainly not mine. Nothing but a corrupt palace built on a hill of corpses.

I should've let the Triad and the kingdom burn.

Horace's magic wrenched my head around to face him. "Who did she work for? Was it you or one of the others? Malthus? Thalindra?"

Horace loved his secrets, and not knowing the truth would drive him mad. It was a poor consolation, but if I were lucky, mutual suspicion would tear the Triad apart.

I pulled my lips into a cruel smile. "I guess you'll never know."

"What a fucking waste." Horace glowered as he rose. "Perhaps the next king will know his place."

Fates help the next king. I'd served the bastards long enough.

A deep, resigned calm came over me, and I closed my eyes, no longer fighting the bonds of his magic. A faint wind drifted across my skin, bringing with it the scent of charred trees. The relentless ringing in my ears began to fade, and another sound brushed against my perception. A pulse.

My senses sharpened instantly. Ella was alive.

Her breath rasped in and out, shallow and labored, and beneath that, I heard the subtle sound of leaves crushing against the grass. Not just alive—she was crawling.

Renewed purpose ignited within me, along with dread. I had to keep Horace's attention long enough for her to get away. My eyes snapped open. "Is this what you did to my brother? Did he tire of your corrupt rule?"

"Figured it out at last, have you?" Horace laughed as he crouched beside me and patted my cheek. "Your brother was almost as much of a disappointment as you are. He thought he might change things after your father died, but we taught him how dangerous change can be."

Rage flared, and I slammed against the bonds of Horace's spell, my hand moving a fraction of an inch. "What the fuck did you do to him?"

Horace chuckled. "Thalindra thought killing him would be a waste of royal blood, so we gave him a choice—learn to obey like a dog or spend the rest of his life as a monster. Poor self-righteous fool. He chose the monster. If he's still alive, he's probably far across the border, cowering in some den in the woods, more animal than immortal now."

Words that would have once enthralled me simply grazed off my mind as the sounds of Ella's movements pricked my senses.

Footsteps. But instead of moving away, they were coming closer.

Panic took me. She needed to *run*. We were in the middle of smoldering trunks. There were no trees here for her to command—only death, waiting to claim her.

I strained against the bonds of Horace's spell. "Get away from me!"

I prayed she'd realize the words were for her, not for him.

"You should've been grateful to us for giving you the crown, yet you've thrown it all away." Looking at me with contempt, Horace slid a wicked knife from the sheath on his belt. "You'll envy your brother's fate by the time I'm done with you."

I spat.

Horace's lips curled up, a sadistic glint in his eye as he twisted the blade in his fingers. "I think I'll start with the girl. I'll make you watch as I carve her up and make her corpse dance like a puppet on a string. How would you enjoy that, Your Highness?"

My heart stilled as Ella stepped up behind him. "I don't dance for bastards like you," she said.

Horace wheeled around and raised his blade, but Ella drove the shattered heel of her glass slipper straight into his eye.

He screamed and stumbled back with his hands clasped over his face. She swung again, this time ramming the sharp heel into the side of his neck. Blood spurted over her arms, but she struck over and over until he crumpled and fell to the earth.

61

Cassius

The spell restraining me unraveled, and I leapt to my feet as Ella dropped the bloody slipper from her hand. Horace lay still, blood from half a dozen wounds pooling on a bed of fallen leaves.

Ella looked away, trembling—not with fear, but with fury. Her gown hung in tatters, bruises and bloody lacerations adorning her skin.

This is my fault.

I pulled her close and pressed her head against my chest, breathing deeply of her scent. "Are you okay?"

"I've...I've never killed anyone before," she whispered as she turned to face the body on the ground.

A shadow passed over my soul. I released her and looked down. "You haven't killed him yet."

Ella drew her lips into a thin line as Horace's wounds started to knit.

I retrieved my blade. "He doesn't deserve a merciful death, but I'll take his head, and it'll be done."

She placed her hand on my arm. "I'll do it."

"No," I said raising the blade. "The duty is mine. It is my blood keeping him alive."

Her eyes became stone as her hand tightened on my arm. "I don't care. Horace may have taken your blood, but he took hope from generations of my people. Restoring it begins here. I need to do it with my own hands."

Fates, she was fierce—yet her heart was pure. Could I really take that from her?

I hesitated, searching her eyes. "Ella, please let me carry this for you."

She shook her head. "I'll carry my own burdens. The duty is mine—to *my* people."

My throat tightened as I nodded. Reluctantly, I handed her the sword. It would be grim work, but if it took her a dozen strokes, so be it. Horace had always been a brute and a butcher. Let him be butchered in the end.

Ella raised the sword high above her head. The blade wavered, but her expression did not. "This is for everyone whose magic you stole."

Then she struck.

I didn't count the blows, but in the end, Horace's head rolled free. Ella's chest heaved from the effort, and tears of anger streaked her cheeks, but her face shone with triumph. She held out the bloody blade. "Is he dead for real?"

"Yes. Neither the mages nor my kind can survive that sort of blow." I knelt and cleaned my sword on Horace's cloak, sickened by the thought of her as his puppet, enslaved to his whims. I'd seen him do it to others.

His death had been too kind by far.

I rose. "We should go. The others may have some way to sense his death. They'll come for us."

"Are they at the castle?"

"No. They were out hunting for you as well. Horace was just the better hound."

A black shadow crossed her face, and she looked up with foreboding. "What happened to the mortals in the castle? When I fled—" Her voice cut off. "My sister is there."

My jaw tightened. Even now, she wasn't worried for herself, but for others. She was better than any of us deserved.

"The slaughter stopped at my word, and I left Aamon behind to enforce it. He may be my second, but he's nearly as strong, and no one will oppose him outright, not with the Triad away." I brushed her hair gently with my fingers. "As for your sister, I sent her to convalesce in the village this afternoon. The Triad had started asking questions again."

Relief flooded her face, and she wrapped her arms around me. "Thank you."

The soft beating of her heart against my chest and the sweet scent of her blood filled my senses—a cruel delight that addled my thoughts. Longing filled me, but I hardened my heart and stepped back. There were questions I had to ask first.

I gripped her arms firmly, locking her in place. "How did you know about the assassins? Were you working with them?"

She gave me a look of despair that twisted my gut. "I tried to stop it, but—"

"But what?"

She clenched her jaw. "But I made it possible without even knowing what I'd done."

Her voice was barely a whisper on the wind, but it could have just as well been a thunderstorm. The noose of betrayal tightened around my neck, and my body became iron.

She searched my eyes. "I'm sorry, Cassius. I didn't mean to betray you or put you in danger. At first, I was just trying to find my sister and collect information, and then—" Her expression melted into despair. "It doesn't matter, does it? I was a spy, and I nearly got you killed."

"Was it for the resistance? Or for one of the houses?" I asked, my voice low and buzzing with an anger I couldn't repress. "Who was it that ordered my death?"

"The resistance," she whispered, and grasped my arms. "Please, have mercy on my people, Cassius. They don't know the truth. They live without hope for change. If you value what I did tonight, if you ever cared for me, don't seek revenge."

If I ever cared for her. The words cut through my anger and betrayal, flooding me with an icy clarity like the winter wind. The resistance. The Triad. The court and the castle. None of it mattered. Only one thing did.

I lifted her chin and looked into her eyes. "And do you care for me?"

Her pupils dilated, her lips parting in a whisper. "Yes. Absolutely, yes."

My breath stilled as I measured her gaze.

Whatever had happened before, whoever she'd worked for, it didn't matter. That *yes* was all I desired or needed. I pulled her close and kissed her, savoring the supple warmth of her lips.

We might not have long in the world with Horace dead and the remaining members of the Triad hunting her, and I refused to waste this moment.

My mouth parted hers, and I closed my eyes, savoring her taste and touch and feel. She pressed herself against me, her scent winding through my senses. Her tongue grazed mine, and I wanted to lose myself in her...

But I couldn't. Even now, I couldn't escape my duty. We were perched on the knife's edge of danger with death drawing in.

I gave myself three heartbeats, then broke away. "We should go." I whistled for Tenebris. "There will be a reckoning for Horace's death, and I don't like our chances. We got lucky with him, but as all three of the mages drew their stolen power from the same source, I'm afraid the others will have grown stronger."

Ella nodded. "Then let's finish this."

My stallion emerged from the woods, with her mare at its side, but rather than head toward them, she began walking toward the ruined building at the edge of the clearing.

"Where are you going?" I asked, catching up and restraining her with my hand. "We need to run."

She shook her head and pulled free of my grasp. "I'm not running anymore. Whatever the Triad did to curse the Bloodvale, it's here. I don't know if we can destroy it, but we have to try. It's our best chance of defeating the others."

"What do you mean?

Ella gestured to the old church. "The source of their power is here."

I lifted my gaze, seeing it for the first time free of the lust of battle. My stomach knotted as recognition sank in.

"Can't you feel the signature of their spell?" she asked quietly. "It's like a heartbeat, but oppressive and draining. You must feel it."

With Horace dead, the spell on her voice had broken, and she could speak of what she knew.

I paused, reaching out with my senses. I could taste blood in the air, and I caught the scents of charred wood and dirt and the sweet aroma of her body. An unnatural host of birds rustled and fidgeted in the trees above, and the deep shadows beyond the clearing concealed foxes and bears and deer, all lurking silently. A waiting army.

Ella's army.

I shook my head. "Immortals have no command of magic. The only heartbeat I feel is yours, and that's the only one I care about right now."

She gave me an appraising look. "Then keep me safe while I end this."

Ella moved toward the ruined church, and I followed, stunned. Rather than flee with the Triad closing in, she was going to take their power head-on.

Who the hell *was* she?

The iron gate had long since been overgrown by ivy. As if sensing her approach, the plants pulled back the gate for her, and it opened with a rusted creak.

I drew my blade and stepped in front of her. "I'll go first. I've been here before."

Her eyes widened. "You have?"

I hesitated at the foot of the stairs, my nerves tingling with tension. "This is an ancient place, from when our clan first came to the Bloodvale. It's where the first king was crowned, and where my brother was to take his oaths of service. But the Triad cursed him and drove him away."

"I heard."

My breath quaked. After centuries trapped with suspicions I didn't dare share even with Aamon, I finally knew the truth—and more importantly, someone else did, too. Ella. For that, I was more grateful than I could explain.

"My brother descended into madness after visiting this place. Whatever secrets lie here, they are what began his fall. It's why I had it boarded up a long time ago."

"But you never knew it was the source of the mages' power?"

Her words iced my skin. My hand tightened around my blade as the fury of my failure wormed through me. "No. If I'd known, I would have burnt this place to the ground with those bastards locked inside."

62

Ella

We climbed the rotting stairs quickly, Cassius creeping forward, quiet as an assassin. All I could hear was the deep pulse of the curse. Each beat thundered through me, shaking my very soul.

He listened at the front door, then stepped back and kicked it in. The heavy board sealing it shut shattered, and the hinges screamed as the door was flung open.

Cassius strode forward, his face a mask of tension. "We're alone, but that doesn't mean there's no danger."

I stepped through the entrance. Dust drifted in the beams of moonlight that sneaked into the church. I could barely see beyond ten feet, but I sensed a deep wrongness about the place. The shadows cast by the moonlight tilted oddly, and the air tasted of rot. The whole building thrummed with corruption, and the steady pulse of the curse dragged me forward like the current of a flooded river, pulling on me as well as my magic.

I shivered. "I can't see anything in this light."

Cassius picked up a wrought-iron candelabra, strode to one of the shuttered windows, and rammed it through the boards like a pike. The rotten planks tore free in a shower of broken slats and splinters, letting moonlight in. He bashed through two more, flooding the church with dim illumination. "Better?"

"So much for stealth." Not that anyone else was here. A heavy layer of dust coated the rows of wooden pews, and cobwebs clung to the walls. The only footprints were ours.

I could make out a raised dais at the front, a stone altar, and high niches for each of the great gods. Their statues had fallen long ago and lay broken at the base of the wall. I turned around slowly. A balcony hung above the entrance, but it was empty, just like the rest.

"I don't know where, but it's here. I can feel it pulling on me."

"Then let it pull," he said.

I closed my eyes and shuddered, sensing the currents in the room. I could feel it draining my strength faster than ever. I stepped forward hesitantly, following the strange sensation up the stairs of the dais to the stone-topped altar. It was like a whirlpool drawing me in.

"Here," I whispered.

Cassius stepped up beside me. "Within the altar?"

"Below."

He braced against the stone and pushed. The massive altar groaned, then scraped across the floor as Cassius heaved it over with a savage growl. The thing tipped up and crashed down onto its back. The floor shuddered, and streams of dust filtered down from the dark ceiling above.

I stared at him, awed by his strength. It would have taken half a dozen blacksmiths to shift that much wood and stone.

The prince bent double and braced his hands on his legs, breathing hard, then glared back at me. "What?"

Despite our current predicament, I couldn't help it. I pursed my lips. "Good thing you were born a prince and not a thief. You're not the subtlest at breaking and entering."

He lifted his brow, mildly irritated. "And what would you have suggested?"

"Using leverage."

Cassius gave an annoyed grunt and crouched down. The altar had left a barren, dust-free patch on the floor of the dais, and amid it was a brass ring inset into the floor. "A trapdoor."

I tilted my head. The stone panel had been carved with runes I couldn't read. "Do you know what it says?"

Cassius frowned. "It's the sepulcher of our house's ancestors."

My breathing stilled as my skin prickled. "Maybe we shouldn't—"

"Doesn't matter," he muttered, then hooked the ring with his fingers and looked up. "We might as well find out what's in there."

Something bad. I stepped back off the top of the dais.

Cassius heaved, and the trapdoor swung open, then crashed backward against the floor. An eerie purple light flooded over him as he stared down into the hole.

My shoulders clenched. "What do you see?"

For a moment, he didn't respond. Then he shook his head as if coming out of a spell. "Light. And it stinks of carrion and rotten flesh."

I opened my mouth to ask for more, but he grabbed his discarded blade and stepped down. I hurried over, practically pulled off my feet by the deep pulsing of the curse.

A stone stairway led downward into a narrow corridor bathed in purple light.

"Be careful!" I covered my mouth with my sleeve, trying to block out the carrion scent, and hurried after him. "There could be traps."

That, or the stench would kill us outright.

Cassius froze as we emerged into a small antechamber. I

stopped beside him, my breath tripping in shock. Beyond the next doorway lay a large sepulcher filled with six sarcophagi carved with ancient runes. The stone walls of the room were lined with massive roots that crept down across the floor and over the caskets.

And in the center of the room was a giant, beating heart.

I gagged, fighting back the nausea twisting my stomach.

It floated, streams of purple light drifting off it with every pulse. The light spilled over the caskets and walls like flames licking the sides of a hearth or sunlight shimmering across the bottom of a lake.

"What the hell is that?" Cassius whispered.

"The curse made manifest, and the source of their power," I said, mesmerized. Its hunger was a current pulling me forward, and although I fought it, I found myself stepping toward the heart.

Cassius grabbed my arm, restraining me. "What are you doing?"

A dull pain racked my body, and the urge to get closer to the heart became undeniable. I braced against him and gritted my teeth. "It wants my magic. And me."

Not just me. It wanted everything—all the magic in the forest and in the humans who dwelt here. It had been feeding off me my entire life and would consume my strength until my last breath. It was ravenous and unquenchable—the perfect tool to keep powerful people in line.

Cassius pushed me back toward the stairs, then strode forward, blade out. "Well, it can't have you. You're mine."

I grasped the lintel to prevent myself from being pulled forward by the spell. "Cassius, wait!"

The moment he stepped across the threshold of the sepulcher, light flashed. His body was hurled back and slammed into the wall, then toppled to the ground.

Shimmering purple light streamed off his skin, and I dropped to his side. "Are you okay?"

He growled and grabbed his fallen blade. "I'm fucking pissed."

Words thundered through my mind: *I will not let you destroy me, Ella.*

My breath stilled. The heart was speaking to me.

"It's alive," I whispered, looking desperately at Cassius. "Can you hear it?"

He stared at me like I was mad. "What are you talking about?"

I know you, Ella, the heart boomed in my mind. *I understand you. You don't need to destroy me. You can use me.*

"You're an abomination," I said, grasping Cassius's arm so that the pulsing thing didn't pull me into its clutches. He watched me, a mix of understanding and horror on his face as I spoke to the heart. "You've taken everything from my people!"

I've been waiting for someone as strong as you. Someone who could control me and use me for good.

"I want nothing to do with you."

The heart flared with a furious purple light. *Think of what you could do with the power I possess. You could end the mages. You could kill the immortals. No one would ever have to give themselves over again.*

"The Triad created you."

They've grown weak. They lack vision, but not you. You see a different future, don't you?

Images of Thalindra and Malthus barged into my mind. They were laughing and drinking blood wine as my people suffered and served their desires. Then I was there, tearing them apart with their own magic.

The lust of vengeance stirred within me, and my pulse

quickened. Cassius's grip on me tightened, an anchor pulling me back.

Give yourself to me, and my power will belong to you forever.

In my mind, I saw the trees and animals bending before me. I saw the sisters begging me for mercy, and then Cassius and his court, all bowing, all serving me.

I sat upon the throne, the mighty queen of the Bloodvale. I could drink the blood of immortals and live forever, and no human would ever have to fear again because I wielded *true power.*

Their power.

A tithe of magic—not my own, but stolen from my people at birth and paid throughout their lives. I'd be given the power to protect them from the world, but they would never know their own strength.

The visions vanished, and cold determination seated itself within my soul. I raised my eyes to the pulsing heart. "You're a thief. The power isn't yours to give."

It is mine to take! the heart thundered in my mind. *Do you think the immortals will ever show your kind any mercy? You could save them!*

As the heart's spell over me grew, I reached for Cassius's hand, his strength giving me fortitude. "No. They can save themselves."

You are a fool.

The heart pulsed, and a wave of magic drove me to my knees. It was Horace's spell, but stronger than his magic had ever been. I pushed against the invisible bonds, and Cassius roared in defiance.

The heart's cruel voice thundered through me. *If you won't take the power, then I will teach you what it means to obey.*

Cassius's eyes suddenly widened, and his hand gripped his blade and rose as if he had no control over it. He strained against the magic, but the blade inched toward my chest. I tried to pull away, but the magic shoved me forward, closer to the steel.

"Ella!" he shouted as his arm quaked. Horror rang in his voice. "I can't fight it much longer!"

You cannot fight me at all, the heart snarled in my mind.

"Yes, I can." I reached for my connection with the trees in the courtyard, but a wave of corrupted power slammed into my body and drove me forward. Suddenly, there was only pain.

63

Cassius

Ella lurched forward beneath a sudden wave of magic, impaling her chest on the tip of my outstretched sword.

Her mouth opened in a silent scream as crimson blossomed beneath my blade.

"No!" I bellowed, terror racing through me.

Desperation sent an unfamiliar strength through my body. My arms and shoulders quaked as I fought the spell binding me, and my blade pulled back half an inch.

Too little. Too late.

"Stop this!" I begged the silent heart. "I will serve you however you wish. Just spare *her*."

Ella's eyes flickered, and a sad smile graced her lips. "Never submit."

Then her eyes closed.

No, gods, not like this.

An earthquake rumbled through the room, and my eyes widened as the roots lining the walls of the sepulcher ripped themselves free and lashed out like serpents. They wrapped around the pulsing heart and pulled back, and seams of white light poured through the spreading tears in its corrupted flesh.

An unearthly screech cut through my mind, and then, in a blinding burst of light, the heart split in two.

The spell binding me vanished, and my sword arm wrenched back. My blade fell from my grasp, and Ella pitched forward.

Streams of magic spilled through the room like a living aurora, and the fallen chunks of flesh began to pulse with a radiant glow. Light flashed, and the world seemed to slow.

Time to run.

Scooping Ella's body into my arms, I thrust myself to my feet and ran. A luminescent wave billowed toward us, and I hurled myself up and out of the hidden stairway, rolling flames on my heels.

Every footstep was leaden, and every moment became an eternity.

The nave of the church disintegrated in a ball of fire behind me, sending shards of stone and burning embers spinning through the air as I raced through the open door. Streams of rampant magic seared my back, and a shockwave rolled beneath my feet, but I didn't stop. All that mattered was her.

The explosion illuminated the tree line ahead of me.

We were out of time.

I launched myself over one of the heavy oaks Horace had felled and dropped down behind it, Ella shielded in my arms. The ground shook, and then the world went white. I shut my eyes, but the searing light streamed through my lids. My body trembled, and my eardrums screamed, but none of it mattered. I felt nothing but her.

When the deluge of fire and light subsided, I leaned back and looked down. Ella lay in my arms, eyes closed and face pale.

A stain of crimson seeped through the pierced fabric of her bodice. *My* blade had made that mark. Her breathing was so shallow that I could barely hear it.

Fear lanced me, and I grasped her shoulders. "Ella, come back to me, gods damn it!"

64

Ella

I gasped, and my eyes fluttered open. Blind.

Pain like I'd never known tore through my body, cold following it. So cold. It was nearly impossible to drag air into my lungs. Though I could sense Cassius nearby, my vision had gone black. I tried to speak, but no words left my lips.

This was it. The end.

There was no question in my mind—*this is what it's like to die.*

And then a surge of strength poured through my veins, driving back the cold and filling me with warmth. The magic felt familiar and welcoming—a power I'd felt before.

The forest.

It was healing me. I could feel the energy from the trees around me, and as sensation returned to my limbs, I realized that the roots themselves had wrapped around my legs and arms. They fed their life into me, healing my wounds.

I hadn't asked, but the forest had offered. It was giving me everything it had. I could feel the life ebbing from the trees. They were also wounded.

I couldn't let them sacrifice themselves. Not after everything they'd done for me already.

"Stop!" The words broke through my lips, and I forced myself upright, tearing the roots from my limbs. "You've done enough. Don't sacrifice anymore."

My body still ached, but I was alive. I could heal on my own.

"Thank you," I said more softly. "Thank you for saving my life."

As the roots released their hold and disappeared beneath the ground, I could feel that the forest understood.

Cassius pulled me to his chest. A wash of emotions crossed his face as he released a shuddering breath. "Thank the gods you're okay."

I hugged him back, so grateful to be alive. I felt like I'd been pummeled by an avalanche. The forest had healed my injuries, but the rest of me ached tremendously, and my muscles quaked with exhaustion. The bright blue of my dress was soiled with dirt and blood. I glanced down at my chest. The wound was gone, though the area still felt tender and bruised.

His arms tensed, and his voice rang with guilt. "I'm so sorry. I had no control over my blade."

I shook my head. "It wasn't you. It was the heart." *The heart.* I shuddered and looked up at him. "Did we destroy it?"

The prince met my searching eyes. "You did."

A great weight slipped from my shoulders, and I relaxed in his strong arms, cherishing the sense of relief that settled over me. "Good."

Whatever happened next, I knew I'd done my part.

Cassius's jaw tensed. "You saved our kingdom, not to mention my life. I don't—"

I reached up and traced my fingers through his hair. "And you saved me. Without you, I'd still be in there, burned alive."

"Ella—"

I pulled myself to him and pressed my lips against his—firmly at first, then as gently as a summer breeze. Tingling waves of sensation traced across my skin, and every touch became new. His arms tightened around me, and I cast tenderness aside, grasping his hair and the shirt on his back. Every kiss was defiance of all that had happened, proof that we had triumphed. That we had lived.

I pulled back. There was no time.

Cassius's lips rose into one of those heartbreaking smiles, some of the tension in him eased. "Who would have thought that a farm girl could take on the realm's most powerful mages and destroy their power? You are truly a wonder, Ella Marquette."

"I didn't destroy anything. The power was stolen. I simply gave it back."

Cassius helped me to my feet. "I'm not one to argue, but *destroyed* might be the more appropriate term."

I looked at the devastation around us, and my stomach tumbled.

The ancient church was gone, and in its place lay a smoldering pile of stone and ash and twisted iron. The blast had consumed the grass and left the clearing a blackened crater. The trees around the perimeter had been flattened, and those beyond were leafless and charred along one side. The heavy trunk that had shielded us from the blast was little more than embers, still glowing in places.

I swallowed around the tightness in my throat. "It seems like it was a rather narrow escape."

"*Narrow* doesn't cut it," Cassius muttered. "I don't think anything could have survived the immediate blast. Not even me."

His words doused my calm like ice water. I grasped his arm, looking around in panic. "Chastity! Tenebris!"

Please, by the Fates, *please*.

A high whinny replied in the distance, and I let out a relieved sigh. "They're okay."

A moment later, the horses trotted into view. Tenebris was fine, but Chastity was worse off. The black scars of Horace's lighting etched her hide, and she had a limp.

Ignoring Cassius's protests, I pulled free and hobbled over to my companion. "I'm so sorry I put you in danger. I never meant for you to get hurt."

She tossed her mane, then nuzzled my hand. *You're far worse off. I'm sorry I couldn't trample that bastard myself.*

I hugged her neck. "Thank you for protecting me and bringing me here."

She rubbed her head against mine. *You've changed everything.*

I paused, taking a long, low breath.

She was right. The world felt different. The hungering pulse of the heart was gone, and in its place was a renewed vibrance. I left the devastated perimeter of the clearing and limped deeper into the woods, my arms out, touching the trees and brush that had survived.

"What is it?" Cassius asked as he followed, concern in his tone. "Is everything all right?"

"Better than all right." I paused with my hand on a tree. "I feel stronger than ever, and the forest does, too. It feels...right."

Beyond the crater of destruction, the magic released by the heart vibrated through every plant and animal—a happy thrum like bees busy about their nest. A handful of little yellow flowers lifted themselves up out of the ash and began to unfold their leaves and petals, and my heart blossomed with them.

Cassius stepped up behind me, his voice soft and reverent. "Did you do that?"

I knelt beside the flowers and brushed their silky petals. "I don't think so. There are centuries of magic at work here. What was taken has been returned, and the woods are already healing."

"And what of the Triad?"

I rose and glanced back at the place the church had been, just to be certain it was gone. "I'm not sure, but we'd better find out. Fast."

Cassius scooped me up and set me in Tenebris's saddle, all before I had a chance to protest. "I think Chasity needs a break. She's done her part. You'll ride with me."

No complaints this time around.

The prince climbed up behind me, his arm looping around my waist and easing me back against him. His body was warm and safe, and for the first time all night, I relaxed and let exhaustion take over.

I bowed my head to the trees as we passed beneath them. "Thank you for your protection. I hope I've repaid your kindness."

The leaves rustled in the still air, and the branches bowed in return.

I grinned back at them. "It was an honor to serve you. Now, if you please, will you show us the way home?"

The woods parted, creating a tunnel through the trees. Cassius drew in a sharp breath, and Tenebris stopped short, but Chastity just trotted ahead into the dark. I looked up and gave the prince a wry smile. "The woods are dangerous and full of monsters, but don't worry, Your Highness. I'll protect you."

65

─────────

Cassius

I slowed Tenebris as we approached the castle an hour later. A full complement of soldiers patrolled the battlements, and the night breeze carried shouts and clamor from the courtyard. My gaze drifted upward. A tall tower rose from the northern end of the castle, dwarfing my own.

The hidden wing had been revealed. Was it because their magic had been broken?

My arm tightened around Ella. She'd been in and out of consciousness since leaving the church, and I'd had to hold her upright for most of the ride. She'd spent everything back there. More than everything. I was certain she'd almost died.

I suspected that in breaking the curse, she'd had to withstand more power than the members of the Triad had ever wielded individually. She was strong—probably stronger than any of them—yet I couldn't help but worry. Her cuts had been healed by the forest, but she was still bruised and beaten. I needed to tend to her soon.

"We're nearly there," I whispered in her ear.

"Are you sure about this?" Ella asked, her voice tired but

determined. "What about the Triad? They may have lost the source of their power, but I'm certain they'll have their own magic. I don't think I'm strong enough for another round—"

"I am." I pulled her closer. "I won't let anything happen to you. I'll kill any immortal who dares to challenge me, and I doubt the Triad will risk an open confrontation—not with their power so suddenly diminished. With the spell broken, my rule is supreme."

Her body relaxed as we approached the walls. "I'll take that as a promise."

"Riders!" A shout rose from the battlements. "His Highness returns!"

A minute later, the castle gate ground open, and we rode through. The gawking crowd in the courtyard parted, servants and soldiers backing away in trepidation.

Aamon forced his way forward as I lifted Ella down from the saddle. "What the fuck is going on?" he demanded. He was covered in blood and sweat, evidence of the grim work he'd done to maintain order.

I cast him a warning glance. "Ella is not to be harmed. She's a hero of the realm and under royal protection."

"She's the least of our worries." Aamon tossed me a twisted object. "Care to explain this?"

I caught it and looked down. It was melted gold, contorted and blackened by flame. "What is it?"

Giving Ella a wary look, he stepped close and murmured, "I watched Malthus disintegrate in a ball of flame. One minute he was shouting orders to our search party, and the next, rays of light burst from his eyes and mouth, and he fucking *melted*."

Ella's eyes widened in shock, and my thoughts raced. Malthus was dead. "What of Thalindra?"

"I'm certain that whoever was with her will have a similar

story." Aamon shook his head. "I won't ever be able to unsee what I witnessed."

"Then that's all of them," I whispered. "We're free."

"I assume you did this?"

I bent to his ear, pitching my voice as low as I possibly could. "Ella killed Horace and destroyed the source of their power. Malthus must have been consumed by his connection to the source—and if he's dead, then Thalindra will be dead also."

"*Ella* did this?"

"Yes."

"My gods." Aamon's expression remained frozen as the thunderous implications sank in. "Then we're no longer under their spell."

I nodded. "And those who knew their secret will now be able to speak the truth. Things are about to get complicated."

Aamon's hand settled around the handle of his blade. "I can handle *complicated* as long as I don't have to grovel to those bastards any longer."

"We need to hunt down the soldiers Thalindra was with," Ella said. "We need to be certain she's gone." Despite her exhaustion and wounds, there was a fight in her yet.

Shaking my head in wonder, I turned to Aamon. "Do as Ella advises and make sure that old witch is dead. Send word of what you find."

Aamon saluted. "It will be a fucking pleasure."

Ella looked up at me. "Should we go w—"

"No." I brushed a smudge of dirt from her cheek. "Not tonight. You need to recover—and that's my first and *only* priority."

Aamon bowed slightly to her. "I don't pretend to understand your role in all this, but if what Cassius says is true...well, then, I owe you my gratitude. The *kingdom* owes you gratitude. An assassination thwarted and a reign of terror ended all in one night. I'm not sure the treasury has enough gold to thank you for what you've done."

"My people," Ella said, suddenly tense. "Protecting them is how you can thank me. Promise not to hurt them. The castle staff weren't involved or even aware of tonight's plot."

Fucking fates, she was better than any of us deserved.

I looked at my right-hand man. "See that the message is clear among the guards and immortals. No servants are to be touched. The same goes for the villagers. Anyone who defies the order will answer to me."

For centuries, the humans in Silverthorn had been faceless things that came and went as the years passed, one no different than the others. Expendable. But then there was *her*. She'd taught me to see their worth and reminded me of my duty to protect all that lived here in the vale.

Aamon lifted his brows at me. "Are you sure that's safe? There could be more assassins, and we need to hunt down whomever—"

"It's an order." I glanced toward the battered front doors of the grand entrance. "What remains of the ball? Is the court still dancing and drinking, or have they have sunk into further debauchery?"

Aamon gave me a knowing look. "The castle is in disarray. While there are a few revelers enjoying themselves in the chaos, most of your guests have fled, including much of the staff. Your wing has been secured with a double guard, however."

"Good. Have Cassandra get anyone else who does not belong here out and keep the sentries on alert."

We left Aamon and ascended the stairs to the grand entrance hall. Shattered glass and flowers littered the floor, and a tapestry hung torn on the wall.

"Fates," Ella said as she scanned the carnage.

"I didn't much care for the decoration, anyway. Let me take

you upstairs." I aimed to carry her up to my chamber, but she insisted on walking herself.

We'd made it halfway up when she clutched my arm, her breathing short and her face paler than it was before. "I just need a moment. I'm a bit dizzy."

I scooped her into my arms, ignoring her protests, and glanced down at her. "You're dizzy because you lost a lot of blood."

Her face hovered near mine, her gaze drifting in and out. "You are really beautiful, you know that?"

I lifted one brow at her as I ascended the stairs. The blue flecks in her eyes were darker than normal, like sapphires under a flame. "Rugged and devastating, I've been told, but never beautiful."

Her lips pulled into a soft smile, and my heart tugged. "You're all of those and more."

Entering my bedchamber, I set her down. I shucked off my boots and coat, then undid the satin bow that kept her bodice tight over her breasts.

"What are you doing?" she asked.

I took her wrist and gently turned it over, pressing a kiss to a deepening bruise. "I'm taking care of you. Your cuts may have healed, but you're still weak and bruised. You need healing, a bath, and a good rest."

She was far more resilient than any human had a right to be. Maybe that was part of her magic as well. Or maybe that was just her—gentle as a willow but strong as an oak.

That playful smile I cherished graced her lips. "The prince of the Bloodvale is waiting on me? What has happened to the world?"

I cupped her face with my palm and looked down into her eyes. "You turned it on its head, my darling."

She'd changed everything—me, most of all—like a mason's

wedge driving a crack through stone. I couldn't catalog or hope to express the storm of emotions raging through me. Instead, I let my instinct take over, and leaned down and kissed her gently.

Now was not the time for talking.

She melted into me, her hands moving up my chest and threading around my neck. I'd almost lost her tonight, and I wasn't going to make that mistake ever again.

She sighed in protest when I pulled away and brushed my thumb across her rouge-stained lips. "Tomorrow, we can talk more. You're hurting. Let me take care of you like a queen."

She gave me a quizzical look at that.

With her consent, I began loosening her bodice. "You wore this dress the day you applied to work here."

"You remember?" She was watching me in the mirror, her brows arching ever so slightly.

"How could I forget? You've made some drastic alterations, but it's still the same dress. I'd never forget it."

I remembered every moment I'd spent with her.

Loosened from its laces, the embroidered bodice gaped as it hung around her waist. I undid her skirt and let it fall to the floor. She wore the black silk chemise I'd given her after her escape from the Triad, and her nipples strained against the fabric.

A torrent of anger doused my desire as I inspected the bruises blooming beneath her skin. It would have been so much worse if the forest hadn't healed her.

My fists tightened. "I wish I could make them fucking pay for this."

Ella brushed her hand over my jaw. "They're dead, and we're alive and together. That's all the revenge I need."

Like water quenching fire, her touch doused my rage, leaving only guilt behind. My throat constricted. "I let this happen to you. You almost died."

She shook her head, her eyes radiating a kindness I didn't deserve. "You saved me, just as I saved you."

I cupped her cheek, wanting to worship every inch of her in gratitude. "I hate seeing you in pain."

Looking up at me through full lashes, she grabbed the hem of my shirt and slowly pulled it over my head. "Then take it away. Show me pleasure the way you did before. I've survived death, and all I want in the world is to be alive with you now."

"I'd do anything for you." My fingers tangled in her hair, and I lowered my mouth to hers, ready to fulfill her every wicked desire.

Ella pressed herself against me, kissing me back. The warmth of her body stiffened me with need, and her arms wrapped around my back as her tongue found mine. I dragged my fingers through her hair, but then they caught. I pulled out a fragment of bark.

She laughed. "I'm afraid I'm a mess."

"Easily fixed."

She shouted in surprise as I swept her off her feet and carried her to the bath chamber. I set her down and stepped into my marble-tiled shower to turn on the hot water.

"What is it?" she marveled.

I couldn't help but smile at the utter wonder on her face. "It's a shower—the only one on the continent. The water is like a warm rain."

She traced her fingers through the falling water and the rising steam. "I don't think I'm ever going to get used to the magic in this place."

I stepped aside, offering the way. "Give it a try."

Her lips curved, one side higher than the other as she flashed me a vixen smile, as if to say, *I know exactly what you want.*

Eyes locked on mine, she grabbed the edges of her silken

chemise and pulled it over her head, freeing her breasts. My breath hitched as she dropped it to the floor. She was beyond breathtaking. A silver-haired goddess whom I was unworthy to touch, let alone gaze upon—but I couldn't tear my eyes away.

Without a word, she turned and stepped past me into the shower, casting a sinful invitation over her shoulder. "Aren't you going to join me?"

Fucking hell. This woman had reduced me to a fool.

I undid my trousers and pulled them down, my cock springing free. Ella's heated gaze traveled down my naked body, her cheeks reddening at the sight of my manhood.

I grinned. "I do believe you're blushing, Ella Marquette."

"It's just that I've never been intimate with a man..."

She'd said as much before, but still, desire streaked through me. The thought of being the first man inside of her was almost enough to make me come right then. Every instinct called for me to grab her and press her up against the wall, but I restrained the urge and gently brushed my knuckles across her collarbone instead. "I'll never take what isn't given freely."

Her chest rose and fell rapidly, her eyes half lidded and full of desire. "I want it to be with you. My first time. And I want it now."

I shuddered with thundering need. It had been ages since I'd bedded a woman, and thinking back, I'd only been going through the motions. I'd never felt such desperation as I did for Ella. Gratitude. Admiration. Hunger. A thousand emotions I didn't fully understand. She was like no one else. I hadn't thought I was capable of emotions—especially not love—but I'd been wrong. I was in love with her, and I knew in that moment that I couldn't live without her.

Unable to restrain myself any longer, I trailed my fingers down the curve of her breast, relishing the way her nipple begged for my touch. "You have no idea how many times I've dreamt of slipping between those pretty thighs."

"I might have some idea," she said coyly, threading one bare thigh around my hip so that her heat was pressing against me.

I groaned, catching her mouth with mine, sinking my tongue inside as I gripped her round ass and pulled her closer.

A soft whimper of pain escaped her.

I released her, shame lancing me for being so careless. "What is it?"

"Just a bruised rib. I'm fine, really."

"Fuck." I pulled away. "I shouldn't be touching you."

She grasped my arm. "No. I want you to touch me, Cassius. To kiss me. To drink from me"—she pressed her palms against my chest, moving them upward until they circled my neck—"and this time, to make love to me."

The thought of her blood passing between my lips while my cock sank into the heat of her virgin body set my mind on fire. My thoughts quaked as I teased my fingers into her hair, tilting her head so that I could see the pulsing artery in her neck. "I will touch you and kiss you, but if I tasted you right now"—my body tensed, and I closed my eyes at the image that rose in my mind—"or slipped inside of you, I might lose control. I could hurt you. I refuse to risk that."

"Because I'm injured?"

"Because you've already given enough of yourself tonight. You need the doctor's ministrations and time to heal." I traced my thumb along her neck. "I'll pleasure you, but I won't feed. Not tonight. Not until you're stronger."

She looked up at me through hooded eyes, her lips curving in the most seductive grin. "I've heard an immortal's blood heals."

I shook my head. This woman was going to fucking destroy me.

"It's more than that," I said gruffly, the words rough and strained. "You don't know what you're asking."

Her lips left a trail of hot kisses on my chest. "Then tell me."

I shook as pure fucking delight shot through my body. It was all I could do to stop from opening my wrist right then and there.

Untangling her arms, I gently pushed her against the heated marble wall, my body caging her in place as water cascaded down my back. "My blood will heal your wounds, but you will be linked to me in ways you'd never dreamed possible. You'd be a part of me forever. I'd be able to track you more easily, to sense your emotions more deeply. Are you sure you want that?"

She placed one hand over my heart, her gorgeous lavender eyes pleading. "I don't want anything to separate us anymore."

66

Ella

The prince of the Bloodvale loomed before me, his arms braced on the marble wall, a rain of hot water pouring off his back. Clouds of steam billowed around us. His expression was as intense as I'd ever seen it, searching my face as a battle raged behind his stormy eyes.

I swallowed. "Why are you looking at me like that?"

His gaze fell to my lips, his brow furrowing ever so slightly. "I'm searching for a reason not to give you what you want."

My pulse quickened. "And?"

"I can't seem to find one." Water droplets glistened on the corded muscles of his chest, each sculpted with precision and tapering down below his navel in a sharp V. He was hauntingly beautiful in a devastating, heart-crushing way.

I'd fallen head over heels for the man. An immortal. The prince of the realm. A male who was destined to be married in a matter of weeks. I didn't know where that would leave us tomorrow, but at this moment, tomorrow didn't matter—only tonight.

Hell, I hadn't expected to see the dawn, let alone break the curse or find myself naked and in his arms.

"I want to be a part of you," I whispered.

His breath caught, and his pupils dilated.

I reached up and took his arm, kissing the underside of his wrist as he'd done to mine earlier. "Let me taste you. Let me feel what it's like to have your blood coursing through me."

His eyes darkened, all his hard-fought restraint crumbling at the touch of my lips.

"Please, my prince. Heal me. Let me be a part of you."

For an eternal second, he hesitated. Then, in a swift motion, he lifted his wrist to his mouth and pierced it with his fangs. A trail of crimson glistened on his lip as he offered it to me, two red dots marring the perfect skin. "I'm yours to take."

My heart pounded as I took his offering, laving my tongue over the two wounds, hesitantly at first—and then I drank.

A rush of euphoria engulfed me, a million bonfires alighting in my body, awakening feelings—*desires*—I didn't know existed. Tingles erupted across my skin, the aches and pains that plagued me suddenly dulling and morphing into something close to pleasure.

Cassius pulled, but I clutched his arm with both hands, swallowing each pulse of life, unable to slake the thirst that he'd awoken in me. *I wanted more.*

He watched me as he submitted, his attention rapt with pleasure and something else—*admiration*? He was enjoying this. Enjoying my hunger.

When he finally extracted his arm from my hungry clutches, my anger flashed briefly at the denial. He wiped a smear of blood from my chin, and his lips curved into a wicked grin. "You're gorgeous when you're ravenous. I like seeing you take what you want."

My chest rose and fell, my blood—and his blood—humming through my veins like bubbles. It was intoxicating and unnerving, and a deep, unyielding ache throbbed at my core. "I want you."

"How do you feel?" he asked, a ghost of concern in his voice.

I glanced down at my body. Where there had once been shades of purple and blue, there was now an unblemished canvas of nearly perfect flesh. My bruises were little more than pale memories. The wonder of it lifted my heart, but the wounds were nothing. I grasped him, meeting his appraising gaze. "I need more."

I pressed my thighs together, hoping to ease the ache inside of me that was becoming almost too much.

"Do you, now?" His rich, velvety voice skated over my heated skin.

My frustration flared. I was certain he'd known exactly what his blood would do to me, how it would amplify my desire to unbearable levels.

I suddenly understood the murals that adorned the great hall.

He palmed my breast, molding it beneath his touch, brushing my nipple with his fingers. My head tilted back against the marble, and I couldn't stifle the moan that escaped my throat. Suddenly, his lips were on my skin, heavy and hot, trailing kisses down my neck, capturing my other nipple and grazing it with his teeth. The sensations rippled through my overly sensitive body, awakening parts of me I'd never noticed, each demanding equal reverence.

"Yes, more," I whimpered. "I need more."

I opened my eyes to find his on me, smoldering like molten fire. He was close, close enough to feel the heat from his body, which branded me like an iron.

He grinned wider, a look of pure wicked sin on his gorgeous face as he slid down my torso, his hands skating my sides while his lips pressed soft kisses along my belly until he was kneeling before me. He slipped his hands between my thighs, parting my legs so that my most intimate parts were on display.

Heat rushed to my cheeks, and I tried to shield myself, but he wouldn't allow it.

"Don't hide yourself from me." He left a trail of soft kisses along my inner thigh, his gaze locked on me. "You are beautiful, and I want to feast on every inch of you."

"Please."

He lowered his mouth, this time finding the bud of my desire, the sensations extinguishing my doubts and turning my legs to jelly. In a quick movement, he braced me against the wall of the shower, wrapping my leg over his shoulder as he began doing devilishly wonderful things.

"Cassius," I moaned.

He answered with one long sweep of his tongue, parting my folds and slipping his fingers deep inside me.

My fingers tangled in his hair, guiding him as he feasted on me like a man starved. Each wicked arc of his tongue brought me closer to the edge, deeper into this blissful haze where it felt like time had stopped. My heart raced, my breath coming in shallow gasps as every sensation became acute.

I whimpered as the liquid tension that had spread through me coiled tighter, a thread pulled taut, ready to snap.

"Come for me, Ella," he growled.

I braced against the wall, my body arching as I shattered beneath him. Torrents of pleasure radiated from my core, engulfing me in a glow of energy.

When the waves of ecstasy slowed, Cassius released me and slid up my body, his eyes dark with need. "You're beautiful when you come."

I kissed him, deeply and slowly. "I want more."

His stiff desire pressed against my belly, and the rising warmth of pleasure built again. His tongue dipped into my mouth, gliding against mine, hungry and unsated. Water cascaded around his shoulders, the heat and steam filling the space and shutting away the troubles of the world outside.

He pulled his lips from mine. "I want to be inside you, Ella. To feel you come around me."

"Yes," I breathed, pulling him greedily toward me.

Gripping my behind, he lifted me like I weighed nothing, and I cried out in surprise. I wrapped my arms and legs around him as he guided the tip of his length between my folds...and then he slid inside. His body tensed, and I gasped as he slowly spread me and filled me until I didn't know if I could take anymore.

Concern and strain etched his face. "Are you all right?"

"Yes. Just move," I breathed. "Don't stop."

Desire flashed in his eyes, but the concern was still there. He slowly eased out of me before gliding back in on a groan. The pain abated, and pleasure spread, and then I was following his movement, my hips meeting each thrust, chasing desire.

"Fuck," he cursed, bracing one arm on the wall as he took me deeper. "You're so perfect."

I shook, demanding more and more of him each time he pushed into me. I wanted it to last forever, but my muscles spasmed with pleasure as my climax neared. "I don't know how long I can hold on."

"I want you to come with me," he said, and claimed my mouth. He kissed me slowly and reverently, like I was a goddess to be worshipped. White-hot desire flared, begging to be released.

And then it shattered.

I flew over the abyss, safe in his arms as he sank into me, his body tensing as he roared my name, giving me everything I wanted and more. I couldn't breathe, I couldn't speak, until I drifted down to reality. My body relaxed, consumed with a contentment I'd never experienced.

Was this what lovemaking did to people?

He lowered his forehead to mine. "You are everything I never knew I needed."

My heart swelled to near-breaking, and a tear slipped down my cheek. "I'm glad it was you. From the first moment we met, I think I knew."

He kissed me, capturing my lower lip between his teeth before releasing it. "I think I did, too."

67

Ella

Long hours later, I woke from a deep, dreamless sleep and stretched out my arms. The aches and pains of the night before were gone, replaced by vibrant energy and the peaceful feeling of being refreshed. A gift of Cassius's blood?

I sighed, rolling over and reaching for him. But the bed was cold, and he was gone. I felt his absence beyond the empty sheets, deep within me, as if he were pulling on me from a long way away. His scent lingered, and it prickled my senses, filling me with a need to be near him.

Was this also the bond of his blood?

My gaze landed on a single red rose on the edge of the mattress, and beside it, a handwritten note.

Rest, my beauty. I'm meeting with Aamon in the study. Come find us after breakfast, if you wish. —Cassius

There was no light coming from the balcony or windows, and I wondered how long I'd slept. Hours? Days? A year? I drifted in and out of a drowsy fog until a light knock sounded on the door, and I sat up with a start.

Still stark naked, I slipped out of bed and wrapped the fur coverlet around me. "Who is it?"

The door cracked open a smidge, revealing one of the royal servants. "I have your breakfast, my lady."

My lady? She was mistaken.

"Come in," I said, pulling the coverlet closer. "And it's just Ella. I'm not a lady."

"Of course, my lady. It's just that the prince insisted that you be addressed as such." The woman looked to be in her thirties, and I thought I recognized her. *Louisa.*

She brought a large tray of coffee, tea, and a selection of fresh pastries and fruits, and set it on a folding table. Blushing, she asked, "Is there anything I can bring you, my lady?"

Embarrassed by her deference, I wanted to correct her again, but I held my tongue. "No, this is lovely. You're very kind. Louisa, isn't it?"

"That's right, my lady. The prince asked me to inform you that there are fresh clothes for you in the wardrobe. Do you need assistance? I could help you bathe, brush your hair, or attend to your toilette."

I nearly choked on the sweet roll I'd dug into. Were the immortals incapable of doing anything themselves?

"No," I said, brushing the crumbs from my lips. "I can dress myself. Thank you, Louisa."

After she left, Pip appeared from beneath a chair cushion, sleepily rubbing his eyes.

"You're okay!" I cried, joy flaring within me.

Of course! He hopped down and nuzzled my ankle. *You're the one I was worried about.*

I lifted him up and set him on the table, and we demolished breakfast together. The prince's blood had satiated my hunger—and more—the night before, but it had returned with a vengeance.

I left him to gorge on the crumbs and headed into the bathroom to splash water on my face. When I looked at myself in the mirror, I stiffened. I was not the woman I had been the day before—and I had done things she'd barely imagined possible. I brushed my fingers across my lips. I could still feel, *taste*, Cassius's kisses. Passionate and filled with so much longing.

My stomach fluttered. Would what happened between us the night before mean anything today, or would our lives continue along their separate paths?

The weight of it pressed down on me as I faced the truth. One night was one night, and the prince still had to marry. At best, he might accept me as his mistress. But could *I* accept that? On the other hand, could I possibly say no? I *loved* him. I was certain of it, more than ever.

I let out a shaky breath. *One thing at a time, Ella.*

The woman the prince chose to marry was the least of my worries, and perhaps even his. So much more was at stake. My breakfast curdled as yesterday came rushing back. Horace's lifeless eyes. The corrupted heart's tainted hunger. The ravaged castle. I hadn't even seen the destruction in the ballroom. Would there still be bodies? I recoiled at the image of the prince painting the floor with the assassins' blood. How many of my kind had died before he'd stopped the slaughter with his command?

I shuddered. No more. Not if I could help it. Cassius had promised protection the night before, but I had to see it through. I had to protect my stepmother and the resistance.

Destroying the Triad was just the beginning of what it would take to change this place.

With renewed purpose, I opened the wardrobe and froze, stunned. A half-dozen dresses in various shades hung in front of me, each more beautiful than the next. Silken undergarments were folded on a lower shelf alongside a riding outfit made of the softest leather. The clothes were more elegant than any courtesan had a right to wear. They were a high lady's clothes— and to my chagrin, most seemed impossible to put on alone.

I pulled out a deep mauve dress with sleeves and no back laces and set to work slipping into it. Unlike the gown from last night, this one was loose and fitted exactly where it needed to be, and was more comfortable than my work uniform. Casting a quick glance in the mirror, I combed my fingers through my hair, then slid on a pair of slippers and headed for the study. I knew where it was located, but even if I hadn't, there was something drawing me forward like an invisible current sweeping me toward him.

His blood.

68

Cassius

A knock sounded on the door, and I stopped speaking as a voice filtered through. "Lady Ella, requesting an audience, Your Highness."

"Send her in," I replied.

Aamon raised his brows inquiringly. I looked from him to Cassandra. "Ella brought down the Triad and stopped the assassination. She should be a part of this conversation."

Cassandra nodded. She was a blood relative and loyal— something that was priceless in our current predicament.

I rose as Ella swept in, and my blood heated at the sight of her. Her heartbeat was like nectar, her scent a heavy wine. The mauve dress I'd hoped she'd wear clung closely to her, sliding over her breasts and hips with each step. She wore no ornamentation, but her silver hair framed her perfect face and enchanting lavender eyes.

She was a goddess. *And she was mine.*

I wanted to wrap her in my arms and claim her there, but the oaken desk, my two advisors, and the last vestiges of decorum that I possessed stood in the way.

"My lady," I said with a dip of my head. "I'm glad you're here."

She blushed at that.

I gestured toward Cassandra. "This is Commander Cassandra, who oversees the forces here in the castle and at the border outposts."

Ella curtsied low. "A pleasure to meet you, Commander."

Cassandra remained stiff. Aside from the Triad, I'd never brought a human into my council before. I'd never seen the point. They lived short lives of little consequence—or so I'd thought. Now, I couldn't imagine the chamber without Ella's voice.

I resumed my seat behind the desk. "We were just discussing the fallout from last night."

"Thalindra?" Ella asked, meeting my gaze with worried eyes.

"She's dead."

"A pile of ash, just like Malthus," Aamon said. "It couldn't have happened to a crueler woman."

Ella released a long sigh, and her shoulders slumped with relief.

"However," Aamon continued, "there's substantial fallout beyond the Triad. We've rounded up the surviving conspirators. There was quite a network behind the assassination attempt."

Ella's eyes flashed with fear, and her heartbeat accelerated. I could almost taste her rising dread through our bond.

I leaned forward, resting my arm on the desk and looking Aamon in the eye. "I gave Lady *Marquette* my word that no more humans would be hurt. The assassins are all dead, and further bloodshed is not the way to fix this."

Aamon lifted his brows and glanced at Cassandra apprehensively. "The court won't be happy. They want justice."

"I think you mean revenge," Ella said, her voice low but filled with fire. Her quiet anger swept through the room, and all eyes turned to her.

"They plotted against the prince," Aamon said. "There should be a trial. The act demands justice."

"Yes," she said, uncowed. "And we want justice for centuries of oppression. For centuries of taking our blood. How are you going to give us that?"

I couldn't restrain my admiration. She was fierce and fearless, and what our kingdom needed. A heart better than mine. A vision unclouded by centuries of arrogance and tradition.

"Rhetoric of the resistance," Aamon scoffed.

Ella spun on him, ferocity in her voice. "If you're going to put the resistance on trial, then you should put yourselves up before a judge as well. Since the Uprising, your kind has treated us as second-class citizens. Worse. You've stripped us of our humanity and our dignity. We've lived lives of oppression and humiliation. What did you think would happen? That people would lie down and take it without a fight?"

"That is a wide net you're casting," Aamon growled. "We're not all animals."

"You're complicit," she said, not missing a beat. "This kingdom is comprised of humans and immortals. It should protect both."

Her words fell like a hammer. A condemnation of our rule, of our laws and pretense and power.

Aamon opened his mouth, but I raised my hand, and the room fell to silence. "Ella speaks the truth. As lords, we've failed in our duty. We can no longer continue to do so."

If we didn't make things better, then the humans would continue to fight. I had no doubt Ella would lead them. Successfully.

"What do you suggest, Your Highness?" Cassandra asked.

Nothing had changed during the centuries my family had

ruled. It was time for new voices. I turned to Ella. "What do *you* suggest? How do I rule both people fairly?"

Her eyes widened at the invitation, and she hesitated.

"Speak, *whisperer*. I value your counsel as much as any here, if not more."

Her voice wavered slightly. "Mandate the fair treatment of humans. And end the blood tithe."

Aamon snorted. "Our people would starve."

Her shoulders tightened, as did her fists. "Then you should *pay* for what you take, and never take it without permission." Ella gestured around the room. "Look at the wealth in this place. Your kind can afford it."

Before my council could continue the argument, I held up my hand. "It will be law. Ella is right. We are rich, and we should pay. It will be the first of many changes I make when I take the throne."

While I'd chafed beneath the rule of the Triad and had only contempt for my father's rule, I'd never imagined a different world. A better world.

Not until her.

She'd opened a path to a better future as surely as she'd made one through the forest the night before.

Aamon poured himself a cup of wine. "I'll follow where you lead, Your Highness, but keep in mind, immortals don't like change."

Cassandra grimaced. "And with the Triad gone, some of the great houses will see it as a chance to depose you and seize power. Lord Perrault certainly will, and these kinds of changes could bolster his support among the court."

I met their gazes squarely. "Which is why I must do my duty and secure my throne first—as well as my line."

Aamon's expression brightened. "Finally, some sense. Before

you declare yourself a complete revolutionary, we need to get you married and your alliances secured."

Ella shifted uncomfortably, and I could taste her sudden misery.

"As it so happens, Eva Marbury is still here," Aamon continued eagerly. "There's time to secure an alliance before she departs."

I shook my head, measuring him and Cassandra both. "Marbury is an outsider. After last night, I need someone who understands the Bloodvale and our troubles. Someone who can rule both humans and immortals with an even heart. Someone I can trust. Someone who is open to change."

The corners of Ella's mouth curved in a frown. "I think you might have trouble finding that woman."

"I already have," I replied, meeting her gaze head-on. "More than anything, I need you. Your strength, your understanding of this place and its people. Your heart."

She stilled. "What are you saying?"

Since I'd met the silver-haired siren, the old woman's words had hung over me, a constant specter. *Choose a bride wisely.* I understood now that what I'd thought to be a warning had been a promise of a new future. *If you fall in love, the woman you choose will destroy everything your father built. And if she ever takes the throne, she will make your people pay the price of their thirst.*

Ella had shaken my world, tearing down the prison of my father's kingdom. She'd destroyed the withering power of the Triad, and now she demanded equality. She demanded justice. Under our rule, any immortal who abused a human would pay —with their lives.

The truth was, Ella had been the answer all along, and the old witch had seen it coming. Not only would her heart heal this place, but her strength would protect it. Together, we would be unstoppable in our quest for change.

I rose and faced the woman who'd saved my kingdom. "Ella Marquette, I want you to be my queen."

69

———————

Ella

The floor felt like it was dropping away, and I reached for the wall to steady myself. He couldn't mean it.

The impossibility of the prince's words was punctuated by Aamon, who spit out his wine and fell into a coughing fit.

"Are you insane?" Cassandra rose from the settee. "You need to marry someone from a powerful house, not make enemies with every immortal in your realm. They won't like this."

"They won't like me taking their heads off if they disrespect my queen," Cassius growled. "And I'd wager they're now as afraid of Ella as they were of the mages. She annihilated their source of power and reduced them to ash."

I felt like my legs were going to give out. Cassius didn't want me as his mistress, but as his *queen*. To sit beside him on his throne. To join him in bed, every night. It was impossible to imagine, let alone hope for, and yet, hadn't he called me as much the night before? *Let me take care of you like a queen.*

Had he been considering this course even then?

I drew in a shuddering breath, forcing my tumbling thoughts to focus. This was about more than just me and my love for

Cassius. It was about my people. This would give me the chance to protect them. To make their lives better.

Aamon and Cassandra still looked skeptical, their brows furrowed in equal expressions of concern.

I straightened my spine and stared them down. "The world we lived in yesterday is gone. The Triad is gone. Their spell repressing magic is gone. I am not the only one who can wield magic. Other humans will wield it again, and soon. Perhaps even more powerfully than I can."

Aamon froze, and Cassandra's face paled. "It will be the Uprising all over again," she murmured.

"Unless we're on your side," I said.

"You want me to make a good alliance?" Cassius added. "Who could be more powerful than the humans of this kingdom with their magic returned, and Ella to lead them? They defeated us once, and unless we change our ways, they will again."

His advisors looked at each other as an oppressive silence fell over the room. To his credit, the prince didn't break the spell, letting the words sink in and work their magic.

Cassandra shook her head in astonishment. "I can't believe I'm actually considering this, but if we put a human on the throne, the *right* human, then I'm certain the army would follow. No amount of bribery from the other houses could buy their loyalty, not with a chance for self-rule. The house retinues would follow suit. It would leave our enemies in the Bloodvale toothless."

"Thousands against a handful," I said. "Any house that opposed us would quickly learn a lesson in mathematics."

Aamon shook his head. "What about the court? How would they ever accept her? Not only is she a human, but she's a *commoner*."

I leveled him with a withering glare.

"There's *nothing* common about her," Cassius rumbled.

"She's a *whisperer*. She drove the entire court from the ballroom with her magic, and I watched the very forest bow before her last night. She destroyed the Triad's source of power. She is, without a doubt in my mind, the strongest and bravest person in this realm. She is the true queen."

His words took the breath from my lungs, the passion of his argument amplified through the bond we shared. I could feel his admiration and faith. The prince truly believed what he was saying.

"No one can debate what she did or her power," Aamon said, eyeing me with a look that felt like it would peel the skin off my bones. "But if you're serious, we can't sell her to the court as *just* a human."

My eyes narrowed. "What's wrong with being *just* a human?"

"Authority," he said, then turned back to Cassius. "We need to emphasize her magic, and that she defeated the Triad. Those bastards gave us precedent in a way. They were technically human, and they ruled for centuries. The court might accept her as a replacement—welcome it, even."

Cassius glared back at him. "Even without magic, I would still want her as my queen. There is no heart as good as hers. Think of what it would be like to be ruled by someone who actually cared for the people here." Then, with a smile that pulled on my heart, the prince took my hand. "Will you rule beside me and help right this kingdom?"

My throat went tight, and it felt like my chest was caving in. I couldn't manage to think, let alone say the words.

Cassius turned on his advisors. "Give us the room for a moment."

Looking deeply relieved, Aamon rushed to the door. Cassandra eyed me for a long time before following, but she paused halfway out and looked back. "You may be the best shot this kingdom has. I'd be honored to serve you, whisperer."

My breath escaped as the door shut behind them, leaving me alone with the prince. The man would be king, and if I agreed, my husband. *I would be queen.*

He cupped my cheek, lovingly rubbing his thumb over my skin. "I'm sorry to put this burden before you in such a fashion. I should have asked you in a beautiful garden or beside a glistening waterfall in the moonlight, but this is the reality of royal life. Backroom negotiations and precarious alliances."

I moistened my parched lips. "I understand."

His stormy eyes thundered. "Will you be my queen? Will you marry me and live with me for the rest of our days?"

It felt like flying too close to the sun, and my limbs trembled with fear and exhilaration. Saying yes would be to dive into danger and a whole new world—but I'd done that before. I could do it again.

"But I'm mortal."

"You don't have to be."

I swallowed hard. Drink his blood and outlive my family and friends? I wasn't sure I could do it.

As if he saw the indecision on my face, he said, "Or I don't have to be immortal."

The breath rushed from my lungs. "You would do that for me? Give up eternal life?"

"There is no life without you. I'd give up the throne if that was what it took for you to say yes. I love you more than anything, more than this kingdom, more than my duty. All I need is you."

"Cassius, I—" Words escaped me. There was nothing in my head or my heart but overwhelming emotion.

"You don't need to make that choice right now. We have time. Whatever we choose, we'll be together."

My heart strained in my chest as an impossible future materialized before me. "Your court won't be happy."

"Fuck them," he said. "You are *mine*, and I will have no one else. I will protect you with my life and honor you with every breath I take, my queen."

I felt his emotions through our bond, an overwhelming torrent of admiration and desire. Could he feel my own? Could he feel the way my heart leapt whenever he drew near? Could he sense the strength he gave me?

His queen.

For all the Fates, I would give anything to be that. I pushed up on my toes, and brushing my lips against his, I whispered, "With all my heart, yes, I will be your queen—now and forever."

70

———

Ella

Two weeks later...

"Are you sure you're going to be able to walk in that thing?" Belle asked from the velvet settee, a bowl of cherries in her lap. Her leg had fully healed, and she was lounging like a barn cat in the sun. Pip sat next to her, happily gnawing on a cherry of his own.

I stared at my reflection in the standing mirror. The silk gown cascaded about me in a waterfall of cream.

Cara's head popped around the full skirt, a pincushion tied to her wrist. "It's not the walking but the getting up that's going to be a problem."

She wasn't kidding. This dress had to be twice my weight. If I fell in a lake, I would drown. I'd probably take Cassius down with me.

The *prince*. The man who was going to be my husband. My king.

Cara looked up at me. "How does it feel?"

Overwhelming. Impossible. A dream.

I skimmed my hands down the cinched waist, my fingers

brushing the crystals that had been sewn into the embroidered flowers. Cara had adjusted the bodice so it didn't squeeze so tightly and hemmed the length of the skirt after I'd tripped on it and nearly broken my face. I'd asked her to be my bridesmaid, and despite her new role overseeing preparations, she'd insisted on making the dress herself—along with a team of overworked helpers.

"It's perfect, Cara," I said honestly. "More beautiful than anything I ever imagined possible. I feel like royalty."

She beamed up at me. "Well, you're going to be royalty soon, so you'd better get used to it."

The wedding was in a week. After that, I was going to *be* the queen of the Bloodvale. My breathing started to come more quickly.

"Getting cold feet?" Belle quirked her brow at me. She always knew when I was nervous. "Just say the word, and I'll run with you."

I laughed. "No, I'm not getting cold feet about the wedding, but I am a little worried about being queen."

"I can't think of anyone better for the job than my little sister." Belle plucked a cherry from the bowl and plopped it in her mouth. "And if anyone gives you trouble, I have no doubt your soon-to-be husband will kill them."

I couldn't help the chill that came over me. She wasn't wrong.

Cassius and Cassandra had purged the court of anyone who'd opposed my ascension or had deep alliances to the Triad. Many had fled of their own accord, including—mercifully—Lorayna and Bianca. It had helped that they'd seen my power during the ball, and rumors about what I'd done to Horace and the Triad had spread like wildfire.

However, I doubted Cassius's blade had remained entirely clean. I *knew* it hadn't.

"It's not all roses and rainbows yet," I muttered, adjusting my skirt to give my nervous hands something to do. "I think it will take time."

Cara perked up. "The villagers and the army are ecstatic. I don't think I've seen the city with this much spirit, not even during the festivals. They've gone all out celebrating. We'll be lucky if half the taverns don't burn down after the wedding. You have the entire populace behind you."

"Most of them," I said.

My stepmother was leaving the valley, along with many of the central figures of the resistance, despite Cassius's pardons. They didn't believe the immortals could change and couldn't forgive them for the past. Perhaps it was fair, but we needed to make a way forward together, as one people, believing in the possibility of change.

And the immortals *could* change. Cassius had already abolished the blood tithe and arranged for reparations from the royal treasury.

For once in my life, I had hope for the future.

I glanced over at Belle as Cara put a few more pins in the back of the gown. "Must you leave as well?"

"I'll stay for the wedding, but after that, I'm going on my own honeymoon." Belle smiled softly and walked over to me, meeting my gaze in the mirror. "This is my chance to see what else is out there. I've been stuck in this valley my whole life, and I want more. It's what we'd always talked about."

It had been my dream as well, but a new dream had found me—one with stormy eyes and the will to change the world.

I just wished she'd be here to see it.

Belle took my hand and squeezed it. "Don't worry. I'll be back before you know it, and I'll have all sorts of stories to share."

She'd always been the adventurous one, and I knew that she

needed this, but it broke my heart to be separated again so soon. "What about the manor?" I asked desperately, letting Cara help me wriggle out of the dress so that I could slip into my riding outfit. Cassius had granted us additional lands and tenants to make us nobles and not, as Aamon put it, *unseemly commoners*.

"There's so much to do," I continued. "Do you really think Tarran can manage it all on his own?"

I'd appointed him steward, though Belle would have to handle the accounts.

Belle gave me that lopsided grin of hers, the one that made a dimple pop out of her cheek. "Tarran will be fine without me for a few months. He did a fair job of managing things while you were seducing the prince, though I'm afraid he's not too happy about you getting married."

A pang of guilt tore at me. "I guess not."

Tarran fancied me, but it was in the way most boys longed for girls. For all his friendship, the truth was, he'd never truly seen me—not in the way Cassius did. To Tarran I'd just been plain Ella, someone to be protected, someone who was just a farm girl and nothing more.

Cassius, on the other hand, made me feel like I was capable of anything, that he *believed* I could do anything—even rule a kingdom. How many people found someone in life who could make them feel like that?

Tarran would easily find another girl. For me, there was only Cassius, and I couldn't imagine spending a day apart from him.

"You're blushing, Ella," my sister teased. "Please tell me you were thinking about your fiancé and not that farm boy."

"What farm boy?" a deep, husky voice said from behind us. Tingles skated over my skin, and I turned toward Cassius. He filled the doorway, one brow lifted as he flashed a devastating smile.

I crossed to him and planted a kiss on his lips. "A dear friend that is looking after our affairs. No one for you to worry about."

"Good. Because I am a terribly jealous man when it comes to you." His arms looped around me, and he kissed me slowly and deeply. Shivers raced down my spine, and I couldn't help but softly moan.

I could feel Belle rolling her eyes behind me.

"What are you doing here?" I asked as soon as he let me go. "Trying to sneak a peek at the dress?

He brushed his knuckles along the curve of my jaw. "A proposition. The night is beautiful, and the moon is out. Come for a ride. I want to show you your kingdom."

Chastity and Tenebris were already saddled and waiting for us at the stable. We guided them out of the castle—soon to be *my* castle—and up into the dark woods, slowing as we met a lone figure hobbling through the darkness.

Siggy.

She paused as we approached, grinning. "It seems that you two found the people you were looking for after all."

My stomach tightened as if tugged by a string from very far away, and I reached for Cassius's hand.

"And where are you going tonight, Grandmother?" Cassius asked with a warmth I'd barely ever heard slip from his lips. "The woods are dangerous, you know."

"Not with this one looking after them," Siggy said, nodding to me. "Bogeyman or none, I had to see what all the fuss was about with my own eye—just to make sure the rumors were real."

"I gather you had a great deal to do with it," Cassius said, a thread of laughter hiding beneath the stony accusation.

She winked. "I just played my part."

I dropped down off Chastity's back and gave her a hug. "Thank you for everything. You're not here to say goodbye, are you?" With Belle leaving, I couldn't lose her as well. The thought sickened me.

Siggy scoffed. "And leave the two of you youngsters to run this kingdom on your own? Absolutely not. I'm invested in the success of this place now." She pointed her cane accusingly at Cassius. "Which is why I expect a seat on the council."

He raised his eyebrows. "Do you, now?"

She straightened her back. "I can see the future. The master of your treasury can't say that. He can barely see his own toes over his belly."

The prince weighed her with his gaze, then slowly nodded. "You shall have it, old woman—for your wisdom, and for all you've done already."

She grunted, but there was a hint of satisfaction in the curl of her lips.

"And what future do you see for us?" I asked as I stepped back toward the prince and took his hand.

Siggy stared into me with her one good eye, like she was peeling away the night around me. Then, as if waking from a dream, she laughed softly. "Why, you'll live happily ever after, of course!"

Thanks for joining us on Ella and Cassius's journey! While their search for love has reached a happy resolution, Belle's perilous adventures are just beginning. You might already have an inkling of who she's destined to meet, but you may not be prepared for the beautiful and devastating monster that the rakish prince has become. To get your hands on Belle's adventure as soon as it releases, preorder *Kingdom of Roses and Flame* on Amazon: https://mybook.to/Roses-and-Flame

And if you just couldn't get enough of Ella and Cassius's story and would enjoy a taste of their life and romance after the wedding, you can sign up our newsletters to read a free exclusive bonus scene that didn't fit in the book: https://story.veronicadou glas.com/Cinder-Bonus

AUTHOR'S NOTE

Thank you all so much for reading Reign of Cinders and Glass!

It's rare in life to get a chance to create something with your best friends, so we hope that you had as much fun reading this story as we all had weaving it together.

Myths and archaeology always go into our writing, and this book had a few real-world inspirations. The beating heart in the church was one of those amazing moments where we both came up with the same idea independently, exclaiming 'that's what I was thinking!' during one of our plotting sessions. The church had several real world inspirations, but one of note was Kostel Svatého Jiří (St. George's Church) in Luková in the Czech Republic. Originally constructed in the 14th century, the church endured fires and was reputably haunted. It was finally abandoned when its roof collapsed during a funeral service. The church was left boarded up for decades without funding for restoration. Then Jakub Hadrava, an artist, sculpted thirty ghosts to inhabit the space, supporting its restoration by turning it into a haunted destination that you can visit today.

The ambiance of Castle Silverthorn was in part inspired by a visit to Dunrobin Castle in Scotland, while we were there for Veronica and Doug's wedding. However, the map and layout of Silverthorn were largely based on Hohenzollern Castle in Germany, the seat of the Prussian royal family. It is a picturesque Neo-gothic fortress perched high on a hill. We'd already started writing the scenes in Silverthorn when we came across the breathtaking images of the Hohenzollern and instantly realized it was the place we were writing about! We hope to one day be able to wander its halls in person.

We hope you enjoyed the book, and if you have the time, we'd really appreciate it if you'd be willing to post a review on either Amazon, Goodreads, or Bookbub. Your reviews keep us motivated and help people find the stories to fall in love with.

Belle's story is coming up next, and if you're interested in getting writing updates, sneak peeks, and early covers reveals, as well as alerts for new releases and giveaways, you can sign up for our vip newsletters here:

https://www.veronicadouglas.com/newsletter

https://linseyhall.com/subscribe

We also have Facebook Reader groups where you can connect with us and chat with other book lovers about new releases, old favorites, and the stories that inspire you:

https://www.facebook.com/groups/linseyhallbooks

https://www.facebook.com/groups/veronicadouglas

Until next time, happy reading!

-Veronica and Linsey

ACKNOWLEDGMENTS

Firstly, we want to thank all our readers, old and new. Whether this is your first journey with us, or you've ridden at our side through the years, we appreciate you more than we can say.

Thank you to Jena O'Connor and Ash Fitzsimmons for your insights and attention to detail. Your edits always help bring the story to life! Thanks as well to Amber Garcia for keeping us rolling on Facebook when we barricaded ourselves in our writing cave, and to Caethes Faron, for her insightful analysis and support. We'd be lost without you both.

We also want to thank the amazing readers on our advanced review team. We love your feedback, and your sharp eyes always make our books better.

Last but not least, thanks to Orina Kafe, who created the amazing cover for this book. We fell in love with it at first sight, and it kept us inspired the entire way!

ABOUT VERONICA DOUGLAS

Veronica Douglas is a duo of professional archaeologists that love writing and digging together. After spending an inordinate amount of time doing painstaking research for academia, they suddenly discovered a passion for letting their imaginations go wild! A cocktail of magic, romance, and ancient mystery (shaken, not stirred), their books are inspired, in part, by their life in Chicago and their archaeological adventures from around the globe.

www.veronicadouglas.com

ABOUT LINSEY HALL

Before becoming a writer, Linsey Hall was a nautical archaeologist who studied shipwrecks from Hawaii and the Yukon to the UK and the Mediterranean. She credits fantasy and historical romances with her love of history and her career as an archaeologist. After a decade of tromping around the globe in search of old bits of stuff that people left lying about, she settled down and started penning her own romance novels. Her series draw upon her love of history and the paranormal elements that she can't help but include.

www.linseyhall.com